Wed on His Terms

CHARLENE SANDS

Published in Great Britain 2015
by Mills & Boon, an imprint of Harlequin (UK) Limited,
Eton House, 18-24 Paradise Road, Richmond, Surrey, TW9 1SR

WED ON HIS TERMS © 2015 Harlequin Books S.A.

Million-Dollar Marriage Merger, Seduction on the CEO's Terms and *The Billionaire's Baby Arrangement* were first published in Great Britain by Harlequin (UK) Limited.

Million-Dollar Marriage Merger © 2010 Charlene Swink
Seduction on the CEO's Terms © 2010 Charlene Swink
The Billionaire's Baby Arrangement © 2010 Charlene Swink

ISBN: 978-0-263-25221-7
eBook ISBN: 978-1-474-00400-8

05-0715

Harlequin (UK) Limited's policy is to use papers that are natural, renewable and recyclable products and made from wood grown in sustainable forests. The logging and manufacturing processes conform to the legal environmental regulations of the country of origin.

Printed and bound in Spain
by CPI, Barcelona

Charlene Sands resides in Southern California with her husband, school sweetheart and best friend, Don. Proudly they boast that their children, Jason and Nikki, have earned their college degrees. The "empty nesters" now enjoy spending time together on Pacific beaches, playing tennis and going to movies, when they are not busy at work, of course!

A proud member of Romance Writers of America, Charlene has written more than twenty-five romance novels and is the recipient of the 2006 National Readers' Choice Award, the 2007 Cataromance Reviewer's Choice Award and the Booksellers Best Award in 2008 and 2009.

MILLION-DOLLAR MARRIAGE MERGER

BY
CHARLENE SANDS

To my husband, Don,
the man I've been sharing chardonnay with for all
our years. A really good man, like a fine wine,
only gets better with age.

One

From the time Tony Carlino was six years old, he'd been infatuated with cars, speed and danger. Back then, the hills of Napa that create award-winning merlot and pinot had been his playing field. Racing his dinged up scooter down the embankment, he'd hit the dirt falling headfirst into a patch of fescue grass a hundred times over. But Tony never gave up when he wanted something. He hadn't been satisfied until he'd mastered that hill with his scooter, his bicycle and finally his motorcycle. He'd graduated to stock car racing and had become a champion.

Newly retired from racing, his present fascination had nothing to do with cars and speed and everything to do with a different kind of danger.

Rena Fairfield Montgomery.

He glimpsed the blue-eyed widow from across the gravesite where dozens were gathered. Valley winds blew strands of raven hair from her face, revealing her heartbroken expression and ruffling her solemn black dress.

She hated him.

With good reason.

Soon he'd walk into a land mine of emotion and nothing posed more danger to Tony than that. Especially when it came to Rena and all she represented.

Tony glanced beyond the gravesite to those hills and Carlino land, an abundance of crimson hues reflecting off foil covering the vines, keeping grape-eating birds from destroying the crop. The land he once resented, the vines that had fed his family for generations was his responsibility now. His father had passed on just months ago, leaving the Carlino brothers in charge of the huge empire.

Once again, Tony glanced at Rena and a face devoid of emotion, her tears spent. She walked up to the bronze coffin, staring blankly, as if to say she couldn't believe this. She couldn't believe that her beloved husband, David, was gone.

Tony winced. He held back tears of his own. David had been his best friend since those scooter days. He'd been there for Tony through thick and thin. They'd kept their friendship ongoing, despite a bitter family rivalry.

Despite the fact that Rena had loved Tony first.

Rena held back a sob and bravely reached out to the blanket of fresh flowers draped along the coffin. She pulled her hand back just as her fingertip touched a rose petal. At that moment, she glanced at Tony, her sad eyes so round and blue that a piece of him unraveled.

He knew her secret.

But Tony didn't give that away. He stared at her, and for that one small moment, sympathy and the pain of losing David temporarily bonded them.

She blinked then turned around, stepping away from the gravesite, her legs weak as all eyes watched the beautiful grieving widow say her final farewell to her husband.

Nick and Joe, Tony's younger brothers, stood by his side. Joe draped an arm around him. "We're all going to miss him."

"He was as good as they come," Nick added.

Tony nodded and stared at the car as Rena drove away from the cemetery.

"Rena's all alone now," Joe said, once Nick bid them farewell. "It'll be even more of a struggle for her to keep Purple Fields going."

Tony drew a deep breath, contemplating his next move. They'd been rivals in business for years, but her winery had been failing and was barely holding on. "She won't have to."

Joe stiffened. "Why, are you planning on buying her out? She won't sell, bro. You know she's stubborn. She's had offers before."

"Not like this one, Joe."

Joe turned his head to look him in the eye. "What, you're making her an offer she can't refuse?"

"Something like that. I'm going to marry her."

* * *

Rena got into her car alone, refusing her friends' and neighbors' well-meaning gestures to drive her home, to sit with her, to memorialize David Montgomery. She never understood why people gathered after a funeral, had food catered in and specialty wines flowing. They filled their plates, chattered and laughed and most times forgot the real reason they had come. She couldn't do that to David. No, he was too young to die. Too vital. He'd been a good man, an excellent and loving husband. She couldn't celebrate his life; he'd had so much more to live. So she spoke the words with sincerity to the guests at the funeral site, "I hope you understand that I need to be alone right now," and had driven off.

She rode the lanes and narrow streets of the valley as numbness settled over her. She knew this land so well, had traveled every road, had grown up in Napa and had married here.

She wept silently. Tears that she thought were all dried up spilled down her cheeks. She found herself slowing her old Camry as she passed the Carlino estate, the vibrant vineyards sweeping across acres and acres.

She knew why she'd come here. Why she parked the car just outside the estate gates. She blamed Tony Carlino for David's death. She wanted to scream it from the hilltops and shout out the unfairness of it all.

A flashy silver sports car pulled up behind her, and she knew she'd made a mistake coming here. From the rearview mirror, she watched him step out of the car, his long legs making quick strides to the driver's side of her car.

"Oh, no." She grasped the steering wheel and rested her forehead there. Biting her lip, she took back her wish to scream out injustices. She didn't have the energy. Not here. Not now.

"Rena?"

The deep rich timbre of Tony's voice came through the window of the car. He'd been her friend once. He'd been her world after that. But now all she saw was a drop-dead handsome stranger who should have never come back to the valley. "I'm fine, Tony," she said, lifting her head from the steering wheel.

"You're not fine."

"I just buried my husband." She peered straight ahead, refusing to look at him.

Tony opened the car door, and she glimpsed his hand reaching out to her. "Talk to me."

"No...I can't," she said with a shake of her head.

"Then let's take a walk."

When she continued to stare at his hand, he added, "You came here for a reason."

She closed her eyes holding back everything in her heart, but her mind wouldn't let go of how David died. Spurred by renewed anger, she ignored Tony's outstretched hand and bounded out of the car. She strode past him and walked along the narrow road lush with greenery. From atop the hill, the valley spread out before her, abundant with vines and homes, both big and small, a hollow of land where many families worked side by side to ensure a healthy crop.

She had promised David she'd hold on to Purple Fields, an odd request from his deathbed, yet one she couldn't refuse. She loved Purple Fields. It had been her parent's legacy, and now it was her home, her sanity and her refuge.

She marched purposely ahead of Tony, which was an accomplishment in itself, since he'd always been quick on his feet. His footsteps slowed. Then he let go an exasperated sigh. "Damn it, Rena. David was my friend. I loved him, too."

Rena halted. Jamming her eyes closed momentarily, she whirled around. "You *loved* him? How can you say that? He's gone because of you!" Rena's anger flowed like the rush of a river. "You should never have come home. David was happy until you showed up."

Lips pursed, Tony jutted his jaw out. Oh, how she remembered that stubborn look. "I'm not responsible for his death, Rena."

"He wouldn't have gotten behind the wheel of that race car if you hadn't come home. When you showed up, that's all David talked about. Don't you see? You represented everything David wanted. You ran away from the vineyards. You raced. You won. You became a champion."

Tony shook his head. "It was a freakish accident. That's all, Rena."

"Your return here brought it all back to him," she said solemnly.

"My father died two months ago. I came home to run the company."

Rena glared at him. "Your father," she muttered. Santo Carlino had been a harsh, domineering man who'd wanted to build his empire no matter the cost. He'd tried to buy out every small winery in the area. And when the owners refused, he'd managed to ruin their business somehow. Purple Fields had seen the brunt of the Carlino wrath for years. Yet her parents had fought him tooth and nail, keeping their small patch of life out of Carlino hands. "I'll not speak ill of the dead, but…"

"I know you despised him," Tony stated.

Rena stuck to her promise and held her tongue about Santo Carlino, but she couldn't help how she felt and made no apologies for those feelings. "Go away, Tony."

Tony's lips curved up, a sinful, sexy curl of the mouth that at one time had knocked her senseless. "This is my land."

She slumped her shoulders. "Right."

Rena inhaled sharply, mentally chastising herself for driving up here—a bonehead move, as David would say. She was even more remorseful that she'd taken this short walk with Tony.

With hasty steps she brushed by him, but his reach was long and painfully tender when he caught her arm. "Let me help."

A lump formed in her throat. He didn't know what he was asking. She'd never accept his help. She glanced into dark, piercing, *patient* eyes. That was something for the record books—a patient Tony Carlino. He hadn't become a national stock car champion from his ability to wait.

She shook her head briskly. "Please don't touch me."

Tony glanced at his hand lying gently on her arm,

then stroked the length of it, sliding his hand freely up and down. "I mean it, Rena. You need me."

"No, I'll never need you." She jerked her arm free. "You just want to ease your guilty conscience."

Tony's eyes grew hard and sharp.

Good.

She didn't need his help or his pity. She'd done without him for twelve years and didn't need anything he had to offer. All she wanted was to curl up in her bed and dream about the day when she'd hold her precious baby in her arms.

Tony rubbed his aching shoulder and stretched out his legs, closing the Carlino books for the day. His racing injuries had a way of coming back to haunt him whenever he sat at his father's desk. Maybe it was because Santo never wanted him to leave Napa. He'd chosen racing over the family business and had left it all behind twelve years ago.

He'd wanted more than grapes and vines and worrying about the weather, crops and competition. Of course, Santo Carlino hadn't taken it lightly. He'd cursed and complained and refused to speak to Tony when he'd left.

Tony pursued his dream despite his father's tirades. Being the oldest of three sons Tony was expected to take over the business one day with his brothers by his side. But as it turned out none of the three sons had stayed home to run the Carlino empire.

Now with Santo gone, Tony had no choice but to return. His father's last will and testament made sure that each of his sons spent some time together running the company. He'd stipulated that in order for any of them to claim their inheritance, the land, the company, the Carlino empire, one of them had to agree to become the new CEO within six months.

It was just another way for his father to manipulate them. But Tony hadn't come back to Napa for the money. He had plenty of his own. He'd come back to lay his father to rest and to let his weary body recover from injuries garnered in a wreck at Bristol Raceway just months before.

He'd called his younger brothers home. Joe, the real brain in the family, had been living in New York, trying to develop the latest software phenomenon. And Nick, the youngest, had been creating havoc in Europe, earning a reputation as a gambler and ladies' man.

Tony smiled at that. Little Nick had a wild streak that could lay shame to a young and virile Santo Carlino in his bachelor days. But if one thing could be said about his old man, it was that he was a loving and faithful husband. Tony's mother, Josephina, had tempered him with love and adoration. Many thought her a saint for putting up with Santo, but only the family knew that Santo would have died for her.

"So when's the wedding?" Joe entered the office at Carlino Wines with his hands on his hips, his studious dark brown eyes visible behind a pair of glasses.

When Tony glanced at him in question, Joe continued, "You told me you were getting married."

Tony shoved the ledger books away and leaned back in his chair. "You need a willing bride for a wedding."

"Wanna tell me why you chose Rena? Is it Purple Fields you're after? Or something else?"

A sigh emerged from deep in Tony's chest. He rubbed tension from his forehead. "Maybe I want it all."

"*Want* or need?"

Tony narrowed his eyes and gave his brother a look.

Joe shrugged in an offhanded way. "You've never spoken of marriage before. And the last thing I thought I'd hear at David's funeral was that you intended to marry his widow. Even if it is Rena. We all know she's not exactly your biggest fan."

Tony scoffed. How well he knew. "Hardly that."

"So, what is it? Do you love her?"

Tony's face crinkled up, despite his efforts to keep a blank expression. The truth was he had loved Rena when they'd been younger but he'd loved racing more. He wound up breaking her heart by leaving her behind to pursue his dreams.

Now he had a chance to make it up to her and honor the pledge he'd made David. At the time he'd made that vow it was a no-brainer. David was on his last breaths, and he'd implored Tony to take care of Rena and the child he'd suspected she carried. Tony hadn't flinched when he'd made that promise.

Did Tony want to marry Rena and raise a child that wasn't his? He simply didn't know. But it was what he planned to do.

"No, I don't love her." He stood and looked his brother straight in the eyes, lowering his voice. "This goes no further."

Joe nodded.

"I made David a promise to take care of Rena, the winery and…and their unborn child."

Joe pressed a finger to the bridge of his glasses, securing them in place. He contemplated a moment staring back at Tony then gave an understanding nod. "Got it. Rena knows nothing about this I suppose."

"Nothing."

"Are you seeing her?"

Tony winced, thinking back on the excuses she'd given him. "I've tried several times since the funeral."

"Not cooperating is she?"

"No."

"Can't imagine why she doesn't want to start up right where you left off twelve years ago," Joe said, mockingly. "She picked up the pieces after you left her. It was a hard fall, Tony. I remember hearing all about it. When she fell for David, everyone thought it was the right move. They were happy for her. Sorry, but your name was mud around here for a long time. Then you started winning races and people forgot about the pain you caused Rena. Except Rena. She never forgot. She really loved David, and now he's gone. You can't blame her for hard feelings. She's had it rough."

"I don't blame her. But I will honor my promise to David."

Joe grinned. "I respect your determination, Tony. How are you going to charm a woman who clearly…"

"Hates me?" Tony huffed out a breath. Unfortunately, what he had in mind didn't require a multitude of charm.

Just blackmail. He would give Rena what she wanted most in life. "I have a plan."

Joe shook his head. "You always do."

"It's time I set that plan in action."

TWO

Rena looked in her closet as tears streamed down her face. It had been three weeks since the funeral, and David's clothes—his shirts and pants, his jackets and sweatshirts—still hung just beside hers. She reached out to touch his favorite blue plaid shirt. Her fingers lingered a bit and an image appeared of sitting by a cozy fire cuddling up next to David and laying her head on the soft flannel, his arm wrapped around her shoulder. She smiled at the memory, even through her tears. "What now, David?" she asked in the solitude of her bedroom.

She was a thirty-one-year-old widow. She never would have believed it. Not when just weeks ago she'd planned on telling David her joyous news...that they were to become parents. She'd had it all planned. She'd silk-screened T-shirts that said, "I'm the Daddy" and another that said, "I'm the Mommy" and the third tiny T-shirt said, "And I'm the Boss." She'd planned on giving David the set of them over his favorite dinner.

She hadn't gone to the doctor yet, relying solely on the pregnancy test she'd taken. She'd wanted David by her side when they heard the news officially. Now she'd be going to all of her appointments alone, facing an unknown future.

The only bright spot in all this sadness was the child she carried. She loved her baby with all of her heart and vowed to protect it, doing whatever it took to make a good life for him or her.

Rena closed the closet door unable to remove and discard David's clothes as she'd planned. "I'm not ready to let go," she whispered. She needed David's things around her, to feel his presence and warmth surround her. It gave her a sense of peace, odd as that might seem.

"Do you want me to help you with David's things, Rena?" Solena Melendez's voice broke into her thoughts. Rena turned to find her friend at the bedroom threshold, a concerned look on her face.

Rena smiled sadly. Since David's death, Solena made a point to check up on Rena every morning.

"Solena, no. But thank you." Solena and Raymond Melendez worked at Purple Fields—Solena in the wine-tasting room, Raymond overseeing the vineyards. They'd been loyal employees since Rena and David took over the winery after her parents' deaths.

"It will take time, Rena."

Rena understood that. She'd lost both of her parents. She knew the process of grieving. "I know."

"And when it's time, I will help you."

She smiled and wiped away her tears. "I appreciate that." She reached for Solena, and they embraced. Their relationship had grown over the years, and now Rena thought of Solena and Raymond as more than employees—they were dear friends. Friends whose salaries she may not be able to pay if she didn't get this bank loan.

"We have orders today," Solena said, breaking their embrace. "I'll make sure they go out on time."

"Orders are good," Rena acknowledged with a nod of her head. Thankfully, Solena reminded her daily that she had a winery to run. Purple Fields was small but well-respected, and they'd been holding their own until a slowing economy and bigger wineries started shoving them out. Smaller vintners weren't able to compete and sustain the same degree of losses as the more established ones.

"I have an appointment at the bank today." Though Rena held out little hope, she had to try. She needed a loan to make her payroll this month and next. She was due a small amount from David's life insurance policy, and that money would pay for her doctor bills and whatever was left over would go in trust for her child's future. No one knew about the child she carried as yet, and she'd planned to keep it that way for the time being. She'd not told a soul. Not even Solena.

"I will pray for good news," Solena said.

"So will I," Rena said.

Rena lingered a bit after Solena left her room, putting a little makeup on a face that had seen too many tears. With dark circles beneath her eyes, no amount of makeup could hide her despair. Her grief would be evident, yet she had enough pride to want to appear in control of her emotions when she met Mr. Zelinski at the bank. Bankers were wary of desperation. Rena understood that and prepared herself with facts and figures she hoped would prove that Purple Fields was holding its own and worth the risk of a loan.

Rena walked down the stone hallway and made it to the living room when a knock sounded at her door. "Who could that be?" she muttered, taking up her purse and the file folder for her bank appointment and tucking it under her arm.

She opened the door to Tony Carlino. More than surprised, Rena blinked. "Tony? What are you doing here?"

He cast her a grim smile. "You wouldn't return my phone calls."

"There's a reason for that. I don't care to talk to you."

"Maybe not," Tony said. "But I have to talk to you."

Rena took in a steady breath and calmed her nerves. Just the sight of Tony brought bad memories. She'd gotten over him once and had moved on with her life. She certainly didn't want anything to do with him now. "What could you possibly have to say to me?"

Tony glanced inside her home. He'd been here before many years ago, but she certainly didn't want to invite him in. She'd never minded that she'd come from humble beginnings and that her family home was cozy and rustic, where the Carlino mansion had four wings of stately elegance, two dozen rooms, Italian marble and ancestral artwork that went back a few generations.

"What I have to say can't be said on your doorstep, Rena."

Rena glanced at her watch. "I'm on my way out. I don't have time to talk to you."

"Then have dinner with me tonight."

"Dinner?" Rena had to focus hard not to wrinkle her face. "No, I won't have dinner with you."

Tony let go an exasperated sigh. "I don't remember you being so difficult."

She hadn't been when she'd first met Tony at the age of sixteen. She'd taken one look at him and had fallen in love. They'd been friends first, Rena keeping her secret that she'd fallen hard for a Carlino. Tony had a smile that lit up her heart, and when they laughed together, Rena thought she'd died and gone to heaven. It had been painful holding in her feelings, not letting on that she loved him. It didn't help matters that Santo Carlino was trying to run her parents out of business.

"You don't know me anymore, Tony." Rena lifted her chin. "If this is about easing your conscience about David, you're wasting your time."

Tony's face tightened. His dark eyes grew cold. He stared at her for a moment, then as if gathering all his patience, he took a deep breath. "I haven't got a guilty conscience, Rena. But what I have to say *is* about David."

Rena glanced at her watch again. It wouldn't do to be late for her appointment, yet he'd caught her curiosity. "What about David?"

"Have dinner with me and I'll tell you."

Pressed for time and jittery about her bank appointment, Rena relented. "Fine, I'll have dinner with you."

"I'll pick you up at eight."

"Okay, now at the risk of being rude, I really have to leave."

With a quick nod of agreement, Tony left and Rena breathed a sigh of relief. She wouldn't think about seeing him later and breaking bread with him. She'd seen the determined look on his face and knew he wouldn't take no for an answer. Frankly, she didn't have time to argue. The bank appointment was all she could focus on. "One hurdle at a time." She mumbled David's favorite words of encouragement every time they'd faced a challenge.

She had more important things to worry about than having dinner with Tony Carlino.

Tony drove out of the Purple Fields gates and turned right driving along the roads that would lead him to the Carlino estate. Vineyards on both sides of the highway spread across the valley rising up hills and down slopes, covering the land in a blanket of green.

He'd only been home about three months, and he still felt disoriented, unsure of his place here in Napa. He'd come home because his father had been ill. And now, as the oldest son, he had to assume responsibility for the business working alongside his two brothers. His father had expected as much from him.

The timing had been right for his return. He'd made his mark on NASCAR and had enjoyed every minute of his career until a crash and injury took him off the racing circuit. Perhaps it had been an omen to quit, but it wasn't until his father's passing that Tony realized he'd had no choice but to leave the racing world behind.

Somewhat.

He still had endorsement deals with various companies, and that could be an advantage to Carlino Wines. The Carlino name meant success, and people identified with that. Yet Tony's life had changed so drastically in such a short span of time, and now he planned on taking on a new responsibility with a wife and child.

Was he ready for that?

He questioned that reality now. His vow to David never far from his mind, Tony admitted, if only to himself, that Rena had been right about one thing. If he hadn't come home and rekindled their friendship, David would still be alive today.

Tony approached the Carlino estate and pressed the remote that opened the wide iron gates. He parked the car in front of the garage house and exited. He met up with Joe in the driveway, his brother ever the optimist wearing a smile and horn-rimmed glasses, slapped him on the back. "You look like you've seen a ghost."

He had, in a way. Visions of David's tragic death played in his head ever since he'd driven away from Purple Fields.

It had been a glorious afternoon in Napa, the temperatures in the low seventies with fresh sunshine warm in the air—a day that made you glad to be alive. Tony remembered thinking that, right before he witnessed David's crash.

Before he knew it, he was riding beside David in the ambulance.

"I think she's pregnant," David whispered, struggling to get the words out.

"Shh. Hang on, David. Please. Save your strength."

Tony's plea didn't register with David. He continued, his voice so low that Tony had to bend over to hear him.

"She won't drink," he'd confessed, and Tony immediately understood. Vintners drank wine like others drank water.

David's coherent pleas gave Tony hope, though he appeared so weak. So fragile.

"Tony," he'd implored.

"I'm here." He knew whatever David had to say must be important.

"Don't leave her alone. She deserves a good life. Promise me you'll take care of her. And our baby."

"I promise, David. I'll take care of Rena," Tony whispered, looking deep into David's fading eyes.

"Marry her," David said, grasping Tony's hand. "Promise me that, too."

And Tony hadn't hesitated. He squeezed David's hand. "I'll marry her."

David gave the slightest tip of a nod and closed his eyes. "Tell her I love her."

"Hang on, David. She's coming. You can tell her yourself."

Frantic, Rena rushed up to David the minute they'd reached the hospital. They'd had time together, spoke their last words and Tony hung back giving them privacy. When David let go, Rena cried out. Her deafening sobs for David shook Tony and reached deep into his soul. He'd never seen a woman fall apart like that.

Tony shifted back to the present and looked at his brother with a shake of his head. "I saw Rena today."

Joe wrinkled his nose and gave an understanding nod. "Which explains the haunted look in your eyes. Thinking of David, too?" he asked with genuine concern.

"Yeah, he's never far from my mind. I'm the race car driver. I'm the one taking risks, yet he was the one to die in a crash."

"People die every day in car accidents." Then Joe caught himself. He didn't have a cruel bone in his body. "Sorry, I didn't mean to sound callous, but you didn't encourage him to get behind the wheel. And it *was* an accident."

"I wish Rena felt that way. It would make what I have to do a whole lot easier."

"So, it didn't go well today?"

Tony shrugged. "She blew me off, but not before I made a dinner date with her."

"That's a start. It should get easier now."

Tony scratched his chin, the stubble grating his fingers. "Doubtful. Rena is as proud as she is stubborn."

"I hear you, Tony. I've learned my lesson with the opposite sex. No more relationships for me."

Tony looked his brother in the eye. "Sheila really did a number on you, didn't she?"

Joe lifted his shoulders in a nonchalant shrug. "I'm over it."

Tony believed him, noting the firm set of his jaw and his cool air of confidence, despite his casual shrug. Joe's gorgeous New York assistant had played him, using her charms to snare him into an engagement. But the minute a wealthier man had shown interest in her, she'd dumped Joe for greener pastures and married a man who was twice her age. Joe had been burned, and he wasn't going near the fire any time soon.

"I'm on my way to the downtown office," he said, changing the subject. "Good luck with Rena tonight."

"Thanks. And Joe, keep this quiet." It wouldn't do for news to get out that Tony was dating his friend's new widow.

"I've got your back, bro."

Rena parked her car outside her home, her hands frozen on the steering wheel as she looked with numbing silence at the house in desperate need of paint and a roof that had seen better days. Her garden had been neglected lately, the grounds and outer buildings weren't what they once were. But the vineyards beyond, whose budding grapes were the mainstay of her legacy, had the best terroir in the vicinity. Their merlot and cabernet wines won awards from the combination of good weather, soil and minerals. The vineyards had never let her down. "All I have left are those vines," she mumbled, her voice shaky. "What am I going to do?"

The news from Mr. Zelinski wasn't good. She hadn't known the lengths David had gone to in order to keep them in business until she'd pressed the banker to be brutally honest. She saw regret in his eyes and sympathy cross his features and knew of his reluctance to tell her the ultimate truth. Both the Fairfield and Montgomery families were part of the tightly knit Napa community and had been personal friends of the banker. She assumed it was out of respect for her mourning that he hadn't been knocking at her door demanding his money.

The grim news she received shook what little hope she had left. Not only couldn't she qualify for a loan but David had taken out a home equity line of credit to keep them going these past few months. Until that loan was repaid and her credit restored, she couldn't even think about asking for additional help from the bank.

She owed more money than she originally thought.

Tears welled in her eyes as the hopelessness of her situation enveloped her. From across the driveway, out among the vines she spotted Raymond checking the leaves, making sure the grapes were healthy.

A sob escaped. She knew what she had to do, and it hurt to even think it. She couldn't pay Solena and Raymond. She'd barely scraped up enough money to give them their last month's salary. She'd let her other employees go, but hoped she could keep her friends on. Now, it was clear she had to let them go as well.

Her heart breaking, Rena bounded out of the car and ran up the steps to her house, tears spilling down her cheeks. She couldn't face losing them, not after losing David so abruptly. Everything around her was changing too fast.

Yet she couldn't expect Solena and Raymond to stay. She knew they'd have no trouble finding employment at another vineyard. Both were efficient, dedicated and knew as much about winemaking as she did. Selfishly, she wanted to keep them close, to have them work the land and be here when she needed them. Rena had sad facts to face, and she didn't know if she was up to the challenge.

Slamming the door shut, she strode to her bedroom, wiping at tears that continued to fall. She tossed her files and purse aside, kicking off her shoes as she flopped down on her bed. She lay looking up at the ceiling, searching her mind for a way to keep her business afloat. What avenues had she missed? Who could she turn to for help? Finally, after a half hour of torturous thought, she came up with the only solution that made sense. She had no other option.

She had to sell Purple Fields.

Three

Tony debated whether to bring Rena flowers, remembering that she'd always loved the tulips that grew in the Carlino garden. "I like the purple ones best," she'd said when they were teens. "They're bright and happy, just waiting to put a smile on someone's face."

But he knew giving Rena her favorite flowers wouldn't put a smile on her face now. Nothing he could do—aside from vanishing off the face of the earth—would do that. He'd opted to knock on her door empty-handed, hoping that she hadn't changed her mind about tonight.

He'd sort of bulldozed her into this dinner date. What other choice did he have? He'd waited a respectable amount of time to approach her, allowing her time to heal from the shock of losing her husband. Yet, with a baby on the way and a failing business, Rena was in trouble. Tony didn't think he could wait much longer.

He'd promised David.

He drove his Porsche through the Purple Fields gates for the second time today and parked in front of the gifts shop-wine-tasting room adjacent to the main house. The quaint shop attracted tourists during the late spring and summer months when the weather was mild and the scent of grapes flavored the air. Rena had worked there during high school, serving sandwiches and cheese and crackers to their customers.

Tony ran a hand down his face, bracing himself for Rena's wrath. She wouldn't agree to his terms lightly, if at all. He got out of the car and walked the distance to the house. Using the metal knocker on the door, he gave three firm raps and waited. When she didn't come, he knocked again, louder.

"Rena," he called out.

He gazed over the grounds as the last remnants of evening light faded. Focusing intently, he glanced around at the other buildings and through the vineyards. There was no sign of her. Tony tried the doorknob, and to his surprise it opened.

She'd left the door unlocked.

He felt a surging sense of alarm. Rena lived alone now. It wasn't like her not to be cautious. Without hesitation, he walked inside the house. The entry that led to the living room was dark. As he took a few steps inside, it seemed the entire house was dark. "Rena?"

He made his way down the long hall and opened one door, peering inside to an empty room. He checked another room without success. When he got to the end of the hallway, he found the last door open. A small amount of moonlight illuminated the middle of the room where Rena slept on her bed.

Tony winced, seeing her sleeping soundly, her chest lifting and falling peacefully, her raven hair spread across the pillow. A few strands curled around her face and contrasted against her creamy complexion. She wore the same austere dress he'd seen her in earlier today, but it couldn't conceal the feminine slope of her breasts or the luscious curve of her hips.

Tony had loved her once. He'd taken her virginity when she was eighteen. When she'd cried, overwhelmed by emotion, he'd clung to her and assured her of his love. Rena had given herself to him one hundred percent and though he'd tried to give her everything she needed from him, he couldn't. He had another great passion—racing. It was in his blood. From the time he was a small boy, Tony needed to feel the wind at his back. He loved speed and thrilled at the danger of being wild and free. Later, he'd learned to harness his passion. He'd learned that precision and accuracy as well as spirit made you a winner.

He'd achieved his goals without much struggle. He'd been born to race. But he'd also disappointed his father by not working alongside him as was expected by the eldest son, and he'd hurt the girl he'd admired and loved most in the world.

Memories flashed again, of making love to Rena and how incredibly poignant and pure it'd been. But Tony's mission here wasn't to rehash the past but to move on to the future. Rena was David's widow now, and the strain of his death was evident on her beautiful face, even in sleep.

His first inclination was to quietly leave, locking the door behind him, but he found he couldn't move, couldn't lift his eyes away from her sad desolate face. So he stood at the threshold of her bedroom, watching her.

It wasn't long before she stirred, her movements lazy as she stretched out on the bed. Tony's gaze moved to the point where her dress hiked up, exposing long beautiful legs and the hint of exquisite thighs.

His body quickened, and he ground his teeth fighting off lusty sexual thoughts. Yet, quick snippets of memory emerged of hot delicious nights making love to her all those years ago.

Rena opened her eyes and gasped when she spotted his figure in the doorway. Immediate fear and vulnerability entered her eyes. She sat straight up, and when she recognized him, anger replaced her fear. "What are you doing here?"

"We had a date."

"A date?" To her credit, she did appear hazily confused. Then the anger resurfaced. "How'd you get in?"

"The door was unlocked. Not a good habit, Rena. Anyone could have gotten into your house."

"Anyone *did*."

Tony chose to ignore the swipe.

Rena swung her legs around and set her bare feet on the floor. She rubbed her forehead with both hands and shook her head. "I guess I fell asleep. What time is it?"

"Eight-fifteen."

She looked up at him. "Were you standing there all that time?"

"No," he lied. "I just got here. I was fashionably late."

She closed her eyes briefly. "I don't know what happened. I felt exhausted and fell into a deep sleep."

The baby, Tony thought. He'd had many a racing buddy speak about their wife's exhaustion during their early pregnancy. "Maybe it's all catching up with you. You've been through a lot this past month."

"You don't know what I've been through." She was being deliberately argumentative, and Tony didn't take the bait.

"How long before you can be ready?"

Her brows furrowed. "Ready?"

"For dinner."

"Oh, I don't think so. Not tonight. I'm not—" she began to put her hand to her flat stomach, then caught herself "—feeling well."

"You'll feel better once you eat. How long since you've eaten?"

"I don't know…. I had a salad for lunch around noon."

"You need to keep up your strength, Rena."

She opened her mouth to respond, then clamped it shut.

"I'll wait for you in the living room."

Tony turned and walked away, not really giving her

a choice in the matter. There were many more things he'd have to force upon her before the evening was through.

Rena got up from her bed, moving slowly as she replayed the events of the day in her mind. First, Tony had visited her this afternoon, a fact that still irked her. Yet he had something to say and he wouldn't leave until he got it off his chest. That's how Carlinos operated; they did what they darn well wanted, no matter how it affected other people. Bitter memories surfaced of her father standing up to Santo Carlino, but Rena shoved them out of her mind for the moment. She couldn't go there now.

Next came thoughts of her conversation with Mr. Zelinski at the bank. He'd been kind to her, confessing his hands were tied. She wouldn't be getting the loan she desperately needed. She wouldn't be able to pay her employees. Purple Fields was doomed.

Her head began to pound. She felt faint. Though her appetite had been destroyed today, she admitted that she really should eat something. For the baby's sake, if nothing else. She couldn't afford to sink into depression. It wouldn't be good for the unborn child she carried.

As quick as her body allowed, she got ready, cringing at her reflection in the mirror. Her face was drawn, her hair wild, her clothes rumpled. She washed her face, applied a light tint of blush to her cheeks, some lipstick to her lips and brushed her hair back into a clip at the base of her neck—just to appear human again. She changed her clothes, throwing on a black pair of pants and a soft knit beige sweater that ruffled into a vee and looked stylish though comfortable. She slipped her feet into dark shoes and walked out of the room. Whatever Tony had in mind, she certainly wasn't going to dress up for him.

Tony closed the magazine he was reading and rose from the sofa when she strode in. She squirmed under his direct scrutiny. "You look better."

She didn't comment yet noted genuine concern in his eyes. Why?

He strode to the door and opened it. "Shall we go?"

"Where are you taking me?"

Tony's expression flattened. He'd caught her meaning. "I've made arrangements, Rena. No one will see you with me."

If she weren't so upset about *everything,* her face might have flamed from his acknowledgment. She lifted her chin. "How's that possible?"

"We own half of Alberto's. It's closed to the public tonight."

"You mean you had it closed for my benefit?"

"You haven't had any use for me since I returned. I didn't think you'd like answering questions about being out with me tonight if anyone saw us."

Rena had almost forgotten that the Carlinos had their hands in other enterprises. They owned a few restaurants as well as the winery. They also owned stores in outlying areas that sold a line of products related to wine.

"This isn't a date, Tony. Just so we're clear."

Tony nodded. "Very clear."

Rena strode past him and waited for him to exit her house before she locked the front door. She moved quickly, and once he beeped his car alarm, she didn't wait for him to open the car door. She climbed into his Porsche and adjusted the seat belt.

"Ready?" he asked unnecessarily. Once they made eye contact, he roared the engine to life. "It's a nice night. Mind if I put the top down?"

"No, I could use a good dose of fresh air."

It's how Tony liked to drive, with the top down, the air hitting his face, mastering the car and the road beneath.

He hit a button, and mechanically the car transformed. He drove the road to Napa surprisingly slowly, as if they were out for a Sunday drive. Every so often, he glanced her way. She couldn't deny his courtesy.

Or the fact that she thought him the most devastatingly handsome man she'd ever met. She'd thought so since they'd first met the day he entered public school at the age of sixteen. Up until that point, the Carlinos had gone to an elite private school. But Tony hated the regimented lifestyle, the solitude and discipline of being in an academy. Finally, his father had relented, granting his sons the right to go through the public school system.

Tony had made a lasting impression on her, and they'd started out as friends. But the friendship had grown as they'd gotten closer, and Rena had become Tony's steady girlfriend two years later.

Despite his obvious wealth and place in Napa society.

Despite the fact that Santo Carlino and her father had become bitter enemies.

Despite the fact that Rena never *truly* believed she could have a lasting relationship with Tony.

"Care for some music?" he asked, reaching for the CD player button.

"If you don't mind, I'd like to be quiet."

She didn't want to rekindle memories of driving in Tony's car with the top down and the music blasting. Of laughing and telling silly jokes, enjoying each other's company.

"Okay," he said amiably.

They drove in silence, Tony respecting her wishes. Shortly, he pulled into Alberto's back parking lot. "I usually don't resort to back alley entrance ways," he said, with no hint of irritation. "Are you hungry?"

"Yes, actually quite hungry."

"Good, the food is waiting for us."

Before she managed to undo her seat belt, Tony was there, opening the car door for her. He reached his hand inside, and rather than appearing incredibly stubborn in his eyes, she slid her hand in his while he helped her out. The Porsche sat so low to the ground she would have fumbled like an idiot anyway, trying to come up smoothly to a standing position.

Sensations ripped through her instantly. The contact, the intimate way his large hand enveloped her smaller one, trampled any false feeling of ease she'd imagined. She fought the urge to whip her hand away. Instead, she came out of the car and stood fully erect before slipping her hand out of his. Composing herself, she thanked him quietly and followed him inside the restaurant.

"This way," he said and gestured to a corner booth lit by candlelight. True to his word, the entire restaurant was empty but for them. She sat down at one end of the circular booth, while he sat at the other.

The few times Rena had come here, she'd always felt as though she'd wandered in from the streets in Tuscany with its old world furnishings and stone fountains. Alberto's was one of finest restaurants in the county, serving gourmet fare and the best wines from Napa.

"I had the chef prepare a variety of food. I wasn't sure what you liked."

"You forgot that I loved pepperoni pizza?"

Tony's mouth twisted. "No one could inhale pizza like you, Rena. But I doubt it's on the menu tonight. Let's go into the kitchen and see what the chef conjured up for us."

Tony bounded up from the booth and waited. She rose and walked beside him until they reached the state-of-the-art kitchen. They found covered dishes on the immaculate steel counter along with fresh breads, salads and a variety of desserts sitting in the glass refrigerator.

Tony lifted one cover and announced. "Veal scaloppine, still hot."

Rena looked on with interest.

Tony lifted another cover. "Linguine arrabiatta, black tiger shrimps with bacon and garlic."

Steam rose up, and she leaned in closer. "Hmm, smells good."

He lifted two more covers displaying filetto di bue, an oven roasted filet mignon, which smelled heavenly but was too heavy for Rena's tastes, and ravioli di zucca, which Tony explained was spinach ravioli with butternut and Amaretto filling. Since entering the aromatic kitchen, Rena's appetite had returned wholeheartedly.

"The ravioli looks good," she said. "And that salad." She pointed to a salad with baby greens, avocado, tangerines and candied walnuts.

"Great," Tony said lifting the covered dish of her choice. And one for him. "If you could grab that salad, we'll eat. Soon as I find us a bottle of wine."

"Oh, no wine for me," she announced. Tony glanced at her with a raised brow but didn't question her. "I'll have water."

"Your poison," he said with a smile. He set the dishes down on the table and took off again, bringing back a bottle of Carlino Cabernet and a pitcher of water.

They settled in for the meal in silence, Rena polishing off the delicious salad within minutes and Tony sipping his wine, eyeing her every move. "Quit looking at me."

"You're the best looking thing in this place."

She squeezed her eyes shut. "Don't, Tony."

He shrugged it off. "Just stating the obvious."

When he turned on the charm, he had enough for the entire Napa Valley and then some. "Do you mind telling me what's so important that you couldn't tell me earlier this afternoon?"

"After dinner, Rena."

With her water glass to her lips, she asked, "Why?"

"I want you to eat your meal."

She gathered her brows and shook her head. "Because…what you have to say might destroy my appetite?"

Tony inhaled sharply then blew out the breath. "Because you're hungry and exhausted, that's why."

"Why the sudden concern about my well-being?"

Tony softened his tone. "I've always cared about you, Rena."

"No, Tony. We're not going there. *Ever*," she emphasized. She wouldn't go down that mental path. She and Tony had way too much history, and she thought she'd never heal from the wounds he'd inflicted.

"Can't you just forget for a few minutes who I am and who you are? Can't we break bread together quietly and enjoy a good meal?"

Rena relented but still questioned Tony's mysterious behavior. "Fine. I'll eat before the ravioli gets cold."

"That's a girl."

She shot him a look.

He raised his hands up in surrender. "Sorry." Then he dug into his filet mignon with gusto and sipped wine until he'd drained two goblets.

After finishing their entrées, Tony cleared the dishes himself, refusing Rena's help. He needed time to collect his thoughts and figure out how he was going to propose marriage to his best friend's new widow and not come off sounding callous and cruel. There was only one route to take and that was to tell her the truth.

Hell, he hadn't ever really thought about marriage to anyone *but* Rena Fairfield. As teenagers, they'd spent many a night daydreaming of the time when they'd marry. But then Rena's mother became ill, and Tony had been given a real opportunity to pursue his dream of racing stock cars. Leaving Rena behind to care for her ailing mother and help her father run Purple Fields had been the only black spot in an otherwise shining accomplishment. Begging her to join him served no purpose. She couldn't leave. She had family obligations. She loved making wine. She loved Purple Fields. She was born to live in Napa, where Tony had been born to race.

He'd hurt her. No, he'd nearly destroyed her.

Each time he'd called her from the racing circuit, she'd become more and more distant. Until one day, she asked him not to call anymore. Two years later, she'd married David. He hadn't been invited to the wedding.

Tony covered a tray with tiramisu, spumoni ice cream and chocolate-coated cannolis. He returned to Rena and answered her skepticism as she watched him place the food on the table. "What? Regardless of what you think, I wasn't born with a silver spoon. We had to do chores at the house. My father was a stickler for pulling your own weight."

"I would think you're one who is used to being served."

"I am. I won't deny it. Life is good now. I'm wealthy and can afford—"

"Shutting down a restaurant for the night to have a private dinner?"

"Yeah, among other things."

"I guess I should feel honored that you served me dinner. You must have a good reason."

"I do." He glanced at the desserts on the table and moved a dish of spumoni her way. "You love ice cream. Dig in."

Rena didn't hesitate. She picked up a spoon and dove into the creamy Italian fare.

Tony dipped into it as well, butting spoons with her. They made eye contact, and Rena turned away quickly. How often had they shared ice cream in the past?

After three spoonfuls of spumoni, Rena pushed the dish away. "Okay, Tony. I've had dinner with you. No one is around. So are you going to tell me why you needed to speak to me?"

"I know you hate me, Rena."

She steered her gaze toward the fountain in the middle of the dining area. "Hate is a strong word."

"So, you don't hate me?" he asked, with a measure of hope.

She looked into his eyes again. "I didn't say that."

Tony didn't flinch. He'd prepared himself for this. "What did David say to you before he died?"

She straightened in her seat, her agitated body language not to be missed. "That's none of your business."

"Fair enough. But I need to tell you what he asked

of me, Rena. I need you to hear his last words to me as I rode beside him in the ambulance."

Tears welled in her eyes. Tony was a sucker for Rena's tears. He never could stand to see her cry.

For a moment, fear entered her eyes as if hearing David's words would cause her too much pain. But then, courageously, she nodded, opening her eyes wide. "Okay. Yes, I do want to hear what he said."

Tony spoke quietly, keeping his voice from cracking. "He told me he loved you." Rena inhaled a quick breath, and those tears threatened again. "And that you deserved a good life."

"He was the kindest man," she whispered.

"His last thoughts were only of you."

A single tear fell from her eyes. "Thank you, Tony. I needed to hear that."

"I'm not through, Rena. There's more."

She sat back in her seat and leaned heavily against the back of the booth, bracing herself. "Okay."

"He asked me to to watch out for you. Protect you. And I intend to do just that. Rena, I intend to marry you."

Four

Tony might as well have said he was going to fly to the moon on a broomstick; his declaration was just as ridiculous. Still, Rena couldn't contain her shock. Her mouth dropped open. She couldn't find the words.

Her heart broke thinking that David's very last thoughts and concerns hadn't been for himself but for her. But at the same time, if what Tony had said was true, then a wave of anger built at her departed husband as well. How could he even suggest such a thing? Asking Tony to take care of her? To protect her? He was the last man on earth she trusted, and David knew that.

Didn't he?

"You can't be serious," she finally got out once a tumultuous array of emotions swept through her system.

"I'm dead serious, Rena." He pinned her with a sharp unrelenting look.

"It's ridiculous."

"Maybe. But it's David's last wishes."

"You're saying he asked you to marry me?" Rena kept a tight reign on her rising blood pressure.

Tony nodded. "I promised him, Rena."

"No, no, no, no, no, no." She shook her head so hard that her hair slipped out of its clip.

Tony held steady peering into her eyes. "Tell me what he said to you. His last words."

"He said," she began, her voice shaky, her expression crestfallen. "He said he loved me. And that he wanted me to keep Purple Fields." She looked down for a moment to compose herself. "He knew how much it meant to me."

"And you promised him?"

"I did. But I—" Flashes of her conversation with Mr. Zelinski earlier today came flooding back. There was no hope of saving the winery. As much as it hurt her, she'd resolved that she had no other option but to sell Purple Fields. Not only would her family's legacy be lost but so would her livelihood. Yet she needed to provide for her baby. That's all that mattered now, and selling out meant that she'd have enough cash for a year or two if she were very careful. "I can't keep it. I've already decided...to sell."

Tony sat back in his seat, watching as Rena tried to compose herself. So many thoughts entered her mind all at once that her head began to ache. She put her head down and rubbed her temples, to alleviate the pain and to avoid Tony's scrutiny.

"You don't want to sell Purple Fields," he said softly.

"No, of course not."

"You know what it would mean to Purple Fields if we marry? You'd have no more worry…I'd make sure of it."

She kept her head down. She didn't want to admit that marrying Tony would solve her immediate problems and she'd be able to keep her promise to David. But she also knew that her emotions would rule it out this time. She couldn't marry Tony Carlino.

He'd abandoned her when she'd needed him most.

He'd hurt her so deeply that it took a decent man like David to heal her and make her trust again. She had no faith in Tony, and marriage to anyone, much less him, was out of the question. Her wounds were still too raw and fresh.

Tony reached over and caressed her hand with his. Again, an instant current ran between them. "Think about it, Rena. Think about the promises we both made to David."

Twenty minutes later, as Tony drove her home, she still couldn't think of anything else. She wanted to save Purple Fields, to see it thrive and be successful again, but the cost was too great.

Tony walked her to the door. She slipped the key into the lock and turned to face him. "Good night, Tony."

Tony's dark eyes gleamed for a moment. He glanced at

her mouth, his gaze lingering there. Her heart pounded, and for an instant, she was that young smitten girl who banked on his every word. He leaned his body closer, his eyes on hers, and she remembered the chemistry between them, the joy of loving him and having him love her. Images that she'd thought had been destroyed came back in a flash. He slanted his head and she waited. But his kiss bypassed her lips and brushed her cheek. He grabbed the doorknob and shoved open her door. "I'll come by to see you tomorrow, Rena."

Rena stepped inside and leaned heavily on her door, her fingers tracing the cheek he'd just kissed. She squeezed her eyes shut and prayed for a way out of her dilemma.

A way that didn't include marrying Tony Carlino.

The next day, Tony knocked on Rena's door at noon. When she didn't answer the knock, he walked toward the gift shop and peeked inside the window. Solena Melendez waved to him, and he walked inside the store. "Good afternoon."

"Hello, Solena." Tony had met her at David's funeral for the first time. He'd learned enough to know that Solena and Rena were good friends, Solena being just a few years older. She lived in a residential area of Napa with her husband, Raymond, and they worked for Purple Fields since Rena and David took over from her parents. A quick glance around told him that though Solena kept the quaint gift shop immaculate, the shelves were only scantily stocked with items for sale. "I'm looking for Rena. Do you know where she is?"

"I'm right here." Rena came out of the back room, her arms loaded down with a few cases of wine.

Tony had an instant inclination to lift those heavy boxes from her arms but restrained himself. Rena was a proud woman.

She set the boxes down on the front counter. "I'll help you with these bottles in a minute." She smiled warmly at Solena and turned to Tony, her face transforming from warm to cold in a flash. "Follow me," she said and walked outside the shop and down the steps.

The air was fresh and clear, the sky above as blue as Rena's eyes. She walked past her house to the vineyards, and once they were out of earshot she turned to him. "Do you plan on showing up here whenever you want?"

Tony grinned. "Are you mad because I didn't call to make an appointment?"

"No. Yes." Her brows furrowed. "I'm busy, Tony. I don't welcome drop-by company unless they are paying customers."

"You're working with a skeleton crew. And working too hard."

Rena rolled her eyes. "I've been doing this work since I learned to walk, practically. Yes, I work hard, but I don't mind. Why are you here?"

"I told you I'd come by today."

"Checking up on me?"

"If you want to look at it that way."

Rena's face twisted in disgust. "I can take care of myself. I hate that David made you promise to watch out for me."

"I know you do. But a promise is a promise."

"And you don't break your promises, do you? Except to young girls you've pledged your heart to. Then you have no problem."

Rena turned away from him, but he couldn't let her get away with that. He reached out and grabbed her wrist, turning her around to face him. "I loved you, Rena. Make no mistake about that. I've apologized for hurting you a hundred times. But I couldn't stay here then, and you know it. And you couldn't leave with me, and you know that, too. We weren't destined to be together back then."

She yanked her arm free and hoisted her pretty chin. "We're not destined to be together ever, so why don't you go away."

"I'm not going anywhere. Not until I make myself clear. I'm offering you a business proposition, not a real marriage proposal. If you let go of some of your anger and pride, you'd see that. I'm offering you a way to save Purple Fields."

She remained silent.

"How long before you have to let Solena and her husband go? How long before you'll have to close the winery? You don't want to sell. Purple Fields is a big part of you. You love what you do."

"Don't," she said, her eyes filling with moisture. "Don't, Tony."

"Don't what? Speak the truth? You know damn well marrying me is the best thing all the way around."

"David's been gone only a short time. And…and, I don't love you." She pierced him with a direct look.

"I don't love you either," he said, softly so as not to

hurt her anymore. "But, in all these years, I've never wanted to marry another woman. I've never even come close."

He put his arms around her waist and pulled her toward him. Without pause, he brushed his lips to hers softly at first. When she didn't pull away, he deepened the kiss, relishing the exquisite softness of her lips, enjoying the woman that Rena had become. Soft, lush and incredibly beautiful.

When he broke off the kiss, he gazed into Rena's stunned blue eyes. "We may not have love anymore, but we have history and friendship."

She tilted her head stubbornly. "I'm not your friend."

"David wants this for both of us."

"No!" Rena pulled away at the mention of David's name. Confusion filled her expression, and she wiped her mouth with the back of her hand, as if wiping away all that they'd once meant to each other. "I can't marry you—no matter what you promised David. I still blame you for his death and, and..."

"And what, Rena? That kiss just proved we still have something between us. You can save your winery and honor David's last wish."

"You don't understand." Then Rena's eyes reflected dawning knowledge, as if a light had been turned on inside her head. She covered her flat stomach with her hand. "Your family prides itself on bloodlines. It's instilled in your Italian heritage. Everything has to be perfect. Everything has to be pure from the wine you make to the babies you bring into this world. Well, I'm pregnant, Tony. With David's baby. You'd be raising David's child as your own."

Tony didn't flinch. He didn't turn away. He didn't move so much as a muscle in surprise. That was his mistake. Rena expected shock. She expected him to change his mind, to withdraw his marriage proposal. It irked him that she thought so little of him.

Rena backed away, gasping at his nonresponse. Her mouth dropped open, and when she spoke, her voice broke with accusation. "You know. How? *How* do you know, Tony?" She pressed him for an answer.

"I didn't know for sure, until now."

Rena narrowed her eyes. "Tell me."

Tony sighed. "It was David. He suspected it."

Rena backed away, her hands clutching at her hair. Her shoulders slumped, color drained from her face. It was as if she relived his death all over again. She looked down at a patch of shriveled grape leaves on the ground. "He knew about our baby."

"I'm sorry, Rena."

Her eyes watered. "David won't ever meet his child."

"No, but he wanted to protect him and…you. I'm capable of doing that for you, Rena."

"But I don't want to marry you," she said softly.

Tony heard the resignation in her tone. She was considering her options. "I know."

She peered into his eyes. "How would it look? I'm barely a widow—and now I'm marrying my husband's friend."

Tony made this decision to protect Rena days ago. "No one has to know. We'll keep it secret."

"Secret?" She looked at him, puzzled.

"For a time, anyway."

She closed her eyes, contemplating. She battled with the idea of marrying him. Her facial expressions reflected her thoughts as they twisted to and fro.

He pressed his point. "Your winery needs help fast," he said quietly, and then added, "but more important, your child needs a father."

"Maybe that's true." Rena's eyes flooded with tears now, her voice filled with surrender. "But I don't need you, Tony. I'll never need you again."

That was the closest she'd come to a yes.

Tony made mental plans for their wedding day.

Rena cried herself to sleep for two nights, realizing the futility in denying the inevitable. She was cornered and had nowhere to run. She'd been waging mental wars inside her head since Tony's proposal for a secret marriage. She couldn't come up with any other viable solution to her dilemma. She was so heavily in debt she doubted she'd find anyone willing to take on such a big risk.

But how could she marry Tony?

How could she allow him to be a father to David's child?

It all seemed so unfair.

Rena stepped outside her house and squinted into the morning sunlight rising just above the hills. Golden hues cast beautiful color over the valley. This was her favorite time of day. When David was alive, she'd often wake early and come outside to tend her garden and open her mind to all possibilities. David would sit on the veranda to drink coffee and watch her. They would talk endlessly about little things and his presence would lend her peace and comfort.

But since his death, Rena had sorely neglected her garden. Today, she hoped she'd find solace working the soil and nurturing the lilies and roses. She needed this time to come to grips with what she had to do.

She put on her gardening gloves and took to the soil, yanking out pesky weeds, and with each firm tug, thoughts of what David asked from her in his death plagued her mind. He hadn't given her what she needed most—time to grieve. Time to try to figure out a way to save Purple Fields on her own. Instead, he'd hidden the facts from her and shielded her from bad news. David had always been a man she could count on, but he hadn't realized the toll his dying request would take on her.

She tugged at a stubborn weed, bracing her feet and pulling with all of her might. Emotions roiled in the pit of her stomach. Feelings she'd held in for a long time finally came forth as she felt the weed break with the ground. "I'm so mad at you, David, I could spit."

The weed released, easing from the soil slowly and Rena held it in her hands, staring at the roots that had once been secured in the earth. "You died and left me with this mess."

And when she thought tears would fall again, instead simmering anger rose up with full force. She was angry, truly angry with David. She was angry with herself.

But most of all, she was angry with Tony Carlino. Her anger knew no rationality at the moment. And for the first time since David's death, Rena felt strong in that anger. She felt powerful. She refused to let guilt or fear wash away her innermost feelings. David had let her down. Tony had blackmailed her.

But she didn't have to take it without a fight. She didn't have to lose control of everything she loved, just because fate had stepped in and knocked her down. New strength born of distress and determination lifted her. She still had a say in what happened in her life. Her primary obligation was to protect her unborn child and secure his future legacy.

Rena whipped off her gloves and stood up, arching her back and straightening out as a plan formed in her mind. With new resolve, she headed back into the house. She had a call to make. She needed expert legal advice and knew that Mark Winters, David's longtime friend, would help her.

She may be down temporarily, but she wasn't out.

For the first time in a long time, Rena felt as though she had some control about her destiny.

And it felt darn good.

Tony glanced at his watch, his patience wearing thin as he sat in a booth by the window at the Cab Café. Rena was ten minutes late. Had she backed out of this meeting at the last moment?

This morning, he'd been happy to hear Rena's voice on the phone. She'd called early, just as he was leaving for work and she'd sounded adamant that he meet with her today. She wouldn't give him a hint as to what the meeting was about, but since he'd proposed to her last week, he figured she'd come to realize that marrying him was inevitable. Not one to ever look a gift horse in the mouth, he'd cleared his schedule and shown up here five minutes early.

The boisterous teenage hangout held a good deal of memories for them both, and he wondered why she'd picked this particular place. At one time the Cabernet Café was a wine-tasting room but when that failed, the owner had changed the café's focus and now it thrived as a burger-and-fries joint.

A waitress wearing an apron designed with a cluster of purple grapes approached and Tony ordered coffee to pass the time. He decided to wait until he'd finished his first cup before calling Rena to see what the delay was.

Less than five minutes later, just as he was pulling out his cell phone, Rena stepped into the café. He rose from his seat and she spotted him. He gave her a little wave, which she ignored.

As she approached, Tony noticed she had shadows under eyes that were haunted and sad, but even that couldn't mask her genuine beauty. Her hair was pulled back from her face in a ponytail and she wore jeans and a blue sweater that brought out the sparkling hue of her eyes. Her purse sat on her shoulder but she also carried a manila folder in one hand. He waited until she reached the table and sat across from him before he took his seat.

"I was just about to call you. Thought you might have changed your mind."

She glanced at him and shook her head. "No, I'm sorry I'm late. I had an appointment this morning that ran a little long."

"What kind of appointment?" he asked, wondering what was so important to keep him waiting.

She glanced out the window, hesitating, and then turned back to him. "I had my first checkup today for the baby."

Tony leaned back against the vinyl booth and stared at her. "How did it go? Is everything okay?"

Rena couldn't seem to keep her joy from showing. She granted him a smile and her voice lifted when she spoke. "Yes, the baby is healthy. I'm due in October."

"That's good news, Rena." But the news also brought home the reality of what he was about to do. He would take responsibility for a child he didn't father. He would marry a woman who didn't love him. All of it hit him hard between the eyes. This was really happening.

He'd loved David as a friend, but he also knew that if it had been any woman other than Rena, he wouldn't have agreed to David's request. He wouldn't be doing this for a stranger. Though Rena would deny it, they had a connection. Their lives had been entwined for years. Marrying her wasn't as much a hardship for him as it was for her. "What else did the doctor say?"

She breathed out quietly. "He told me to try to stay calm. Not to let stress get me down."

"That's good advice, Rena. You've had a lot to deal with lately and you should try to relax for—"

"I don't need a lecture, Tony."

Her abrupt behavior had him gritting his teeth. Pregnant women were temperamental at times, at least that's what he'd heard from his married friends, but it was more than that with Rena. His proposal to her was nothing more than sugarcoated blackmail. Hell, he hated to add to her stress. But he owed David this and he had to see it through.

She looked at him and inhaled a deep breath. "I'm sorry. This isn't easy for me. Believe me, I have the baby's well-being in mind every second of the day. That's why it's been such a tug of war."

Tony had thicker skin than to be offended, but most women wouldn't consider a proposal from him a terrible thing.

The waitress walked up to the table again. "Hi, what can I get for you?"

Rena faced her without opening the menu. "I should have the California café salad."

"One California café salad, got it. And for you sir?"

"But," Rena interrupted and the waitress turned back to her, "I'm craving a chili cheeseburger with extra pickles."

The waitress grinned. "That's our specialty. Got it. And I'll make sure you get those pickles."

"Thank you. I'll have a lemonade too."

Tony ordered the same thing, and after the waitress left, he glanced at Rena. "You're having cravings? I wondered why you wanted to meet me here."

She lifted a shoulder and shrugged. "It's been a long

time and this morning when I got up, I couldn't stop thinking about having a chili cheeseburger."

"We sure ate our share of them when we were kids. We used to close down this place, remember?"

"Yeah, I do."

And for a moment, Rena's face softened. Tony remembered what it was like being with her back then. The fun times they'd had together. They'd been so close and so much in love.

Rena stared at the manila folder she'd set down on the table and her expression changed.

"What's going on?" Tony asked, glancing at the folder. "What's in there?"

"It's something I want from you."

Surprised, Tony looked at her, arching a brow. "Okay, so why don't you tell me?"

She slid the folder toward him. "It's a prenuptial agreement." Her eyes met his directly.

Tony hid his surprise well. He didn't react, though a dozen thoughts popped into his head all at once. He decided to hear her out and not jump to conclusions.

"If I marry you, I want Purple Fields to remain in my name. I want full ownership of the winery and vineyard. I want to have the final say in every decision having to do with it. My child will own Purple Fields one day, no questions asked. Have your attorney look it over. It's legal and there shouldn't be any problem."

Tony sighed heavily. "Rena, you do see the irony in this, don't you?"

Rena searched his eyes. "How so?"

"First of all, I don't want Purple Fields. Marrying me

has nothing to do with me getting my hands on your winery. The fact is, I'm worth tens of millions, Rena. Everything I own will be yours. I'm not asking for a prenuptial agreement from you."

"If you want one, I'd sign it."

"I don't want one, damn it! I'm not entering into this marriage lightly. If we marry, it'll be for keeps. We'll have a child and we'll be a family. Do you understand what I'm saying?"

"Yes, of course. But you've made promises to me before that you've broken, and now I have no choice in the matter. I want some control. You should understand that, being a Carlino."

Tony's lips tightened. He didn't want an argument, so he chose his words carefully. "This time it's different. This time, I'm not going to break any promises I make to you."

"I'd sleep better at night if I believed you."

Tony let go a curse.

Rena continued to explain. "I'm only protecting what's mine. Can you blame me? It's all I have left and I don't want to lose it."

Angry now, Tony didn't bother reading the agreement first. "Fine. I'll sign it."

He reached into his pocket and pulled out a pen. Then he slid the papers out and gave them only a cursory glance before signing his name at the bottom.

"Don't you want your attorney to look it over?" Rena asked, her expression incredulous, watching him slide the papers back into the folder.

He shook his head. "I know you well enough to

know there's nothing in this agreement that I'd find questionable. I *trust* you."

Rena sat back against the booth, her chin bravely raised. "I won't let you make me feel guilty about this."

"I'm not trying to make you feel guilty," Tony remarked gruffly. Then when he saw Rena holding back tears, he softened his tone. "I signed the papers. You're getting what you want—at least as far as Purple Fields is concerned. I never intended on taking that away from you." Then he braced his arms on the table and leaned in. Their gazes locked. "We have to make this work, Rena. If for nothing else but that child you're carrying."

Rena closed her eyes briefly. Her silence irritated him, as if she were trying to believe and trust in him. He wasn't like his ruthless father, but would Rena ever acknowledge that? "I know," she said finally.

Tony settled back in his seat. What was done, was done. He didn't want to rehash the past. It was time to look toward the future.

And live in the present.

Tony changed the subject as soon as the food was delivered. He wanted Rena to enjoy the meal she'd craved. Lord knew she needed to build her strength. She also needed some calm in her life and wondered if he could ever provide her that.

Without Rena actually saying so, the existence of the prenuptial agreement he'd just signed was an acceptance to his proposal.

Tony resigned himself to the fact that soon he'd be a husband to a pregnant and reluctant bride.

* * *

One week later, Rena stood beside Solena, Tony beside his brother Joe as they spoke vows before a Catholic priest in a little church just outside of San Francisco. Rena's mind spun during the entire mass thinking this was some kind of a bad joke. She couldn't believe she was actually marrying Tony Carlino, the boy she'd once loved beyond reason. The boy she'd dreamed of marrying with every breath that she'd taken. Now that dream seemed more like a nightmare.

As the priest blessed their union, Rena reminded herself of the reasons she'd made this decision.

Marrying Tony meant saving her winery from ruin. It meant that she could honor David's last wishes.

It meant that her baby would never want for anything, much less a roof over his head or a meal on his plate.

They were good solid reasons. No sacrifice was too great for her child.

Father Charles finished the ceremony. "You may kiss the bride."

She hardly felt like a bride. She wore a pale yellow dress suit. Tony had provided her with a small calla lily bouquet and had placed a simple platinum band on her finger during the service. Out of reverence to David, he hadn't given her a diamond—she'd only just last week removed her wedding ring from her finger and tucked it away safely in her jewelry case. It had been excruciatingly hard letting go.

Tony's lips brushed hers softly. He smiled when he looked into her eyes. She granted him a small smile in return.

Joe and Solena congratulated them, their mood solemn. If Father Charles noticed the austere atmosphere at the altar, he didn't mention it. In fact, he pumped Tony's hand hard and embraced Rena.

Raymond approached with a handshake to Tony and a hug for her. Nick approached her with arms open and a big smile. "Welcome to the family. I've always wanted a sister. But I'll let you in on a little secret. I had a big crush on you in high school."

Rena chuckled and flowed into his arms. "No, you didn't."

"I did. But you were my big brother's girl." They broke their embrace and Nick stepped away, turning to Tony and slapping him on the back. "He's a lucky man. Be good to her or I might steal her away."

Tony glanced at her. "I'd like to see you try."

Rena bit her lip, holding back a smile. She'd seen the Carlino boys' teasing banter, and at times she had been a part of it. If anyone could make her laugh, it was Nick. He'd always been too clever for his own good. All the Carlino boys had their own brand of charm and she'd learned early on that each in his own way was a lady-killer.

The six of them dined in an out-of-the-way restaurant on the outskirts of San Francisco, and everyone sipped champagne when Nick proposed a toast. Rena pretended to sip hers, letting the bubbly liquid touch her mouth before she set her glass down. She was among her closest friends here, and though she'd explained to Solena and Raymond her reasons for this sudden secret marriage to Tony, she hadn't confessed about the baby yet. She needed time to come to grips with all that had changed in her life.

When the dinner was over, Rena walked outside with Solena, bidding her farewell. "I hope I'm not making a mistake."

Solena took her hand and squeezed gently. "Remember, David wanted this for you." She glanced at Tony who stood beside Raymond and his brothers. "Give him a chance," she whispered. "You loved him once."

"It's different now, Solena. There's so much hurt between us."

"I know. But if you find forgiveness, your heart will open."

Rena doubted it. She didn't know if she was capable of forgiving Tony. He'd destroyed her life not once but twice. Was she supposed to forget all that? Emotions jumbled up inside her, and she fought to control them. "I can't believe I married him."

Solena reached out to hug her tight. "It will work out as it's meant to. Be patient. And remember, I am always here if you need me."

Rena faced her and gratitude filled her heart. "I know you are." She reminded herself that if she hadn't married Tony, she wouldn't be able to employ her dear friends, and that was enough consolation for now.

Tony approached and put a hand to her back. "Are you ready to leave?"

She nodded to him and bid farewell to her friend, squeezing her hand tight. "I'll see you tomorrow, Solena."

"Yes." Solena glanced at Tony. "Congratulations."

"Thank you."

Once Raymond and Solena left, Tony took Rena's hand and guided her to his car. "You're not going to your own execution, you know."

"Did I say anything?" she quipped, slipping her hand away.

"Not in words."

She shrugged. "It's all so strange."

But before Tony could respond to that, Joe and Nick walked up. Nick smiled. "You did it, you two. *Finally.*"

Joe cleared his throat. "Let's leave them alone, Nick."

"Just wishing them well," he said. "I guess we'll see you at the house later."

Tony shook his head. "I'm not going back to the house tonight."

"You're not?" Rena's nerves jumped. She hadn't discussed with him what they'd do after they married. She'd only assumed that since the marriage was secret, he'd stay at his house and she'd stay at hers.

"No." He turned to her. "I've booked a suite at the Ritz-Carlton in San Francisco."

Joe grabbed Nick's shoulder and gave a little shove. "Let's go."

"I guess I'm going," Nick said with a cocky smile. "Congrats again, Rena. Big brother."

Rena watched them both get in the car and leave. She turned to Tony, dumbfounded. "Why did you get us a room at a hotel?"

"It's our wedding night."

She closed her eyes, praying for strength. "Surely, you don't expect—"

"You're my wife now, Rena. Did you expect me to remain celibate the rest of my life?"

Five

Rena sat stonily silent in the car all the way to the hotel, her expression grim and her pretty mouth deep in a frown. She said nothing as he checked in or on the ride in the elevator to the Presidential Suite.

A private servant opened the door and showed them inside. In awe, Rena gasped when she entered the suite.

Rich furnishings, stately artwork and a Steinway grand piano filled the living room. Tony put a hand to her back and guided her inside. The servant showed them around the suite, walking them through French doors to the master bedroom with an amazing view of San Francisco Bay, the master bathroom highlighted by a sunken whirlpool bath filled with scented flower petals, a second bedroom and an elegant dining room with seating for eight.

Once back in the living room, Tony dismissed him. "We won't need your services for the rest of the evening."

"Yes, sir," he said, and once he left the suite, Tony opened the French doors to the terrace.

"It's massive," Rena said, stepping outside and taking a deep breath of air. The sun began a slow descent on the horizon. "You could fit two of my gift shops in the terrace alone." Then she turned to him. "Why did you do this?"

"You deserve it, Rena."

Before she could respond, he turned her shoulders and pointed out toward the ocean. "Look, there's Alcatraz."

Rena focused on the island that had once been a notorious prison. "The view is amazing. All of this is amazing."

Tony kept his hands on her shoulders for a few seconds, caressing her lightly. The air fresh and clear, he breathed in and caught the subtle scent of her exotic perfume. She'd put her hair up for the wedding ceremony, giving him access to her throat. He took in another breath before he felt her stiffen. He backed away, giving her space and time to adjust to the situation and pulled out a white iron patio chair. "Sit down and enjoy the fresh air."

She did and he sat facing her. "I'm not the big bad wolf, Rena. I know this is difficult for you."

"Difficult doesn't begin to describe it. I never thought

I'd see this day." Her eyes appeared strained. Her body slumped with fatigue.

"What day?" he asked.

"The day that I'd be your wife."

"I'm not the villain here. I'm trying to do right by you and David. I'm going to save your business, take care of you and raise...our child."

Rena flinched, and regret filled her eyes. "You're trying to ease your conscience and fulfill an obligation."

Tony shook his head. "You won't cut me any slack, will you?"

"I'm sorry I'm not the doting wife you'd imagined. I can't be...this is all so unfair."

"I wish to hell David was alive, too. He was my best friend, damn it." Tony rose and paced the terrace. He hadn't planned on any of this. But he was trying to make the best out of a bad situation. He'd been patient with Rena, though she still blamed him for David's death. He'd tried to please her. He'd tried being the nice guy, yet she wanted no part of it.

Okay, the gloves were coming off.

"You're exhausted. Why don't you take a bath? It's waiting for you. Then get into bed."

Rena hoisted her chin. "I'm not sleeping with you tonight, Tony."

"Wrong," he said pointing a finger at her. "*I'm* not sleeping with *you*, but I'm your husband whether you like it or not."

"What does that mean?" She asked with real fear in her voice.

Tony was too annoyed with her to care. "It means that I don't plan to tiptoe around you anymore, Rena."

He left her on the terrace and strode over to the wet bar, pouring himself three fingers of scotch. He hated that Rena had it right this time. He *had* married her out of obligation and a sense of duty to David. But he hadn't expected her resentment to irk him so much.

Hell, he'd never had to beg a woman for sex in his life. And he wasn't about to start now.

Rena had never stayed in a hotel as extravagant as this one and decided to take advantage of her surroundings. True to Tony's word, the bathtub was steaming and waiting for her. Her body craved the warmth and tranquility a nice hot soak in a tub would provide. She closed the bathroom door and lit the candles that were strategically placed around the tub, sink and dressing area. The Ritz-Carlton knew how to pamper and she wasn't going to deny herself this pleasure. She kicked off her shoes, then stripped out of her clothes folding them neatly and setting them on the marble counter. She turned on the large LCD screen on the wall, finding a music station that played soulful jazz. All lights were turned down but for the flashing abstract images on the flat screen and the candles that burned with a vanilla scent.

Naked and relishing her impending bath, Rena stuck her toe in the water. "Perfect," she hummed, sinking the rest of her body into the exquisite warmth. For the first time in days, she relaxed.

She closed her eyes and obliterated all negative

thoughts. Instead, she thought of the baby growing inside her. She wondered if it was a boy or a girl. She hoped it would have David's kindness and intelligence and maybe her blue eyes. She hoped for so many things, but mostly she hoped her child would be happy.

A smile surfaced on her face as she pictured a sandy blond-haired little boy or a raven-haired little girl. Or perhaps a boy would have her coloring and a girl would have her father's. Either way, Rena would love that child beyond belief.

The door to the bathroom opened and Tony strode in. She gasped and sunk farther down into the tub. "What are you doing in here?"

Tony unbuttoned his shirt and dropped it onto the floor. He looked her over, his gaze following the valley between her breasts. "I'm taking a shower."

Her heart rate sped. "In here?"

"This is the master bathroom, right?"

Rena narrowed in on him. "How much have you had to drink?"

He cocked her a smile and shook his head. "Not enough, honey."

His shoes were off in a flash, and when he reached for his belt, she closed her eyes. She heard him stepping out of his clothes, open the glass shower door, then close it. The shower rained to life, and steam heated the room.

Rena opened her eyes slowly. Tony was deep into his shower, soaping himself up. She took a swallow and watched, unable to tear her gaze away. At one time, Tony Carlino was everything she wanted in life. Those old feelings surfaced, and she tried to shove them away, but it was darn hard to do. Not when he was built like a Greek god, stunningly masculine and boldly beautiful. He moved with grace and confidence, comfortable in his own skin. And so she watched him lather his body, wash his hair and let the water pelt down in streams over his broad shoulders, down the curve of his spine and into the steam that hid the rest of him from view. He turned abruptly and caught her staring. His brows elevated into his forehead, and the corners of his mouth lifted ever so slightly.

Rena turned away then, afraid that if he read her expression, he'd know what she was thinking. He'd know that some feelings can't be destroyed. Some feelings just simply…stay, no matter how hard you try to abolish them. They hide under the anger and pain, waiting.

When the shower spigot turned and the water shut off, Rena tensed. She didn't know what Tony expected. His comment about not tiptoeing around her had her perplexed. The shower door opened, and Tony stepped out, naked. Rena refused to let him intimidate her. She didn't look straight at him, but she didn't look away either. Instead she focused on a point beyond his head.

After wiping down his body, he wrapped the towel around his waist and glanced at her. "You should get out. You're getting cold."

His gaze lingered on her chest. No longer covered with flower petals and bubbles, her nipples were now visible beneath the water. She covered up and nodded. "I will, as soon as you're through in here."

Tony scrubbed the stubble on his face, contemplating.

"I guess I'll shave tomorrow. You can get out now." He reached over and handed her a plush chocolate-colored towel.

She grabbed it and hoisted it to her chin. "Well?"

"I'll be sleeping in the second bedroom. Get some rest, Rena." He bent over and kissed her on the cheek then cast her a rather odd look.

"What?" she asked, curious.

"When we were together, neither one of us would have imagined our wedding night to be anything like us."

She sighed. "No, not back then."

He nodded and left the room, leaving her with poignant and erotic memories of making love to him years ago when they'd been hot and wild for each other.

Rena slept heavily, her body needing the rest. When she woke, she snuggled into the pillow recalling her dream. She'd been out in the vineyards, the grapes ripe and ready to be picked, the air flavored with their pungently sweet aroma. She turned and David was beside her, his smile wide as he looked at the vines, then at her. "We'll have a good year." But then, David's face became Tony's. Somehow, within the eerie images of her mind, it had always been Tony out in the vineyard with her.

Disoriented, she popped her eyes open and gazed out the window as the San Francisco Bay came into view. She clung to cotton one-thousand-thread-count sheets and sat up in bed, looking around the master suite of the

Ritz-Carlton Hotel. It all came back to her now. David was dead, and she'd married Tony Carlino yesterday.

"Oh, God," she whispered.

"I see you're up." Tony stepped out of the bathroom, his face covered with shaving cream, his chest bare, wearing just a pair of black slacks.

Rena blinked, trying not to stare at his tanned, broad chest or the way he casually strode into the bedroom as if they'd been married for twenty years. "Did you sleep well?"

"Like a bab— Um, very well."

"You look rested," he said, then turned around and entered the bathroom again. She craned her neck to find him stroking a razor over his face. "Breakfast is ready if you're hungry," he called out.

She was famished. She'd discovered the first trimester meant eating for two. Finally, her appetite kicked in full force and that was good for the baby. Her child needed the nourishment and so did she. She'd been so terribly strained lately, with David's death, the failure of Purple Fields and her financial situation, that she'd lost her appetite. She'd had to force herself to eat. It was so much easier when she actually *felt* like eating.

"I'll get out of here in a sec," Tony said. "Give you time to dress. I'll wait for you in the dining room."

"Okay," she found herself saying.

Rena entered the bathroom shortly after Tony finished his shave. She splashed water on her face and combed her hair. While she'd often stay in her bathrobe during her morning breakfast routine, she found that too intimate to do with Tony. She dressed in a pair of slacks and a thin knit sweater that Solena had picked out of her wardrobe when Tony had secretly asked her friend to pack a bag for their stay here at the hotel.

Rena suspected Tony hadn't mentioned their wedding night at the Ritz to her, knowing she'd refuse. But yesterday after the wedding dinner, he'd just sprung it on her, catching her off guard. Just one more reason she didn't trust him. While others might see it as a romantic gesture, Rena felt as though she'd been deceived.

She entered the dining room and found Tony relaxing at the head of the table, reading the newspaper and sipping coffee.

He stood when she entered the room. "Morning again."

She managed a small smile then glanced at the antique sideboard filled with platters of food. "Where did all this come from?"

Tony shrugged. "It's the Presidential Suite."

"And that makes food magically appear?"

He laughed. "Yeah, I guess so."

"You might be used to being treated like this, but this is…overwhelming to me."

Tony walked over to stand before her. He searched her eyes. "I don't live like this, Rena. But it's a special occasion. I thought you deserved a little pampering." He stroked her cheek, his finger sliding along her jaw line tenderly. It had been so long since she'd been touched like this. So long since she'd had any real tenderness. She was nine weeks pregnant, and though she'd tried to be strong when David died, there were times when she just needed some gentle contact.

She looked into Tony's dark beautiful eyes, then lowered her gaze to his mouth. It was all the encouragement he needed. He took her carefully in his arms and bent his head, bringing their lips together in a soft kiss.

Rena relished his lips on hers, the gentle way he held her, the warmth and comfort he lent. It wasn't a sensual kiss but one of understanding and patience.

He surprised her with his compassion, and that made her wary. She couldn't put her faith in Tony—he'd destroyed that years ago. If she'd had any other way out of her dilemma she wouldn't have married him, despite gentle kisses and kind overtures.

"Rena, don't back off," he said.

"I have to. You offered me a business proposal. Your own words were, 'this isn't a real marriage.' And now, now…you're expecting me to fall into the role as your wife." She shook her head, and her emotions spilled out. "Don't you understand? At one time, I would have trusted you with my life, but now there's not much you could say or do to make me trust you. My heart is empty where you're concerned. I was forced to marry you… otherwise I wouldn't be here. I'm protecting myself, and my baby."

"That's what *I* intend to do, Rena. Protect you and the baby."

"No, you're going to help build my company back up. Period. I can't let you get too close to my child. I can't let you hurt my baby, the way you hurt me."

"How could I ever hurt your child?"

"The same way you hurt me. By walking out. By

leaving. By finding something more exciting than being a husband and father. While I've recovered from you leaving, it would be devastating to a child to be abandoned that way. My son or daughter may never get over it."

Anger flashed in his eyes. His jaw tightened, and his body went rigid. "I don't intend on abandoning either of you."

"What if you get the racing bug again? What if you're called back? It's in your blood, Tony. You love racing."

"That part of my life is over. I did what I set out to do. I'm not going back, ever."

Rena shook her head, refusing to believe him.

"You have my promise on that," he said. Then he spoke more firmly. "Did you hear me, Rena? I'll never leave you or the baby. It's a promise."

Tony stared at her for a long moment, and when she thought he was so angry he'd walk out of the room, he handed her a plate. "Eat up," he said. "We're going to have some fun today."

Rena glanced at him. "We are?"

"Yeah, even if it kills me."

Rena chuckled, despite the tension in the room just seconds earlier. She had to hand it to Tony for lightening the mood. "That's not my intention."

"Can I bank on that?"

She shrugged as she filled up her plate. "Sure," she offered. "You can bank on that."

They exited the hotel, and because it was a glorious day, they decided to walk the crowded streets. A few times, Rena and Tony got separated in the onslaught of foot traffic, so he grabbed her hand and they strolled along that way, browsing through shops. When Rena took a lingering look at a ruby necklace, her birthstone with a setting that was beautifully unusual, Tony dragged her into the store and purchased it for her. "You don't have to do this," she said.

"Consider it a wedding gift, since I didn't get you a diamond ring."

"I know, but I don't need this. What I need is for my vineyard to thrive and be solvent again."

"That'll happen too, Rena. You don't have to give up one to get the other."

Rena sighed inwardly. She'd been doing that most of her life, sacrificing her own needs and wants in order to assure Purple Fields' survival. It had been years since she'd known what it was like to simply have something she wanted without guilt.

Next they took the trolley to Fisherman's Wharf and ate clam chowder in sourdough bread bowls, then stopped at an ice cream parlor and ate sundaes until Rena thought her belly would expand out of her pants. "Oh, I'm so full."

"Me, too," Tony said, looking at her empty dish. "I guess you never get over loving hot fudge over strawberry ice cream."

"With nuts on top."

"Hmm and whipped cream. Remember the whipped cream fight we had?" Tony asked.

Rena remembered how they'd each taken out a can of Reddi-wip from Tony's refrigerator. No one was home and they'd just finished eating sundaes. "Yeah and you cheated!"

"I did not. I fight fair. I couldn't help it that your nozzle got stuck."

"You took advantage then and squirted me until I was covered with it. That stuff even got in my hair."

"You were sweet from head to toe," Tony said with a nostalgic smile.

The memory popped into her head of Tony kissing it off her until kissing wasn't enough. He'd taken her to his bedroom then, stripped her down and licked every bit of the whipped cream off. They'd made love in the shower, deciding that strawberry sundaes were their favorite dessert.

"I never have whipped cream without thinking of you," Tony said, his eyes fixed on hers.

Her cheeks heated and she inhaled sharply. "That was a long time ago." What she didn't add is that the same held true for her.

"But a good memory."

"I don't think about the past anymore," she fibbed.

He watched her intently. "Maybe you should. We had something special."

"'Had' being the key word." She refused to let Tony get to her.

Tony leaned over and kissed her on the lips. "Let's go," he said abruptly, taking her hand again. They rode the trolley back and checked out of the hotel. Rena took one last look around, feeling oddly sentimental. She blamed it on her fickle hormones.

When Rena thought they'd head back to Napa, Tony

drove her to a four-story shopping mall and parked the car. "What are we doing here?"

He grinned. "We're getting baby things."

"Baby things?"

"I promised you a fun day, and I figured a new mother-to-be would enjoy picking out furniture and clothes and whatever else the baby might need."

"Really?" Tempted by such an elaborate offer, Rena's heart raced with excitement. Offhand, she could think of dozens of items she'd need for the baby's arrival, and quite frankly, she didn't know how she'd manage to pay for all of it. Other than shopping at thrift stores, she was truly at a loss.

"I haven't a clue what a baby needs," Tony said, getting out of the car and opening the door for her.

"I'm on new ground here, too." She took his outstretched hand. "We'd always talked about having children, but—" Rena stopped and slipped her hand from his, her heart in her throat. How could she do this? How could she look at cribs and bassinets and baby swings when this was a dream she and David shared together? They'd always wanted a family. The time had never been right. She refused to think of the life growing inside her as an accident, but they hadn't really planned on this baby.

Rena ached inside thinking that David would never know his child. He'd never change a diaper, kiss its face or watch it take its first step. He'd never go to a ballet recital or little league game. He'd never know the joy of seeing his child develop into a smart-alecky teen or fall in love one day. David would have been there for his child. He'd have seen his son or daughter through the good times and the bad, because David was loyal and devoted. He would have made a wonderful father.

Rena's legs went weak suddenly. Her body trembled, and she knew she couldn't do this. She glanced at Tony, her voice a quiet plea. "I'm sorry. I don't think I'm ready for this."

Tony drew in a breath. "Right." He closed his eyes briefly, and Rena noted genuine pain there. "Okay, we'll do this another time. When you're ready."

She sighed with relief. "It's not that I don't appreciate—"

"I get it, Rena. I'm not the baby's father. Enough said."

Tony got back into his car and revved the engine, waiting for her to climb inside. She bit her lip and held back tears as she sank into the car. They drove to Napa in silence, Rena glancing at Tony's stony expression every once in a while.

She knew in her head that David was gone. He was her past, while this angry man sitting beside her was her future.

The irony struck her anew.

How many times had she hoped to be Tony Carlino's wife? Only to find now she should have been more careful what she'd wished for.

Six

Tony drove to Napa, a debate going on in his head. On one hand, he knew Rena still grieved, but on the other hand, he'd taken responsibility for her. She was his wife now. He couldn't let her dictate the terms of their relationship, not if he planned to really honor David's dying wish. So he drove past Purple Fields and down the highway leading to his home.

"Where are we going?" she asked.

"To my house."

Rena slanted him a dubious look. "Why?"

"Just stopping by to pick up some of my clothes to bring to Purple Fields."

Rena blinked before realizing his intent. "This was supposed to be a secret marriage, Tony. We can't live together."

Tony expected this argument. He pulled to the side of the road and stopped the car. Immediately, Rena's shoulders stiffened. She sat up straighter in the seat and faced him. Before he spoke, he searched her face for a long moment, reining in his anger. "Rena, we're not announcing to the public we're married. But I can't possibly work with you at Purple Fields and—"

"Watch out for me," she finished for him with a twist of her full lips.

She tried his patience, but Tony held firm. He'd made up his mind about this and decided it was best for both of them. "We'll be discreet. Purple Fields isn't exactly bustling with crowds."

"Thanks for the reminder."

"Rena, listen. All I'm saying is that you don't have a big staff that will spread gossip through the county. The place isn't on the main highway. In fact, you're in a remote location."

Rena's voice held quiet concern, and she refused to look at him. "I didn't think we'd live together."

Tony reached over to gently turn her chin his way. She lifted those incredible eyes to him. "You're my wife. I'm your husband. We *are* married. We'll keep the secret for a while, but make no mistake that I intend for us to live as man and wife. Now, if you'd rather move into the Carlino estate with me, we can—"

"No!" She shook her head. "No, Tony. That makes no sense. I need to be at Purple Fields."

Tony wasn't fooled. Rena's hatred for his father was evident in her blatant refusal. After Tony had moved away, Santo Carlino had tried to ruin all the local vintners in the area, and Rudy Fairfield hadn't been the exception. Once Tony was gone, his father had ignored Tony's protests to leave Purple Fields alone. The Fairfields had suffered, but they'd never fully succumbed to his father's ruthless business tactics.

Rena hadn't stepped foot in his house since. It seemed his new wife hated *everything* Carlino.

"Well then, it's settled. I'll move into your house."

Rena swallowed and gave him a reluctant nod.

He bounded out of the car and opened her door. She looked up and announced, "I'll wait for you out here. It's a nice day. I need the…fresh air."

Tony didn't push her. He helped her out, making a mental note that his Porsche wasn't a family car or comfortable for his pregnant wife. "I'll be a few minutes."

She nodded and stretched out, raising her arms, shaking out the kinks, confirming that he'd been right about the car.

Tony bounded up the steps and entered the arched wrought iron doors decorated with delicate metal vines that led to a breezeway. The house, set more like an Italian villa atop the hill, had four wings that met in the center by a large expansive living room and dining area overlooking the vineyards. Tony liked his privacy, and each of the Carlino men had lived in separate sections of the house once they'd grown up.

"Hey, I thought I heard you come in. How are the newlyweds?" Joe asked, approaching him as he began his ascent up the stairs.

Tony sighed. "Fine."

"That bad? I take it the wedding night didn't go so smoothly."

Tony knew Joe meant well. He wasn't prying; he was simply concerned. "She's still grieving."

"Understandable. Where is she?"

"Outside. She won't come in. But I plan to rectify that soon. She's not thrilled that I'm moving in with her."

"I wasn't sure of your plans. I guess it makes sense for you to live there for a while."

"I'll divide my time between here and there, Joe, but I'd appreciate it if you and Nick could hold down the fort for a few days without me."

"Sure, no problem."

"Thanks. You know," he began with a slant of his head, "if you'd have told me six months ago I'd be married to Rena and raising a baby, I wouldn't have believed it."

"Am I hearing a little bit of awe in your voice?"

"Yeah, well, maybe I'm adjusting to the situation a little better than my wife is."

"She'll come around. In fact, I think I'll step outside and say hello to my new sister-in-law. Maybe put in a few good words for you."

"I can use all the help I can get. Rena thinks she married the devil." He chuckled as he took the steps up to his bedroom. He'd been called even worse by some of the women he'd dated in the past.

And it had all been true.

"Tony?" Rena questioned him immediately when she realized where they were going. Tony hadn't taken her directly back to Purple Fields after he'd picked up his clothes from his estate. Instead, he'd driven to the cemetery where David was buried.

"Are you okay with this?" he asked.

Rena squeezed her eyes shut. Right after David died, she'd made daily trips to the cemetery to lay wildflowers by his grave. She'd come and sit on the grass just to feel close to him again. But after she'd learned about the promise he'd asked of Tony, she'd gotten so angry with him for his manipulation that she hadn't come back since. Now she realized the folly in that. David had tried to protect her. Even in death, he'd tried to take care of her. Guilt assailed her for being so shortsighted and selfish. She should have come more often. She should have honored the man who'd loved her. "Yes, I'm okay with this."

Once out of the car, Tony met her on the lawn and put out his hand. She glanced down at it and then into his reassuring eyes. "We'll do this together."

She slipped her hand into his, and silently they walked to the center of the Gracious Hill section of the cemetery. A new bronze headstone with David's name and birth date embossed in gold stared up at them. Rena sank to her knees and said a prayer. She sat there for a minute, looking down, running her fingers over the headstone, touching David's nameplate with infinite care.

Tony helped her up, and taking her hand, he spoke with reverence as his gaze drifted down toward the grave. "She's safe, David," he whispered. "We're married now. I'll take good care of her."

Overwhelmed with emotion, Rena let out a sob. Tears she couldn't hold back, spilled down her cheeks. The reality of the last few weeks came crashing down on her.

"It's okay, honey," Tony said softly. He turned his body and encompassed her in his arms, cradling her as she cried into his chest. She sobbed deeply, the pain emanating from deep within. Guilt and sadness washed over her.

Tony tightened his hold on her. "Let it out, Rena."

Cocooned in Tony's strength and warmth, she cried and cried until she finally managed to control her emotions. She sniffed and gulped in oxygen and stopped crying after several minutes, yet she couldn't let go of Tony. Wrapped up in his arms, she was grateful for the comfort, the gentle assuring words, the soft kisses to her forehead. She gave herself up to Tony allowing him to be strong for her. She needed this. She needed for once to let someone else take the brunt of her heartache.

"He's okay with this, Rena," Tony whispered. "It's what David wanted."

She knew that to be true. But she also realized she had just married a man who had hurt and betrayed her once—a man whom she blamed for her husband's death, a man who'd felt obligated to marry her. How could she find comfort in that?

"I was mad at David for asking this of you. Of me," she whispered painfully. "I haven't come here in weeks."

Tony stroked her back again and again, keeping her head pressed to his chest. "Don't beat yourself up, Rena.

You're a strong woman, but you have a right to all your feelings."

"Even the ones that scream I shouldn't have married you?"

Tony looked down into her eyes. "Yeah, even those."

"I don't intend on cutting you any slack," she said quietly.

"Planning on making my life miserable?"

"Not deliberately, Tony. But yes. You may want to move out before the week is over."

"Doubtful. I'm not going anywhere."

Then he leaned down and kissed her softly, exquisitely on her lips, and for the first time, Rena came close to believing him.

With arms folded, Rena watched Tony set his bags on the floor beside her bed. He faced her, his gaze direct and piercing. "I told you, I won't tiptoe around you anymore. We're going to live as man and wife."

Rena drew in a breath. Exhausted, she had no more tears to shed. She'd used up her quota and then some at the cemetery. Though her insides quaked and her head ached, she knew she had no choice but to accept Tony in her home and in her bed. He had pride. He was virile and strong and extremely sexy. She suspected women had thrown themselves at him all the time. He was a race car champion, an appealing bachelor who was definitely easy on the eyes. He'd probably had women in every town he traveled.

Though he'd been patient and kind to her the past few

days she knew she'd pushed him pretty far. And soon, he'd start pushing back.

He must have noted her fear, because his jaw clenched and he swore. "For God's sake, Rena. I'm not about to force myself on you. But we will sleep in the same bed."

Rena glanced at the bed, then up at him. "I understand."

"Ah, hell." He rolled his eyes at her robotic answer. "You'd think we'd never had sex before. Mind-blowing, earthmoving,   do-it-until-we-can't-breathe-anymore sex."

Rena nearly tripped over her own feet backing up, his statement stunning her. Her face heated, and her body shook a little. Speechless, she lowered her lashes, fighting off memories of their lovemaking. He'd been blunt but accurate in his description. "That's when..." she began, almost unable to get the words out. "When we were in love."

"Right." Tony tossed his overnight bag on the bed. He pulled out aftershave lotion, deodorant, razors and a hairbrush. "You have a place I can put these?"

She pointed to the master bathroom. "It's small, but you should find some room on the counter."

She'd taken David's things out of the bedroom, unwilling to have that daily reminder of his absence. But she'd yet to remove his clothes from the closet. She'd be forced to now. Tony would need the room, and unlike his home with massive walk-in closet space, her closets were barely big enough for two people.

She held out hope that he'd get disgusted with her

small three-bedroom house and move back to the estate where he'd be ensconced in luxury.

Rena opened her closet and began gathering up David's clothes to make room for Tony's. Before she knew it, Tony stood beside her and placed a stopping hand on hers. "You don't have to do it now. You're exhausted."

"It needs doing. I just never could fa—"

"If it makes you feel better, I'll do it."

"No," she said with a shake of her head. "I should do it."

Tony grabbed both of her hands while they were still on the hangers. He stood close. So close that she noted the golden flecks in his dark eyes. "Okay but not today. It can wait. Agreed?"

She nodded, breathing in his subtle, musky scent. A lump formed in her throat thinking of his stirring kiss before. She didn't want to be attracted to Tony. She'd gotten over him a long time ago, yet when he touched her or looked deep into her eyes or kissed her, emotions rolled around inside. And made her nervous. "I'll make dinner."

"Thank you."

She strode out of the room, confused by what she was feeling and angry for feeling anything at all.

Rena stirred the spaghetti sauce, watching as little bubbles broke on the surface sending a pungent, garlic scent into the air.

"Smells great." Tony came up behind her, his body close again, surprising her in how quietly he appeared in her kitchen. He reached for the wooden spoon. "May I?"

She handed it to him. "I hope you don't mind pasta tonight."

"Are you kidding? I'm Italian. You know I love pasta." He stirred the sauce, then lifted the spoon to his mouth, tasting it.

"What do you think?"

"Needs a little salt," he said, then grabbed the salt shaker and added a few shakes. "There."

"You like to cook, don't you?"

He shrugged. "I get by. When a bachelor wants to eat, he's got to know more than how to boil water."

"I didn't think you'd ever have to cook a meal for yourself."

Tony continued stirring the sauce. "When my gourmet chef was off, I had three other servants waiting on me hand and foot." He turned to her and grinned.

"You're teasing."

"Yeah, I'm teasing." Then he set the wooden spoon down and stared at her. "I'm not going to apologize for how I live. I've earned it. Racing has afforded me a good life. But there were sixteen-hour work days, long lonely times on the road. Times when I had to cook for myself when I longed for a home cooked meal. Eating out is overrated."

"There must have been plenty of women happy to cook for you. Never mind," Rena said, catching herself. She didn't really want to know. "Forget I said that."

Tony's expression changed, and he gave her a quick shake of the head. "Your image of me is way off."

CHARLENE SANDS   93

Rena pursed her lips. "It really doesn't matter."

Tony grabbed her arms gently as steam rose up from the sauce and bathed them in heat. "Yes, it does matter. I'm your husband. I care what you think of me."

Rena stared into his eyes, unable to answer. She had mixed emotions when it came to Tony Carlino, but for the most part, she didn't want to see any good in him. She wanted to keep him a safe distance away in her mind and heart.

When he realized she wouldn't respond, he let her go and she went about filling a big pot of water for the pasta noodles.

Tony watched her work at the stove for a long while before he spoke again. "What can I do to help?"

Grateful to give him something to do, she barked orders. "Take out the romaine and tomatoes from the refrigerator. I think there's a cucumber in there, too— and anything else you can find for a salad."

She heard him going to work, and much to her surprise, he fixed a delicious salad, and, adding black olives and herbs, he made his own olive oil-based dressing.

When she walked over to taste it, she cast him a nod of approval. "Yummy."

"My mother's. One of a few recipes I learned from her before she died."

Tony's mother died when he was fifteen. Rena hadn't known her, but she'd heard she was a saint among women. She'd have to be in order to be married to Santo Carlino. Rumor had it she'd kept him in line. When she died, Santo poured himself into building his business taking no prisoners along the way.

"And you remembered it," Rena said. "It's funny the things we remember about the ones we love."

"What do you remember about your mother?" he asked.

Rena smiled wide, recalling her mother's favorite pastime. "That's easy. She had a morning and nightly ritual of walking three miles. No matter how tired she was, no matter the weather. She'd get into her walking clothes, put on these beat-up old shoes and go for a walk. She said it cleared the mind, cleansed the soul and kept the weight off." Rena grinned, confessing. "My mama liked to eat."

Tony chuckled. "That's a good way to remember her. Walking, I mean. Not eating."

"Hmm, yeah." Rena blinked herself back to reality. Even with all her exercise, her mother still contracted a deadly disease. She'd lingered for years, missing her daily walks and everything else that required a bit of effort. It was a brutal reminder of the unfairness in life.

Once the meal was ready, they sat down to eat at her country oak kitchen table. She wondered what Tony thought about this rustic house. To her it was home, and she wasn't ashamed of it. Through the years, she'd put personal touches throughout, cheerful curtains, comfy sofas with throw pillows she'd sewn, refinished tables, armoires and cabinets. When she looked around her home, she saw bits and pieces of her parents' life here as well as her life with David.

Facing Tony at her kitchen table reminded her once again how it had all changed so quickly.

Tony ate up heartily. There would be no salad-only dinners for him. He was a well-built man who enjoyed a good meal. He was halfway through a large dish of pasta when he lifted his head. "I want to see your accounts tomorrow. I hope to get through them by the end of the week. Then I'll know better how we can get your winery back on track."

Grateful that he'd taken the first step, Rena discussed with him her conversation she had with the banker. Tony hadn't even blinked when she told him her financial situation and how much money she owed.

"I'll take care of it," he said, without pause. "You'll make your payroll, and any other debts you have will be dealt with."

"Thank you." Humbled by his generosity, she put her head down.

"Rena?" She looked up into his dark eyes. "We're in this together from now on. You don't have to worry about the winery."

"I know. I appreciate everything, really. I just can't help feeling like a failure. I tried. David tried. We had some bad luck, equipment that needed replacing, problems with distributors and well, the bigger wineries tried to shove us out."

Tony covered her hand, and the instant spark jolted her. "Carlino Wines being one of them. That's not going to happen anymore."

She tried to ignore sensations rippling through her. "The Fairfields have always taken pride in their livelihood. *I* have a lot of pride. I feel like I let my parents down. I had to remarry to save the business."

Tony stroked her hand, his fingers caressing hers. It felt good—too good—to pull her hand away. Lord help her, she needed to feel his touch.

"I won't take offense to that," he said. "I know I'm the last person on earth you'd want as a husband."

She watched as his fingers slid over her knuckles so gently. "At one time, I wanted nothing more."

"And now?"

She gazed deeply into his eyes and lifted a shoulder in confusion. "Now, I don't know, Tony. I really don't know. I'm just so tired."

Tony rose from the table with concern in his eyes. "Go. I'll take care of this." He took up their plates and headed toward the dishwasher. "You need to rest. It's been a long day."

Rena got up, ready to argue, but Tony had already rinsed their dishes and began loading them into the dishwasher. With his back to her, she noted his broad shoulders tapering down along his back and slim waist-line. His slacks fit perfectly over his buttocks, and she recalled the quick flash of excitement she felt when he'd stepped out of the shower yesterday, buck naked. She'd only caught a glimpse, but oh, that image wouldn't leave her anytime soon.

"I, uh, thanks. I'll take a quick shower and go to bed. What will you—"

He turned sharply and met her gaze. "I'll come to bed later, Rena."

She gave him a clipped nod, turned around and strode

out of the room. Her exhaustion catching up with her, she was too tired to think of the implications of sleeping with her new, extremely sexy secret husband.

Seven

Rena snuggled deeper into her bed, rebelling against thin rays of dawn creeping into the room. She closed her eyes tighter, rolling away from the light and into familiar warmth. Cocooned in the heat now, she relaxed and let out a stress-relieving sigh.

Her eyelids blessedly shut, she breathed in a pleasing musky scent and smiled. A warm breath brushed her cheek, then another and another. She popped her eyes open. Tony was there, inches from her face, his eyes dark and dusky. He lay stretched out on his side, apparently watching her sleep. "Morning, beautiful."

Alarm bells rang out in her head. She couldn't believe she was in bed with Tony. And enjoying it. His warmth surrounded her. She focused on the firm set of his sculpted jaw, then opened her mouth to speak, but

Tony placed his finger to her lips, stopping her words. "Shh. Don't overthink this, Rena." He wrapped his arms around her waist and drew her closer.

She remembered putting on her most unappealing nightshirt last night, a soft, brushed cotton garment with tiny cap sleeves just in case Tony held true to his word to sleep with her. But Rena liked to feel feminine in bed, so the least suggestive nightgown she owned was still a far cry from head-to-toe flannel.

"Don't overthink what?"

"This," he said, moving closer and touching his lips to hers. The heat of his mouth and the intimate contact should have caused her to panic. Yet, she didn't resist, her body and mind not fully operational at the moment. He pulled away long enough to search her eyes and must have been satisfied with what he saw in them.

Tony knew how to kiss a woman, and he held nothing back with the next kiss. He drew her in with expert finesse, coaxing a reaction from her. His hand on her waist, she felt his strength through the thin cotton fabric of the nightgown. He squeezed her gently, and immediate tingles coursed through her body. She sighed aloud, a throaty little sound that emanated from deep within. Tony moved his hand up, stroking her side slowly up and down, his fingers brushing the underside of her breast.

Oh God, it felt good to have him caress her, teasing her breast until she ached for his touch.

Rena loved the physical act of making love. She loved the intimacy, the joy of having her body succumb to infinite pleasure. Tony had taught her that. He'd taken her virginity and taught her to enjoy sexual intercourse. Of course, back then they'd been so much in love that holding back wasn't an option. She'd given herself fully to him, surrendering her heart and her body. She'd only been with two men in her life, and each in their own way had taught her about loving a man. Where David had been sweet, patient and dependable, Tony had been irresistible, hot-blooded and sexy.

Tony's passionate kisses unnerved her. His touch drew her like a magnet. She moved closer, arching toward him, her breaths heavier now. He nibbled on her lips, whispering how beautiful she was, how much he wanted to touch her.

She gave him permission with a sigh.

His hand came up and cupped her breast over the fabric of her cotton nightie. He flicked a finger over the tip, rubbing back and forth, sending shock waves through her body. Intense heat swamped her, and she longed for more.

She knew the instant Tony's body went taut. His breaths deepened, and his kisses became more demanding as he parted her lips. His tongue beckoned hers, and she met him halfway. They sparred in an endless search for satisfaction.

While her body craved the physical release, her heart and mind screamed no. Torn by indecision, she stilled, forcing herself to think this through.

"You're overthinking again, Rena," Tony said in a low rasp. He continued to stroke her breast, unraveling her mind.

She mustered her willpower and covered his hand with hers, stopping him. "One of us has to."

"I told you I don't plan on being celibate in this marriage," he said quietly. "If I thought you weren't ready, I'd back off. But the woman I was just kissing wasn't protesting at all. You were enjoying having my hands on you. In another second I would have taken off your nightgown, and we would have been skin to skin. I want that, and I know you want that, too."

Rena's heart pumped hard. He was right, but she had to voice her innermost thoughts. "Wanting and having are two different things."

"Rena's rules, not mine."

Rena drew oxygen in. "I can't forget who you are. I can't ignore what you did to me. My heart is empty where you're concerned."

"So you've said." Tony flopped onto his back and looked at the ceiling. "What's done is done, Rena. I can't change that."

"I know. And I can't change how I feel. I may want you physically, but you'll never really have me. I can't love you again. I won't. You'll never own my heart."

"As long as you're faithful to me, that's all I'll ask for now."

Stunned by the statement, Rena lifted her head off the pillow. "You know me, Tony. I'd never even consider—"

He turned onto his side again to face her. "What you don't know about me is that I'd never consider it, either. But I'm a man with physical needs, and since we're married and compatible in bed, there's no reason not to make love."

"You mean, *have sex?* Because without love, it's just sex," Rena pointed out.

He lifted a strand of her hair, eyeing it as he let it fall from his fingers. "Just sex?" Tony cocked her a playful grin. "Even better."

Rena shook her head in bewilderment.

"C'mon, Rena. We've cleared the air. I get it. You don't love me, but you crave my body."

"I never said that!"

"Oh, no?" he said innocently. He was such a tease. He crushed his mouth to hers and kissed her passionately. She'd hardly come up for air when he grabbed her hand and set it on his chest. "Touch me."

Crisp scattered hairs filled her palm and underneath muscles rippled. She wove her hand up along his sculpted shoulders then down to tease his flattened nipple. His intake of air let her know he enjoyed her flicking her finger over him, the way he had to her.

Laying her hand against his torso, she inched her way down, tempted by a perfect body and powered by the sounds of Tony's quick jagged breaths. Okay, so maybe she did crave his body. She had memories that wouldn't go away. Sexual flashes that entered her mind at the most inopportune times. She'd remembered how he'd made her feel, how potent his lovemaking was, how satisfied she'd been afterward. If anything, Tony had matured into a stunning male specimen. He knew how to give pleasure, and he knew how to take it. He'd always made Rena feel special and cherished, no matter what act they performed.

She slid her hand farther down, slipping below Tony's waistline. When she reached the elastic band of his boxers, she hesitated, tentative in her approach. Myriad thoughts flitted through her mind one right after the other, but Tony interrupted that train of thought. "Just let go, Rena," he whispered. "We both need this."

Rena touched him then, her hand gliding over silken skin. His arousal shocked her, though she didn't know why it should. He was a virile man, and they were in bed together, ready to consummate their marriage.

"I want you." Tony's low tone held no room for doubt. He cupped her chin and brought her lips to his. There was a sense of urgency to his kiss, yet he remained gentle and patient, waiting for her to respond. She stroked him with trebling fingers, bringing him to a fuller state of arousal.

"This is not—" Rena began, but Tony kissed her again, his mouth generous and giving, coaxing her to fulfill their destiny. Torn by indecision, she shoved all thoughts of the past years aside and tried to focus on the future.

"We'll have a life together, Rena." Tony's words mirrored her own. Her life included him now, whether planned or not, whether she liked it or not. She had no other option now.

"I know," she said, finally resigning to her fate.

Tony removed his boxers then placed her hand back on him, skin to skin, and her insides turned to jelly. There was life to Tony, a vitality she'd missed during these past months. He filled the void, the hollowness that beseeched her since she'd become a widow. She had her precious child, yes, but this intimacy fulfilled her need to feel alive again.

She stroked him until his pleasure heightened. Instincts, or perhaps recollection, told her that he'd reached his limit. He flipped her onto her back, and in one quick sweep, he removed her nightgown, pulling it up and over her head. His kisses burned her through and through, and his hands roamed over her, touching, tormenting, caressing and teasing every inch of her skin. His voice was low and consumed with passion. "You're as beautiful as I remember."

He brought his mouth down to suckle her breast, his tongue wetting her with long swipes. After laving each nipple, he blew on them, and every ounce of her body prickled with need. Her pulse raced with exquisite excitement. Unmindful of any repercussions, she relished the thrill of the moment.

Tony praised her body with quiet expletives and cherished every limb before moving on to touch her at the apex of her legs. His palm covered her, and she arched up.

"You're ready for me, sweetheart," he acknowledged. Without hesitation, he rose over her. She gazed up at him, and images of their past, of doing this very thing with nothing but love in their hearts, played out in her mind. She'd relished their joining, eager to show the man she loved how much he meant to her. It had been perfect. Blissful. Exciting.

Tony stared into her eyes in the dawn light, and she

witnessed that same spark. The memories had come back to him, as well. His lips lifted and his eyelids lowered. Then he gripped her hips and she squeezed her eyes shut, ready for him to take her.

"Look at me," he commanded.

"Tony," she murmured, popping her eyes open. It was clear what he wanted. No memories of any other man. No memories of David.

He nodded when their eyes met, apparently satisfied, then he moved inside her with extreme care. Rena adjusted to his size and accommodated him with her body. It wasn't long before his thrusts magnified, their bodies sizzled hot and the burn she'd remembered from long ago returned fiercely.

Infinitely careful and recklessly wild, Tony made love to her, seeing to her needs, giving as much as taking, gentle at times and feral at others. He was the perfect lover—that much hadn't changed. And all the while, Rena gave up her body to him but held firmly onto her emotions.

It was *just sex*.

And as Tony brought her to the peak of enjoyment, her skin damp, her body throbbing for the release that would complete her, she wrapped her arms around his neck and arched up, her bones melting but her heart firmly intact.

Tony wrapped Rena in his arms. They lay quietly together on the bed after making love, each deep in thought. It had been months since he'd had sex, and his release had come with powerful force. Rena had responded to him as she always had, with wild abandon. At least her body had reacted as he'd hoped. He knew what she liked and how to please her. She'd been his first love, too, and a man doesn't easily forget how to please the woman he loves.

They'd been so young back then, full of dreams and plans for the future. But Tony had been a rebel. He'd hated being under his father's thumb. He hadn't wanted any part of the family business, not when racing cars meant so much to him. He'd never planned on leaving Rena behind. It just happened. While his professional life had been great, his personal life had suffered.

Once he'd become a champion, he had women knocking at his door at all hours of the night. They followed him from race to race. They'd called him, showed up when he least expected it. Beautiful, sexy, outrageous women. He'd never fallen in love with any of them. He'd had flings and a few casual relationships that never lasted more than a couple of months.

He'd held hope for Rena in the early years, but he hadn't blamed her for giving up on him. He hadn't known what the future held for him other than racing cars. He was on the road a great deal of time, thrilled by his success but heartbroken about Rena.

His gaze fell to Rena's face, her expression glum, her eyes filled with regret. Hardly the loving wife in the aftermath of lovemaking.

Hell, he felt like crap himself, guilt eating at him. He wanted to do right by David, but he couldn't forget that a few months ago, his friend was alive and well and living with the woman he loved. He was to become a father, something that David always wanted.

Tony had suspected David had feelings for Rena early on. They had been good friends in school, yet all three understood in an unspoken agreement that Rena and Tony were meant for each other. When Tony left town, David stayed behind to pick up the pieces of Rena's shattered heart. He'd loved her that much to forego a chance to enter the racing circuit with Tony. To Rena's way of thinking, David was her white knight coming to her rescue, where Tony was the villain who'd abandoned her.

Now they'd consummated a loveless marriage.

Her remorse irritated him more than it should. Was it ego on his part? They'd just made incredible love, and now Rena looked so darn miserable.

Damn it, what did she expect? She was his wife. He would raise her child as his own. They'd both agreed to honor David's last wishes. That meant living as man and wife and sleeping together. He blinked away anger and guilt then rose abruptly, mindless of his state of undress. "I'll grab a shower, then I want to go over your accounts."

Rena glanced at him for an instant, bit down on her lip then focused her attention out the window. "I'll make breakfast."

"I'm not hungry," he said. "Coffee will do. Meet me in the office once you're dressed."

Rena nodded without looking at him.

Tony showered quickly and dressed with clothes he'd taken from his bag. He put on a pair of faded jeans and a black T-shirt then shoved his feet into a pair of seasoned white Nike shoes.

He heard kitchen sounds as he walked down the hallway, the aroma of hot coffee brewing, whetting his taste buds. But instead of greeting his new wife in the kitchen, he strode outside and closed the door. The northern California air was crisp and fresh, the brilliant sky laced with white puffy clouds.

He filled his lungs several times, breathing in and out slowly, enjoying the pristine air. The vineyards were far removed from the city, elevated to some degree, the vistas spread out before him, glorious. Funny, as a young boy, he'd had no appreciation for the land or its beauty and solitude. He'd never seen this country as his father had seen it.

Now he'd make a life here. The irony that his father was getting what he wanted in death, rather than in life, was never far from his mind.

Tony entered the office adjacent to the gift shop with the key Rena had left for him on her dresser. He glanced around, noting two tall file cabinets, an out-dated computer, a desk that had seen better days and shelves displaying certificates, wine awards and pictures of Rena and David. He walked over and picked one up that was encased in a walnut frame. He looked at the image of the couple standing among the vines ripe with cabernet grapes.

"It was a good year for cabernet. Our fifth anniversary." Rena walked into the office with a cup of coffee and set it down on the desk.

Tony stared at the photo. "You look happy."

"David made me dinner that night. He set up twinkling lights out on the patio. We danced in the moonlight."

Tony put the frame back, deciding not to comment. What could he say to that? "Thanks for the coffee."

She shrugged. "Well, this is the office. Our accounts for the past ten years are in those file cabinets."

Tony picked up the coffee cup and sipped. The liquid went down hot and delicious, just what he needed. "I'll start with the past year and work my way backward."

"Okay, I'll get those for you."

"Are they all paper files? Do you have anything loaded into the computer?"

Rena glanced at the machine. "We have our inventory computerized now. And David had started to enter the paper files. But he didn't get very far, I'm afraid."

Tony sat down at the desk and signed on. "Want to show me where everything is?"

Rena came close, her hair still slightly damp from her shower. She bent over the computer, clicking keys. Her clean scent wafted in the air. "What is that?" he asked.

She looked at him in question. "What?"

"You smell great."

She smiled softly. "It's citrus shampoo."

Tony met her eyes, then took her hand gently. "Rena... listen, about this morning."

She squeezed her eyes shut and shook her head. "Don't, Tony. I can't help how I feel."

"How *do* you feel?"

She hesitated for a moment, but Tony fixed his gaze

on her and wouldn't back down. She sighed quietly. "Like I sold my soul."

"To the devil?"

Her lips tightened as if holding back a comment.

Tony leaned in his chair, releasing her hand. "Physically, are you okay?"

"Yes," she said. "I'm fine. I see the doctor next week, but I'm healthy."

She continued clicking on keys, showing him where the files were kept and how to access them. Then she came upon a document and lingered, her gaze drawn to the words on the screen: *Vine by Vine*. "Don't worry about this," she said, her finger on the delete button.

"Wait." Tony stopped her. "What is it?"

"It's nothing." Rena said, but he wouldn't let it go. Something in her eyes told him, whatever it was, it was important to her.

"I need to see everything, Rena. If I'm going to help you."

"It's got nothing to do with the accounts, Tony. Trust me."

"So why won't you let me see it?" Determined, he pressed her.

"Oh, for heaven's sake!" Rena straightened, her eyes sparkling like blue diamonds. "It's just a story I was writing."

"A *story?*" That sparked his curiosity. "What's it about?"

"It's about a girl growing up in the wine country."

"It's about you?"

"No, it's a novel. It's fiction, but yes, I guess some

of it is about what I know and how I feel about living here. It's sort of a wine guide but told from a different perspective. It's an analogy of how a girl grows to womanhood—"

"And you relate that to how a vine grows? Sort of like, how you need to be cared for and loved and nourished."

"Yeah," she said, her expression softening. "Something like that."

"You're not finished with it?"

She made a self-deprecating sound. "No, I'd forgotten about it. There's too much to do around here." She shrugged it off. "I never found the time."

"Maybe someday you'll have time to finish it."

Rena stared deeply into his eyes. "Right now, I'm more interested in saving my winery."

Tony glanced at the computer screen, satisfied that she'd removed her finger from the delete button. "Agreed. That's the first order of business. We have to find a way to keep Purple Fields afloat."

Rena walked into the gift shop through a door adjacent to the office, leaving Tony to work his magic on their books. She'd given him all the files, answered his questions and left once he was neck-deep in the accounts, unaware of her presence any longer.

Her small little haven of trinkets and boutique items always perked up her spirits. She loved setting up the displays, making each unique object stand out and look desirable to the customer. They made very little profit on the shop, but it complimented the wine-tasting room and made the whole area look appealing.

Rena sighed with relief rather than anguish this time. For so long she'd had the burden of saving Purple Fields on her shoulders, and the weight had become unbearably heavy. Now she knew that with Tony's assets backing her up she had salvaged the future of Purple Fields, thus insuring her baby's future as well. She could only feel good about that.

But saving the winery had come at a high price. If it weren't for the promise she made to David, she wondered if she'd be standing here right now. She'd been set to sell Purple Fields and move away, making a fresh start with her child. Now she was tied to Tony Carlino, and the notion prickled her nerves.

She didn't want to enjoy being in his arms this morning. She didn't want to admit that having sex with him made her world spin upside down. She *hated* that she'd liked it. That she'd responded to him the way she always had. Tony wasn't a man easily forgotten, but she'd managed it for twelve years. Now he was back in her life and planned to stay.

Solena entered the gift shop, thankfully interrupting her thoughts. "Hey, you're up and out early this morning."

Rena smiled at her friend, happy to see her. "It's just another workday."

Solena eyed her carefully. "Is it? I thought you got married two days ago."

"Seems longer," Rena said, lifting her lips at her little joke.

"That bad?"

Rena glanced at the door leading to the office. "I shouldn't complain. He's in there right now, going over all our files and accounts. He's owning up to his end of the bargain."

Solena walked behind the counter and spoke with concern and sympathy. "Are you doing the same, my friend?"

Rena lowered her lashes. "I'm trying. I'm really trying. I never thought we'd live together like this. We, uh—" Heat reached her cheeks, and she realized she'd blushed, something she rarely did.

Solena spoke with understanding. "Tony's a very handsome, appealing man, Rena."

"So was David." Tears welled in her eyes.

Solena leaned over the counter to take her hands. Rena absorbed some of her strength through the solid contact. "David is the past, Rena. As hard as that is to hear, it's true. You have to look forward, not back."

"But I feel so…guilty."

Solena held firm. "Remind yourself that David wanted this."

"There are times when I really hate Tony," she whispered. "And I'm ashamed that I'm not too thrilled with David for making me do this."

"But we both know why he did."

Rena tilted her head to one side. "There's more. I should have told you sooner."

"What?" Solena's dark eyes narrowed with concern.

Rena hesitated, staring at her friend. Finally she blurted, "I'm pregnant."

Solena drew in a big breath then let it go in relief. "Oh! You had me scared for a second there, imagining the worst." Quickly, she walked around the counter to give Rena a hug. "This is good news…really good news."

"Yes, it is. I know." A tear dropped down her cheek. She'd already fallen in love with her baby. "I'm happy about the baby, but now do you see why I'm so, so—"

"You're torn up inside. I can see that. But you have hope and a new life to bring into this world. Oh Rena, my dear friend, I couldn't be happier for you."

She glanced at the office door and lowered her voice, speaking from the heart. "David should raise his child, not Tony."

Solena's eyes softened with understanding. "But that can't be. Your feeling bad isn't going to change that. It takes a remarkable man to raise another man's child. Tony knows?"

"He knows."

"You resent him."

"Yes, I do. I resent him for so many reasons. I'm so afraid."

"Afraid?" Solena met her gaze directly. "You're afraid of Tony?"

She shook her head. "No, not of him. Of me. I'm afraid I'll forgive him. I don't want to forget the hurt and pain he caused me. I don't want to ever forgive him."

Tony spent the morning loading the Purple Fields files into a new database program. His first order of business was to update the computer. He wasn't a genius at business like his brother Joe, but he knew the value of state-of-the-art equipment. Rena needed a new computer, but for now he'd do what he could and download everything to a flash drive.

Rena walked into the office holding a plate of food. "It's after one, and you haven't eaten lunch."

Tony glanced at his watch, then leaned back in his seat. "I didn't realize the time."

She set the plate down onto the desk. "Ham and cheese. I have chicken salad made if you'd prefer that instead?"

Tony grabbed the sandwich and took a bite. "This is fine," he said, his stomach acknowledging the late hour. "Did you eat?"

"Solena and I had a bite earlier. Since David's death, she's been babysitting me. She thinks I don't know it, but it's sweet. We usually have lunch together."

"What about Ray?"

"He eats a huge breakfast at home and skips lunch."

"Do you have time to sit down?" he asked. "I could use the company."

He rose from his chair, offering it to her. He waited until she took the seat before he sat on the edge of the desk, stretching his legs out. He wasn't used to poring over a computer screen for hours. He wasn't used to being holed up behind a desk in a small office either.

He gobbled his sandwich and began working on the apple she'd cut into wedges. "How's your day going?"

"Good," she said. "I gave a wine tour at eleven, and we sold a few cases today. Want something to drink?"

"I'll have a beer later. I'll need it."

She tilted her head, her pretty blue eyes marked with question. "Too many numbers?"

"Yeah. I'm inputting files. Setting up a database. My eyes are crossing."

She laughed. "I know what you mean."

Tony liked the sound of her laughter. He stared at a smile that lit the room. "You do?"

"All those numbers can make you crazy."

He grinned. "I think I'm there now." He gobbled up the apple wedges. "Thanks for lunch."

Rena watched him carefully. "You're welcome."

"You need a new computer and some stuff for the office. This thing is outdated. We'll work out a time to do that."

Rena's eyes widened. "A new computer? I, uh, we never could afford—"

"I know," Tony said softly. "But now we can."

"And you need me for that?"

"Yes, I need your input. Look, we can drive into the next town if you'd feel more comfortable, but—"

"I would." She offered without hesitation.

Tony's ego took a nosedive. He'd promised her a secret marriage and he'd stick to it, but he wasn't accustomed to women not wanting to be seen with him. Usually, it was just the opposite—women enjoyed being seen around town with him.

Irritated now, he agreed. "Fine."

"So what are your plans?" She stood and picked up his empty plate.

"I loaded the info to a flash drive. I'm going to have Joe take a look at everything. Though I have my suspicions, I need his opinion."

"You're going home tonight?"

Her hope-filled voice only irritated him some more. With legs spread, he reached out and pulled her between them, the plate separating their bodies. "Yeah, but I'll be back." He kissed her soundly on the lips reminding her of the steamy way they'd made love early this morning. He nuzzled her neck, and the devil in him added with a low rasp, "I have more inputting to do."

Rena's eyes snapped up to his.

He smiled and then released her.

He'd told her no more tiptoeing around and he'd meant it.

Eight

Tony entered the Carlino offices, a two-story building set in the heart of Napa Valley. The older outer structure gave way to a modern, innovative inner office filled with leather and marble. The mortar and stone building had been classified as a ghost winery, once owned by an aging retired sea captain who had run the place in the 1890s until Prohibition put him out of business, along with nearly seven hundred other wineries in the area. While some wineries had been turned into estates and restaurants, some held true to their original destiny, haunted not by ghostly spirits but by the passage of time and ruin.

The place had lain dormant and in a state of wreckage until Santo Carlino purchased the property then renovated it into their office space.

Tony walked into the reception area and was greeted by a stunningly gorgeous redhead. "Hi, you must be Tony Carlino." The woman—her cleavage nearly spilling out of her top—lifted up from her desk to shake his hand. "Joe said you'd be stopping by. I'm Alicia Pendrake, but you can call me Ali."

"Hi, Ali." He grasped her hand and shook.

"I'm Joe's new personal assistant. Today's my second day on the job."

"Nice to meet you," Tony said, curious why Joe didn't mention hiring anyone new when they spoke, especially one who looked like an overly buxom supermodel, with rich auburn curls draping over her shoulders, wearing a sleek outfit and knee-high boots.

She pointed to the main office door. "He's inside, crunching numbers, what else?"

Tony chuckled. The woman was a spitfire. "Okay, thanks."

"Nice meeting you, Mr. Carlino."

"It's Tony."

"Okay, Tony." She granted him a pleased smile that sent his male antenna up.

He found Joe seated behind his desk, staring at the computer screen. He made sure to close the door behind him. "Whoa…where did you find her?"

"Find who?" Joe said, his attention focused on the computer.

"Alicia…Ali. Your new PA."

Joe's brows furrowed and he took off his glasses, rubbing his eyes. "I met her in New York last year. She's efficient and capable."

"I bet. What happened to Maggie?"

"I had to let her go. She wasn't doing her job. This place was in chaos when I got here. I remembered Ali, and I called her. Offered to pay her way out here, gave her an advance on her salary to get set up. I didn't think she'd take the job."

"But she did. Just like that?"

"Yeah, I got lucky."

"*You got lucky?* Joe, the woman is beyond gorgeous. Haven't you noticed?"

Joe rubbed his jaw. "She's attractive, I suppose."

"You suppose? Maybe you need better glasses."

"My glasses are fine. I'm not interested, Tone. You know that I've sworn off women. After what happened with Sheila, I'm basically immune to beautiful women… to all women actually. Ali is smart. She's dedicated, and she does her work without complaint. She's very organized. You know how I am about organization."

Tony's lips twitched. "Okay, if you say so."

"So, what's up? You said you needed a favor?"

Tony tossed the flash drive onto the desk. "I need you to compare these accounts from Purple Fields with ours, for the same dates. I've been going over Rena's books. I just need your expert opinion."

"How soon?"

"Today?"

"I can do that." Joe inserted the flash drive into his computer. "I'll upload the files and let you know what I find out."

"Great, oh and can you burn them to a CD for me? There's something else I want to check on."

"Sure thing. I'll do that first."

While Joe burned the information to a disk, Tony walked around the office, noting the subtle changes Joe had made to Santo Carlino's office. Joe had secured even more high tech equipment than his father had used and updated the phone system. He was determined to make the company paperless, sooner rather than later.

It would seem that the only thing left from the older generation of the winery were the vast acres of vineyards—six hundred in all—the grapes that couldn't be digitalized into growing faster and the wine itself.

After a few minutes, Joe handed him a CD of Rena's accounts. "Here you go."

Tony tapped the CD against his palm. "Thanks."

"So how's married life?"

Tony shrugged, wishing he knew the answer to that question. "Too soon to tell. I'll be back later. You don't have plans tonight, do you?"

Joe shook his head. "Just work."

"Okay, I'll see you around six."

Tony walked out of the office after bidding farewell to Ali, who was as intent on her computer screen as Joe had been. He drove out of town and up the hills to the Carlino estate, waving a quick hello to Nick as he drove off the property with a pretty woman in his car. Tony only shook his head at his happy-go-lucky brother, thinking "been there, done that."

Tony entered the house and grabbed a beer out of the refrigerator. Taking a big swig from the bottle, he walked upstairs to his quadrant of the house, entered his private office and sat down at his desk. He logged onto his computer and inserted the CD into the slot.

He stopped for one moment, contemplating what he was about to do. Taking another gulp of beer, he sighed with indecision, but his curiosity got the better of him. He searched the files and finally found what he'd been looking for. The screen popped up with the title *Vine by Vine* by Rena Fairfield Montgomery.

Tony began reading the first chapter.

Roots.

In order to make great wine, you need good terroir, meaning the soil, climate and topography of a region that uniquely influence the grapes. A wine with a certain terroir cannot be reproduced in close resemblance of another, because the terroir is not exactly the same. Much like the DNA of a person each wine has a one-of-a-kind profile.

I guess I came from good terroir. That is to say, my parents were solid grounded people, rich, not by monetary standards but by life and vitality and a grand love of winemaking. My roots run deep and strong. I come from healthy stock. I've always been thankful for that. I've had the love of the best two people on earth. A child can't ask for more than that.

My parents, like the trellis system of a vine, show you the way yet cannot dictate the path you will ultimately choose. As I grew I felt their protection, but as I look back I also see the strength they instilled in me. After all, a new vine needs to weather a vicious storm now and again. It needs to withstand blasting winds, bending by its might but not breaking.

I remember a time when I was in grammar school...

Tony read the chapter, smiling often as Rena portrayed anecdotes from her childhood, relating them to the ever-growing vines, taking shape, readying for the fruit it would bear.

He skimmed the next few chapters until he came upon a chapter called "Crush and Maceration."

The crush in vintner's terminology is when the grapes are harvested, broken from the vine by gentle hands. The crush happens each year between August and October, depending on the kind of grapes that are growing in your vineyard. For me, the crush happened only once. It's that time in your life when you break off from the ones that graciously and lovingly nourished you to become your own person. I was sixteen when that happened. I grew from an adolescent girl to womanhood the autumn of my sophomore year. The day I met my first love, Rod Barrington.

I had a big crush on Rod from the moment I laid eyes on him. He was new to our school, but his family was well known in the area. Everyone knew of the wealthy Barringtons, they owned more property in our valley than anyone else.

While my friendship with Rod grew, I fell more and more in love with him. For a young girl, the pain of being his friend nearly brought me to my knees. I couldn't bear seeing him tease and joke with other girls, but I kept my innermost feelings hidden, hoping one day he'd realize that his good friend, Joanie Adams might just be the girl for him.

Tony read a few more passages, skimming the words on the page quickly, absorbing each instance that Rena relayed in the story, vaguely recalling the circumstances much like Rena had written. It was clearly obvious that though Rena had changed the names, Rena had written about his relationship with her, reminding him of the love they once shared. As he read on, the smile disappeared from his face, Rena's emotions so bold and honest on the page. He knew he'd hurt her but just how much he hadn't known until this very moment.

In winemaking once the grapes are gently crushed from the skins, seeds and stems, allowing the juices to flow, maceration occurs. The clear juice deepens in color the longer it's allowed to steep with its counterparts, being in direct contact with stems and seeds and skins. Time blends the wine and determines the hue and flavor, intensifying its effect.

And that's how I felt about Rod. The longer I was with him, the more direct contact I had with him, the more I loved him. He colored my every thought and desire. I knew I'd met the man of my dreams. We blended in every way.

Tony skimmed more pages, his stomach taut with regret and pain. He stopped when he came to a chapter titled "Corked."

He knew what that meant. He forced himself to read on.

Wine that is "corked" has been contaminated by its cork stopper, causing a distinctly unpleasant aroma. The wine is ruined for life. It's spoiled and will never be the same. Fortunately for wine lovers, only seven percent of all wine is considered corked or tainted. A sad fact if you'd invested time and energy with that bottle.

Wine shouldn't let you down. And neither should someone you love.

Tony ran his hands down his face, unable to read any more. But a voice inside told him he had to know the extent of Rena's feelings. He had to find out what happened to her after he'd left her. He continued to read, sitting stiffly in the chair, woodenly reading words that would haunt him.

"Rod called today, after his first big sale. It killed me to talk to him, I felt selfish for wishing he'd flop in his high-powered position in New York. I was dealing with my mother's terminal cancer, needing him so badly."

After reading Rena's story, which ended abruptly when Rena's mother died, Tony slumped in the seat.

Drained, hollowed out by what he'd learned, he simply sat there, reliving the scenarios in his mind.

Eventually Tony logged off of his computer, leaving the disk behind, but Rena's emotions and her silent suffering while he was winning races and pursuing his dreams would stay with him forever.

He met Joe at the office at six o'clock as planned, his disposition in the dumps. "Did you find anything unusual?" he asked his brother.

"No, not unusual. Dad did screw a lot of people over, but I've never seen it so clearly as now."

Tony groaned, his mood going from gray to black in a heartbeat. "I was hoping I was wrong."

"No, you're not wrong. Your instincts are dead-on." Joe shuffled papers around, comparing notes he'd written.

"Looked to me like Dad deliberately undersold cabernet and merlot to the retailers to drive Purple Fields out of business. We make five kinds of wine, but he chose the two Purple Fields are famous for to undercut them. From what I've found, he sold for a slight loss for at least ten years. He knew he could sustain those losses without a problem, while Purple Fields couldn't compete."

Tony winced, hearing the truth aloud. "I'd asked Dad to leave Purple Fields alone. To let them make a living. But I'm betting he did it to spite me."

Joe's brows rose. "You think he singled them out because you chose a different career?"

"He'd never approved of my choices. He didn't want me to succeed. He wanted to dictate the course of my life, and it pissed him off that I wouldn't listen to him. I chose racing over him."

"Yeah, Dad was angry when you took off. He wanted to hand down his business to his firstborn son. Hell, he wasn't too fond of me not sticking around either. I've got a head for business, not grape growing."

Tony's lips curved halfway up. "You're a computer geek, Joe."

"And proud of it," Joe added, then focused his attention back on the subject at hand. "Dad was an all-around brute. I bet he used the same tactics on half a dozen other small wineries to drive them out of business."

"Doesn't make it right. Hell, he made millions. He didn't need to shut down his competition."

"Apparently, he didn't see it that way."

Tony let go a frustrated sigh. "At least there's something I can do about it. I'm going to renegotiate those contracts. We'll sell our wine at a fair price, but we won't undercut anyone, especially Purple Fields."

Joe nodded and leaned back in his chair. "That should make Rena happy."

"Yeah, but it won't make up for all the past pain this family put her through."

"You're not just talking about Dad now, are you?"

Tony took a steadying breath and shook his head. "No. But I plan to make it up to Rena. Whether she likes it or not."

"Those sound like fighting words, Tone."

Tony rose from his seat. "They are."

"Oh, before I forget, someone called for you today."

Joe shifted through a pile of notes, coming up with one. "Something about your racing contracts. They've been calling the house and couldn't reach you."

He handed Tony the note, and when he glanced at the name, he cursed under his breath. He didn't need this right now. "Okay," he said, stuffing the note in his pocket. "Thanks. I'll take care of it."

Now he had three things to deal with, the note he tucked away being the least of his worries. At least he knew now how to save Purple Fields, but after reading *Vine by Vine,* Tony wasn't sure how he could repair the damage he'd done to Rena.

The promise he made to David far from his mind, Tony wanted to save his hasty marriage for more selfish reasons. He couldn't deny that reliving the past in these last few hours made him realize how much Rena had once meant to him.

He got in his car and drove off, speeding out of town, needing the rush of adrenaline to ward off his emotions and plaguing thoughts that he was falling in love with Rena again.

Tony entered the house, and a pleasing aroma led him straight to the kitchen. He found Rena standing at the stove top stirring the meal, her hair beautifully messy and her face pink from puffs of steam rising up. She didn't acknowledge his presence initially until he wrapped his arms around her waist and drew her against him. He kissed her throat, breathing in her citrus scent. "Looking good."

"It's just stew."

"I meant you," Tony said, stealing another quick kiss. Coming home to this domestic scene, something grabbed his insides and twisted when he saw her. "You're beautiful behind the stove. I want to come home to you every night."

She frowned and moved slightly away. "Don't say those things."

"Why?" he asked softly. "Because I've said them before and now you don't believe me?"

Rena kept stirring the stew. "You're astute."

"And you're being stubborn."

She shrugged, moving away from the stove to grab two plates from the cabinet. Tony took out cutlery from a drawer and set two glasses on the table.

So now they were resorting to name-calling? This certainly wasn't the scene Tony pictured in his mind when he first entered the house.

"Did you find out anything from Joe?" Rena asked.

"Yeah, I did. But let's eat first."

"Whenever someone says that to me, I know the news is not good."

"There's bad news and there's good news. I think we should eat first before discussing it."

Rena brought the dishes to the stove top and filled their plates, adding two biscuits to Tony's plate. She served him and sat down to eat. Her long hair fell forward as she nibbled on her food. She wore jeans and a soft baby-blue knit blouse that brought out the vivid color of her eyes. She hardly looked pregnant, except for a hint of added roundness to her belly.

Sweeping emotions stirred in his gut. He wanted to protect Rena. He wanted to possess her. He wanted to make love to her until all the pain and anger disappeared from her life. So much had happened to her in her short thirty-one years from losing her mother and father, to losing David, but it had all started with him. And Tony determined it would all end with him as well.

After the meal, Rena started cleaning up. Tony rose and then took her hand. "Leave this. We'll take care of it later. We need to talk."

She nodded and followed him into the living room. Oak beams, a stone fireplace stacked with logs and two comfortable sofas lent to the warmth of the room. Tony waited for her to sit, then took a place next to her.

They sat in silence for a minute, then Tony began. "What I have to say isn't easy. Joe and I went through the records and have proof now of how my father manipulated sales in the region."

"You mean, my father was right? Santo set out to destroy us?"

Tony winced and drew a breath. "I can't sugarcoat it, Rena. My father undercut Purple Fields, even at a loss to his own company to drive you out of business. Joe's guess is that it wasn't personal. He'd been doing the same to other small businesses for years."

Rena closed her eyes, absorbing the information. "My father knew. He didn't have proof. His customers wouldn't talk about it, except to say that they'd found better deals elsewhere. They'd praised our wine over and over but wouldn't buy it."

"My father probably strong-armed them into silence," Tony said.

Rena opened her eyes and stared at him. He couldn't tell what was going on in her head, but he suspected it wasn't good.

She rose from her seat and paced the floor. "My mother was worried and anxious all the time. She loved Purple Fields. She and my father poured everything they had into the winery. They worked hard to make ends meet. She held most of it in, putting up a brave front, but I could tell she wasn't the same. My father noticed it, too. He'd stare at her with concern in his eyes. And that all started around the time when we broke up and you left town."

Tony stood to face her. He owed Rena the full truth or at least the truth as he saw it. His voice broke when he made the confession, "I think he targeted Purple Fields after I left."

She stiffened and her mouth twisted. "My God," she whispered, closing her eyes in agony. "Don't you see? The stress might have triggered my mother's illness."

Tony approached her. "Rena, no."

She began nodding her head. "Oh, yes. Yes. My mother was healthy. There was no history of that disease in our family. Mom was fine. Fine, until the winery started going downhill. She worried herself sick. The doctors even suggested that stress could be a factor."

Rena's face reddened as her pain turned to anger. She announced with a rasp in her voice, "I need some air."

Tony watched her walk out of the house, slamming

the door behind her. He ran a hand through his hair, his frustration rising. "Damn it. Damn it."

He'd never hated being a Carlino more than now. He could see it in Rena's eyes—the blame, the hatred and the injury. When she'd looked at him that way, he understood all of her resentment. He knew she'd react to the truth with some degree of anger, but he'd never considered that she'd blame his family for her mother's illness.

Could it be true?

Tony couldn't change the past. All he could do now was to convince her he'd make things right. He gave her a few minutes of solitude before exiting the house. He had to find his wife and comfort her.

Even though in her eyes, he was the enemy.

Nine

Rena ran into the fields. The setting sun cast golden hues onto the vines, helping to light her way. She ran until her heart raced too fast and her breaths surged too heavy. Yet she couldn't outrace the burning ache in her belly or the plaguing thoughts in her mind. She stopped abruptly in the middle of the cabernet vines, fully winded, unable to run another step. Putting her head in her hands, tears spilled down her cheeks. Grief struck her anew. It was as if she was losing her mother all over again. Pretty, vivacious Belinda Fairfield had died before her time. Her sweet, brave mother hadn't deserved to suffer so. She hadn't deserved to relinquish her life in small increments until she was too weak to get out of bed.

Rena's sobs were absorbed in the vines, her cries

swallowed up by the solitude surrounding her. Her body shook, the release of anguish exhausting her.

Two strong arms wrapped around her, supporting her sagging body. "Shh, Rena," Tony said gently. "Don't cry, sweetheart. Let me make it right. I'll make it all right."

"You…can't," she whispered between sobs. Yet Tony's strength gave her immeasurable comfort.

"I can. I will. We'll do it together."

Before Rena could formulate a response, Tony lifted her up, one arm bracing her legs and the other supporting her shoulders. "Hold on to me," he said softly, "and try to calm down."

Rena circled one arm around his neck and closed her eyes, stifling her sobs, every ounce of her strength spent.

Tony walked through the vineyard, holding her carefully. In the still of the night all that she heard was the occasional crunch of shriveled leaves under Tony's feet as he moved along.

When he pushed through the door to her house, her eyes snapped open. He strode with purpose to the bedroom and lay her down with care, then came down next to her, cradling her into his arms once again. "I'm going to stay with you until you fall asleep."

Rena stared into his eyes and whispered softly, "I hate you, Tony."

He brushed strands of hair from her forehead with tenderness then kissed her brow. "I know."

The sweetness of his kiss sliced through her, denting her well-honed defenses.

He took off her shoes and then his own. Next he undressed her, removing her knit top over her head and unzipping her jeans. She helped pull them off with a little tug, ready to give up her mind and body to sleep.

Tony covered them both with a quilted throw and tucked her in close. She reveled in his warmth and breathed in his musky scent despite herself. "Just for the record, sweetheart," he began, "I'm not here just because of the promise I made to David. It goes much deeper than that. And I think you know it."

Rena flinched inwardly, confusion marring her good judgment. She should pull away from Tony, refusing his warmth and comfort. She couldn't deal with his pronouncement. She couldn't wrap her mind around what he'd just implied. Yet at the same time, she needed his arms around her. She needed to be held and cradled and reassured.

Was she that weak?

Or just human?

"Good night, Rena." Tony kissed her lips lightly, putting finality to the night. "Sleep well."

Rena slept soundly for the better part of the night but roused at 3:00 a.m. to find Tony gone from bed. Curious, she slipped on her robe and padded down the hallway. She found him sprawled out on the living room sofa with his eyes closed. He made an enticing sight, his chest bare, his long lean, incredible body and handsome face more than any woman could ever hope to have in a mate.

Rena shivered from the coolness in the room. She

grabbed an afghan from the chair and gently covered Tony, making sure not to wake him. She lingered for just one moment then turned to leave.

"Don't go," he whispered.

Surprised, Rena spun around to meet Tony's penetrating gaze. "I thought you were asleep."

"I was—on and off." Tony sat up, planting his feet on the ground and leaning forward to spread his fingers through his hair.

"Sorry if I disturbed your sleep."

Tony chuckled without humor. "You did. You do."

Stunned by his blunt honesty, Rena blinked.

"Sleeping next to you isn't easy, Rena." Tony shook his head as if shaking out cobwebs. "Sorry, I wish I could be more honorable, but you're a handful of temptation."

Rena's mouth formed an "oh."

Tony stared at her. "You shouldn't find it shocking that I want to sleep with you. You remember how we were together."

Rena's spine stiffened. "Maybe you should sleep in another room."

"I have a better idea." He took her wrist and tugged her down. She landed on his lap. Immediately, he stretched out on the sofa, taking her with him. "Maybe I should make love to my wife."

A gasp escaped from her due to his sudden move. "Oh."

He untied the belt on her robe, his tone dead serious. "I want you."

His hands came up to push the robe off her shoulders,

revealing the bra and panties she'd slept in. His appreciative gaze heated the blood in her veins. "You can't blame me for that."

"No. But for so many other things," she said quietly.

"I get it, sweetheart. I understand." Tony pulled the robe free, exposing her fully.

Positioned provocatively, feeling his hard length pressing against her, excitement zipped through her system. Her breathing rough, she barely managed to utter the question. "Do you?"

"Yes, I do. And I want to make it up to you. Let me do that," Tony said, cupping his hand around her head and bringing her mouth to his. He kissed her softly. "Let me wipe away the pain." Again his lips met hers. "Let me help you heal, sweet Rena. You've been through so much."

His sincerity, his tone, the breathtaking way he looked at her softened the hardness around her heart. She wanted to heal, to release her defenses, to feel whole again.

"Tony," she breathed out, unsure of her next move.

"It's your call, sweetheart," he said, stroking her back in a loving way that created tingles along her spine. Another notch of her defenses fell.

Images flashed of the good times she'd had with Tony. The fun, the laughter and the earth-shattering lovemaking they'd shared. As much as she wanted to forget, the good memories came back every time he touched her. "I want the pain to go away," she whispered with honesty. Even if it was only for a short time tonight.

"Then let me take you there."

She closed her eyes, nodding in relief, surrendering herself to the moment. "Yes."

Rena touched his chest, her fingers probing, searching, tantalizing and teasing. He felt incredibly good. Strong. Powerful. She itched to touch him all over.

Bringing her head down to his, she claimed his mouth in a lingering kiss. She took it slow, pushing aside her misgivings. His body seemed in tune with hers. Every little action she took brought his sexy reaction. Every moan she uttered, he answered with a groan. She liked being in control. It was the first time she'd ever taken the reins so fully, and Tony seemed to understand what she needed. He encouraged her with a gleam in his eyes and a willing body.

"I'm all yours," he whispered.

Her breath caught. She knew he meant it sexually, but Rena seized on the reality of that statement. He was all hers. But what she didn't know was, could she ever be *all his?*

"You're thinking again," Tony scolded with a smile.

"Guilty as charged." Rena reached around to unhook her bra, freeing her breasts. Letting her bra drop, she freed her mind as well, pushing all thoughts away but the immediate here and now.

Tony reached for her then, his touch an exquisite caress of tenderness and caring. He kissed her lovingly, cherishing every morsel of her body with his lips and hands until his unexpected compassion seeped into her soul.

Their lovemaking was sedate and measured, careful and unflappable one moment, then crazy and wild, fierce and fiery the next. They moved in ups and downs, from highs to lows, they learned and taught, giving joy and pleasure to one another. The night knew no bounds. And when it came time to release their pent-up tension, Rena rose above Tony, straddling his legs. He held on to her hips and guided her. Taking him in felt natural, familiar and so right. She enjoyed every ounce of pleasure derived from their joining. She moved with restless yearning, her body flaming, all rational thought discarded.

Tony watched her, his eyes never wavering, his body meeting her every demand. He was the man she'd always wanted, the man she'd been destined to love. He'd pushed his way back into her life, but Rena couldn't trust in him, not fully, not yet. But each time they came together, her resolve slipped just a little, and her heartache slowly ebbed.

When she couldn't hold on any longer, her skin prickling, her flesh tingling and her body at its absolute limit, she moaned in ecstasy.

"Let go, sweetheart," Tony encouraged.

And she shuddered, her orgasm strong. She cried out his name when her final release came. Tony tightened his hold on her and joined her in a climax, taking them both to heaven.

Rena lowered down, spent. Tony wrapped her into his arms and kissed her forehead. "Do you still hate me?" he asked.

"Yes," she replied without hesitation. "But not as much as before."

Tony squeezed her tighter and chuckled almost inaudibly. "Guess, I'm going to have to work on that."

During the next week, Tony left Rena during the day to work on saving her winery. He made calls out of his Napa office, meeting with customers personally to explain the new pricing structures. Tony liked winning but not at the expense of others trying to eke out a living. If there was a contract he could renegotiate, Tony was on top of it.

He made sure that their company held their own in the marketplace, but with Joe's help they'd come up with a pricing plan that would realize profits and still allow the smaller wineries to compete.

Unlike his father, Tony didn't need to crush his opponents. The company's profits would go up on certain types of wine while the other local wineries of comparable quality would also make a profit on their specialties. It was a win-win situation in his opinion.

Satisfied with what he'd accomplished today, he called it quits, gathering up the papers on his desk. He was anxious to get home to Rena. Little by little, she was coming around, softening to him, smiling more and looking less and less guilty about their circumstances.

As he got ready to leave, he pondered how at night he'd join her in bed, and more times than not, they'd make love. Slow and sweet one time then wild and hot another time. Tony never knew what the night would bring. Some nights, when both were exhausted, they'd just fall asleep in each other's arms.

Tony enjoyed waking up next to Rena in the mornings. With her hair messy and her eyes hazy with sleep, she'd look at him and smile softly for a second or two before her memories returned and a haunted look would enter her eyes.

He clung to those few seconds in his mind, telling himself that one day that troubled look would be gone forever and she'd accept him completely as her husband and the father of her baby.

Tony smiled at the thought. Rena's stomach showed signs of the baby now. He was amazed at how quickly her body had transformed, her belly growing rounder each day.

"Excuse me, Tony," Ali said, stepping into his office.

Tony glanced at her, and as usual, the same thought flitted in his mind. He couldn't believe Joe wasn't interested in this vital, gorgeous, very capable woman.

"There's a call for you. From your agent. A mister Ben Harper? He says it's important. Line one."

Tony's smile faded. "Okay, thanks." He glanced at the flashing red light. He couldn't ignore Harper anymore. "I'll get it in here."

He waited until Ali walked away before picking up the phone. "Hello, Ben."

His agent read him the riot act for not returning his calls. Tony slammed his eyes shut, listening to his tirade.

"You know damn well you're under contract. My ass is on the line, too."

"It's not a good time right now," Tony said.

"You told me that two months ago. They gave you an extension because of your father's death, and you were recovering from your injuries, but I can't put them off much longer. They're threatening a lawsuit, for heaven's sake. You need to give me something. *Now,* Tony."

Tony sighed into the receiver, caving in to these last few contractual commitments. He still had an endorsement deal with EverStrong Tires and was expected to do interviews for a few of the races. "How long will it take?"

"Filming could take up to a week for the commercial."

"When?"

"Yesterday."

"Make it for next week, Ben. I'll do my best."

"You better be there, Tony. You've pushed them too far as it is. And don't forget, you're expected at Dover International Speedway for the first interview."

"I'll be there."

"I'll call you with the details."

"I'm holding my breath," he mumbled and hung up. He paced the office, shaking his head. Things were just getting better with Rena, and he didn't want that to end.

Rena hated anything to do with racing. Understandably so, but Tony had no choice in the matter. The last thing he needed was a lawsuit. And, if he were truly honest with himself, he missed the racing scene. Tony had recognized that it was time to leave it behind. Exit while still on top, they say. He'd accomplished what he'd set out to do, but a man doesn't lose his passion that easily. His blood still stirred with excitement when he stepped foot on the raceway.

The difference was that now Rena and the baby took precedence over racing. He was committed to his marriage and determined to get that same commitment from her.

Tony left the office and drove to Purple Fields, eager to see Rena. He entered the house and found her finishing a conversation on the phone in the kitchen. He came up behind her and wrapped his arms around her waist, his hands spreading across her stomach. He caressed her tiny round belly and nibbled on her throat. It had only been a few days that she'd allowed him this intimacy, and Tony couldn't get enough. "Who was that?" he asked, setting his chin on her shoulder.

"The doctor's office. I have an appointment tomorrow."

"What time are we going?"

"We?" Rena turned in his arms. "You can't go with me, Tony."

He blinked. "Why not?"

Rena stared at him. "You know why."

Tony's brows furrowed. "No, I don't. You tell me."

She moved out of his arms and shrugged. "This is David's baby."

Tony rolled his eyes. "I'm aware of that." She reminded him every chance she could. "So?"

"No one knows we're married. How would it look if I showed up with you?"

Tony summoned his patience and spoke slowly. "It would look like a good friend is supporting you at your doctor's appointment."

"No," she said adamantly. "I can't. Solena is taking me."

"No, *I'm* taking you."

Rena's eyes closed as if the prospect disturbed her sanity. Tony's ire rose, and he calmed down by taking a few breaths. "Maybe it's time to expose our marriage. Then you'd have a legitimate reason to have me there."

She shook her head. "I'm not ready for that."

"Why, Rena? Why not stop this ruse? We're living together. *We're married.* Don't worry about what people think. It's no one's business. This is about us, our lives and our family."

"It's not that," she rushed out, giving him her uplifted chin.

Tony stared at her. Then it dawned on him. "Oh, I see. You're not ready to accept me as your husband. As long as no one knows, you can pretend it isn't so. You can stay in your own world and not face reality."

Rena didn't deny it. She put her head down, refusing to let him see the truth in her eyes.

"Tell Solena I'm taking you tomorrow. I promised David and I won't break that promise."

But Tony's truth was that he wanted to be beside Rena during her appointment. He wanted to provide for her and protect her. He wanted to lend her support. And more and more, he found his desire had nothing to do with the vow he made to his best friend.

"Everything looks great, Rena. You're in good health. The baby has a strong heartbeat," Dr, Westerville said, smiling her way.

"Thank you, Doctor." Sitting upright in a green-and-white checkered gown on the exam table, Rena sighed in relief. Though she felt fine, hearing it from the doctor relieved her mind.

After he'd finished the checkup he'd reminded her of the do's and don't's regarding her pregnancy. Eat smaller meals, more times a day. Keep on a healthy diet. Stay active, but don't overdo anything.

Rena had been doing all those things since even before her first appointment with the doctor. The second she realized she was having a baby, she'd read everything she could about pregnancy and gestation.

"I'll let your friend in now," the doctor said.

She gave him a small smile.

The doctor opened the exam room door and let Tony inside. She'd relented in letting him take her to the appointment, but absolutely refused to have him in the room during the examination.

Tony walked a few steps into the room with his concerned gaze pinned on her. Before she made introductions, she answered his silent questions. "I'm fine and the baby is healthy. Dr. Westerville, this is David's good friend, Tony Carlino."

"Of course." The doctor put out his hand. "Nice

to meet you Mr. Carlino. I've been a fan of yours for years."

Tony nodded and shook the doctor's hand. "I appreciate that."

"All of us locals have rooted for you since day one."

Tony accepted his compliment with grace. "I've had a lot of support from this area. It means a lot. But now I'm retired and home to stay." He turned to Rena and she shot him a warning look. "Rena's a family friend. I plan to help her as much as possible."

"That's good. She's doing fine. She's very healthy and I don't foresee any problems. With all you've been through these past few months," the doctor said, focusing back on her, "it's very good to have a friend go through this with you. I recommend childbirth classes in a month or two, but for now, just follow the list of instructions I gave you."

"I'll do my best."

"Still running the winery?" he asked.

She nodded. "I promised David I'd keep Purple Fields going. Not that I want anything different myself."

"Okay, good. But in your later months, you may have to back off a little. Delegate duties more and—"

"I'll see to it," Tony chimed in. "I'll make sure she takes it easy."

The doctor glanced at Tony, then at Rena. He smiled warmly. Heat crawled up her neck, and at the same time, she wanted to sock Tony into the next county.

Dr. Westerville patted her shoulder. "I'll see you next month, Rena. I know your husband would be proud of you and glad you're going to have the support you need." He turned and shook Tony's hand once again. "David was a good man and it seems that he picked his friends wisely."

When he left the room, Rena glared at Tony. "I need to get dressed."

"I'll help." He grinned.

She shot him another warning look.

"Come on, Rena. Lighten up. The baby is healthy and so are you. That's good news."

Rena sighed and admitted joy at her baby news, but it struck her anew that she'd be going through all of this with Tony. "Can't you see that this is hard for me?"

"I know, Rena. You remind me every half an hour."

Rena twisted her lips. "No, I don't."

"Seems like it," Tony muttered. "I'll wait for you outside."

She stepped down from the table and walked into the small dressing area, untying her gown and throwing on her clothes. Had she been too hard on Tony? At times, she felt like a shrew, but it was only because every time she softened to him, she felt like she was losing another piece of David. Little by little, David's memory was fading. And that wasn't fair to him or to her. A woman needed time to grieve and recover. But Tony had bounded into her life, hell-bent on keeping the vow he'd made to David.

Her feelings were jumbled up inside and half the time she didn't know which emotions were honest and true. She'd never been in a situation remotely like this. She chuckled at the absurdity—she was a secretly married, pregnant widow.

Not too many women could say that.

After Rena's doctor's appointment, Tony took her to lunch at her favorite little café in town. Thinking about the new life growing inside her, she couldn't deny her happiness. Seeing Dr. Westerville made it all seem real, and knowing that the baby was healthy and hearing the due date for the birth lightened her heart. The joy and love she held inside couldn't be duplicated.

After they ate their meal, they stopped at an electronics store where she and Tony ordered a top-of-the-line computer with all the bells and whistles. To overcome her resistance to such a complex-looking computer, Tony had promised to set it up when it arrived and get her acquainted with it. Whatever they couldn't figure out, his brother Joe would certainly be glad to explain to them.

Tony made other purchases as well—new phones for the house and office and a four-in-one fax machine he insisted they needed at Purple Fields. She certainly couldn't fault her husband his generosity. Where she and David had pinched pennies to make a go of the winery, Tony had no trouble spending money for the cause. Of course, he was a millionaire in his own right, famous in the world of racing, and he could afford these things.

They strolled down the street past a baby store, the window displaying a white crib and matching tallboy dresser, strollers and car seats. Rena lingered for a moment, aching with yearning.

"Rena, any time you're ready," Tony said.

Her emotions kept her from taking the next step. Something held her back. "Maybe soon. First I have to clean out the room and paint it. I thought we'd use the room across from ours to be closer to the baby."

Tony surprised her with a kiss. "It's a great idea."

Her gaze lifted to his noting the pleased gleam in his eyes. She'd *surprised* both of them with her comment, but more and more she was learning how to trust him again. So far, he hadn't given her any reason not to. He'd made good on his promise to fix Purple Fields. He'd spoken with customers and renegotiated contracts all in order to save her from ruin. He'd been patient with her. He'd been kind. He'd been a magnificent lover and a good friend.

He'd set out to prove that he wasn't like his ruthless father, and so far, he'd succeeded. If she could put the past behind her, they stood a chance. For her baby's sake, if not her own, she wanted to take that chance.

"I'll help you with the room. I'm pretty good with a paintbrush. What color?"

Rena grinned, letting go a little bit more of the pain trapped inside. "Sage-green or chiffon-yellow."

"What, not pink or blue?"

Rena tilted her head and sighed. "We don't know the baby's sex yet." She glanced inside the store again, then placed her hand over her belly and admitted, "I don't want to wait until we find out."

"Me, either," Tony said, taking her hand. "Let's go find us some sage and chiffon paint. There's a hardware store up ahead."

By the time they returned home, Rena was in the best mood she could remember. They'd picked out paint colors together—unable to decide, they'd bought gallons of each shade—paintbrushes, rollers and drop cloths.

"Do you really want to help me paint the bedroom?" Rena asked after dinner as they retired to the living room. The day had exhausted her physically. Tony sat beside her on the sofa, and he brought her into the circle of his arms. She rested her head on his chest.

"You doubt me after I badgered that salesman with questions about baby-safe paint for half an hour?"

A wave of excitement stirred as she envisioned her baby's room all fresh and clean, filled with furniture, just waiting for his or her arrival. And Tony had been there every step of the way. She'd resisted giving him anything more than her body, but Tony wasn't a man she could easily put out of her mind. Ever so slowly he was making inroads to her heart. "I'm anxious to start."

"I'll clear my calendar, and we can start tomorrow," Tony said. "We'll have it done by the weekend."

"Oh, I can't. I have a vendor coming for an appointment tomorrow. We have three wine tours booked this week, and I can't leave Solena to do it all. Can we start on it first thing next week? Monday?"

Tony looked into her eyes, hesitating. Then he rose to stand before the large double window facing the front yard, his hands on his hips. "I can't do it next week, Rena."

His tone alarmed her. "Why not?"

He scrubbed his jaw a few times, as if searching for the right words. "I was going to tell you tomorrow." He paced the room, walking slowly as he spoke. "I'm up against a wall. I have commitments I made a long time ago, and my agent can't find any wiggle room. I'm going out of town on Sunday. I'll be gone at least a week."

"A week?" Rena's heart plummeted. A serious case of déjà vu set in.

I won't be gone long, Rena. I'll come back as soon as I can. Or you can come meet me. We'll be together somehow, I promise.

"What are you going to do?" she asked.

"Some interviews and a commercial. It's one of the last endorsements I'm contracted to do."

Rena felt numb. "Okay," she said once she'd gathered her wits. She kept her voice light, her tone noncommittal. "You don't need my permission." She rose from the sofa. "I have some work to do to prepare for my meeting to-morrow."

"I'll help you," Tony said, gauging her reaction.

Rena could only manage a curt reply. "No. I can do it myself."

Tony approached her. "Rena?"

She halted him with a widespread hand. "It's okay, Tony. Really. I understand."

"Damn it! You don't understand." Frustration carried in his deep voice. His olive complexion colored with heat. "I've put this off for as long as I can. They'll sue me if I don't show up, and that's not what either of us needs right now."

"You don't have to explain to me." She hoisted her chin and straightened her shoulders. "I never wanted any of this to begin with."

Tony strode to face her. Taking her into his arms, he yanked her close and narrowed his eyes. "This isn't twelve years ago. The situation is different. You think I won't come back?"

"Darn right, it's different. I'm not that love-smitten young girl anymore. Whether you come back or not, I know I'll survive. I did it once and I can do it again."

Tony released her arms and then barked off a dozen curses, each one fouler than the next.

"As far as I'm concerned, you owned up to your obligation to David. You married me. Purple Fields is on its way to becoming solvent again. I won't fool myself into thinking we have anything more. You did your duty, Tony. Congratulations."

"Anything else?" Tony asked, clearly fuming.

"Yes," she said, unmindful of his state of anger. She was plenty angry, too. To think he'd nearly had her fooled that they might have something to build on. But somehow, racing had always come between them. David was gone to her. But Tony? She'd never really had him to begin with, and this was a brutal reminder that she would always come in second place. "Thanks for ruining the best day I've had since my husband died."

Ten

Nick and Joe were relaxing outside on the patio overlooking the Carlino vineyards when Tony strode in. The stone fire pit provided light and heat on this cool spring night. The weather was always cooler atop their hillside than in the valley below, and tonight, Tony welcomed the brisk air.

His brothers welcomed him with curious stares. "Want a beer?" Nick asked.

Tony shook his head. "I need a real drink." He strode over to the outside bar and poured himself two fingers of whiskey. Without pause, he gulped down one finger's worth of the golden liquid before returning to sit on a patio chair facing the flames. He slouched in his seat, stretched out his long legs and crossed one ankle over the other, deep in thought.

After several moments of awkward silence, Nick asked, "What's up, Tony?"

Tony sipped his whiskey. "What? Can't a guy come home to spend some time with his brothers?"

Joe and Nick chuckled at the same time.

"Seriously, why are you here?" Joe asked.

The fire crackled, and Tony watched the low-lying flames dance. "I had to tell Rena I still have racing obligations. I'm leaving on Sunday for a week. She didn't take the news well."

"She's mad?" Nick asked.

Tony shook his head. "Worse. She's indifferent. She's not sure I'll come back and pretty much told me she doesn't care."

"She's recalling past history, Tone. She's protecting herself," Joe said.

"I know. But the hell of it is that we were working out our problems, getting closer, until this came up. What am I supposed to do? My agent's butt is on the line. Ben's been with me since the beginning, and he's been a loyal friend. I owe him. If I get sued for breach of contract, it reflects on him, too."

"It's not like you can tell anyone you have a pregnant wife at home," Nick added. "Ben doesn't know?"

"No, he doesn't. There's no need to tell him." Tony finished his whiskey, not revealing his opinion about the subject. He'd tell the world about their marriage, if Rena would agree. "The problem is that we were getting closer. I took her to the doctor today. We'd planned on fixing up the nursery together. It's the first time she's let me in. And it felt good. Damn good. If I had any choice at all, I'd stay here and paint the baby's room instead of flying off to do a commercial."

"Wow," Nick said, catching his gaze. "I didn't realize you were in love with Rena."

Tony couldn't deny it. He set his glass down and stared into the flames. "I don't think I ever stopped loving her."

"You two are a perfectly matched set," Nick offered, his statement hitting home.

Joe sighed. "I'm the last one to give advice on romance, Tony. But it seems to me from a logical standpoint that you need a gesture of some sort. Some way to show her how much she means to you."

"You mean like blowing off this deal?"

"No, by asking her to go with you."

"She won't go. She hates anything to do with racing. It would just remind her of all the bad things that have happened in her life."

"Then I suppose you'll just have to make it up to her when you get back."

Tony agreed. He'd have a lot of making up to do. "Listen, will you two check on her next week while I'm gone?"

"Sure." Joe nodded.

Nick added, "No problem. I like Rena. She's family now, and I don't have much on my nightly agenda at the moment."

"Which means you're not dating three women at the same time," Joe said, with a teasing grin.

"Never three." Nick leaned back in his chair and

sipped his beer. Thoughtful, he added, "I only date one lady at a time. I like to keep things simple."

"You're not off to Monte Carlo anytime soon, then?" Tony asked.

"No. I'm here for a while. The contractors have the renovations at my house under control and it'll be ready soon enough. At least dad's timing was good in that respect."

Tony exchanged a glance at Joe. Of the three, Nick held the deepest grudge against Santo Carlino. With good reason, but the damage was done and they all had to move on with their lives.

"Besides," Nick added, "I told you I'd help out with the company for as long as it takes. Once we figure out which of you two will be running the company, I'm moving back there."

"What makes you think it'll be me or Tony?" Joe asked.

"Because it sure as hell won't be me. You know how I feel about this place."

Tony raised his brows. "It's just us now, Nick. Santo is gone."

Nick ignored him. "You're both invited. You've never seen my place in Monte Carlo. I want you to come as soon as you can."

Tony rose from his seat, ready to get back home to Rena. Talking with his brothers had helped. He'd gotten his dilemma off his chest, but he wasn't at all sure that they'd come up with a solution. "I'll feel better leaving knowing you both will call Rena and stop by Purple Fields for a visit."

"We have your back," Joe said.

"Thanks. I appreciate it."

"You leaving already?" Nick asked.

"Yep, I'm going home to my wife." He needed to see her. He had to sort out their differences and try to make his marriage work.

Rena's last parting comment had stung him.

Thanks for ruining the best day I've had since my husband died.

He was her husband now.

It was time Rena realized that.

The next three nights Rena claimed exhaustion, turning in early and falling asleep long before Tony came to bed. In the morning, she'd find herself tangled up in his arms. He hadn't pressed her for more. In fact, she admired the patience and consideration he'd shown her. He'd kiss her hello in the morning, then rise from bed early.

They lived life like a married couple. He'd shave in front of her, and she'd catch glimpses of him showering, the vision often lingering in her mind long after he'd toweled off and dressed. She cooked for him and cleaned his clothes, and he thanked her politely.

Often, he'd take a cup of coffee and buttered toast into the office and not come out until well past noon. He spent a great deal of time working on her books, but once in a while she'd spot him out in the vineyards speaking with Raymond or checking the vines.

She found him today amid the merlot grapes. "The

computer just arrived. And all the other things you ordered."

"Great," he said, squinting into the bright sunshine. "I'll be right there. With any luck, I'll get it up and running before I leave tomorrow."

"Okay," she said, not in any hurry to return to the office. Her mind was in a jumble. On the one hand, she didn't know if she could trust Tony's intentions, but on the other hand she hoped she wasn't making a big mistake by misjudging him.

She'd spoken with Solena about Tony leaving for a week to keep his contractual obligations. Rena had been honest about her feelings and concerns, and while Solena had always been supportive, this time she hadn't seen it Rena's way.

"Are you sure you're being fair to him?" she'd asked. "Doesn't seem like he has much choice in the matter. Or maybe there's more to your anger than that?"

"Like what?" Rena had asked.

Her friend had given her a knowing, yet sympathetic, look. "Like maybe you want to keep friction between the two of you because you're falling in love with him again."

Tony broke into her thoughts, staring at her over her obvious reluctance to leave. He cast her a big smile. "Is there anything else?"

Her heart lit up. "No, nothing else. I'll be giving a wine tour in a few minutes. I'd better go."

"Yeah, me too. I'll walk with you."

He put his hand to her lower back, and together they left the fields.

"Tony?" she began, as they headed for the house.

He looked up. "Hmm?"

She stopped at the very edge of the vineyard and peered into his eyes. Sunlight cast a glow over his dark hair and deepened his olive skin. He was gorgeous-times-ten, and that never hurt his cause. But she had loved the man *inside* that hunky body, the one who'd slay dragons for her. Or so she'd believed.

"I may have overreacted the other day."

His brows rose.

"I'm not saying I did, but just that there's the possibil—"

"Shut up, Rena." The softness of his tone belied his harsh words.

He grabbed her waist and yanked her against him, taking her in a crushing, all-consuming kiss. When the kiss ended, she opened her eyes and swayed in his arms, feeling quite dizzy.

"How long before your tour group shows up?" he asked in a rasp, nuzzling her throat.

"Ten minutes."

Tony groaned. Then he kissed her once more, bringing her body up against his again, fitting them perfectly together. "Tonight, after dinner."

Rena's breath caught in her throat. She couldn't pretend she didn't know what he meant. She wouldn't protest. Sleeping next to him and waking up wrapped in his arms, pretending indifference hadn't been easy on her. She was a mass of contradictions when it came to Tony. But she wouldn't deny him. She wanted him. Not that her sexy husband would take no for an answer.

Judging by the hot gleam in his eyes or the way he'd just kissed her senseless, Rena knew they were in for a memorable night.

Dinner seemed to take forever. Rena fumbled with the meal, undercooking the potatoes and forgetting the garlic toast in the oven. They ate raw potatoes and burnt bread, and all the while Tony's gaze never wavered as he watched her stumble her way around the kitchen. She apologized a half dozen times, but Tony continued to eat her nearly inedible meal. "I'm not complaining, sweetheart."

Once they finished, he helped clear the dishes, moving about the kitchen and touching her whenever he could, a casual graze here, an accidental bump of the shoulders there. Rena's nerves stood on end. This was foreplay, Carlino style. And it was working! His dark, enticing eyes made her wish she was tumbling in the sheets with him rather than doing dishes by the sink.

Tony came up behind her, pressed his hips to her rear end and wrapped his arms around her, his hands just teasing the underside of her breasts. His warm breath teased her throat. If anyone could make her feel desirable wearing an old apron with her hands in soapy dishwater it was Tony.

"I know what I want for dessert," he whispered, nibbling on her neck.

The glass she'd been rinsing slipped from her hand and shattered in the sink. "Oh, no!"

Tony chuckled and turned her around to face him, his body pressed to hers. "Calm down, Rena. It's not as if you broke your parents' prized antique goblet. Like when you were a kid."

Rena's brows furrowed. "What?"

"You know, your great-grandmother's goblet that you broke when you were trying to surprise your mother by washing the whole set."

"I know what I did, Tony." Rena chewed on her lip, her mind reeling. She'd never told anyone about that incident. She'd replaced all the glasses in the curio praying her mother wouldn't notice that one of the eight were gone. "But how did you know? I never told a soul about that."

Tony blinked. A guilty expression crossed his features.

Rena shoved at his chest and moved away from him. Anger bubbled up. "You read my story, didn't you?"

Tony hesitated for a moment then nodded, not bothering to lie. "I did."

"How could you do that, Tony?" Rena's voice rose to a furious pitch. "That wasn't meant for anyone to read. I can't believe you'd invade my privacy like that!"

"Sorry, but I had to know."

"Know what?" she shouted. "That losing you had devastated my life? That when my mother was sick I cried for her every night, needing you so badly? That after she died, I was at my wit's end and David, poor David, came along and picked up my shattered life and made me whole again." Rena paced the kitchen floor, her temper flaring. "I needed to write that for myself, Tony. Don't you see? Those were my innermost, heartfelt thoughts. Those were mine and mine alone!"

Rena whipped her apron off and tossed it aside, her body trembling. Regret and remorse set in. "Damn it, Tony. You were never meant to read that."

"Maybe I needed to read it, Rena. Maybe it made me see what a big mistake I made back then."

"No," Rena said, shaking her head. She didn't want to hear any of this. Not now. It was far too late. "Save it, Tony. For someone who cares." She directed her gaze right at him. "I thought that maybe this marriage could work, but now I see it never will. You abused my trust one too many times. I want you to go, Tony."

Tony shook his head. "I'm not going anywhere."

"You did what you set out to do. You saved my winery. I'll make it on my own from here on out. I'm not afraid of hard work. You've repaid your debt to David."

"This isn't about David anymore, Rena. You know it and I know it."

Rena faced him dead-on, her bravado slowly dissipating. Tears threatened and she held them back yet her voice cracked with anguish. "I know nothing of the kind. Now I'm asking you to please leave my home. You were leaving me anyway tomorrow. What's one more night?"

"You're my wife, damn it. I'm not leaving you to-night."

"Fine, do whatever you want. That seems to be what you do best. Just leave me alone."

Rena walked out of the room with her head held high. She slammed the bedroom door and fell onto the bed, tears spilling down her cheeks.

Tony's vivid curses from the living room reached her

ears. She curled her pillow around her head, blocking
the sound of her husband's frustrated tirade.

At least she knew that tomorrow morning he would
be gone.

Eleven

Stubbornly, Tony refused to leave Rena's house. He'd made himself comfortable on the sofa, listening for her. Once he was sure she'd shed all of her tears and had fallen asleep, he opened the bedroom door to check on her.

She looked peaceful tucked in her bed, her face scrubbed of makeup, her thick, dark hair falling freely onto her pillow. She made an enticing picture, one gorgeous leg extending out of the tousled sheets, her body glistening in the slight moonlight streaming in.

Tony's heart lurched seeing her alone in that bed. Certainly the night hadn't ended on the happy note he'd planned. He wouldn't join her tonight. She'd made it clear what she thought of him. She'd made it even clearer that she didn't want him near her.

As complex as their situation was, Tony believed that they belonged together. He hoped that the time they'd spend away from each other would help her see that. He wouldn't even consider the possibility of not having Rena in his life.

Right now, she was angry with him. She had a temper. And so did he. They were both passionate people, and that's one of the things he loved most about Rena—her zest for life. She wasn't a wilting flower. Not by a long shot.

She'd been hurt many times by him and by his family, but she refused to let him make it up to her. It was as if she'd relished the rift they'd had so she wouldn't have to face facts. She wouldn't have to realize that she had strong feelings for him.

Tony closed the door quietly and took up a place on the sofa with a bottle of Purple Fields' award-winning merlot. He poured a glass and knew he wouldn't be sleeping any time soon. The wine would lull his senses somewhat, but Tony couldn't shake a bad feeling that had wedged its way into his gut.

Before sunrise, Tony rose from the sofa. He stretched out the kinks in his shoulders, slanting his head from side to side and shaking out the rest of his body. With stealth, he moved through the house to peek in on Rena again.

She slept.

Tony cast her one long look before turning back around. He showered in the bathroom down the hall, and once he was dressed in the same clothes he'd worn the night before, he made himself a cup of coffee and walked outside. Sipping the steamy brew, he glanced toward the winery, glad to see Raymond's car parked in front.

He found him checking on the crusher. "Morning," he said.

Raymond glanced at him. "It's a beautiful one."

Tony nodded, his mood not so bright. "Listen, I have a favor to ask. I have to go out of town for a while. Can I depend on you to check on Rena for me?"

"Sure, you can count on me. And Solena will be around all week, too. Those women are like two peas in a pod."

"Yeah, Solena's a good friend. Both of you are."

Raymond removed his latex gloves. "Is there any reason you're asking? Is Rena feeling poorly?"

"No, she's fine. It's just that," Tony began, scratching the back of his head, hating to admit this, "I doubt she'll take my calls when I'm gone. We had a disagreement, and she's being stubborn."

Raymond laughed. "I hear you. I'll keep an eye on her. You can call me anytime."

Relieved, Tony slapped him on the back. "Thanks. I appreciate it. Well, I'd better get going. I've got a plane to catch."

Tony drove to the Carlino estate and packed his clothes in a suitcase, hoping to find his brothers there. No one was around but the housekeeper and gardening crew. He'd been on his own, traveling from city to city for the better part of twelve years but had never felt the sense of desolation he felt now.

Tony knew it was a short trip and that he'd be back,

but leaving with Rena angry at him didn't sit right. He was sure no amount of persuading would change her mind. He conceded that they needed time away from each other, yet as his driver dropped him off at the airport and he boarded the plane heading for his first on-screen interview in Charlotte, North Carolina, as the retired champion, a sense of foreboding clutched him.

And as the plane landed and Tony was picked up by ESPN's limo driver, he couldn't shake the strange feeling in his gut.

Rena deliberately waited until she heard Tony's car pull away before she rose from bed and showered. Her anger had turned to sadness in the light of day, and her heart ached at the sense of loss she felt.

She'd tried trusting Tony, and he'd once again disappointed her. The situation was so darn tangled up in her mind, the past and present mingling into a giant miserable heartache. She had every reason to feel the way she did. Tony would always put *his* career and *his* life ahead of hers. He looked out for *numero uno*.

Even if she were able to put the past behind her, how could she trust him to raise her child? She couldn't bear the thought of him disappointing her child again and again. Scenarios played out in her head, and she envisioned Tony simply not being available when they needed him.

Rena dressed in a pair of stretch jeans that accommodated her growing belly and a loose tank top. She pulled her hair up in a ponytail and secured it with a rubberband.

She didn't have to give any wine tours today, which she deemed a good thing. Her heart just wasn't in it. She'd cried so hard last night that even now her breathing was less than even.

Digging deep in her soul, she'd have to admit that the house seemed empty without Tony here. He had a presence about him. Life wasn't dull when he was around. But Rena would have to get used to that. She'd be alone again. She'd come to the realization that maybe she wasn't meant to have anyone in her life.

She'd endured so many losses, and if it weren't for the new life she nurtured, she wouldn't know how to go on.

But the baby above all else gave her hope.

When a knock resounded at her door, her nerves jumped, and images of Tony returning home to her flashed instantly in her head.

She opened the door wide and faced Raymond. Disappointment registered, surprising her. She'd analyze that feeling later. "Oh, Ray. I didn't think you'd come to work today."

"I wanted to check in. Uh, I was checking the crusher and destemmer yesterday, and I didn't like the way they sounded."

"Is there a problem?"

"No, not really. They're just old. Don't work like they once did. I fiddled with the crusher a bit. We sure could use a new one."

"Well, maybe we'll be able to get one soon." Rena hoped so. They'd be making a profit again, thanks to

Tony. Purple Fields was due for some refurbishing. "There's a few things I'd like to change around here."

"Sure would be nice."

"Want to come in? I was just going to have some orange juice and toast. You're invited if you have time."

"No thanks, Rena. Solena fed me a big breakfast already." He patted his flat stomach.

She chuckled, shaking her head at the dark-haired man who'd become such a good friend. "I don't know where you put it." Raymond could eat like a truck driver, yet he remained lean and fit.

"One day it will catch up with me," he said, with a certain nod. "Well, I just wanted to say hello. Everything okay here?"

"Just fine. I plan to have a quiet day. Maybe do some reading."

"We're home today if you need anything."

"I won't. But thank you. I'll see you both tomorrow."

Rena bid farewell to Raymond and finished her breakfast. She sat down on her sofa and read five chapters of her book on what to expect as a new parent, did a load of laundry and as she walked down the hallway to put the folded linens away, she passed the empty nursery filled with paint cans. Excitement stirred in her stomach. Distraction kept her loneliness at bay, and she'd run out of things she'd wanted to do. Except for one.

"Why not?" she asked herself. "I have all the supplies I need."

You were going to paint the room with Tony.

"Can't wait around for something that might not happen," she grumbled, answering aloud her innermost thoughts.

Rena put on one of David's old shirts, grabbed a ladder from the supply room behind the winery and set out the drop cloths on the floor of her baby's room.

Sunshine beamed into the undressed windows, and warmth flowed into the room. She imagined a few months ahead, when her baby cooed with happiness in his crib, surrounded by all his things, the room a very light shade of sage-green.

"That's it," Rena said with a smile. "Not yellow, but green."

She grabbed her father's old boom box from the hall closet, dusted it off and plugged it in. She sang along with the pop music blaring from the radio, humming when she didn't know the words. She opened the paint can with a screwdriver and stirred the lead-free paint feeling assured that the fumes wouldn't hurt the baby.

When the phone rang, Rena turned the radio down and listened to the voice speaking into her answering machine.

"It's Tony. Just wanted you to know that I'm here in North Carolina. Rena, we need to talk when I get back. I know you won't believe me, but I miss you."

Rena squeezed her eyes shut. She nibbled on her lip, putting the paint roller down, wishing Tony wouldn't say those things. Though he sounded sincere, his words always contradicted his actions.

"Well, I guess you're not going to pick up the phone. I'll call you tomorrow. Goodbye, Rena."

Rena sunk down to the floor and sat there for a long time, rehashing everything in her mind. But the bottom line, whether she deemed it rational thinking or not, was that Tony had once again left her. He hadn't put her needs first.

Rena's mood shifted then. She'd been enjoying painting the baby's room until Tony ruined it—like he seemed to ruin everything else in her life. She had a good mind to tell him not to call again, but that would warrant her picking up the phone and speaking to him. She couldn't do that for fear of what she might say.

In truth, she didn't know how she'd react with him saying nice things to her from miles away.

She had no faith in him.

And yet she was deeply in love with him.

Yes, she finally admitted that she'd fallen in love with him when she'd been a lovestruck teen, and those feelings just wouldn't go away. Having him back in her life had rekindled that love, as much as she had fought it. As much as she didn't want it to be true. As much as she thought herself a fool for allowing him back into her heart.

"Why is it so complicated with you, Tony?" she whispered. "Why do you constantly torture me?"

On a deep sigh, Rena stood and decided to fight those feelings. She wouldn't allow Tony's phone call to mar the joy she'd felt just moments ago. She picked up the paint roller and continued on until she'd finished painting two walls. After an hour, she stopped and stepped back to view her work.

"Not bad," she said, her mood lightening. The sage paint on the wall dried to the prettiest hue of green.

She took a quick water break and peeled an orange she'd picked from her kitchen fruit basket. Sitting down at the table, she gobbled up orange wedges and rested for a while, flipping through a baby magazine, getting decorating ideas.

Eager to finish, she headed back into the nursery and turned the radio volume up. Frank Sinatra crooned, "Our Love Is Here to Stay," the disc jockey deeming the song ageless. Rena saw irony in the song's lyrics as she hummed the melody.

She positioned the ladder against the third wall where an opened window faced out toward acres of vineyards. Late afternoon air blew through the screen and cooled the room. "This is the best room for you," she said, laying a loving hand over her tiny round belly. It gladdened her heart that her child would see Purple Fields at its finest, when the leaves grew strong and tiny beads of grapes flourished to plumpness.

Rena filled the tray of paint atop the ladder and began rolling the uppermost part of the wall. When the news broadcast came on the radio, Rena tuned it out, too enthralled in baby thoughts to focus on anything the broadcaster had to say until she heard Tony's name mentioned. She stopped to listen.

"And in sports news, retired race car champion Tony Carlino is back on the scene. In an interview today in Charlotte, North Carolina, amid thousands of fans, Carlino admitted that he'd been contemplating a return to racing...."

The paint roller dropped from Rena's trembling hand. Sage-green paint splattered the walls in big drops as the roller hit the ground. Woozy, she swayed and grabbed for the top of the ladder, but her light-headedness won out. She lost her balance and fell backward, landing on the floor with a solid thud. Pain throbbed in her head just before the world went black.

Tony removed the microphone from his shirt the second the interview with the jackass newscaster was over, the whole time wishing he were back in Napa instead of sitting in a press booth in North Carlolina, thousands of miles away from his wife. His mood had gone from resigned to irritated in two seconds flat, when the newscaster spun his words in a continual effort to press Tony about his nonexistent return to racing.

After a heated off-air exchange between them, Tony left the press box fed up with all the hoops he'd had to jump through today just to meet the terms of his contract.

He wasn't looking forward to spending the next few days making a commercial either. He didn't want to be here, not when he'd been making headway in his marriage to Rena. Day by day, in small increments, they were working through their problems. There seemed to be some light at the end of the tunnel. She'd started to trust in him again.

Now, she wouldn't return his calls.

And he couldn't blame her. He'd let her down, going back on promises he'd made to her.

His agent followed him outside the press booth

and they left the racing venue together. "Tony, what's eating you? I've never seen you react that way to an interviewer."

"You heard him, Ben. He wouldn't let up on me. How many times does he have to hear no?"

"You made your point." Ben, always the diplomat, tried to appease him, but Tony wasn't ready to let it drop.

"He misconstrued my words and circled around the truth. Make a note, I never want to do another interview with him." Hell, he didn't want to do another interview with *anyone*. It was becoming more and more clear where Tony's place was.

"Well, it's over and done with now. Forget about it." Ben slapped him on the back. "Come on, let me take you to dinner."

Tony shook his head. "No thanks. I'm beat. I'm going to head back to the hotel."

"Okay, get some rest. I'll see you in the morning for the commercial shoot."

Tony bid his agent farewell and took a limo back to his hotel. When he arrived at the Hyatt, instead of going to his room, he headed straight for the cocktail bar and ordered a double whiskey.

He sat there, thinking about his life and all he'd accomplished. He wasn't one to ever give up when he wanted something. He'd had obstacles in his way, but he'd never had much trouble overcoming them. At least, not until now, with Rena.

He felt a tap on his shoulder and turned to find a

beautiful young blond woman taking a seat beside him. "You're Tony Carlino, the racecar driver, aren't you?"

"That would be me." He sipped his drink.

"Would you like to buy me a drink?"

Tony stared at her and saw the bold, provocative look in her eyes. She made no bones about what she wanted; she had "groupie" written all over her meticulously salon-tanned body. At one time, he might have indulged her and welcomed the fringe benefits that would've come afterward. Now, his thoughts were of his pregnant wife and the miles between them.

He finished off his drink and set a fifty on the bar. "Sure, have whatever you want on me. I'm going home to my wife."

And hours later, Tony put the key in the lock and turned the doorknob to Rena's house. The three-hour time difference from the East Coast put him back in Napa in the late afternoon, and he was grateful for regaining those hours. He'd spent more time in the air today than he'd spent on the ground in North Carolina. Wondering about Rena's reaction when she saw him, Tony opened the door slowly.

"I'm the last one to give advice on romance, Tony. But it seems to me from a logical standpoint, you need a gesture of some sort. Some way to show her how much she means to you."

Joe's words had stayed with him, and grand gesture or not, Tony knew in his gut that he had to return home to Rena tonight—it had to be tonight.

There were things he had to say. He needed to

clear the air between them. Especially after what had happened in North Carolina earlier today.

"Rena?" he called out, noting how quiet the house seemed. Again, he called her name and was met with silence. He hadn't seen her in the fields when he'd driven up, but then he wasn't really on the lookout at that time. He strode down the hallway and heard static coming from a radio. "Rena, are you here?"

He followed the sound to the room across from their bedroom. One look inside made his skin crawl. "Oh my God." A pool of green paint oozed from an overturned paint tray, the drop cloth doing its best to contain the puddle. Near the radio on the floor, Tony spotted something red. Initially, he froze and prayed that it wasn't what he'd thought. He moved quickly and bent to touch the crimson liquid and bring it to his nose. It wasn't wine or paint.

It was blood.

"Rena's blood," he breathed out. Plaguing thoughts of her being injured and bloody raced through his mind. "No," he said, shaking his head. "Please, God."

His cell phone rang.

Tony answered it immediately. "Tony? It's Solena. I've got some news—"

"Where's Rena?" he bellowed into the phone.

"We just arrived at Napa Hospital. I'm in the ambulance. She took a fall—"

"I'm coming. I'll be there in ten minutes."

"Ten minutes? Where are you and how—"

"I'll explain later." Tony shut off the phone and ran out of the house. His main concern was to see Rena.

He climbed into his car and hit the road, driving twenty miles an hour above the speed limit. Luckily, the roads were nearly empty, but even if they hadn't been, it wouldn't deter him. Nothing was going to stop him from getting to Rena.

He arrived at the hospital in eight minutes and strode with purpose to the emergency room desk. The clerk questioned his relationship to Rena Montgomery. "Damn it, she's my wife." He clenched his fists.

"There's no paperwork to support that," the woman said, glancing once more at her files, then slanted a look at the security guard standing in the corner. Sometimes his fame made his life a living hell. Everyone thought they knew everything about him. "Her name is Rena *Carlino* now. We just got married."

The clerk blinked. "Oh, uh. Well, then Mr. Carlino, I'll let you right through."

She buzzed him in. "Third door to your left."

Tony was there in seconds. He found Rena on the hospital triage bed, her eyes closed, her head wrapped in a white bandage. Solena stood by her side and smiled when she saw him. "How did you get here so fast?" she whispered as she strolled over to him. She gave him a hug then guided him just outside the door. "We all thought you were in North Carolina."

Tony glanced back at Rena. It pained him to see her looking so frail and weak. "I was already home when you called. I found the room a wreck and panicked. What the heck happened?"

"I don't know, other than she fell off the ladder. I

stopped by with dinner for her. When she didn't answer the door, I got worried and used my key to get inside.

"Apparently, she hit her head on the radio when she fell. She was unconscious when I found her."

"How long ago?"

"You missed us by fifteen minutes."

Tony's heart ached. He was to blame for this. He knew it in his gut. "Has she woken up?"

"Yes, in the ambulance. We've been speaking on and off. She's a little woozy. The doctor wants her to rest while they are preparing for the CT scan."

"What did she say?"

"She was worried about the baby."

Tony closed his eyes and nodded. Immense fear coursed through his body and he sent up silent prayers. "Me, too."

That baby, that beautiful new life growing inside Rena was Tony's responsibility, too. But it was so much more. It was to be his first child. He already knew he loved that baby. Rena had been through too much pain in her life to endure another tragedy. Tony wouldn't allow it. As irrational as that sounded, he would make sure that Rena never knew another bad day.

"The doctor was optimistic. She has a concussion and a little bump on her head, but they don't think the fall affected the baby."

"That's good," Tony said with relief. He'd never forgive himself if something happened to the baby. Rena would be inconsolable, and he wouldn't blame her.

"I'm going in now. I'll stay with her," Tony said.

"Do you want me to stay, too?" Solena asked.

Tony shook his head. "No, I have to speak to her. There are things I really need to say."

Solena smiled. "I understand."

"It's a good thing you found her when you did. I can't thank you enough."

"You were only minutes behind," she said. Then she cast him a curious stare. "Why *are* you here? I thought you'd be gone a week or more?"

Tony drew oxygen into his lungs. "That's why I have to speak with Rena. I'm here, and I'm not leaving her again."

Rena lay with her eyes closed in the hospital bed feeling slight relief, the throbbing in her head much less painful now. She remembered the reason she was here. Solena had called for emergency help and had traveled with her in the ambulance. The events of the past day came to mind at a snail's pace—but with surprising clarity.

A gentle touch to her hand brought her eyes open. She knew that touch. It was the person she'd dreamed about. The one person she'd wanted to have by her side.

"Hi, sweetheart," Tony said. "You're going to be okay."

"Am I?" she whispered on a breath.

Tony nodded, his dark eyes soft and glistening. Had he teared up? "Your CT scan is perfect. Dr. Westerville said the baby is fine. You can go home later this morning if you feel up to it."

With a slight nod of her head, she choked out, "That's good news. I'm so relieved about the baby. If something happened…" She couldn't even manage the words. She couldn't go there, couldn't think of the possibility of another loss in her life. This one would crush her.

Tony took her hand and squeezed. "It didn't, honey. You both are going to be fine."

Rena sat up a little straighter in the bed, grateful the movement didn't cause her pain. "What time is it?"

"Five o'clock in the morning."

"Have you been here all night?"

"Right here," he assured her. "All night."

"But how? You were in North Carolina last I remember."

"Yeah, well. I shouldn't have gone in the first place. The minute I landed there I knew I'd made a mistake. I knew where my place was. And that place was with you."

"Tony?" Rena couldn't believe her ears. "What do you mean?"

"I did that interview, the whole time wishing I was with you."

Rena looked away then, unable to meet his eyes. She removed her hand from his. She remembered the reason for her fall now. She remembered the pain and shock she felt, hearing that news report on the radio. His presence here confused her. Why had he come back? None of it made sense.

"Rena? What is it?" His question was marked with concern.

She stared out the hospital window, looking at the new dawn breaking through. Birds chirped and tree branches swayed in the breeze. It was a glorious day to be alive, yet Rena's stomach knotted with heartbreaking anguish. "I was so hurt when you left. I guess I never got over you leaving me. And I thought it was happening all over again. I didn't know what to do with myself, so I started to paint the baby's room." She turned her head slightly to gaze into his eyes. Might as well give him the whole truth. "I figured I was on my own again. I wasn't meant to be with anyone. It would just be the baby and me from now on. I didn't want to rely on you or anyone else."

Tony clenched his teeth. Pain entered his eyes, but she continued. "The radio was on when I climbed the ladder, and I heard a news report about you. They said you were contemplating a racing comeback. When I heard that I felt faint. It was like my world was spinning in ten different directions. I couldn't get a grip. My worst fears had come true. That's when I fell."

Tony's eyes rounded. Shock stole over his face. He let go a vivid curse then took her chin in his hands and ever so gently lifted her face to his. "I'm so sorry, Rena. Sorry for everything. But you have to believe me. What you heard is not true. None of it is. My words were misconstrued. The press never gets anything right. That's why I had an argument with the newscaster. We almost came to blows, Rena. I called him every four-letter name in the book and then some.

"I swear to you that after the incident I took the next flight home. I didn't want you to hear that news report. It was a flat out falsity. But I didn't know if I could convince you how much I care about you from thousands of miles away."

"What about your obligations? You signed contracts."

He shrugged, his eyes hard. "Let them sue me. I can afford it. Losing a lawsuit is a million times better than losing you." He cast her a warm, sincere look. "I love you, Rena. I love you with all my heart."

He removed the sheet covering her and bent his head, laying the sweetest, most gentle kiss on her belly. "I love this baby, too. I love you both. I'll spend the rest of my life trying to convince you. But I'm asking for another chance. Give me a chance, sweetheart."

Tears entered her eyes. The loving gesture broke down all her defenses. Every wall she'd constructed against Tony fell to ruin, and her heart swelled. "Tony, is it true? Really true?"

"Yes, it's true. I love you. I want a life with you. A *real* life and not because of David's dying wish but because I have genuine love in my heart for you. I've always loved you, Rena."

He kissed her then, and it was the most tender brushing of their lips.

"I love you, too, Tony. I always have. Through everything, all the wrongs your family imposed on mine and all the hurt we've shared, I've never really stopped loving you. I think—" she began, admitting this truth to herself as well as to Tony "—I think David knew that. I think he knew that what we had couldn't be matched. And yet, I did love him. He was a good man."

"Yes, I know. He was the best. And I think he really wanted this for us. His child—*our* child—will have two parents who love each other as much as we love him or her."

Rena stroked Tony's dark hair, staring into his eyes, loving this strong powerful man with all that she had inside. "We can have a beautiful life."

"We will. I promise you. You and the baby will always come first."

"I believe you, Tony." She laughed as joy entered her heart. "I never thought I'd say that, but I really do believe in the strength of our love."

"And can you forgive me for everything in the past?"

Rena drew in a breath. "I think so. I think I already have."

"You won't be sorry, sweetheart. I will love and protect you the rest of my life. It's my solemn vow."

"Then I'm ready, Tony," she said decidedly.

"I am, too," he agreed, then shot her a puzzled look. "For *what*, exactly?"

"To shop for baby furniture. I want to fill our house with every baby thing imaginable."

Tony chuckled and drew her into his arms. "Now, I *know* you really love me."

"I do. I really, really do."

* * * * *

SEDUCTION ON THE CEO'S TERMS

BY
CHARLENE SANDS

To Bill, Carol, Angi and Eric—the Petti.
Thanks for being my biggest fans and source of
love and support. I'm happy to call you family!
With special gratitude to my sister Carol and
brother-in-law Bill for making me an auntie!

One

Ali Pendrake sat at her desk at the Carlino Wines office, hitting the computer keys in rapid succession. She'd been at the top of her keyboarding class in college seven years ago, being not only a speedy typist but an accurate one. Today her usual tenacious focus waned and mistakes abounded.

"Darn it, Ali. You dummy," she muttered under her breath. She hit the backspace key and fixed her error, her concentration lost today.

Stealing a glance at her boss, Joe Carlino, Ali sighed. Joe's attention was glued to the computer screen in his executive office as he mumbled and crunched numbers. Deliberately, she'd positioned her desk in the outer office to afford herself this view of him.

No matter how hard she'd tried, she couldn't get Joe off her mind. Working alongside him in New York last year for a software giant, Ali had come to know him fairly well. Tall, dark-haired and extremely handsome behind the glasses he wore, Ali admired his intelligence, dedication and honest work ethic more than his good looks. He'd always treated her with respect, and Ali appreciated that.

Usually men took one look at her and discounted her intellect and ability. All they saw was a rather buxom auburn-haired woman with a pretty face and nice legs, so of course, she couldn't possibly have any brains. Most male employers had never given her a chance. Oh, they'd pretended to hire her for her capabilities, but all too soon harsh reality would set in when they made nonprofessional overtures.

The last thing Ali wanted was to be like her mother. Umpteen boyfriends and five husbands later, Justine Holcomb, a one-time beauty queen, gloried in the attentions of men. The former Miss Oklahoma never missed a chance to scope out wealthy, powerful men and manipulate them into marriage.

Ali only wanted *one* real good man. And that man wouldn't look at her twice.

"Ali, could you come in here?" When Joe popped his head out of his office, his thin black-rimmed glasses slipped down his nose Clark-Kent style.

Excitement buzzed within her at the sound of his voice. She'd never wanted her feelings for Joe to show. She'd enjoyed working with him in a professional manner in New York. It had been a rarity and an experience she'd valued. But then his father died, and he'd been called home to help run the family wine empire.

She'd driven him to LaGuardia Airport as her last official act as his personal assistant. He'd taken her in his arms and kissed her goodbye. Now memories of the exquisite press of his mouth on hers, his musky scent, the scratch of his day-old beard on her skin and the way he held her tight in his arms flashed through her mind. In that instant, everything inside her had gone hot; her body had oozed with desire. She'd looked up and met the gleam of desire in his eyes.

They'd stared at each other for a long time, saying nothing. She didn't know what to say. He'd obviously felt the same awkwardness in the situation after that kiss and had left her standing there pondering what had happened.

Since then, there wasn't a day that went by when she didn't think of him, and to her great surprise those thoughts weren't G-rated. In fact, her traitorous mind conjured up sexy images of Joe that stole her breath.

So when he'd called, offering her the opportunity to uproot her life and work to join him in northern California, the decision hadn't been difficult. She'd been ecstatic and jumped at the offer. She figured she'd have another chance with Joe. She happily left the Big Apple's rat race behind.

But after three weeks on the job, Ali was sure the potted plant in the corner of the room got more attention from Joe than she did. He was all business, pretending that the kiss they'd shared at the airport hadn't blown them both away. In truth, no man she'd met recently had been *less* interested in her.

"Sure, Joe. I'll be right in." She picked up her notepad, her BlackBerry and her wits and followed him into his office.

He waited for her to sit down before taking a seat behind his desk. His warm smile devastated her. "I realized that I haven't asked you how you're settling in here in Napa." He leaned back in his leather seat, waiting for her to reply.

"Just dandy, boss." She returned his smile. "It's different and all, but you know what they say, a girl's gotta do what a girl's gotta do."

Joe peered over his glasses at her. "How's that?"

She shrugged, and her white peasant blouse slipped off her shoulder. Joe didn't appear to notice when she adjusted it back into place, his focus staying on her face. "I like working with you," she said truthfully. "I'm glad to be here. I think we make a good team."

Joe nodded slowly. "I appreciate that. So you have no problems? No questions?"

Yes, you don't seem to know I'm alive.

"Not really. Not about work. I would love to learn more about the Napa area, though. I thought I'd start venturing out on the weekends."

"Sounds like a good plan."

She straightened her calf-length skirt. She'd gone for the gypsy look today. Hoop earrings and her bright auburn hair down in curls added some flavor to her outfit. She had smarts and was proud of her achievements, but she also loved fashion. Her flamboyant style often garnered compliments from the other Carlino Wines employees. If nothing else, it was an icebreaker and a way to meet people who had worked for the family for a long time.

Joe stared at her for a moment. She sat, waiting for him to voice the reason he'd called her into his office. Usually, it was to go over accounts, check monthly reports or give her an assignment. His silence made her wonder. "Is there anything I'm doing wrong?"

"Hell, no," Joe said. "You're the best employee we have on-site."

"Well, thank you."

"That's the reason I've asked you in here today. I, uh, well, I have a favor to ask. And I won't hold it against you if you can't help me out with this."

Ali waited for a moment before the suspense got to her. She gestured impatiently with both hands. "Spit it out, Joe."

He chuckled and shook his head.

She grinned.

"Okay, okay. I've offered to give Rena and Tony a wedding reception. You've met my brother and sister-in-law, right?"

"Great people," Ali said.

"It's a long story, but they got married secretly a short time ago, and well, now they want to renew their vows and have a reception."

"You offered to throw it for them?"

"More like my brother Nick roped me into it. What do I know about planning a party like that, right?"

She nodded.

"That's where you come in. I need your help. I'll understand if you're too busy to help me out with this—"

"Are you kidding?" Ali stood, excited at the prospect. "I love a good party. You won't have to ask me twice. What's the timetable on this?"

"Well, the sooner the better. Tony mentioned he wanted to do it ASAP. Say, in three weeks?"

"That's doable."

"Really?" Joe stood, too, an expression of relief washing over his features. "It may mean working together some weekends—that's if you're not too busy."

"I'm not too busy." *Was he joking?* She'd sat around her apartment at night bored to tears. Not that she couldn't have company, but the men who'd asked her out didn't compare to the computer brain—she refused to call Joe a geek—who seemed to occupy her mind lately.

"You might not have time to check out the sights around here."

Ali's mind clicked into high gear. "I'll make you a deal. If I help plan this successfully, then you can show me the sights in wine country. Fair is fair, Joe."

Joe adjusted the glasses on his nose, and Ali recognized that sign. Whenever Joe needed extra time to contemplate a question, he played with those glasses. "I can show you the inner workings of a computer better than I can be your Napa Valley tour guide."

"Joe," Ali said, refusing to let him off the hook, "you grew up here. You *know* this area." This was her opportunity to see Joe in less sterile surroundings. She really wanted to get to know him better. Her recent work relationship with Dwayne Hicks made her extremely wary of all men. Dwayne had exacted more from her than secretarial skills, and things had gotten ugly. Joe was the only man she'd trusted to take a chance with. And she really did love a good party. "Are we on?"

"I really appreciate this, Ali. Yes, we're on."

After returning to his office, Joe picked up his phone and dialed Nick's number. He reached him on the second ring.

"Hey, Joe. What's up?"

"Tony's wedding reception is in the works as we speak."

"That's good news. I knew you'd come through."

"Hey, not me. I'm not the wedding planner. I've got a one-woman task force, and I know she'll do a great job."

When his father died, his brother Tony had called both he and Nick home to honor the terms of Santo Carlino's will. All three sons were to take the helm at Carlino Wines for a period of six months and figure out which son would be better suited to run the family empire. It was his father's dying wish. Joe had left his life behind on the East Coast to help Tony and Nick, but he'd never have guessed part of his job description would be as a wedding planner.

Secretly, Tony had married his first love and high school

sweetheart, Rena Fairfield, shortly after her husband's death in order to save her winery and provide for her unborn child. After they fell back in love with each other, Rena had finally come around to letting their secret out. And Tony didn't trust anyone outside the family to see that his renewal of vows and reception were done right. He'd entrusted his brothers with the honor.

Joe sighed with relief. With Ali's help now, he knew it all would work out. She was always up for a challenge, and he had faith that she'd do a superb job.

"And you're going to come in on deadline with this?"

"Yeah, we'll be in the right time frame," Joe replied.

"You talked your gorgeous assistant into helping you, didn't you?"

"Nick." Joe sighed. "Her name is Ali Pendrake. And yes, she's taking on the project. We'll need a female's input, and she's very capable."

Nick chuckled. "So you've told me about a hundred times. Beauty and brains is a dynamite combo in a woman, Joe."

"I guess so," Joe said, fidgeting with his computer keyboard. He didn't like the direction this conversation was taking.

"So, you're *really* not interested in her?" Nick asked.

"No, of course not. She's my employee. I thought I made myself clear on that."

Joe dismissed the one time he'd held Ali in his arms and kissed her. His gesture of farewell at the New York airport that day had gotten a little out of control. But his emotions had been running high at the time. His father had just passed away, and he'd been called home. His life had changed drastically, and Ali was there for him, lending support and comfort. Kissing her had been impulsive—and so damn good that his head had spun.

He'd thought of her often after that. But after his assistant and ex-fiancée Sheila's betrayal, an office romance of any kind was out of the question. She had cut his heart out when she'd dumped him for another man. Joe had a will of iron, and though Ali was beautiful and had traits he admired, he knew he'd never pursue anything with her but a working relationship. He'd offered her the job in Napa only because he knew he could work beside her and not get emotionally involved. It was hard for both of his brothers to understand that he just simply didn't see Ali that way.

"So, you wouldn't mind if I asked her out?" Nick questioned.

Joe furrowed his brows. He hadn't seen this coming. Nick had his fair share of women. He wasn't one to spend his nights alone. But Ali and *Nick?* Joe couldn't picture them together. His jaw clenched, and he contemplated for a moment.

"Joe? Did you hear me?"

"I heard you, little brother."

"We've never stepped on each other's toes when it came to women, but if you're clearly not interested in Ali—"

"I'm not."

"So, I can ask her out without causing you sleepless nights?"

"No, you can't ask her out."

"I can't?" Nick didn't sound too upset. "Why?"

"No offense, but I wouldn't subject any of my employees to dating you, especially Ali. You'd likely break her heart. And then she'd leave town, and I'd be out one damn good personal assistant."

"You don't give me much credit."

"History doesn't lie."

"Maybe I'm a changed man."

"Maybe…but I don't want you to use one of my employees as your test subject."

Nick laughed. "Man, you really don't have a good opinion of me, do you?"

"In any other arena, you're a great guy. Just *not* when it comes to women." Joe was ready to leave this subject behind. "So when are you leaving for Europe?"

"In a few days. But have no fear, I'll be back in time for the big hoopla. I wouldn't miss Tony's wedding reception."

"Yeah, your timing is impeccable. Leaving me to deal with all the details, while you're off—"

"Selling wine, schmoozing with customers and making sure Carlino Wines stays on top."

"Among other things," Joe muttered.

In truth, it bothered him how glad he was that Nick would be out of the picture for a couple of weeks. If he wasn't around, he couldn't be romancing Ali. In his analytical mind, that shouldn't be a factor. But he was damn glad of it just the same.

"I'll see you at home tonight," Nick said.

"I'll be working late with Ali."

"Hey, I can't blame you, bro." Joe visualized his brother's smirk. "Regardless of all your denials."

Joe hung up the phone and shook his head.

Ali came in then, holding a calendar in her hands. "Joe, I think we'd better set a date for the wedding reception."

Ali's darn blouse had slipped down again, and it was all he could do to keep from staring at her soft shoulder. She had such beautiful creamy skin. He'd have to be blind not to notice.

Every day with Ali was a fashion extravaganza. Today she looked like a gypsy princess—a very sexy, approachable one. He'd never noticed her style much in New York, but now, Nick and Tony's prodding was making it hard for him to *keep* from noticing her.

But the more he noticed, the more he was determined to keep her off-limits. She wasn't his type of woman anyway. She reminded him too much of Sheila with her quick wit, flamboyant nature and sense of adventure. He'd been playing with fire in his office relationship with Sheila, and he wasn't about to jump back into the flames anytime soon. A broken engagement and being left for a flashy billionaire wasn't his idea of a good time. Joe had been smacked down by that betrayal, and he had no intention of bounding up on the ten count to take another knockout punch.

"I think that's a good idea. Sit down, and we'll go over some dates. Then I'll check with Tony to make sure it'll work for them."

"I'm already on it. I just spoke with Rena. She's coming into town today, and we're having lunch. I'll cross-check the dates with her once you and I come up with something feasible."

Joe smiled and leaned back in his seat. He wasn't sorry he'd asked Ali to come work for him. Time and again, she'd proven to him that hiring her was the smartest thing he'd ever done. "I'm glad you took me up on my offer to come to Napa, Ali."

Ali's jade-green eyes lit up. "You are?"

"Yeah, you're in line for employee of the year."

Ali's gaze dropped to the calendar in her hands. "How nice."

Joe drew his brows together. Ali wasn't thrilled with his pronouncement. Somehow he'd disappointed her, but he couldn't figure out how. If anyone understood an honest work ethic, it was Ali Pendrake.

He thought she'd be happy that he'd recognized her many capabilities.

Rena Carlino was beautifully pregnant. The minute she walked into the office, Ali noticed the bright beam of happiness on her face and the lightness in her step despite sporting a rounded belly.

From all she'd gathered from Joe, Rena hadn't had an easy life and Tony had caused most of her trouble. The former race car champion had left Rena in the dust years ago to pursue his dream of racing stock cars. Jilted and heartbroken, Rena had married David Montgomery, Tony's best friend. She'd come to blame Tony for David's untimely death, faulting him for her heartache and the terrible things done to ruin her family's winery.

But when Tony returned to Napa twelve years later and honored the vow he made to Rena's dying husband to marry his pregnant wife, their rocky road had smoothed out. To his credit, Tony had come through in the end. Now, Tony loved both mother-to-be and baby and the evidence of that love beamed in Rena's eyes.

"Hi, Ali."

Ali stood and smiled. "Hi." She walked around the desk to embrace Rena. "You look fabulous."

Rena rubbed her belly and grinned. "Thank you. Most days, I'd disagree with you. But I made an extra effort today, since I was meeting you for lunch."

"I don't believe that for a minute."

"Oh, believe it. I feel *fine,* it's just that I'm moving so much slower these days. I'm used to doing a lot of work. I was always up early, working hard at the winery, but now things have slowed down. It's to be expected. And Tony is so protective that he won't let me lift anything heavier than my purse."

Ali chuckled, and a slight wave of envy coursed through her system. Tony adored Rena, and Ali wondered when her time would come to feel that same sort of love from a man. "I hear the baby's healthy as a horse."

"Yes, and I plan to keep it that way. Did you hear we're having a boy?"

"Oh Lord, love him. Another male Carlino in the world? I feel sorry for the next generation of baby girls."

Rena grinned. "I know what you mean. The Carlino men are a handful. I guess I'll have my work cut out for me."

Ali really admired Rena. She'd been given a lot to deal with lately, and she'd taken it all in stride. She'd finally come to accept the role as Tony's wife without giving up her own dream of saving her family's legacy, Purple Fields Winery. But even more amazing was that she'd forgiven Tony for all the hurt he'd caused and accepted him as the father of her child.

Ali grabbed her knockoff Gucci handbag and her briefcase. "Excuse me a second. I'll just let Joe know we're leaving for lunch." Ali turned and bumped smack into Joe, stepping on his toes and bumping heads. "Oh!"

Joe grabbed her arms to steady her, his touch sending lightning bolts straight through her. She was so close to him that their breaths mingled. The subtle scent of Hugo cologne was heaven to her senses.

"Are you okay?" he asked with concern.

Ali stared at him and nodded. "I didn't see you. That's what you get for sneaking up on me."

"I wasn't sneak—" But he stopped when he noticed her smile.

"I'm fine, Joe," she said. "You?"

Joe straightened. For a computer whiz, Joe didn't have an ounce of jelly on his body. He was granite hard, but rather than speculate, Ali would like firsthand knowledge. *If only...*

Joe dropped his hands from her arms, blinked and then took a step back. "I'll let you know if I develop a headache later."

"I'm really sorr—" Then Ali stopped when she realized Joe was joking, something he rarely did.

He walked around her to give Rena a hug. "Hi, sister-in-law. How's my brother treating you?"

Rena sighed. "Like a queen. I've got no complaints, Joe. And I can't thank both of you enough for taking on the wedding details. I'm afraid with all the construction we're doing to the house now it's a bit much for Tony and me."

"No problem," Joe said. "With Ali's help, it should run like clockwork." Joe glanced her way, and her heart did a little flip.

"You're welcome to join us for lunch, Joe," Rena said, "but I'll warn you, we'll be talking wedding and baby, and there's no getting around it."

Fear entered his eyes for a moment. "I'll leave you two to hash out the details. Once you have a plan, then I'll chime in. Thanks, anyway."

"Sure, Joe." Rena glanced at Ali and they both giggled.

"What's so funny?"

"Having three root canals without anesthesia sounds better to you than having lunch with us today. Admit it, boss."

Joe shrugged his shoulders in feigned innocence, which made him look sexier than all get-out. "Have a nice lunch, ladies."

They bid him farewell, and twenty minutes later after a nice walk along the main street of town, they were seated at an outside café that served sandwiches, salads and specialty coffees.

Ali ordered a double vanilla latte, while Rena opted for a glass of cranberry juice. They sipped their drinks while waiting for the salads they'd ordered.

"So how do you like Napa?" Rena asked.

"From what I can tell, I like it. It's a far cry from New York."

"Did you grow up there?"

She shook her head. "Heavens, no. I'm a southern gal from Oklahoma originally. My mama and daddy divorced when I was just a kid. Seems Mama wanted a better life for us, and Daddy just wasn't up for the task. She was Miss Oklahoma after all and figured she deserved better than a man who worked for the county as a deputy sheriff. As soon as she could, she moved us to the East Coast. I grew up in a string of big cities from Boston to New York. We never really settled anywhere for long."

"Sounds like you had it tough as a kid."

She shrugged. "It is what it is. I still keep in touch with my dad. He's remarried now and perfectly happy and still working in law enforcement."

"And your mom? Do you see her?"

"We see each other whenever we can." Ali wouldn't tell Rena her mother was on husband number five now. Ali had been bounced around from one household to another, from city to city, her mother never finding satisfaction in the men she married. She'd always wanted to elevate herself and thought money and power would be the ticket. Now, she was married to a millionaire attorney with political ties. "My mama leads a very busy social life." Ali shook her head and shuddered. "That life's not for me. So yeah, Napa's a nice change of pace."

"I wondered why you'd agree to uproot your life to work here…for Joe." Rena's brows raised, and her blue eyes beamed with clarity. "Can I ask you a personal question?"

Ali nodded.

"Are you and Joe…"

She shook her head. "Nothing."

"Really?" Rena sounded truly puzzled. "Because I swear, I thought I saw sparks between you two at the office."

"That's just me being me. Joe isn't interested."

Rena opened her mouth to reply but then clammed up.

"Were you going to say something?"

Rena stared at her for a moment. "No, it's not my place."

Darn it. "I understand," Ali said.

Ali opened her briefcase and took out her calendar. "Shall we set a date for the big occasion?"

"Sure," Rena said, and leaned over to glance at the calendar.

They settled on a Saturday three weeks away. The celebration would be held on the Carlino estate, the renewal of vows under an arbor of flowers in the backyard and the reception on the grounds.

"I'm doing this for Tony," Rena said. "For years, I wouldn't step foot on Carlino land. This is one way for me to show Tony that I've truly let the past go."

"You're very lucky to have this second chance, Rena." Ali cast her a small smile, suddenly feeling that life was passing her by.

Rena reached over and took her hand. "If I've learned one thing about life it's that you've got to make the best out of every moment and go after what you want." She lowered her voice. "If you have a goal in mind, don't let anything stop you."

Ali blinked. It was a lightbulb moment for her. She'd never been a quitter. Joe Carlino had enticed her to come to Napa, and she'd jumped at the chance because she cared about him. Ali wasn't one to wait around for things to happen.

If Joe needed a little push, then Ali wouldn't mind giving her sexy employer a shove in the right direction.

Two

As soon as Ali opened her front door, Joe realized his mistake in coming to her apartment tonight.

"Hi, Joe." She beamed him a smile. "I can't thank you enough for coming by. I'm in computer hell at the moment. Your timing is perfect, I just finished my Pilates workout."

He'd *noticed*. She wore spandex, a tight midriff top that pushed her cleavage to its limits and black pants that hugged her tiny waist. A glittering sheen of moisture coated her exposed skin.

Damn Nick and his constant jabbing. Joe didn't want to notice Ali as anything but his assistant. Feeling beholden to help when she'd complained about her computer problems today, he'd offered to stop by to look at it. "Happy to help out, Ali."

She stepped aside to let him in as she sipped from an Arrowhead water bottle. "I don't know what happened to it. Like I explained at the office, it just froze up on me. But I'm glad you came by anyway. You've never seen my apartment."

"River Ridge has a great reputation," Joe said. He'd gone out of his way to find her a good location that suited her when she'd accepted the job.

"It's a great place. I've always wanted a fireplace. I love the view from my living room window, too. Come take a look," she offered, and walked over to a wide picture window overlooking a garden setting. "There's a little pond out there. Can you see it?"

Joe stepped beside her and gazed out the window, indulging her. He'd made sure she'd gotten an apartment with the best view. He'd checked out this apartment before Ali had moved in. Adjusting the glasses on his nose, he narrowed his eyes. "I see two ducks splashing around."

"Let me see," Ali said, brushing up against him. "Oh, how sweet."

Her joy at such a little pleasure touched him. Joe stepped away from the window. "Different from living in New York, isn't it?"

"That's an understatement," she said with a groan. Then she sipped her water again. "Well, I'd better get showered and changed. I'll show you my computer, and maybe you can work your magic while I'm cleaning up. Can I get you anything?"

Joe kept his focus on her face and shook his head. "No, I'm good." He wouldn't allow his mind to conjure up images of her showering.

"Okay, then follow me." She walked down a short hallway. "This is my bedroom," she said, pointing and continuing to move.

Joe caught a glimpse of soft yellow hues, a large inviting bed and mismatched furniture that somehow looked perfect together. A fresh scent of lavender emanated from the room.

He followed her into a smaller bedroom down the hall. "I haven't fixed it up yet. It's sort of my office, slash, junk room, slash, guest room."

Joe scanned the room. "It's not very messy."

"You haven't seen what's stashed in the closet." She grinned.

"Shoved everything in there, did you?"

"*And* under the bed."

"All this to impress me?"

"Well, I didn't want you to see how unorganized this room is. I have a rep to protect, you know."

Joe shook his head in amusement.

"Okay, boss. I'll get out of your hair now. Just twitch your nose and fix the darn thing."

"I'll try."

Ali turned to exit the room and offered as a parting shot, "If you can't fix it, nobody can."

Joe grinned. He appreciated the compliment. Joe was good with computers and had been fascinated with them since he was a young boy. While all the other kids were involved in sports or getting into mischief, Joe stayed at home, learning the intricacies of the newest form of technology. He'd never felt he'd missed out on his childhood, though his father would often look in on him in his bedroom and frown.

Fifteen minutes later with the computer problem solved, Joe strode out of the office/junk room/guest room and walked down the hallway, passing Ali's bedroom. The door was closed, the shower had stopped and a vision of Ali towel-drying her naked body entered his mind.

His will of iron allowed him only two seconds to enjoy that image before he proceeded to the living room. He sat down on the sofa, picked up a *People* magazine then flipped through the pages. When the doorbell rang, Joe stood, glancing at Ali's room down the hallway.

"Ali," a male voice carried through the doorway. "It's Royce. And I have something for you I think you're going to like."

Joe stared at the door for a moment. When Ali didn't come out of her room to answer it, Joe walked over and yanked the door open.

A man wearing oven mitts holding a casserole dish raised his eyebrows. "Sorry, I didn't know Ali had company. I'm Royce."

"Joe."

The shaggy blond-haired Brad Pitt lookalike didn't seem happy to find Joe in Ali's apartment. And Joe didn't make it easy on him.

"I'm Ali's neighbor."

Joe nodded.

"I brought her my newest creation. Ali tests out some of my meals for me."

Joe narrowed his eyes. "Hold on. I'll get Ali."

"I'm here," Ali said, coming into the room dressed in jeans and a white knit top, still towel-drying her gorgeous auburn hair. As she whizzed by him, he caught the scent of fresh citrus. "Oh, hi, Royce. What did you bring me this time?"

Royce seemed relieved to see her. "Champagne chicken with a touch of cognac."

"Yum. Smells great. Come in and set it down on the stove. Joe, this is Royce, my neighbor. He's a chef at Cordial Contessa. Royce, this is my...uh, Joe."

"We've just met," Joe said, watching how Royce's gaze fixed on Ali. "Ali works for me at Carlino Wines," Joe said.

Ali furrowed her brows and stared at the two of them. "Well, thanks, Royce. I'll give you my review of your latest creation tomorrow. Unless you want to join us?"

"Join you? What are you two doing?"

Ali looked his way. "Joe's a computer genius. He's fixing my senior-citizen computer. Poor thing is on its last legs."

"*Fixed* your computer," Joe corrected.

"You fixed it already?" Ali's eyes lit up, and Joe took immense satisfaction in her reaction. "There, you see," she turned to Royce. "He *is* a genius."

Ali returned her attention to Joe, her green eyes round and bright. "Thank you so much."

"No problem. Your computer has a lot of life left in it. You just need to upgrade a few things." Joe took the list he'd jotted down out of his pocket and handed it to her.

Ali's smile faded when she glanced at the items he'd listed. "Okay."

Joe gently grabbed the list from her hand. "You know what, I'll take care of it for you."

"Really? But you've already—"

"It's not a problem, Ali. Consider it payback for helping me with the wedding."

"The wedding?" Royce interrupted, casting Ali a curious look.

"Joe's brother is getting married, and he needs a little help with the planning."

"Is that part of your job description?" Royce asked with a disingenuous smile, directing his attention solely to Ali.

"She's doing this off-the-clock, as a favor to me. Not that it's any of your business," Joe said.

Ali intervened, appearing a little nervous. "I'm happy

to do it. I love planning fun events. I know parties the way
Joe knows computers."

Joe met Royce with a hard stare. Who the hell was this
guy anyway? Why was he so damn protective of Ali? He
tested Joe's even-keeled temper in the span of just a few
minutes.

Ali placed her hand on Royce's arm and guided him
toward the door. "Thanks for the champagne chicken,
Royce."

"Anytime, Ali," he said. "Let me know what you
think."

"I will," she said, closing the door behind him.

Joe walked up to her. "Is he your boyfriend?"

Ali shook her head. "No."

"Gay?"

She laughed. "Hardly."

From her laughter and the surprised expression on her
face, Joe surmised Royce had ulterior motives for bringing
Ali his latest culinary creation.

"I think he's just a little protective of me."

"You think?" Joe asked between tight lips.

She shrugged. "I've confided in him about some things
in my past, and well now, I think I shouldn't have."

What sort of things? Joe had been work-close to Ali, but
they'd never confided in personal matters before. He felt
a twinge of jealousy that shouldn't be. But still, it gnawed
at him all the same.

"He's interested in you, Ali," Joe said with blunt honesty.

"I've made it clear that we're just friends."

Hell, men never took that "just friends" garbage seriously. If they were interested in a woman, eventually it
would come out.

Ali walked over to him and stared straight into his eyes.

Her fresh scent surrounded him. Her hair had dried in curls around her pretty face. She glanced at his mouth, and Joe had a difficult time keeping his focus. If she made another move toward him, he didn't think he'd stop her. And that could spell disaster.

He reminded himself that office romances never worked out. An image of Sheila flashed in his mind. He and his bright, feisty, flamboyant onetime fiancée were complete opposites. It had taken months to realize that marrying her would have been a big mistake.

"Can we forget about Royce?" Ali asked. "We have work to do on the wedding."

"Right, the wedding." Joe pushed his glasses farther up his nose and nodded. "Royce who?"

Ali went to bed that night thinking of Joe. For once, she noticed a chink in his armor. He'd actually seemed perturbed with Royce showing up. She could only find a bit of hope in that.

Royce had offered friendship when she'd first moved into River Ridge. He'd helped her settle in and was always around if she'd needed anything. After a couple of weeks, he began asking her out, but Ali had always made it clear that she wasn't looking for a relationship.

Royce had backed off and offered his understanding. He'd been so compassionate, and one night over a bottle of zin and his delicious shrimp scampi à la Contessa, Ali had confided in him about her past history. She'd explained about her tumultuous childhood with her mother and her latest office fiasco with her employer, Dwayne Hicks, a man who'd hired her under false pretenses, pursuing her sexually and giving her grief at the office because she'd denied him.

She'd filed harassment charges against him, and the

whole ordeal had left her somewhat scarred. No matter the right or wrong of it, lawsuits against employers didn't build great resumes.

That's why working for Joe Carlino had appealed to her. He'd been flawless as a boss and seemed to have no other agenda. Working alongside him, her feelings had grown out of respect and admiration.

Ali snuggled deeper into her bed. Joe was becoming more and more important in her life. Instead of fearing those feelings, she welcomed them with her whole heart. He was the only man on her radar, and she wished they'd met outside of the office environment. They'd had a strictly professional working relationship. Until he'd kissed her at the airport, Ali held no hope for a relationship with him. But after that kiss—and if she'd read his jealousy right tonight—all was not lost.

The sun shone warm and bright into her apartment when Ali rose from bed the next morning. The Napa news report called for record-high temperatures today. With that in mind, Ali slipped on a sleeveless white eyelet sundress, tied it at the waist with a red leather belt, added beaded red jewelry around her neck and wrists and tucked her feet into matching three-inch sandals.

After a quick slurp of orange juice, Ali set out for the Carlino estate for her morning meeting with Joe. If she was going to plan a renewal of vows and a reception at the estate, she needed to see the house and grounds. When she'd come up with the idea last night, Joe hadn't balked. Always logical, Joe saw the value in her visit.

After being buzzed inside the gates, Ali drove up the stone driveway and parked the car. The estate and well-groomed grounds were massive, and the colorful rolling vineyards beyond lent a beautiful backdrop for the house.

A housekeeper named Carlotta met her outside the arched Mediterranean-style breezeway and showed her inside the house. She found herself face-to-face with Nick Carlino, who'd just descended the stairs. "Hey, Ali."

"Hi, Nick."

"You're here early. Joe said you'd be coming over for a meeting." He cast her an assessing look. "You look beautiful today."

"Thank you."

"What's the meeting about?" he asked.

"We're going over plans for the wedding before our real workday begins."

"Joe would be lost without you." He eased into a smile. "He really relies on you, doesn't he?"

"I guess so."

"He's always singing your praises to anyone who's willing to listen."

"And is that all he says about me?" The question slipped out much to her surprise "Sorry, I shouldn't have asked you that."

"No need to apologize. As far as I'm concerned, Joe's got rocks in his head." Nick winked. "Come on, I'll take you to him."

Nick led her outside to a covered stone deck overlooking a swimming pool that blended into the landscape so well it appeared born of the earth rather than man-made.

"Joe does laps in the pool every day. Clears his mind for all the numbers he crunches," Nick explained.

Ali spotted Joe gliding through the pool. Sleek and well-muscled, Joe dipped in and out of the smooth blue waters, and Ali's heart swelled.

"Hey, Joe. You have company," Nick called out. He

turned to Ali. "Unfortunately, I've got a plane to catch. Thanks for helping Joe out. He needs it." Again, Nick winked, and before he turned to walk away, he offered one last parting comment. "Just so you know, my brother isn't as noble as he seems."

"Meaning?"

"Don't give up on him."

Ali opened her mouth in denial, but Nick's astute look spoke of the futility in that. He wouldn't buy it, and Ali wasn't all too sure she could sell it to him.

Oh God, was she that obvious?

"I'll be right there," Joe called to her from the far end of the pool.

Joe bounded out of the pool, and she caught her first real glimpse of another side of Joe—the stunning, well-built, tanned and gorgeous man who looked as if he could conquer an enemy in one fell swoop.

Ali's throat constricted.

Her Clark Kent had just transformed into Superman.

Three

Morning sunshine cast a golden sheen over Joe's entire body as he stood by the pool's edge. Water dripped from his hair to his shoulders and then slowly drizzled down his rock-hard torso. She could compare him to a Greek god, but nothing topped Superman in her estimation.

She watched him towel off, then throw his arms into a shirt and head her way. Ali got a grip real fast. She couldn't be caught drooling.

"Sorry," he said as he approached. "I didn't realize the time."

"How many laps do you do?"

"One hundred."

Her mouth gaped open. "One hundred? Every day?"

"Just about."

"No wonder."

"No wonder what?" He looked puzzled.

Ali had to learn to stop thinking out loud. "Oh, um. I

was thinking about your stamina…you must have great stamina."

Joe smiled. "I've built it up over the years." He walked over to a large inlaid stone and iron patio table and picked up his glasses. Taking a second to clean them with the end of his shirt, he narrowed his eyes. "So what do you think?"

"About your stamina? Very impressive."

"No," he said, running a hand through his hair. He put his glasses on, and this was the Joe Ali had come to know. "I mean, about using this place for the wedding."

"Are you kidding? It's a girl's dream come true, Joe. Your home is amazing, and I've only seen a small part of it."

"I'll rectify that in a few minutes. First let me shower and change. In the meantime, have a cup of coffee. I cooked you up some breakfast to have during our meeting."

"You cook, too?" Ali couldn't believe Joe had culinary skills, as well as his other talents.

"I get by. After my father died, our longtime cook retired, and we just never replaced her. Tony's living at Purple Fields now, and Nick and I are rarely home."

Joe walked over to a coffeepot on the patio counter. "What'll you have?"

"I'll get it, Joe. Don't worry about me."

"Okay, I'll be back in five, then I'll give you the grand tour."

Ali watched him leave, her heart in her throat. She couldn't fight her feelings any longer. All shreds of rationality escaped her. She'd never before met a man like Joe Carlino. Before, she'd welcomed the challenge to get him interested in her. But now, it went deeper than that. She admired Joe, found him unique and intelligent and sexy as sin. Emotions washed over as a question entered her mind.

Could she be falling in love with her boss?

"I think your home will work out nicely," Ali said after a cup of coffee and not-half-bad eggs Benedict. Joe cooked like he did everything else, with honed precision and accuracy.

She sat at the patio table after he'd given her the grand tour of his home. Stunning was an understatement. Joe's mother must have had a hand in decorating the house. He'd always spoken so fondly of her sweet, calming ways, and her talent for making a house a home was evident everywhere.

The entire home, though updated with modern conveniences, oozed warmth and love, giving off a Mediterranean flair from the polished carved wood furniture and colorful sofas to the pale golden walls and inlaid stone flooring.

Where the first floor was set to bring in the harmony of the family, the upstairs was laid out to accommodate privacy, each wing being a home within a home. The parents and three sons could enjoy their private suites and never bump into one another.

Silly, but Ali pictured herself here with Joe, living in the east wing of the house. It wasn't the grandeur that appealed to her but the sense of stability. Seeing Joe's brothers interact with each other—witnessing their family ties—had touched a sentimental chord within her.

She'd never had a real place to call home.

She fought her resentment tooth and nail, yet Ali couldn't forgive her mother for her lifestyle. She'd dragged her young child from town to town, marrying men who'd look upon Ali as a burden. At least, she'd always felt like a necessary evil that Justine's husbands had to endure.

Ali had inherited her mother's feisty, bubbly nature. She wasn't shy by any means. But unlike her mother, Ali had a career that she enjoyed. She'd worked hard for everything she'd achieved in life including her bachelor's degree in business. She had brains, thank goodness, and liked to use them.

But now, she was at a complete loss with her strong feelings for Joe. She'd never been in love before and wondered if the impeding sense of dread and earth-shattering excitement she felt was normal. The conflicting mix of emotions put her on unsteady ground.

And other than that one kiss, he really hadn't laid a hand on her. She'd never want to resort to her mother's means for snaring a man, and therein was her problem.

"Where should we hold the renewal of vows?" Joe asked, his focus and those dark piercing eyes intent on her. He'd changed from his swim trunks to black casual trousers and a white button-down shirt. Joe the Hunk had changed back into Joe the Boss.

She came out of her stupor to reply to his question. "Poolside. I think that'll be perfect," she said, the notion in her mind gaining momentum. "The sound of the rock waterfall and the glistening water below will be a great backdrop. We'll have a flower archway made for them to say their vows underneath but nothing too elaborate. The grounds are enough."

Joe looked out at the pool, giving a nod of agreement. "I think you're right."

"I'm always right," she teased.

"I know." Joe didn't blink as he shot back his response.

Ali stared into his eyes. Did he really have that much

faith in her abilities? "I think Rena will be pleased with what I have in mind. Do you think Tony will like my ideas?"

"Without a doubt. He has the woman he loves. That's all he cares about."

"I wish," Ali began, then bit down on her bottom lip.

"What do you wish?" Joe asked, touching a finger to his glasses. Ali knew his gestures and that one meant true curiosity. She couldn't relay her innermost wish, but she could turn the tables on him.

"Have you ever been in love, Joe?"

He blinked and shot his head back in surprise. "Me?"

She held her breath and nodded.

Joe pursed his lips and answered in a clipped tone. "Once. It didn't work out."

Ali was floored by his admission. He was a gorgeous, thirtysomething man who had a lot going for him, but somehow she couldn't picture Joe being in love.

Unless of course, it's with you, Ali.

"I'm sorry."

"Don't be," he said. "It was for the best." He dismissed the subject by flipping through a batch of menus she'd brought with her. "Now, what about the reception? Any ideas?"

"I have a few thoughts on the subject."

He nodded. "Good."

Ali stood and walked around the grounds, conjuring up images of how to best use the backyard and surrounding vineyards for the reception. But more so, she had to move away from her sexy boss to come to grips with the fact that Joe had been in love once. And maybe, he was holding on to that love. Maybe that's why he'd kept his distance. A knot twisted in the pit of her stomach.

Joe came up behind her. His nearness made her heart pound against her ribs. "What's your plan, Ali?"

In the world-according-to-Joe, you always had to have a plan.

Ali turned to find him close enough to touch. She searched his eyes, dying to know the truth. Ali made a decision right then and there to go for broke. "I'm working on it. But you can be sure when I come up with a good plan that you'll be the first to know."

Ali stood in the wine-tasting room at Purple Fields, browsing through the items on the shelves. The quaint shop spoke of decades of winemaking, a family legacy that Tony Carlino had a hand in saving.

Ali looked out of the shop's window to view the construction crew outside. It appeared every effort was being made to update the house without losing its original rustic style.

"Hello, Ali. This is a pleasant surprise."

Ali turned to face Rena, who had walked in from the backroom. "Hi," Ali said. "I hope you don't mind me stopping by."

"Not at all." Rena walked over to her. "It's good to see you again. Sorry about the mess outside. Tony needed more space. And with the baby coming, we thought it best to do the construction before he's born. Tony wanted to add a playroom for the baby, an office for himself and a full remodel of the kitchen for me."

"Wow! All that will be done before your little bambino enters the world?"

Rena nodded. "Carlinos have a way of making things happen."

Ali glanced out the window again and sighed. "If they want something badly enough I suppose."

Rena stared at her, furrowing her brows. "Ali, is something wrong?"

She shook her head. "No." She plastered on a big smile. "I came to give you an update on the wedding plans."

"Wonderful. I'm getting excited about it. Come, have a seat and let's talk."

Rena guided her to one of the three small round tables set in the corner portion of the room. "I'll get us something to drink first. Grape juice for me and our best merlot for you."

Rena returned shortly, handing her a wineglass. Ali sipped from it. "This is fabulous." She set the glass down on the cheery cornflower blue-and-white tablecloth and waited for Rena to take her seat. "Thank you."

"I should be thanking you for all you're doing. I hope Joe isn't working you too hard on this."

"Not at all. I, uh, listen, Rena, I have a confession to make," Ali said. She was never good at fibbing. "I could have called you with the update. We're just beginning with the plans, and there's not much to tell."

"Okay," Rena said, looking a little confused. "But you don't need a reason to stop by to say hello. You're new to Napa, and I'm happy to be your—"

"I do have a specific reason for coming here. Dang it, I'm so confused, and now I'm confusing you!"

Rena chuckled. "Ali, just tell me."

Ali chewed on her lower lip and took a deep breath. She was never one to hesitate about anything. "Okay, I think I'm in love with Joe," she finally blurted out.

Rena's eyes snapped wide-open. "Oh, wow."

"Yeah, wow. It's wonderful and terrifying."

Rena smiled and nodded in full agreement. "I know. That's exactly how I felt about Tony. I didn't want to love him, but those feelings just creep up on you and there's no denying them."

"Joe doesn't suspect anything. He barely knows I'm alive."

"Joe's involved in his work, but he knows you're alive, Ali. I can guarantee it."

"Yeah, I'm nominated for employee of the year."

Rena's smile faded and she cast her a solemn look. "You're serious about this? About him?"

"Very. I've never been in love before. I think Joe's perfect for me. Unfortunately, the only sheets he's interested in me slipping between are the Carlino Wine's tally sheets."

A chuckle burst from Rena's lips. "Sorry. You do have a way with words, Ali."

"It's a curse. I spit out exactly what I'm thinking."

"But not in a demeaning way. You're honest, and that's refreshing."

"Do you think I scare Joe?"

Rena thought about it a few seconds, and Ali was sorry she asked. Perhaps, she didn't want to know the answer to her question.

"No, it's not that," Rena said finally. "I know you don't frighten Joe. He may be a computer geek, but women don't intimidate him. In case you haven't noticed, beyond those brains, Joe's quite a hunk."

"Oh, I've noticed. But that's not the reason I think I love him."

Ali went on to explain to Rena that her reasons for loving Joe went way beyond his sexy good looks. What she'd noticed about him first and foremost was that he'd always taken her seriously, respecting her intelligence, treating her as an equal and *not* coming on to her five minutes after she'd been hired. Ali explained about her former employer. For all intents and purposes, she'd never thought she'd ever get involved with someone in the workplace, much less her boss. But she and Joe had a unique work relationship.

"I flat-out asked him if he's ever been in love, and he told me that he had, once. He didn't want to talk about it. Do you think he's still in love with her?"

"No," Rena said adamantly, bringing hope to her heart. "He's been over Sheila Maxwell for quite some time."

"So what is it?"

"Well, I can tell you this. Joe was burned really badly. Apparently, he became engaged to Sheila while she worked for him at Global Software. She was very beautiful and clever, from what I've been told. Joe thought the sun rose and set on her shoulders. His millions hadn't been enough for her. As you know, of all the Carlino men, Joe is the least flashy. He drives a hybrid car, wears conservative clothes and doesn't have a pretentious bone in his body.

"It wasn't enough for Sheila, though. As soon as an oilman from Texas with billions became interested in her, she dumped Joe like a hot potato."

"How awful for him."

"He didn't take it well. He felt duped and foolish for falling for her. I think Joe is just a little gun-shy right now. And for the record, Ali, he's vowed to never get involved with someone who works for him ever again."

Ali put her head down. "I get it now."

"Well, that's the bad news. The good news is that I think Joe is way off on this. If the right woman comes along—no matter where, when or how—he should act on it. I think he's interested in you, but he's holding on to the promise he made to himself."

"Nick told me Joe's not as noble as he seems. Maybe that's what he meant?"

"Maybe. You're a beautiful woman, Ali. You have flair and style, and if you don't mind me saying, you're sassy. I think Joe looks at you and warning bells go off in his head that scream, 'Stop!'"

"Wonderful," Ali said, feeling hopeless.

"All is not lost. Nick told me he wanted to ask you out, and Joe wouldn't hear of it. Joe was pretty adamant about it."

Ali's antenna went back up. "Did he say why?"

"Something about not wanting Nick to break your heart, but I think it's more than that. I think Joe was jealous."

"That's something," Ali acknowledged. She sipped her merlot, contemplating. "But what can I do about it other than jump his bones?"

Rena shook her head. "I think the opposite approach would work much better. We've got to remove that stop sign in his head. You've got to tone down your appearance and become less of a threat in his mind."

"You mean, a makeover in reverse?"

Rena smiled. "That's one way to put it. But yes, he may notice you more, if you're not on his mental do-not-touch list. Sort of like Cinderella turning back into a plain Jane."

Blood surged through her veins as Ali mulled the idea over. "I think it might work. I'm ready to try anything at this point."

"Trust me, Ali. If I didn't see sparks between you, I wouldn't encourage this. But Joe's a great guy and deserves love in his life again," Rena said, daring Ali with the gleam in her eyes.

"Nothing I've been doing so far has worked."

"If you decide to do this, I'll help in any way I can."

"Hah, so *Ali,* has an *ally.* Okay, I'll do it. If I succeed, I'll name our firstborn after you."

"And I'll hold you to that."

"When should this all happen?" Ali asked.

"Well, I think you should make a few subtle changes during the next few weeks."

"Like toning down my hair and makeup and my sass mouth?"

Rena shook her head with laughter. "Yes, but slowly. The change should happen over time and then—"

"Then?"

"The real transformation will happen when it will be noticed the most." Rena leaned in and curved her lips into a wickedly satisfied smile. "Cinderella will turn into a plain Jane, at the ball…my wedding!"

Four

Dressed in a Brooks Brothers suit and ready to stand up for Tony as best man, Joe glanced around the grounds of the Carlino estate. The backyard had been transformed into an elegant wedding venue, the changes subtle and well-designed thanks to Ali Pendrake.

Joe had spent the past weeks working on the wedding details with her, but she hadn't really needed his input. Ali's organizational skills and her instincts were right on. She'd ordered the cake, taken care of table seating arrangements, hired a five-piece band and a florist and arranged for her neighbor, Royce, to head up the catering.

Joe hadn't said much about her choice of chef, but he hadn't loved the idea.

She'd gotten here early this morning, dressed in jeans and an old sweatshirt, making sure everything would go according to plan. Joe couldn't commend her highly enough, but he also felt a personal sense of pride in her accomplishments. He hated to admit it, but Ali would make an expert wedding planner. Thank goodness, she seemed content working at Carlino Wines with him. He'd never be able to replace her.

"The place looks great," Tony said with a smile, coming to stand beside him on the patio. Guests milled around the grounds, conversing.

"You should tell Ali that. She did it all."

"I will. She's in with Rena now, getting dressed. They've become friends."

"Ali has no trouble making friends." Satisfaction hummed through him. Inexplicably, that his sister-in-law liked Ali made Joe feel good.

"Rena and I owe you both a big thank-you."

Joe nodded. "It wasn't as hard as I thought it'd be."

"Hell, I wouldn't think so. I hear you spent your weekends with Ali."

Joe shot his brother a warning glance. "It's not like that."

Tony shook his head. "I know, and I can't figure that out."

"Sometimes, neither can I." Joe muttered aloud what he'd kept his mind from thinking.

The band started playing, and guests began to take their seats. Tony straightened his tie and took a deep breath. "It's time to do this. I'd better get Rena."

Joe embraced his brother. "I'll see you up there," he said. "I'm happy for you, Tony."

Ali's plan was for both Tony and Rena to walk down the white aisle runner together. They'd had a hard road getting to this place, and their trip down the aisle together would be more meaningful and show unity.

Joe had the urge to grab Ali from the dressing room and have her stand beside him. He wanted her next to him.

They'd been together in this from the beginning, but he held back. Logically, his place was beside his brothers and not with his personal assistant. And damn it, if Ali had a way of making him think illogically.

Joe took his place next to Nick to the left of the flowery archway. The setting sun reflected off the pool waters, and he squinted as he waited for the wedding couple. The band stopped playing, and the entire group of guests hushed their voices. Then a harpist began playing a melodic tune.

Joe searched the dozens of guests for Ali. When he spotted her standing by the last row of chairs, their eyes locked.

His heart pounded.

His breath caught in his throat.

Dressed in a soft jade-colored satin dress, covered with a jacket of the same material, her hair spun up in a demure twist and her face nearly free of makeup, Joe almost hadn't recognized her. Her appearance stunned him. Flashy Ali, usually with all the bangles, beads, boots and exotic hair, looked soft and elegant tonight.

"That's a new look," Nick whispered. "Ali sure can keep a man on his toes."

Irritated by the truth of that comment, he ignored his brother and focused on Ali. She'd been on his mind too much lately. True, they'd spent a good deal of time together these past three weeks planning the wedding. Joe hadn't faltered, keeping his relationship perfectly professional the entire time. Whenever his mind would wander, he reminded himself that she was his employee and a woman who was off-limits. He denied feeling anything but pride for Ali and her accomplishments here today.

Joe turned his attention to his brother, who had reached the arbor of flowers along with Rena. Without the benefit of clergy, they renewed their wedding vows to each other with deep emotion and honesty. At times, they laughed; at times, tears stung their eyes. When it was all said and done, Tony took his pregnant wife by the hand and turned to their guests, receiving a round of applause.

Rena's face beamed with joy, and Tony looked happier than Joe had ever seen him. A bit of envy crept into his heart. At one time, Joe thought he could be that happy. But he'd learned a hard lesson. No woman would ever make a fool of him ever again.

After shaking his brother's hand and hugging Rena, Joe turned to face Ali, who had walked up and also congratulated the couple.

"You did it, Ali," he said.

"*We* did it, Joe," she said softly.

"You did most of the work. The place looks great. I can't give you high enough praise."

Ali put her head down, then glanced out toward the vineyards. "Thank you."

Joe was at a loss for words. Usually Ali did most of the talking. Today she appeared unusually melancholy. "Can I get you a drink?"

"That would be nice."

"I'll be right back."

Joe flagged down a waiter holding a tray of bubbly champagne and returned to Ali with two flutes. "Here you go." He handed her one and then made a toast. "To you, Ali, for all your hard work. The wedding was perfect."

Ali touched his glass and then sipped champagne.

Joe stared into her eyes, wondering what was up.

Ali smiled softly at him, and for some odd reason, dread entered his heart.

Ali's neighbor, Royce, came out of the kitchen and approached them. "Ali, can I speak with you for a minute? I need your opinion about something."

"Sure," she said to Royce. "Excuse me, Joe."

The chef put his hand to Ali's back and escorted her into the kitchen. With a clenched jaw, Joe watched Ali walk away from him. He polished off his champagne in one huge gulp and searched for something stronger.

He headed for the bar inside the house and poured himself two fingers of Scotch. It went down smooth and easy, and Joe sighed, relaxing his tense body.

Laughter from the kitchen had him walking that way. He stopped just outside the door, recognizing Royce's amusement and Ali's quiet chuckling. He heard Ali reassuring Royce about the main dish he planned to serve, complimenting his choice, and then they seemed to share another private joke.

Jealousy burned in his gut.

He clenched his teeth again and headed outside, his blood boiling.

Ali sat next to Joe at the Carlino table during dinner. She met Rena's good friends, Solena and Raymond, who worked at Purple Fields, and several of the Carlino cousins as they dined on Royce's amazing dinner. She'd had her doubts about hiring him since she sensed Joe didn't like him, but Royce's entrées were a big hit, and she felt justified in her choice.

She was sure she was only asked to join the head table because of the work she'd done on the wedding, yet everyone she'd met had been cordial to her. She'd bitten her tongue a dozen times dying to dive in and get to know her dining partners better, but she'd taken Rena's advice to stay under the radar instead of flashing her friendliness like a neon sign.

She'd spent the past three weekends with Joe, creating a wedding and reception that Tony and Rena would cherish in their memories. All that time, Joe had been eager to help, but he hadn't shown one iota of interest in her personally, even though she'd become more reserved, put her hair into sedate styles she'd never have dreamed up before and dressed herself like a churchgoing schoolteacher.

Her ego had taken a deep plunge.

This was her last-ditch effort to get Joe to notice her as more than his employee. If the makeover in reverse was her ticket to gain Joe's attention, then she'd give it her best shot. Unfortunately, patience was a virtue she hadn't been born with. She'd wanted this to happen the second she'd slipped her feet into her first pair of lackluster pumps.

"In case I haven't said it yet, you look very beautiful tonight," Nick said from across the round table. Rena had done the seating cards and had deliberately put Joe next to her and Nick as far away as possible. "Joe, don't you think so?"

Joe shot Nick a hard look and then turned to Ali. Needlessly, he pushed his glasses up his nose. They were already as far as they could go. "Yes, Ali, you look very pretty tonight."

Nick grinned, and Ali didn't know which Carlino brother she should clobber first.

"Thank you both."

Ali looked at Rena, who gave her a nod of approval. Rena had been a saint, helping her pick out a new conservative wardrobe and giving her tips on how to subdue her outgoing personality. Rena warned it might take some time for this plan to work, but Ali wondered how long she could endure loving Joe and not having that love returned.

After dinner, the band started up again, and people began to approach the large redwood decking overlooking the vineyards, which served as the dance floor.

Ali rose from the dinner table to listen to the music,

and immediately, a friend of the family approached her. "Would you care to dance?"

Ali didn't have time to respond. Joe appeared beside her and clasped her hand in his. "I think she promised me the first dance, Allen."

Ali's heart pumped overtime. Joe squeezed her hand tight, and she nearly stumbled when he brought her onto the dance floor. "I don't do fast," he warned.

How well she knew. But she was sure he meant fast *dances*.

"But I think I can manage not to break your toes with this song." He pulled her up against him, and she thought she'd died and gone to heaven. Hugo cologne and dancing practically cheek to cheek with Joe was a sexy mix. Consumed with being in his arms, she couldn't name the artist or the song they danced to, barely hearing the music at all as Joe swirled her slowly around the dance floor.

"You're a good dancer, Joe."

"Am I?" he asked, his voice a low rasp in her ear.

Tingles broke out all over her body, and she relished each amazing second of the dance.

Joe tightened his hold on her. "How can I thank you for tonight?" he whispered.

She had a few suggestions that didn't involve touring Napa. Lusty images filled her head. She could barely put together a coherent thought with him holding her so close. But she couldn't push her luck. She had to stick to the plan. "You didn't forget our bargain, did you?"

"No. I'm a man of my word."

"I know that about you."

Joe pulled away to gaze into her eyes. He blinked a few times and then shot her a killer smile. That smile, his sexy scent, the way he held her—Ali wanted to pull him into his bedroom and make love to him until the sun came up.

"I'm glad, Ali, but I just don't know how much you'll get out of me being your tour guide."

Nick and Royce both offered to show her the sights, but Ali was holding out for numero uno. She wanted to spend time with Joe and only Joe. Ali had pressed him to this bargain, and she couldn't let him off the hook now. Normally, she'd goad him into it—a promise is a promise—but the new Ali had to take a different turn. "It's all right if you'd rather not. I understand."

Joe's brows arched. "I wasn't weaseling out of it, Ali. I'll do my best to show you around."

Ali smiled, warmth overflowing. "That's all I ask."

Joe seemed satisfied with that and took her back into his arms until the dance ended. When they parted, Ali hated the separation. She could have stayed on the dance floor with Joe all night.

"Thanks for the dance," he said, escorting her back to their table.

"It was nice, Joe. Thank you."

Joe nodded, and when he pulled out her chair to sit down, Ali changed her mind about staying at the table. "I think I'll take a little walk."

"Would you like some company?"

She would love it! She hesitated one second then with a slight tilt of her head, she answered. "Okay."

They walked past the reception area lit with twinkle lights and lanterns, down an inlaid stone pathway that led to steep steps. Only moonlight guided their way now, the party music fading.

"They're tricky without much light." Joe took her hand and helped her down steps that seemed to go on forever. He'd touched her more today than in the past year since she'd met him. Ali held out some hope that progress was being made, small as it may be.

Once they reached the floor of the vineyard, which was still pretty high up on the hillside, he released her hand. Ali gazed out at the endless rows of vines that columned Carlino land. She sighed in awe. "Most people have swing sets in their backyards."

"We had those, too. We were privileged as kids, but believe it or not, we had a pretty normal childhood. My father was a taskmaster. We had chores to do and had to bring home good grades, just like anybody else. We got grounded. Well, I didn't so much, but Nick and Tony? They were always causing the old man conniptions."

Ali wished her childhood involved having a mother and father who loved her unconditionally. Someone who loved her enough to ground her or make sure she was doing her homework. She'd never had stability in her life. There was never much normalcy, either. Joe—living up here on a hill, with all his wealth and privileges—probably did have a more normal childhood than she had.

"He cared about the men you were to become."

Joe scrubbed his jaw. "I guess so. He was a hard man. My mother softened him, though. He loved her so much. He'd have died for her."

"They were lucky to have each other."

Ali turned from Joe to absorb what he'd just said. She pretended to look out at the vineyards, but she looked beyond them to her own life. That kind of love—that close family bond—was completely foreign to her. People looked at her and assumed she had everything she wanted. But that was far from the truth. Her childhood hadn't been a fairy tale. She wanted the kind of love that Joe's mother had—that unconditional commitment and devotion. Ali had been on her own in one way or another most of her life.

She could easily live a superficial life, the kind her mother lived, bouncing in and out of relationships, grasping for the brass ring that would make her happy momentarily, but never fully content. Ali had vowed to never be like her mother. She wanted something real. Money didn't matter to her. Oddly, she'd fallen for Joe, a man worth millions, but he could just as well have been broke and she still would've loved him. That was the difference between her and her mother.

"Ali, are you okay?" Joe came up behind her, his voice soft and tender. She felt his solid presence at her back. Maybe that's why she loved him. Joe was a rock of stability. "You're different tonight."

Tears entered her eyes, and she fought them. She couldn't break down in front of him. She didn't want his pity. She didn't want to tell him about her mother, her past and the love she'd never received as a child.

Taking a deep breath, she turned to him and gave a little shrug. "Weddings do that to me. I'm fine."

"You're quiet. I thought you loved a good party." Joe searched her eyes. He looked puzzled and sweetly concerned.

Oh, how she hated all this deception. She just wanted to blurt out that she loved him. She loved him, and her heart was breaking. But it was the last thing Joe would want to hear. She'd destroy their relationship. She had to follow through with "the plan."

"I'm enjoying myself."

Joe cast her a dubious look. "Have I done anything to upset you?"

She shook her head. "No."

To her surprise, Joe reached for both of her hands, clasping them tight. An unexpected jolt shot clear through her. She held her breath, her heart hammering.

Joe slanted his head, staring deep into her eyes and

leaned toward her. "Maybe I'm about to," he whispered into her mouth.

Then he pressed his lips to hers.

The kiss was gentle and giving, but that didn't stop fireworks from exploding in her head. She could hardly believe this. Joy entered her heart, and she wanted to wrap her arms around his neck and press her body against him.

Please let this moment never end.

Joe must have heard her silent plea. He slid his hands up her arms and gently squeezed, tugging her closer, his hips crinkling her satin gown as he deepened the kiss.

The rich taste of liquor made her head swim, and images of bedrooms and silken sheets flashed in her mind. Joe parted her lips and their tongues mated, then a deep groan of pleasure rumbled from his throat and Ali's joy doubled.

It was finally happening.

"Hey, Joe? You down there?" Nick called from above. "It's time to toast the bride and groom."

Ali gasped when she heard Nick's voice and backed away.

"I'll be right there," Joe called toward the stairs. She couldn't see Nick, which meant he couldn't have seen what Joe and Ali had been doing.

Joe turned to her. "Sorry. We'd better get back. You okay?" he asked, blinking behind his glasses.

She couldn't utter a word, so she bobbed her head up and down.

"I, uh, should explain," Joe began, his voice a rasp in the breeze. "You looked like you needed…comforting." Joe's brows furrowed as if he was as confused by his confession as she was.

"Comforting?" Ali questioned on a low breath.

"Yeah." Then Joe turned his attention toward the stairs. "C'mon." He took her hand, and they climbed up the steps, Ali following behind him. Before they reached the top of the stairs, he turned to her, his gaze fastened to her mouth. "When I said I was sorry, I didn't mean about kissing you. I meant sorry we were interrupted."

"I think I knew that," Ali replied, just catching her breath.

Joe's lips curled up slightly. "You're astute, Ali, but if I was out of line, you'd tell me, right?"

Heavens, he was so *in* line, it wasn't even funny. "Yes, I'd be sure to tell you."

Joe looked at her mouth one last time with regret in his eyes, and Ali wanted to skip right over the moon.

After the toasts were made by Joe and Nick, everyone sipped champagne and wished the newlyweds the best. Rena sidled up next to Ali by the dance floor. "How's it going, my friend?"

Ali beamed her a smile. "I'm no longer in the potted plant category."

Rena's brows rose, and she looked on with interest. "Really?"

"Joe kissed me down in the vineyards," she gushed out. She'd wanted to scream it from the rooftops that Joe Carlino finally showed some interest in her. "It was *the best*."

"What did he say?"

"Not much. He was worried about me. I think this change really threw him off. He's looking a little bit puzzled."

"He noticed you. That's all that matters."

Ali drew in a deep breath and sighed. "Oh, I know, but I'm not patient enough to wait. I want more."

Rena's chuckle turned a few heads in her direction.

"Calm down, Ali. You're doing fine. And you look stunning in that dress."

"Who knew that I could wear something so...not me and pull it off?"

"I did."

"Well, I'm not counting my chickens yet."

"It takes time, Ali. If it's meant to be, it'll happen." she said. "And look who's coming straight toward us, with you in his sights."

Ali glanced across the decking and spotted Joe, heading her way. Every time she looked at him dressed in that striking black suit, his dark hair groomed just so, his handsome face marred by just a hint of a beard and wearing those glasses that made him look sexier than a man had a right to look, her heart rate sped up like crazy.

Rena leaned over to whisper. "Remember, weddings have a way of bringing out the best in people."

Ali swallowed hard.

Joe focused his attention on her as he approached. "Is it time to cut the cake?"

Joe was always spot on when it came to schedules. "Yes, I think it's time." She turned to Rena. "Ready?"

"I'm ready. I'll find Tony and meet you over by the cake table."

Both watched as Rena walked away. "I think everyone had a great time tonight," Joe said.

"I know I did."

Joe gazed into her eyes. "I'm feeling a little bit guilty," he began, and Ali prayed he didn't regret their kiss from a few minutes ago. She waited for him to explain. "A few people asked me if you were a party planner. You could have a very lucrative business here, if you wanted it."

"So why are you guilty?"

"Because I told them you're not interested in outside work. You did this as a favor to the family."

"That's not a lie."

"Well no, not technically. But I shouldn't have answered for you. The fact is, I don't want to lose you," then Joe hesitated before adding, "as my personal assistant."

Ali smiled inwardly. Joe was slowly coming around. "You won't."

Joe stared at her, unblinking then glanced at her lips. She returned his stare, wishing he'd kiss her again. But she knew that he wouldn't in full view of the guests at the reception. Too many people knew Ali worked for Joe, and his reputation was at stake, along with hers.

The irony struck her anew. Ali never wanted an office romance. She'd shied away from them all of her adult life, wanting to be treated as an equal in business and respected for her intellect. And as soon as she found a man who'd done that, she'd fallen hard for him.

"I'm in the mood for something sweet," Joe said, still glancing at her mouth.

"Hmm?" She cast him a curious look. It wasn't like Joe to make innuendo. Could he have been teasing?

He gestured with a slight nod toward the fondant cake decorated with white roses and greenery. "Cake. Let's go and see how good your pastry chef is."

He's not *her* pastry chef. She'd simply hired him, but Ali stifled her comment. "I'd like that. Royce recommended him highly."

Joe's lips twisted but he didn't reply.

And ten minutes later, Ali sat at their table in sugar heaven. The mango-filled white cake was too delicious for words. "Mmm."

"It's pretty damn good." Joe had his piece of cake polished off in seconds.

Ali scooped up the last bit of frosting with her fork, relishing every bite, aware that Joe watched her every move. When the owner of a neighboring winery stopped by the table asking to speak to Joe for a second, he agreed and rose from his seat, bending to whisper in her ear. "Excuse me, I'll be right back."

Goose bumps erupted on her arms, and Ali's body sizzled. She cast him a quick acknowledgment and watched him leave. This was new for her. She'd never received so much attention from Joe, and she wanted it to continue. The handsome prince had kissed her and stolen her heart. But she feared her reverse Cinderella night was quickly coming to an end. Now what?

The final dance of the evening was announced. Everyone stopped their conversations and mingled around the dance floor. The band played an old classic tune "I Want to Walk You Home," and Rena, dressed in an ivory-colored satin maternity dress, swirled around on Tony's arm, glowing with joy.

Their happiness was contagious, and as Ali glanced around, she found smiles on all the guests' faces. Out of the blue, Royce appeared next to her.

"Give me a rain check on a dance," he said. "I couldn't get away long enough to show you my dance skills."

He'd changed from his chef's uniform into dark slacks and a black shirt. She couldn't deny her neighbor his good looks. She'd noticed more than one female's head turn in his direction during the night.

"That's okay, Royce. You showed me your culinary skills."

"Well?"

"Absolutely perfect. Every dish was delicious."

Royce closed his eyes, savoring the compliment. "Thank

you, Ali. You recommended me for this event, and I didn't want to let you down."

"You didn't," she said. Then she tilted her head. "In fact, you exceeded my expectations."

"The same can be said about you. You put this party together in record time, and it looked as if you'd worked on it for months instead of weeks."

They shared a moment of mutual admiration.

"Let me finish up in the kitchen, and I'll drive you home," Royce said.

"I'm taking Ali home."

Ali turned to find Joe beside her, his jaw tight as he faced Royce. Where had he come from? Ali hadn't seen him since he'd taken off to speak with that elderly winemaker.

"It's not a problem," Royce said. "We live in the same building."

Joe removed his glasses slowly, squaring off with Royce. Neither one of the men looked like they'd back down. Ali felt like a pawn in some macho game. "Actually, I have my own car. But thank you both for the offer."

There, she'd settled it.

Joe hesitated, eyeing Royce, then slipped his glasses back on. "The food was exceptional tonight."

Royce seemed surprised at the compliment. His rigid stance relaxed some. "Thank you."

That's what she loved about Joe. He was fair-minded. "Ali recommended you, and I trust her judgment."

"I'm happy to have the honor." Royce glanced at Ali. "I've got to see to the cleanup in the kitchen. Catch you later, Ali."

"See you, Royce."

Ali turned to face Joe, his expression noncommittal. "I'll be leaving shortly, unless there's anything else you need me to do?"

"No, you've outdone yourself with this party. Tony and Rena are thrilled with how it all turned out. I am, too."

"It was a pleasure," she said. "Well, then I'd better say good-night to them." She turned to leave.

"Wait," Joe said firmly. "It's a difficult drive down the hill at night. You don't know the roads. I'll follow you."

"But you don't have—"

"No arguments, Ali. I'm following you home."

Five

Joe followed behind Ali's car until she parked in her garage. He watched her get out. He debated for a half second whether to get out of the car and walk her to the door, a little war waging in his head.

The kiss they shared earlier was still on his mind. He'd been foolish to do it, yet he hadn't been able to stop himself. Ali had looked vulnerable and a little sad, something he'd not recognized in her before. The change in her made him want to comfort and console her. He'd meant to plant a little peck on her lips, but the minute he'd taken her into his arms, something snapped inside him. He wanted to hold her and go on holding her. To kiss her and go on kissing her.

He wanted to do more.

Warning bells rang out in his head. His mind screamed that she was off-limits. He wasn't ready for any relationship, much less one with his employee. How many times had he reminded himself of that?

Joe stepped out of his car and leaned against it. "Thank you for following me home, Joe. It wasn't necessary, but I do appreciate it."

"Just wanted to make sure you got home safely, Ali."

She faced him and leaned over to give him a little kiss on his cheek. "That's sweet."

Sweet? Joe's hackles went up. He spread his legs and braced Ali's waist with his hands, pulling her closer. Her exotic scent scurried up his nose and went straight to his brain. "Can you forget that I'm your boss for one night?"

His gaze dropped down to the ripe fullness of her mouth.

Ali blinked. Then a beautiful smile emerged. "I think so. Why?"

Joe answered her by wrapping a hand around her neck and bringing her mouth to his. "To show you I'm not that sweet," he whispered before he crushed his mouth to hers.

A tiny whimper of pleasure arose from Ali's throat, her lips inviting and lush. Joe deepened the kiss and brought Ali even closer, meshing their hips together.

Pressure built in his groin, his breathing sped up and the urge to take Ali inside her apartment and finish this overwhelmed him. He mated their tongues, all the while stroking his knuckles along her smooth cheekbones and then capturing her face in his outspread hand.

"Still think I'm sweet?" he asked, nipping at her lower lip.

"Not at the moment," she answered without hesitation.

"Am I out of line?" he whispered.

She sighed into his mouth. "Very."

But she wasn't complaining, and that's all the fuel Joe

needed to continue. His mind went on autopilot, and he kissed her again and again, each time bringing her closer, crushing her beautiful breasts to his chest, his arousal hard to restrain.

He stroked her lower back, gliding his hands up and down, damning the satin material and wishing he could put his palms to her creamy skin.

Ali pulled away slightly, her breathing labored, a soft sheen on her face. She searched his eyes and shook her head. "I don't do one-night stands, Joe."

Joe loosened his hold on her. It was hard to let her go. Already, he missed the sweetness of her mouth on his and her erotic scent filling his head. He pursed his lips and nodded. He'd let his lust get in the way of what he knew to be right. "When I asked if you could forget that I was your boss for one night, that's really not what I had in mind. I, uh, things got a little carried away."

"They seem to, whenever you kiss me," Ali stated quietly.

Joe knew better than to mess with Ali's emotions. Nothing could come of their relationship. He was her boss, and she was his most trusted employee. "Listen, uh, I, don't believe in workplace relationships. I did that once, and let's just say that it was painful and destructive."

Ali listened patiently, her gaze intent on him. She looked so lovely tonight, and any other man would have found it easy to seduce her into bed. Joe still wanted to. He wanted to make love to Ali tonight.

But it wasn't fair to her, and he'd vowed that he'd never put himself in that situation again.

He reached into his pocket and pulled out a jewelry box made of gold velvet. "This is what I'd meant." He handed Ali the box, laying it on her palm. "It's a thank-you for all you've done to help me."

Ali gazed at the box she held. "I don't understand."

"A pay bonus didn't seem quite right in thanking you for what you've done tonight. You helped my family, and that called for something more personal. I can't tell you how much I appreciate, well…you. Open it."

With trembling hands, Ali opened the box. The look on her face made it all worthwhile. "It's beautiful."

"I picked it out, but I wasn't sure you'd like it."

Joe had gone to the best jeweler in the county to find just the right gold and diamond bracelet. He was used to seeing Ali wearing bangles and jewelry that made a big statement. But that wasn't what he'd wanted for her. When he'd spotted this bracelet, he knew it was right for her. It wasn't gaudy—the small, but perfect diamonds were set within the gold framework of the delicate piece.

"I love it," she said softly. Then her eyes filled with moisture. "This is a thank-you?"

He nodded. "For everything, Ali. But mostly for making my brother's wedding so memorable. Do you want to try it on?"

She nodded and Joe lifted the bracelet from the box and took her wrist in his hand. He secured the clasp, his head bumping hers as they looked on. Her subtle exotic scent dazzled him. Their heads came up at the same time, and they stared into each other's eyes.

Joe's heart thumped, a spark of something more than lust making its way in. He kept thinking of the torturous night ahead while he slept alone in his bed, yet knowing he'd made the right decision.

I don't do one-night stands.

And that's all Joe could offer her. He released her hand.

"It fits perfectly." Ali's voice lowered until it was barely audible. "You *are* sweet."

Joe cringed inwardly.

Ali smiled, and he wasn't sure what to make of it. She blinked and took a deep breath that was almost a sigh of disappointment. "Well, I'd better get inside. I'll probably fall asleep the minute my head hits the pillow."

Joe wished he'd be that lucky. He already knew what his night would be like. "Good night, Ali."

"Good night, Joe."

He waited for her to get inside and close her garage door before he got into his car and drove away.

Ali leaned against the garage door of her condo, listening as Joe drove off. She fingered the bracelet on her wrist, with love bursting from her heart. She'd never been given such a beautiful, thoughtful gift and yet, she'd let Joe leave tonight, making it clear that she wasn't a woman who slept with men unless there was a commitment.

It was the vow she'd made to herself after watching her mother's social-climbing ways. If Joe wasn't ready to give her more, then Ali would have to wait.

But the waiting was killing her! She could be in bed with Joe, making love with him at this very moment if she hadn't stopped him, yet she'd had to express her feelings. He hadn't offered her more than a night of passion, and Ali wouldn't settle for that. She wanted Joe—but not just for one night. She wanted his love and respect, too.

She learned a hard lesson allowing a man to call all the shots. Ali knew better now. Judging by the press of Joe's arousal while kissing her, Joe would have definitely made her night memorable. Sadness filled her heart for a moment, but then she remembered what Rena said.

Be patient.

She realized Rena was right. After all, she'd made progress, and turning Joe away tonight might not have been a bad thing. All things considered, the night had been magical, and Joe had certainly noticed her.

Ali took a quick hot shower and dressed for bed. She climbed in, tucking herself in cozily, and laid her head back, relishing the softness of her pillow. When the phone rang, she groaned and let it ring again, pretending she hadn't heard it. On the fifth insistent ring, she grabbed for it grudgingly, glancing at the clock. It was after midnight, and she couldn't imagine who'd be calling this late. "Hello."

"Ali, it's me."

Those three words instilled fear in her heart when she recognized the voice. She bolted up from bed. "Mom, what's wrong?" Her mother lived on the East Coast, and it was three in the morning there. Concern rippled through her. Guiltily she realized she hadn't talked to her mother in over a month. "Are you okay?"

"No, I'm not okay. I'm terrible." Her mother sobbed into the phone, alarming Ali all the more. Visions of her contracting a rare disease or having a car accident flashed through Ali's mind.

"What is it?"

"It's Harold. He's being impossible. I don't think I can live with him anymore."

Ali's rigid shoulders slumped.

Not this again.

She recognized her mother's tone and the sobs that were more complaint than anguish. What was it this time? Was his work interfering with their playtime? Or was Harold smoking too much? Maybe he liked his dog more than her. Ali had heard it all before. Her mother's need for attention and adoration was monumental, and whenever she didn't get it from one husband, she'd move on.

At forty-nine, her mother was still a beauty, and she had no trouble attracting men. Her problem was keeping them.

She expected perfection from her mate, when she was far from it herself. She wanted to be placed on a pedestal and admired by her man. It had become increasingly clear to Ali that the main trouble with her mother's relationships with men was that *life* got in her way.

There were times when her mother couldn't be the main focus in her husband's life. Times when their work took precedence and times when outside influences that couldn't be helped, interfered. Ali had always believed that the men Justine had married truly loved her, but they couldn't keep up with Justine's need for attention.

"Mom, what's wrong with Harold?" Ali had actually *liked* Harold Holcomb. He was a man of honor and integrity and had always treated her mother well in their three years of marriage.

"He's being so…so, stubborn."

"Mom, please stop crying."

"Okay," she said immediately, catching a sob. "I know you hate when I cry."

"I do. You know I've always liked Harold. I think you should calm down and think about what's important in life. *Really* important."

"I know you think I'm flighty, but this time I'm really worried. We're always fighting and… Ali, *I really love Harold.*"

Her mother seemed a little stunned by her own revelation. Maybe she'd finally figured out what love was all about.

"He loves you, too, Mom."

"I know."

"Then whatever it is, you two can work it out."

"I know, I know. You've already said you won't come to any more weddings so I'd better make this one stick."

"Mom," Ali said, sighing into the phone, "can we discuss this in the morning? I'm really tired."

"It's only midnight there, sweetie."

"That's late for us working girls."

"But surely you're not working tomorrow—on Sunday?"

"No, I'm not." Yes, she actually was. She'd brought home a stack of work to look over. She'd been so busy with the wedding reception this week that she'd put a few projects on hold, knowing she'd get to them on Sunday.

Not that her mother had asked her how she liked her new job or her new home. When Ali had moved here from the East Coast, her mother had called her once to make sure she was settled and safe. Once she was assured of that, she hadn't called again, leaving it up to Ali to make the calls from then on.

Her mother really did love her, but she showed it in odd ways sometimes. This call tonight was a perfect example of her love. Justine confided in Ali when she wouldn't confide in anyone else. Ali had always shared that bond with her mom. She'd listen to her and give advice and encouragement, and her mother always made it clear that Ali was the only one she trusted to vent her frustrations.

Maybe Ali had been far too understanding with her mom over the years. Justine needed a hefty dose of reality. "I had a big day today, Mom. I helped my boss plan a wedding reception all week, and tonight was the big event. I just got in a few minutes ago, and I'm really pooped."

"Your boss? You mean, Joe Carlino?"

"Yes, I mean, Joe."

"How was the affair?"

"Spectacular, even if I do say so myself."

"If you had anything to do with it, I'm sure it was stylish and fun."

"Thanks, Mom." Justine was loyal and thought Ali could

conquer the world. Another example of how she showed her love.

Ali wondered what her mother would think of the "new-and-improved" Ali Pendrake, the one with the conservative clothes and reserved demeanor. The one who'd sink to fraudulent behavior to ensnare the man of her dreams.

Justine never had to resort to such measures. She'd simply flirt and tease a man to garner his interest, but Ali was sure her mother had never come up against anyone like Joe before. A man like Joe wouldn't interest her enough to make overtures.

Yet, Joe held Ali's heart in the palm of his hand.

"Okay, sweetie," her mother said. "I'll call you in the morning." She sniffled. "It was good to hear your voice. I miss you, Ali."

Ali closed her eyes and savored the sentiment. "I miss you, too, Mom."

She really did.

"Good night. Sleep tight. You're my beautiful princess."

Ali smiled into the phone. "I know. Good night, Mom."

On Monday morning, Joe walked into the Carlino Wines office, amazed at how this century-old building had survived to modern times. The building on Main Street was well known as one of the "ghost wineries" of the past that had been nearly crippled by age and ruin. The exterior built of mortar and stone, refurbished to its original vintage architecture, spoke of winemaking in its earliest form in the Napa region.

While the exterior held the ambience of old times, the interior had been transformed into offices that represented the most modern and up-to-date technology and equipment in the country. For all his old ways, Joe's father, Santo Carlino, had also been a forward thinker.

Joe headed past the reception area and aimed his way toward his office, stopping short as he approached Ali's outer office. He blinked his eyes then drew his brows together.

Ali sat at her desk, her gaze focused on her computer screen. Her auburn hair was drawn severely back and clasped at the nape of her neck with a band, and her face, free of makeup was adorned with plain, wire-rimmed eyeglasses. He approached with caution. "Ali?"

"Hi, Joe," she said, barely casting him a glance. "Just catching up on work."

He swallowed. "I didn't know you wore glasses."

Ali stopped what she was doing to grant him a little smile. "My contacts were bothering me under the fluorescent lights. I think I need to see my eye doctor." She shrugged. "It's just easier to wear glasses at work." She tilted her head to one side. "Do you mind?"

"Mind?" Joe stepped back a half step. "No, of course not." He pushed his own glasses farther up his nose. "I just didn't realize you wore them."

Ali stood up and came around the desk. "I came in early to finish up those reports you'd asked for." She handed them to him, and Joe noticed the diamond bracelet around her wrist.

His heart gladdened at the sight.

She wore no other jewelry but a pair of tiny heart-shaped gold earrings.

Joe took the files from her. The brush of her hand against his created an immediate spark. They stared at each other, their eyes behind their eyeglasses, locking. Then he scanned her body, taking in her soft pink knit sweater and straight-leg, gray slacks. Something was way off, and it had little to do with the clothes she wore. Joe couldn't put a finger on it until his eyes ventured farther down her body to her feet.

She wore flats. Aside from the glasses and clothes being different, Joe realized he towered over her by three *extra* inches. "You're shorter today." He hadn't meant to blurt that out.

Ali stifled a giggle. "That's what happens when I don't wear high heels."

Joe smiled, reminded of the night he'd fixed her computer, after she'd come out of the shower. She'd been barefoot, but he hadn't noticed how he'd towered over her. He'd had other things to focus on then. In the workplace, though, it caught him off guard. "I guess so."

"Anything else?" she asked.

"No, not at all." Joe tapped the file against his other hand. "Thanks for this. There was no rush on it."

Ali sat behind her desk. "It wasn't a problem. I came in early."

Joe continued to stare. He couldn't help from peering at her mouth and remembering how her lips felt pressed up to his. The kisses they shared the other night couldn't be repeated, yet they'd stayed with him all weekend long. If he were honest with himself, he'd have to say the memory had haunted him.

He remembered holding her and pulling her against him, having her body pressed to his, his desire evident and obvious to both of them. He shoved that memory aside and instead recalled the joy he'd witnessed on her face when he'd given her the bracelet.

Putting it on her.

Seeing her green eyes sparkle as bright as those diamonds.

Feeling contentment that he'd made her happy.

"Joe," Ali was saying, holding the phone to her ear. "You have a call, line two."

"Oh," he said, coming out of his reverie. "Thanks, I'll get it in my office."

"Mr. Carlino will be right with you," Ali said into the phone, and Joe strode to his office and closed the door.

The rest of the week had been pretty much the same. Joe found himself immersed in Ali. He stole glances at her whenever the mood struck, watched her talk on the phone or interact with other employees. She'd play with a rebellious lock of her upswept hair as she studied something on her computer screen, and Joe's methodical mind would wander to the land of Ali Pendrake.

"This is crazy," he muttered to himself on Friday afternoon. He'd been avoiding spending more time with her than necessary, but he owed her. And Joe was a man of his word.

He shot up from his chair and walked over to her desk. She peered up at him over her glasses, and Joe thought she looked adorably sexy.

Don't go there, Carlino.

Those thoughts were exactly why he'd procrastinated all week long.

"Do you need something, Joe?"

"Ali, this is really short notice."

"What is?" She looked puzzled and glanced at her watch. "If you need those invoices sooner, I'm on top of it. They're almost done."

"No, it's not about invoices." Joe scratched his head. "Do you have plans tomorrow?"

"Saturday? Well, nothing that can't be changed. I can come in if it's urgent."

Joe shook his head and stared at the diamond bracelet

he'd given her. She'd worn it every day this week. "This isn't about work."

She stopped what she was doing and took off her glasses. Her eyes were the prettiest shade of light jade. Joe leaned over her desk, bracing his hands on the edge. "I thought you might like to see some of the sights in Napa."

Realization dawned, and Ali pursed her lips, drawing his attention there. Her mouth looked glossy and soft pink, kissable. He forced his attention back up to her eyes.

Ali drew in a breath, then sighed. "Joe, I know you don't want to do this."

The disappointment registering on her face made him feel like a heel. He shouldn't have waited until the last minute. From the look in her eyes, he could tell she'd let him off the hook. Yet, suddenly, that's the last thing Joe wanted. "I do, Ali."

"Because you owe me?" she asked softly.

"Because we made a deal, and I want to show you—"

"Show me?"

"Around. I'd like to show you around wine country. I've been checking out some places during the week that I thought you'd like to see." The fib flowed easily through his lips.

"Really?"

Joe nodded. "Just tell me what time you can be ready."

"I just need to make a phone call to cancel a lesson."

"A lesson?"

She shook her head. "With Royce. He was going to teach me how to cook a—" Ali stopped in mid-sentence and made a slight gesture with her hand "—it's not important. He can show me another time."

Royce again? Joe was glad he'd foiled her plans with

Royce. He felt no compunction whatsoever, and a sly smile curved his lips. "How strong are your legs?"

Ali snapped her eyes to him. "My legs? Pretty strong, I guess. Why?"

She worked out. Joe remembered the night she'd opened the door to him in her workout clothes, her body gleaming with moisture. He'd also seen her going into the on-site gym during her lunch hour. "We're going on a bike trip. It'll take the whole day and into the evening. Are you up for it?"

Ali's expression brightened, and for a second, he thought she'd jump out of her chair. Then she took a deep breath and sent him a sweet smile. "Yes. I'm up for it."

"I'll pick you up at nine."

"Do I need to bring anything in particular?"

Joe shook his head. "I've got it covered."

Joe walked back to his office and sat behind his desk and waited until Ali left her desk. Then he called his friend from high school who ran the Napa Wine and Dine Bike Tour Company. "Hey, Benny. I'm calling in a favor. I need to arrange a private bike tour ASAP. Can I count on you?"

After his phone call with Benny, Joe leaned back, arms behind his head, and rocked in his leather seat, thinking about Ali and looking forward to spending the entire day with her.

An unexpected peace washed over him.

Joe bolted upright in his seat, coming to grips with what he was feeling for her.

Lust, Carlino, he told himself.

That's all it was.

He could deal with it.

He refused to admit it was anything more.

Six

Ali spent Friday night floating on air. She'd had a dickens of a time restraining herself when Joe had approached her at the office about the bike tour. She'd wanted to jump for joy, but instead she'd kept a reasonable sense of decorum. She sensed that when Joe gave her the diamond bracelet it was his way of getting out of their deal, yet he'd surprised her with the offer.

Excited, Ali picked up the phone and dialed Rena's number. She had to share the news with someone. When Rena picked up, Ali greeted her in a rushed voice. "It's Ali. Guess what? I'm going out with Joe tomorrow!"

"Oh, Ali. That's wonderful. So is our little plan working?"

Ali's joy ebbed a little, reminded of the deception that she'd engaged in with Joe. If there was any other way to get Joe's attention she would have tried it, but she couldn't look this gift horse in the mouth. "Apparently so. I'm so happy now that I could throw a party."

"You already did, for me. And it was perfect, Ali. So tell me all about this date."

Ali told her about the bike tour and then relayed the events of the past week and remarked that Rena had been right. Joe seemed to notice the more demure, subdued Ali more. At least, they'd been interacting on a personal level now.

Ali would do anything within her power to have her love returned by Joe, yet as she spoke with Rena, a thought wiggled into her subconscious that she wanted Joe to love her for herself—the woman she truly was.

Rena's bright voice broke into her thoughts. "I can't wait to see you in glasses, Ali. Nice touch."

"You'd hardly recognize me, Rena."

"You're beautiful with or without glasses, Ali. With or without flashy clothes. Joe will come to see this. Right now, you're giving him a very loud wake-up call."

Ali immediately felt better. Rena was right again. She'd needed to change things up a little to get Joe to look at her as more than his devoted assistant. Who'd have thunk she'd needed a reverse makeover to achieve her goals.

Yet, Joe wasn't like most men. And that's what she loved about him.

"I guess you're right, Rena. I hadn't really thought about it that way. I'm glad I called you. I was about to burst outta my seams."

Rena chuckled. "Hey, you're giving an old pregnant lady a thrill."

"Glad to help. Now, if only I could get some sleep tonight."

"Look who's talking about not sleeping. What if you had

twenty pounds of extra baby weight around your middle and no way to get comfortable."

"I wish," Ali said with longing.

Rena's tone sobered a minute. "You'll get there, Ali."

"Will I?"

"Remember what I said about being patient."

"I'm trying. But with every beat of my heart I want to jump Joe's bones and tell him how I feel."

Rena laughed. "Your time will come. Have faith."

"I do."

After Ali finished her conversation with Rena, she felt much better. She poured herself a glass of milk and grabbed an organic oatmeal cookie Royce had brought over the other day.

She sat down on her sofa, propped her feet up and clicked on the television remote. She found her favorite cooking show, munched on the cookie and sipped milk, settling in for a relaxing evening.

Not five minutes into *The Rachel Ray Show,* breaking news flashed on the screen. Images of a yacht off the Florida waters appeared, and the newscaster's somber tone alerted Ali immediately—she recognized the yacht. She leaned forward and turned up the volume on the television.

"While Senator Rodney Holcomb and his family vacationed off the coast of Florida on his yacht, Harold Holcomb, the senator's younger brother, had what is alleged to be a heart attack. The senator acted quickly administering CPR, but it is unknown whether his attempts helped to save his brother's life. Harold Holcomb was airlifted to West Palm Beach Memorial Hospital, along with his wife. The senator will be making a statement in the morning...."

Ali bounded up from the sofa and reached for her phone, dialing her mother's number. Thoughts of their last conversation ran through her head.

We're fighting all the time.

He's so strong-willed. He never gives in.

Her mother married a powerful man, a man who was accustomed to making all the decisions. Justine wouldn't let him get away with bulldozing her. She needed to have a say-so in their lives. Originally, according to her mother, it was what Harold liked best about her. She'd always challenged him.

And what had Ali told her mother to do?

Take a vacation. Get away from their routine and daily life. Take a cruise and talk things out.

Apparently, that's what they'd been doing, trying to work out their differences, perhaps.

Her mother's cell phone rang and rang. Ali's nerves went raw. After the sixth ring, finally someone picked up. "Mom, Mom, is that you? Are you okay?"

"This is Judy Holcomb. Is this Ali?"

It was the senator's wife. "Yes, it's me, Judy. Where's my mother?" Ali couldn't keep the panic out of her voice.

"We're in West Palm Beach Memorial Hospital. Your mom's in with Harry. She's pretty shaken up."

"And what about Harold? The news report said he had a heart attack."

"Yes, they've confirmed it now. They are running tests."

"I'm so sorry. Mom must be beside herself."

"Well, yes. I won't lie to you. She's quite upset. It was a shock to all of us. We were having such a nice time after dinner. Harold and your mother were walking on deck, and she came running for help, crying that Harry had collapsed. We assumed it was a heart attack, and Rodney gave him CPR. We don't yet know the damage, if any, to his heart."

"Oh, I pray he'll be all right. Thankfully your husband acted quickly."

"That's what the doctors are saying. He may have saved Harry's life."

"I should be there," Ali said, thinking aloud.

Judy didn't hesitate to reply. "Ali, I've never seen your mother so frightened and nervous. I tried my best to calm her down. Perhaps you should come."

"I'll take the red-eye. Please tell my mom that I'm on my way."

"I will. I know she needs you, Ali," Judy said. "She's trying to be so brave, but having you here would really help."

"I should be there early in the morning."

"I'll tell her you're coming. I think it's going to be a long night."

For both of us, Ali thought. She hung up and made reservations at Sacramento International Airport. Then she packed an overnight bag. If she left right now, she'd have just enough time to make her flight.

Ali waited until she checked in for her flight before calling Joe. She'd almost forgotten about him and their weekend plans. She couldn't imagine having Joe show up at her door in the morning and realize he'd been stood up. It was either that or calling him at midnight.

He answered on the third ring. "Hello," he grumbled, his voice raspy. It was clear that she'd woken him up. "Sorry to call so late, Joe."

"Ali?"

"Yes, it's Ali. I'm at the airport. My stepfather had a heart attack. I'm on my way now to be with him and my mom."

"Oh," he said, his voice sounding more alert now. "Sorry to hear that." He seemed a little confused.

"I'll be in Florida this weekend. Just wanted you to know in advance so you could cancel the bike tour for tomorrow. I'm sorry. I was really looking forward to it."

"Yeah, I was, too," he said. "But that can be rescheduled. You need to be with your family now, Ali."

Ali's heart surged. She didn't have much family, and she hadn't had a great childhood, but she loved her mother, even with her flaws. And she knew that she needed to be by Justine's side now. "I hope to be back by Monday."

"Don't worry about it. I can manage at the office without you for a few days," he said, and then added, "barely. Take the time you need."

Ali smiled for the first time since she'd seen that newscast on television tonight, and her mood lightened a bit. "Thank you, Joe."

"Have a good flight. I'll see you when you get back."

"Okay."

Ali hung up the phone, and her good mood immediately vanished. Oh, how she wished Joe were here, lending comfort and holding her, telling her it was going to be all right. How she longed to hear him say he loved her. The bike tour would have been a means for them to get closer, to spend time together outside of work.

Then a distressing thought struck. Could this be an omen of some kind? Maybe the deception and her plans to entice Joe into noticing her were backfiring. Maybe it just wasn't meant to be. After all, she was forcing every situation with Joe, and that's not how she normally operated.

Ali shoved those plaguing thoughts aside when she boarded the plane. She dozed during the flight, and before she knew it, she had arrived in West Palm Beach.

* * *

At precisely 9:00 a.m. Ali walked into the hospital, eager now to see her mother and praying that Harold had held on during the night.

"Ali!" Her mother dashed across the waiting room when she spotted her, tears flowing down her cheeks. Ali feared the worst.

When her mother reached her, she wrapped her arms around her and hugged her tight. "I'm so glad you're here."

"I am, too, Mom. How's Harold?"

Justine began crying again, and Ali walked her over to a bench seat and guided her down. Ali sat next to her and offered her a tissue. "He's holding on. I'm to blame for this. His heart attack is all my fault, Ali."

Ali's mother broke down, crying so hard, Ali had to hold her as if she were a baby. She cradled her in her arms and held her, rocking her back and forth. "No, Mom, it's not your fault. It's not."

"We were always arguing," she said between sobs. "I wouldn't give in."

"But that means he wouldn't give in either, right?"

"Right, but what if I caused this? What if…he dies? Oh, Ali. I couldn't live with myself."

Now was not the time for blame, and Ali understood that. "Let's hope he survives this, Mom. Then you both will have to change your ways. But let's not think about that. Let's focus our energy on Harold getting better."

"I just wanted him to slow down," her mother said quietly, her voice drifting. "We're not getting any younger, and I wanted him to stop working so much. He needed a vacation. We both did. It was the best advice, Ali. I finally got him to go on that cruise and we were having—" she stopped to take a breath and dab at her eyes with the tissue

"—we were having such a lovely time. We hadn't argued once on the yacht. Then all of a sudden, he collapsed, right there on the deck, and I thought he'd died."

"You got him help quickly. The senator might have saved his life."

Justine looked at her with soulful eyes. "I've been praying so hard for him, Ali. Lord, I love him so much."

Ali had never seen her mother react this way. Justine had always been indulged. Her husbands had spoiled her, and she'd relished their attention and gifts. In some ways, her mother had been selfish and self-indulgent.

But Justine Holcomb was a different woman now. Ali saw the truth in her eyes and heard the sincerity in her tone. Her mother had finally and fully fallen in love.

Ali's heart ached thinking her mom might lose Harold now, after she'd found the right man to share her life with. It had taken her five tries to do it and all those years of searching. Ali was convinced that her mother would fall apart if she lost her husband.

Though Ali would never want to walk in her shoes, she believed her mother was ultimately a good person. She refused to believe any of the hushed rumors that Justine was a gold digger.

She shuddered at the thought. It was such an ugly label.

"Mom, let's go grab a cup of coffee. I'm operating on a few hours' sleep."

Her mom nodded and they rose, Justine taking one quick look at the critical care room where Harold rested.

"C'mon, Mom. He's not alone. And I bet you've been in there all night with him. Let's get you some breakfast."

On Saturday, Joe rose early and swam his usual one hundred laps in the pool. He ate a breakfast of cooked oats, toast, eggs and orange juice on the patio then showered and dressed. Glancing at his watch, seeing the time approach when he would have been picking up Ali for their bike tour, disappointment registered.

He admitted how much he'd been looking forward to spending the day with her. He wondered how she was faring, taking the red-eye and flying across the continent in the middle of the night, not knowing what she'd find when she arrived. He realized he didn't really know much about Ali's family life. He'd never asked. Had she been close to her stepfather? How would she handle it if the worst happened?

Joe hoped, for Ali's sake, that she wouldn't have to deal with any loss. Having lost his mother and father, he knew firsthand about grieving and heartache.

He didn't want Ali to go through that alone.

Joe drove to the office and finished up some work he'd had to do. "Busy work," he muttered, staring at his computer screen after he'd accomplished his goal in thirty minutes.

He felt at loose ends today with thoughts of Ali never far from his mind. But Joe was resolute, if anything. His vow to keep his distance and not get involved with her was imperative to his sense of well-being. Unfortunately, he couldn't stop thinking about her. He'd glanced at the phone a half dozen times since walking into his office, tempted to call her.

But wouldn't she read something more into that than he intended?

When his phone rang, Joe's heart sped up. He grabbed his iPhone and quickly saw Tony's image pop up on the screen. He felt a measure of disappointment and almost laughed aloud at how ridiculous that was. Had he really thought Ali would call him? She'd barely been gone twelve hours.

"Grapes to grow," he answered.

Tony chuckled. "Wine to flow."

And Nick's line was always "Cash to blow." Typical of Nick, Joe thought. He shook his head. "I don't know why I said that."

"It's been years. Reminds me of high school."

"Yeah, the old man didn't appreciate our little jingle," Joe mused.

"He was more bark than bite. I'd catch him with a grin, when he thought I couldn't see him."

Joe surmised that people tended to remember the good about a person after they were gone, choosing to forget the bad.

"I thought I'd be speaking into your voice mail. Rena said you had a hot date with Ali today."

"Nothing hot about it, Tony. Unless you call a bike tour around Napa a big deal. Ali had an emergency last night. She flew to Florida."

"What kind of emergency?"

"Her stepfather had a heart attack."

"That's rough. How's he doing today?"

"I don't know. I haven't heard from her."

"You haven't called her?"

Joe inhaled sharply. "No."

Tony was silent for a few seconds. "Okay. So what are you doing today? Don't tell me you're at the office."

"Okay, I won't."

"Joe, you can't spend all your time there. Give yourself a break."

"Just clearing up some last-minute things." Joe didn't know why he had to defend his efficiency, yet both of his brothers taunted him about it, until they needed his help with something. Then, they praised his abilities and work ethic.

"Rena and I are coming into town for lunch. Why don't you join us?"

"Yes, join us," he heard Rena call into the phone.

"There," Tony said. "You can't very well refuse a pregnant lady."

"Well, in that case, sure. I'll have lunch with you."

"My wife's got a craving for Italian food. Meet us in a half hour at the Cordial Contessa," Tony said.

"I'll be there," he said.

Thirty minutes later, Joe strode into the quiet, dimly lit restaurant and found his brother nuzzling Rena's neck at a table set for three. "Maybe I should bow out gracefully and let you two get a room."

Rena chuckled and lifted her arms up in welcome. "Come here, Joe, and give your sister-in-law a hug."

After giving her a gentle embrace, he kissed her cheek. "It's good to see you, Rena." Then he turned to shake Tony's hand.

"I'm glad we dragged you outta that pit," his brother teased.

"You mean, the pit with state-of-the-art technology that keeps a roof over all of our heads?"

"The very one," Tony replied. "What brought you into the office today?"

"I'm finishing up a weekly accounting, that's all. Crunching numbers."

"What else is new." Tony looked at Rena and winked. "You need to get a life, Joe."

"I have a life. *A good life*. And I'm trying to keep it that way."

"Meaning?"

"I've been following current buying trends and working

up graphs. Even in today's lackluster economy, people are still drinking wine—to drown out their troubles, maybe. But sales are holding strong."

"That *is* good news," Rena said. "I'm happy to say that Purple Fields is holding its own, too." Rena glanced at the menu. "I'm famished. It all looks so good. Today, I'm going to eat for two and not feel guilty about it."

They gave their orders to the waiter, and the meal was delivered shortly after. They sat in silence for the most part, gobbling down their meals. The veal scallopini was the best Joe had ever had.

"Mmm," Rena said after finishing off her meal. She leaned back and patted her stomach. "So good."

"My pasta primavera was perfect," Tony said. "This place is giving Alberto's a run for the money."

"Yeah, why aren't we eating there?" Joe asked. The Carlinos owned half interest in an Italian restaurant that served Tuscany fare.

"My fault," Rena said with a quick smile. "After having this yummy lemon sesame chicken pasta dish at our reception, I've been craving it all week. The chef is a genius."

And just as she spoke of him, Royce walked out of the kitchen, holding a tray of pastries. "For the newlyweds," he said, placing the delicate tray onto the table. "I'm so happy you came to the Contessa for lunch."

"I told you we would," Rena said. "I've been craving this dish all week. Oh, and these pastries. I can't possibly pass them up."

Royce looked pleased. "Enjoy them."

"Thank you," Tony said.

Royce glanced at each of them. "Would any of you like some coffee?"

"I'm fine with water," Rena said.

"I'm fine, too," Tony added.

"No thanks," Joe said, inexplicably miffed that Royce had made such an impression on Rena and Tony.

"Royce," Rena began. "I know I told you this before, but I'm very glad Ali recommended you for our reception. Everyone complimented the food."

"That's very nice of you to say. Ali's been a good friend."

Rena nodded. "She's a special friend to me, too. I hope she's doing okay."

"She's fine. I spoke with her this morning."

Joe's head snapped up, and he narrowed his gaze on Royce. "How's her stepfather?" he asked. But what he really wanted to ask was why the *hell* did she call you?

"Out of danger, but looks like he'll have a long rehab period. Ali said her mom was really upset, but they are both relieved that he'll make a full recovery in time."

"Oh, that's good to hear," Rena said, glancing at Joe. She seemed to read his mind. "Did she say when she'd be coming home?"

"Probably in a few days. I'm picking up her mail and newspapers and watering her plants for her."

Joe sat there, keeping a steady noncommittal look on his face, while inside his gut churned. "I told her to take as much time as she needs."

"She's planning on calling you tomorrow."

Joe didn't want Royce's blow-by-blow accounting as to Ali's plans. The guy really irked him. Or rather, as Joe mulled it over methodically in his mind, Ali's relationship with Royce was the true source of his irritation.

He nodded and looked away.

"Well, I'd better get back in the kitchen. Enjoy the rest of your meal."

Once Royce walked away, Rena and Tony stared at him.

Joe adjusted his glasses on his nose then spoke when he couldn't ignore their stares another second. "What?"

Tony grinned. "You should see the look on your face. The Grinch has nothing on you."

"Tony," Rena said, grabbing his arm. "Let's drop it."

"Your wife is a smart lady," Joe said.

Tony aimed a headshake at him before digging into a raspberry tart. "Royce sure knows what he's doing," he added after he finished.

The hidden message in his brother's comment wasn't lost on him. "I told you I'm not interested in Ali."

"Who said anything about Ali?" Tony feigned innocence.

"Joe," Rena began. "I was hoping you could do us a favor. Tony and I were scheduled to go to San Francisco for the Annual Grapegrowers Convention. But I'm really feeling tired lately."

"You are?" Tony looked at her with surprise.

Rena turned to her husband and gave him a small smile. "I am, honey. I didn't want to worry you. It's just a combination of the pregnancy and not getting good sleep. I think the trip would exhaust me." She turned her attention toward him. "Would you mind going in our place?"

"You haven't missed that event since you took over Purple Fields," Tony said.

"I've never been pregnant before, either," Rena shot back a little too quickly. Joe had a sneaking suspicion this was a setup, but he couldn't refuse Rena the favor.

"I'll go. Don't worry, Rena."

"I know it's a lot to ask on short notice." Rena seemed really contrite.

Joe gestured away her worry. "I'll have help. I'll take along a secretary."

"That's a good idea," Rena said, seemingly satisfied.

"I think Jody Millwood might be available."

Rena's eyes went wide with shock, and Joe gave himself a mental pat on the back. Rena's expression spoke volumes. He knew what she was up to.

"The woman from your sales office?" Rena's voice elevated slightly. "She's...well, she's a bit—I think she spends her weekends with her grandchildren."

Grinning, Tony caught on and shook his head. "Sweetheart."

Joe frowned. "You two don't give up, do you?" He didn't give them time to protest. "You know what, if I take Ali to the convention and come out of it unscathed, then will you both get the message and quit matchmaking?"

Rena clamped her mouth shut and nodded.

Tony smiled.

"Fine, then," he said. "I'll hold you to your word."

Seven

On Sunday night, just as Joe was retiring for bed, his cell phone rang. He answered it and heard Ali's voice on the other end. "Hello, Joe. It's Ali." She sounded somber, so unlike herself.

"Ali? Are you okay?"

"I'm doing fine, I guess. Just a little tired." He heard the sigh in her voice and wanted to kick himself for not calling her. He glanced at the clock. It was after one in the morning in Florida. "I wanted you to know that I won't be coming back until Tuesday night. I'll take some personal time, if that's okay."

"Don't worry about that, Ali." Damn it, she sounded so businesslike, calling her boss to report her absence at work. Joe thought they'd progressed beyond that. "Take all the time you need."

"Thank you."

"How's your stepfather?"

"He's out of the woods, right now. There was some damage to his heart, but thankfully he'll recover with rehab and a lifestyle change."

"And how's your mother doing?"

"She was overwrought when I first got here, but she's doing much better now. She's taken hold of the situation, making plans for when Harold comes home and how things will change for the better. I'm really proud of her."

There was a lull, and Joe sensed Ali was ready to end the conversation. But he wasn't. He missed talking to her. During the past four weeks, they'd spent a lot of time together at the office and working on the wedding reception. He didn't like how he felt at loose ends without her. "What are you doing now? It's late there, isn't it?"

"Yes, it's past one. I'm getting ready for bed."

Joe's mind took a U-turn, envisioning her slipping off her clothes, donning a sheer nightie that would keep her cool in the humid Florida climate, her hair unrestrained and flowing in curls past her shoulders. He stifled a groan.

"What are you doing?" she asked softly.

"The same. Getting into bed." He flashed a vision of Ali joining him under the sheets and couldn't deny how much the thought pleased him.

"Sorry if I disturbed you."

"Not at all." He missed her. And it was on the tip of his tongue to say so. He should have called her. He should have at least expressed his concern for her stepfather and checked in on her. But his vow to steer clear of her had stopped him. "I'm glad you called."

"You are?" She sounded doubtful.

"The fact is," he began, fumbling with the right words to say, "it's good to hear your voice. I was concerned for you."

"Oh, well, I'm fine. I appreciate your concern."

Joe winced. They were speaking as if they were total strangers, their conversation stilted and deliberate. And had he heard a note of disappointment in her voice? Should he have said more? "I'd better let you get to sleep."

"You, too. Sleep tight, Joe."

He didn't know how much sleep he'd get, but one thing was certain—his entire body was as *tight* as a hangman's noose.

"Good night, Ali."

Frustrated, Joe climbed into bed, realizing his hands-off approach with Ali was backfiring. The more he kept to his resolve, the more he wanted her.

And this wasn't a problem he could solve with his unique mathematical skills.

As soon as the plane landed at Sacramento Airport, Ali grabbed her overnight bag and scooted down the narrow aisle, glad to be back in California. She'd had an exhausting four days and felt like the scourge of the earth in her clothes. She'd tossed together only one outfit change in her hurry to get to Florida, and she hadn't had time to do any laundry while she was there. The clothes on her back were beyond wrinkled.

Ali walked down the long corridor leading to the airport terminal, her body aching and her eyes burning from the little bit of sleep she'd gotten these past days. But the minute she glanced up and saw Joe, standing there waiting at the gate, a burst of stunned joy entered her heart.

He tipped his head when he spotted her. She'd never been so glad to see anyone in her life. Joe, with his hair slightly disheveled, wearing jeans and a black T-shirt, looking better than any of God's creations, was the one and only person who could lift Ali's spirits. She wanted to run to him with outstretched arms and kiss him silly.

But the new Ali would never do something like that. Fake Ali, as she called herself, would simply approach him with a smile, which was exactly what she did.

"Hi, Joe," she said, her breath nearly catching.

"It's good to see you, Ali."

She blinked and waited. Joe noted her hesitation. Then he opened his arms, and she walked straight into them. "Are you okay?"

She nodded, digging her head into his chest and holding on. Tears stung her eyes. She kept telling herself he'd never be here if she hadn't begun this ruse. Somehow that justified her actions. "How did you know what flight I was on?"

"I didn't. But this was the only evening flight coming in from Florida. It seemed logical."

God, how she loved him. "Thank you for coming. But I have my car here."

"Don't worry about your car. I'll have someone pick it up for you. I brought a limo. Thought you'd like a quiet drive home."

Ali nodded. "Sounds like heaven. This is very kind of you."

Joe squeezed her tight and then looked into her eyes. "You've had a rough few days, haven't you?"

Ali cringed. She must look awful. "Yes."

Joe hadn't called her during those four days, and as ridiculous as it seemed, her feelings had been hurt. She'd thought they were closer than that. She'd thought that Joe would have given her more support. Those few kisses they'd shared had given her hope, but she'd come to realize that maybe Joe would never come around. Not in the way she wanted.

"I'm sorry." There was a depth to his tone she hadn't heard before.

"Sorry?"

"That you had to go through that alone."

She shrugged. "At least, my mother is handling it better now."

"Thanks to you, Ali. I bet you being there meant the world to her. You have a way of making people feel better."

When Joe said things like that to her, it made her want to shed tears. He could be so sensitive at times. "I hope so."

Joe snatched her bag from her hand and guided her out to the parking lot. True to his word, a black limo was waiting with a chauffeur who had opened the door the minute he'd spotted Joe.

"After you," he said to her, then handed over her bag to the driver. Joe slid in beside her, and the door was closed.

Ali couldn't keep from asking, "I thought you were the green guy in the family."

Joe laughed. "I am," he said as if he'd just been caught cheating on an exam. "But some things are just worth the carbon footprint."

Ali smiled. "Thank you, Joe."

"Lean back and relax. You must be exhausted."

Ali did just that. She slid down in her seat a little and rested her head back. "Do I look that bad?"

"No, actually you look amazing."

She tilted her head to gaze at him. Those dark eyes behind the glasses appeared sincere. It was on the tip of her tongue to tell him how much she'd missed him, but Ali held back.

Joe slid a little closer and opened his arms to her. "Lean against me, and close your eyes."

The invitation was too tempting to refuse. Silently, she

did as she was told. The minute she rested her head on his chest and his arm wrapped around her, a sense of peace and fulfillment washed over her. "Mmm."

"Try to sleep," he whispered.

"You make the best pillow, Joe," she said, cuddling into him. "I think I will."

Ali knew the exact moment the limo rolled to a halt. Her eyes snapped open. Joe held her against him as she slept, and now she wished she hadn't woken up at all. She wished she could stay in his arms forever.

"You're home," Joe said quietly.

She *felt* at home in his arms. At least now, she could say she'd slept with Joe—or rather *on* him. She slid out of his grasp and straightened in her seat. Oh God, had she snored? "How long was I out?"

"Just about the entire way, Ali."

"Was I, um—"

"Peaceful. And quiet as a mouse."

Thank God. She blinked then nodded, trying to wake up fully.

"If you need another day to rest, take it."

"No," she said shaking her head. "I'm eager to get back to work. I, uh, missed it."

Joe smiled and looked deep into her eyes. "Good, because things don't run smoothly without you."

Ali searched his eyes. Should she read more into his compliment? "That's nice to hear."

The chauffeur opened the door on her side. "Well, this is my stop."

"I'll walk with you." Joe got out on his side of the limo, grabbed her overnight bag from his driver and then met up with her. They walked to her condo in silence. When she reached her front door, she turned to him. "Thanks for the ride. It meant a lot."

Joe searched her eyes and nodded. "You're welcome." He hesitated for a moment, then scratched his head and let go a deep sigh. "Ali, maybe now's not the best time to ask, but are you free this weekend?"

This weekend? Ali's sluggish body registered a happy alert. Was he going to reschedule their bike tour? There wasn't anything she had planned that she wouldn't cancel for him. "Yes, I think so."

"I'm afraid it's a working weekend in San Francisco. I'm elected to go to the Annual Grapegrowers Convention. Rena and Tony were planning on going, but Rena isn't up to it."

"So, they asked you to go?"

He nodded. "And I need your help, if you're willing to work the weekend."

Ali held her smile inside. An entire weekend in San Francisco with Joe? Every tired nerve in her body jumped for joy. This was a dream come true. "I can manage it. Sure, I'll go with you."

Joe seemed relieved. "I appreciate it, Ali. You never let me down."

Ali reached up and kissed him on the cheek. "Thanks again," she whispered, her breath caressing his throat.

Joe blinked and leaned closer, his intense gaze focused on her mouth.

Ali opened her door and slid inside, popping her head out. "I'll see you tomorrow."

She closed the door and held her breath. "Fake Ali," she muttered, "this better work because you just left the man of your dreams hanging outside your door."

Friday night hadn't come fast enough for Ali. She'd spoken with Rena out of concern for her well-being, only to have been assured that her pregnant friend was doing just fine. Rena confessed that begging off from this trip was a perfect way to get Ali together with Joe in a romantic setting. She'd been darn proud of her plan, and Ali had thanked her matchmaking friend.

Each day since Ali had returned to work she'd found Joe staring at her from his desk, his expression intense. The minute they'd make eye contact, Joe would glance away as if he'd been caught with his hand in the cookie jar. She'd been encouraged and at the same time, felt like a complete con artist, gaining his attention by deceptive means. The subdued hair, the glasses and the conservative clothes were everything she was not.

But now as Ali put her clothes on hangers, her room just a few steps away from Joe's in San Francisco's luxurious Four Seasons Hotel, hope filled her thoughts. She couldn't keep from smiling. Joe, the rock-solid man who held her heart, would be picking her up soon for the Welcome Dinner in the Grand Ballroom.

She knew Joe didn't like these stuffed-shirt affairs. Neither did she, really. Though she'd never have refused this invitation, she wished that they were here for a romantic weekend rather than rounds of business dinners and lectures. "A girl can only dream," she said softly.

She had just enough time to freshen up and dress before Joe would be knocking on her door.

Ali swept her massive hair back into a tight ponytail, allowing a few curly tendrils to fall demurely along her cheeks. She applied a light coat of makeup, just a hint of green shadow to bring out the color of her eyes and a soft peach lip gloss to tint her lips.

She slipped into a black chiffon dress that Rena helped her pick out for tonight's formal dinner. With a square neckline that dipped just a little below her throat, no one could accuse her of looking indecent. The bodice accented her narrow waistline then flowed in wispy folds to just above her knees. An antique pearl necklace complimented the dress and of course, Ali wore the diamond bracelet Joe had given her. She put her feet into two-inch black pumps and finished the whole look by putting on her glasses.

She glanced in the mirror. "You fraud," she whispered.

The knock at the door came precisely at seven o'clock.

Excitement coursed through her system. She dashed to the door, then remembered to compose herself, taking a steadying breath before opening it slowly.

When she glanced at Joe standing at her threshold in a black tuxedo, his dark hair smoothed back and curling at the base of his neck, his face tanned from morning swims and those dark eyes, intense once again, she might have swooned had she been faint of heart.

"You look very nice, Joe," she said quietly.

Joe's lips curved up in a killer smile. "Thanks. And you look beautiful tonight, Ali."

She did? She thought otherwise—the mundane dress was boring with a capital *B*. "Thank you."

"Are you ready to schmooze?"

Ali smiled. "As ready as you are."

Joe frowned. "Not the best way to spend your weekend, is it?"

Was he kidding? There was no place she'd rather be. Ali tilted her head. "I'll survive."

Once at the Welcome Dinner, Ali remembered that this was indeed a working weekend. She kept her eyes and ears open and networked with several winemakers along with Joe. They took their seats after the cocktail hour and listened to the keynote speaker's views on winemaking and the economy.

They dined at a table with three CEOs and their wives, Ali entering into light conversation with the women about West Coast versus East Coast fashions. Ali engaged them while Joe spoke with the men at the table, and after a sumptuous meal, all business was concluded.

A seven-piece orchestra began playing what Ali could only describe as nondescript music. The mellow tunes allowed for close proximity on the dance floor, and as men swept their partners to the center of the room, Ali found Joe deep in conversation with the head of Paladino Wines.

When she was tapped on the shoulder from behind, she turned to a man with hopeful eyes. "Would you care to dance?"

Ali hesitated for one second, glancing at Joe, who seemed oblivious to anything but the deep conversation he engaged in. She couldn't see refusing the middle-aged man, whose name tag revealed him to be a master sommelier. "Yes, thank you."

The man pulled out her chair and waited as she rose and headed for the dance floor. "My name is Juan Delgado," he said.

"Ali Pendrake."

He nodded with a smile and guided her to the dance floor, then took her into his arms as the music played on and literally swept her off her feet. Juan Delgado was not only a wine professional but a marvelous dancer.

Juan took dancing seriously, and there was no time for talking. Ali was curious about him, the man with kind eyes and exquisite dance steps. She'd never felt so weightless while dancing before.

"You dance with spirit, Ali," he said as the dance ended. "If I could confess, I'd love to dance with you all evening."

Juan continued to hold her waist, and his interest deepened to another level, one Ali recognized as dangerous. She glanced at her table and found Joe gone. Scanning the room, she locked gazes with him on the edge of the dance floor, his face tight, his body held in a rigid stance.

Ali had never seen that expression on Joe's face. Her pulse raced with dread. Had she done something wrong?

She turned back to Juan. "You're a wonderful dancer, Juan, and I did enjoy the dance, but I'm afraid I'm not here to dance. I must get back to my table. I'm…working."

"Aren't we all?" The casual tone in his voice belied the passion in his eyes.

Ali broke all contact with him. "Really, Juan. I have to go. Thank you for the dance."

Ali turned and walked straight into Joe, smacking into his chest. "Oh!"

He took her hand. "I need to speak with you," he said, leading her off the dance floor, then out of the ballroom entirely. Ali's heels scraped the floor trying to keep up.

Joe kept walking at a brisk pace, and Ali's mind whirled with confusion. Once he found a secluded alcove in the hallway, he pulled her inside and turned her, pressing her back to the wainscoted wall.

Ali had no time to react. Joe braced the wall behind her with both hands, brushed his hips against her, then crushed his mouth to hers, claiming her in an all-consuming kiss.

The kiss went long and deep, and tears of joy filled her closed eyes. Her mind screamed her love for him, her body turning to jelly in an instant.

Whatever this was, Ali had never experienced such intense passion. This kiss was urgent and fiery beyond her wildest dreams.

Joe didn't let her come up for air. He kissed her again and again, his musky scent filling her nostrils, his powerful body taking full control. Ali relished every second of his passion. Then finally, when both of them were ragged and nearly breathless, Joe broke away to look at her, his eyes gleaming with dark intensity.

"I like you, Ali."

"I like you, too, Joe."

"Wanna blow this damn convention?"

She thought he'd never ask. "Blow it?"

"I want you, Ali," he said, his voice a deep rasp.

Ali's brows rose in response.

He cupped the nape of her neck and eased her head back, planting tiny mind-blowing kisses along her throat. "I want to make love to you all weekend."

"Oh, Joe," she whispered. Her heart nearly burst from her chest.

"I don't want to see you in the arms of another man. I want that right for myself." His next kiss curled her toes. "You have to know I didn't plan this, but it's happening and I can't stop it."

"I know," she whispered. "I know. I don't want you to stop."

Joe gazed into her eyes for a brief moment and smiled. "Then let's go."

He grabbed her hand and led her to the elevator. They waited impatiently, and once the elevator dinged and the doors opened, Joe strode inside, punched the button and took her into his arms again. He kissed her like there was no tomorrow, and they were both breathless when they reached the sixteenth floor. Joe kissed her all the way to the room, both stumbling, and Ali thought she'd truly died and gone to heaven.

They fumbled with the keycard to open the door between kisses, and once inside, Joe shoved the door closed behind them. "I'm usually smoother than this."

Heart pumping like crazy, Ali smiled. "You're doing just fine."

Joe laughed. "Then in that case." He lifted her up in one fluid motion and strode into the bedroom. She wrapped her arms around his neck. Once he reached the king-size bed, he lowered her gently, and Ali released her hold on him.

He took his glasses off and then reached down to take hers off, as well. Then he pulled off the band that confined her auburn hair. He fingered through her tresses, watching the hair spread out across the pillow. "Amazing." He stood tall, straightening out, his gaze fixed on her. Loosening his tie, he removed his tux jacket and unbuttoned the first few buttons of his shirt.

Ali's breath caught. How many times had she dreamed of being with Joe like this?

Joe kicked off his shoes and joined her on the bed, crushing her again with kisses that left no room for doubt about where they were heading.

All the while, Ali held back. She wanted to strip Joe of his clothes, wiggle out of hers and unleash her own fiery passion. But Fake Ali couldn't do that. She had a role to play, and she reminded herself of the journey that had gotten her to this point.

Let it go, Ali. You're where you want to be.

Ali shoved her guilt and self-loathing out of her mind. With Joe beside her, it was easy to do.

He parted her lips and drove his tongue into her mouth. Ali let out a little moan of pleasure. The kisses went on and on until Joe's body went completely rigid with need.

He pulled away and yanked off his shirt, tossing it aside, then worked the back zipper of her dress. He eased it up and over her head, leaving her naked but for her black bra and bikini panties.

Joe took a good look and inhaled deeply, "Ah, Ali."

Ali gazed at him, consumed with love.

"You're beautiful."

So was he. His chest bare, she filled her gaze with broad shoulders, powerful arms and a ripped torso. Every ounce of her wanted to jump his bones right now, but Ali only reached for him and laid his hand on her breast.

Joe took it from there—his passion intensified, his eyes narrowed. The look he shot her was so steamy her insides melted.

He released her full breasts from their bonds and palmed her firmly, his hand rough against her soft skin. Next he grazed over her nipple, the tip pebbling hard. Over and over he touched her, his hand flat against her skin as he moved, explored, caressed and admired her body.

Her breaths shot out in short bursts, her pulse raced. "Oh, Joe," she murmured.

"Hang on, Ali." And before she knew it they were both fully unclothed. Joe slid his hands all over her naked body, kissing her senseless. Gliding his hand lower, anticipation built and every nerve ending tingled with intense awareness. This is the moment she'd wanted for so long—the moment when she and Joe would come together.

He cupped her between the legs and touched her gently at first, then with more and more intensity. Fireworks shot off in her head, and she moved under his ministrations. He stroked her like he would a keyboard with quickness and efficiency, his fingers masterful.

Ali returned his kisses, moved in harmony with him and clung to him as he lifted himself over her. Protection—that had almost magically appeared—was fixed in place. He spread her legs apart.

Ali held her breath and welcomed him with an arch of

her back. And then Joe was joined with her, his erection full and thick, driving into her with a slow deliberate thrust.

Joe's body shook. A low guttural groan of pleasure released from his throat. The union brought tears to Ali's eyes. Then she forgot all else as Joe deepened his thrust, filling her full.

He cursed, and she knew it was from the sheer awe of satisfaction he experienced. She felt it, too. Nothing in her life would ever compare to this.

He gazed down at her, and she curved her lips in a smile of encouragement. Then Joe let loose, his thrusts quick and fiery. He braced his hands on her hips and lifted her even higher, his body coated with moisture, his expression beautifully intense.

Ali relished his lovemaking, moving with him and enjoying each bit of stirring pleasure he brought her. She gave him full command of her body. His stamina amazed her, and she thought of all those early-morning workouts in the pool.

Ali's body reached an explosive point, and she threw her head back and arched way up, letting go of her control. Her release came in exquisite short bursts of surrender. She huffed out quiet little moans and looked up at Joe.

Controlling his own need, he held back until she'd been fully sated. Then his pace and rhythm changed to a frenzied assault, his thrusts hard and demanding until he, too, met with a powerful orgasm.

She watched his face change, his passion release and his body contract. It was stunning and magnificent, and Ali was sure she'd never witnessed anything so inspiring.

Joe eased down onto her, taking her head in his hands, and kissed her soundly. "Did I mention how much I like you?"

"You mentioned that," Ali answered with a chuckle.

Joe rolled off her, and her heated body cooled considerably without him. He turned toward her, his head braced on his hand. He seemed to have something on his mind. Ali recognized when he was in deep concentration. Then he blinked and shot her a serious look. "Stay with me tonight."

The only way she'd leave is if he threw her out. "Yes."

Joe took her into his arms, and they lay in silence together. Shortly after they climbed under the sheets, Joe fell asleep first and Ali watched him take deep breaths, wrapped in his arms.

She wished every night could be this perfect.

Eight

Joe's natural alarm clock woke him at six in the morning to the soft sound of Ali breathing. Her back was toward him, and the uniquely feminine curve of her body next to his was a sexy sight to behold. Her hair fell in wispy waves past her shoulders. On impulse, Joe reached out and touched a few strands, curling his fingers into the thick locks.

He closed his eyes and breathed in her scent.

He hadn't wanted this to happen. He'd fought it with all of his might, telling himself she was off-limits. And he'd been immune to her for a long while, looking at her through eyes that had once been deceived by a gorgeous face and killer body. He'd associated Ali with Sheila, perhaps unfairly, and he didn't want to go down that road of employer/employee ever again.

As a defense mechanism, Joe had dismissed Ali in his mind as nothing more than his very loyal business associate.

Then something changed.

Ali had changed, and he began viewing her differently. The changes in her weren't subtle, and he hadn't figured them out entirely. But Ali had become important to him—and not just because of how well they worked together.

Her neighbor Royce had given him a nudge, the irritating man who had more than friendship on his mind. Then last night, as she danced with her partner, who had all the grace of a swan, another man had approached Joe and asked if Ali was unattached.

"Is she fair game?" Those were the man's exact words.

Joe shot the guy a hard look, deciding right then and there that he couldn't let Ali go. He'd booted the man with a cold and foreboding "no" and claimed her the moment the dance ended.

Joe nibbled on her shoulder, impatient for her to wake up, and when she turned around, he wasn't disappointed. Her green eyes sparkled when she gazed at him, the light in those orbs as brilliant as the sun.

He smiled. "Good morning, beautiful."

Ali's grin went wide, then as abruptly as she'd brought it on, she pulled back on her smile. The light in her eyes faded. "Good morning, Joe."

They'd had an incredible night of lovemaking, yet all the while, Joe felt something was wrong. Not that he could call her on it. He wasn't going to look a gift horse in the mouth. He was where he wanted to be, in bed with an intelligent, gorgeous woman.

He caressed her arm, gliding his hands up and down. "How did you sleep?"

"Very well. You?"

"I always sleep well. But this morning, I woke up and there you were. Sorry, but I couldn't keep from touching you." He leaned closer and kissed her. "You okay with this?"

Ali smiled again, and Joe felt better seeing genuine joy on her face. "I'm great with this."

She turned and braced up on her elbow, her hair flowing over her bare shoulder. She painted a lovely picture draped in the sheets. He could go on looking at her, but when the sheet slipped down and exposed her full breasts, his body reacted instantly.

She covered up, almost shyly, and Joe's sanity returned. "Ali, listen. I don't know where this is going and I want to be fair to—"

"Shh," she said, pressing two fingers to his mouth. "Joe, let's not analyze this. If this is only for the weekend then I'm good with that. And if Monday comes and we have to go back to business as usual, I'll be fine."

Joe took all of that in, wondering if he'd misunderstood her the other night when she'd told him she didn't do one-night stands—not that Joe wanted that with her anyway. He realized he was ready for more. Maybe even a relationship with Ali.

It'd be tricky at work, but they'd find a way.

"And what if we don't?"

"Don't?" she asked.

"Don't go back to business as usual?"

The brightness in Ali's eyes returned full force, transforming her expression into one of pure joy. "I could manage that, too."

Purposely now, she let the sheet slide lower down, and Joe's mind went on temporary vacation. He kissed her on the lips then rolled them both until she was under him. "How am I going to see you at work and not think of you like this?"

Ali pressed her hands to his chest. Oh God, it felt so

damn good. He wished she'd done more of that last night. "I could ask you the same question."

Joe wanted to make love to her slowly, leisurely this time, and devour every inch of her body. He wanted to kiss her into oblivion and then bring them both to simultaneous satisfaction.

But all of that would have to wait. "We can't do this anymore," he said, climbing off her.

Ali appeared stunned. "The convention?"

"Hell no," Joe said, unable to hide his smile. "We're blowing it off, remember?"

"Then?"

"I need to make a trip to the hotel gift shop. I told you I didn't plan any of this. I'm out of protection."

Ali nibbled on her lower lip in that adorable way of hers. Then she smiled. "I'll be waiting."

"Sleep, Ali. I'll take my swim, make that pit stop and be back here before you know it. I'll send up breakfast."

Joe rose from the bed and then leaned down to kiss her again. She watched him move around the room bare naked, her eyes softly following him, and that was enough to send his wicked mind into overdrive.

He dressed into swim trunks, threw his arms into a shirt and headed out. His mind conjured images of Ali waiting for him in bed. It was damn hard to leave her.

Doing one hundred laps in the hotel's junior Olympic-size pool would be his only salvation.

He needed a cold splash of reality.

Ali rested her head against her pillow and sighed. Blissfully happy, she thought about the past twenty-four hours. Joe had finally come around, but was the cost of his ardor too high? She didn't have an answer, and right now, maybe she shouldn't care. All of her dreams were coming true.

Too restless to lie there, Ali rose from bed and realized all of her clothes were still in her hotel room. She donned the dress she wore last night, finger-combed her hair, slipped her feet back into her pumps and left the room.

Once she got to her hotel room, just steps down the hall, she flopped onto her bed, in a quandary. "What now?"

She didn't want Joe to come back and find her gone. She would love to dress in her sexiest lingerie and seduce him the minute he returned to his room. The whole scene played out in her mind in erotically vivid details.

But that wasn't in the plan. And she couldn't tempt fate. The woman Joe was attracted to wouldn't take the reins like that. She wouldn't be the aggressor and let loose. It saddened her to think that Joe might never be attracted to the Real Ali.

She'd give him more credit than that but for the fact that they'd worked together for one year and the Real Ali had never interested him. She'd fallen in love with her boss, and he'd never known it. He wouldn't allow himself to see the truth, much less give the idea any credence at all. He'd had his heart broken by a woman who'd worked for him, and he wasn't going there again. She understood that.

Ali glanced at the digital clock. She didn't have much time. She rose and quickly showered then dressed in a pair of slacks and a soft scoopneck knit top. She pulled her hair back and put on her fake eyeglasses.

She entered Joe's room, and shortly after, room service knocked. She let the waiter in and watched as he set up the table by the large bay window. The food smelled wonderful, and Ali's stomach growled.

Joe walked in just as she nibbled on toast and sipped orange juice. "Hi," she said. "How was your swim?"

He swept into the room, looking magnificent, his dark hair wet and curling at the nape of his neck, his shirt

rumpled and buttoned up only partway. Glancing at the
clothes she'd put on, he tossed a bag onto the nightstand
then strode over to her. "Too long." He bent down to take
her face into his hands. Searching her eyes first, he brushed
his lips to hers. "I missed you. Couldn't you sleep?"

"No, I, uh…I couldn't." She was still recovering from
Joe's admission that he'd missed her. "I didn't have any
clothes and with room service coming—"

"It's okay, Ali." He kissed her deeply this time, his mouth
making love to hers in a slow deliberate way that curled her
toes. Her mind went on autopilot, and she returned his kiss.
She was becoming accustomed to Joe kissing her, taking
liberties that only made her love him more.

"You should have seen the look on the clerk's face when
I walked in dripping wet and bought condoms."

Ali laughed. "I wish I'd been there." Then she thought
about it. "On second thought, no, I don't."

Joe grinned. "No, I guess you don't." He lifted the covers
from the food plates and seemed satisfied with what he
found. "Go on and eat if you're hungry. I'll take a quick
shower and be right back."

"I'll wait for you," she said softly. "We'll eat together."

Joe inhaled and peered at her as if she'd granted him
knighthood. "Thanks. I won't be long."

Ali heard the shower going on, and all sorts of erotic
images played out in her mind. She imagined steamy water
raining down his body, his skin sleek and slippery as he
soaped up.

Ali rose from the table and peered out the window,
trying to thwart her wayward, X-rated mind. The view from
the sixteenth floor was inspiring. She wrapped her arms
around her middle and enjoyed the rise of the sun over the

Pacific Ocean. The San Francisco Bay was a sight she'd only seen on postcards.

"I'll take you wherever you want to go today." From behind, Joe put his hands on her shoulders and planted little kisses on the nape of her neck.

Goose bumps rose up her arms from the thrill. He smelled fresh and clean, the subtle scent of lime on his skin.

Could she tell him she only wanted to see him between the sheets again? "I'll go wherever you want to take me, Joe."

Joe chuckled. "Then we won't get very far."

She turned around in his arms and stared into his eyes. "Oh, no?"

"The bedroom beckons, Ali." Then he gestured to the table. "And so does the food. C'mon," he said, taking her hand. It was only then she realized he had nothing on but a fluffy white towel around his waist. How would she get through the meal? "I know you're hungry. Sit," he ordered. "Eat up."

"Yes, boss."

Joe squeezed his eyes shut. "Ouch. Let's forget I'm your boss this weekend."

She wanted to ask him, but then who are you? My boyfriend? My lover? But Ali was too distracted by his ripped upper body to formulate any questions. And his lower body and the pleasures he'd evoked last night made her head swim. "I can do that."

She sat down and he joined her, sitting across the table. She had the most appealing view of a nearly naked Joe with San Francisco's famous skyline in the background. A girl couldn't ask for more.

Joe waited for her to fill her plate before he took his share. They dined on eggs Benedict, roasted potatoes and crepes with fresh summer fruit compote. The coffee was heavenly.

Once they finished the meal, Joe rose from the table and reached for her hand. She lifted up and stood before him, puzzled by the solemn look on his face. "I'm not the crafty old lecher trying to seduce my hot secretary, Ali, but I'd be lying if I said I didn't want to make love to you again."

Ali gulped air. She knew what Joe was trying to say. "I'm not doing anything I don't want to do, Joe. As far as I'm concerned, the sights in this room are pretty darn appealing. I don't need anything else."

He drew her in slowly, placing both hands on her waist. "I know how to compromise. We'll do a little of both. Well," he amended, "we'll do a *lot* of exploring in here and some exploring out there."

He sealed the deal with a long, lazy kiss. "How does that sound?"

Explore away, Joe, and leave no stone unturned, she wanted to say. "Wonderful."

Joe led the way, removing her clothes between kisses, and once inside the bedroom, he backed her up against the bed. They fell down together amid laughter, and Joe took his sweet time, discovering all of Ali's erotic zones.

He stroked her throat, tonguing his way up to her chin. Then he kissed her again and again in a sensual frenzy of lips and tongues. His hands inched their way down, and he caressed her breasts, flicking the tips until she bit down with silent urgent need.

Next, he traveled farther down, kissing her torso, her hips, her navel, gently easing his way lower. When he parted her legs and positioned himself, raising her hips to meet his mouth, he made love to her soft folds, until she nearly melted on the spot.

Joe didn't let up. He touched her everywhere, his hands roaming over her skin as he whispered soft endearments, his words muddling in her mind. He stroked her legs and arms with the same heat and passion, and once she was certain he'd caressed her everywhere, he stroked her apex again and again, this time pressing his palm against her silken, needy flesh.

"Joe," she huffed out, holding back her innermost desire to unleash her passion.

Joe removed his towel, and she watched as he rose above her like a magnificent animal ready to claim his mate. He was so beautiful that she wanted to cry.

Then he made love to her, entering her body and deepening his place in her heart. He owned her soul, and there was nothing she could do about it.

After, they stayed in bed and munched on the leftovers from breakfast, then on each other again. Morning became afternoon, and after they'd dozed in each other's arms for a few hours, she heard Joe stir beside her.

She opened her eyes to find him stretched out before her, his hands clasped behind his head. He'd put his glasses on, and the sexy picture he made with the silken sheet draped across his lower body and a look of pure contentment on his face, stole Ali's breath.

"It's almost three," he said.

Was that a hint for her to leave? She wasn't sure where she stood with him. They'd had hot sex, but he hadn't made any declarations to her other than soft stirring murmurs during the throes of passion. "Hmm. I guess I should go."

Joe turned to her. Shaking his head, his voice soft but commanding. "You're not going anywhere. I'll have your bags sent to my room. I want you here with me."

It was music to her ears.

"Don't you want that, too?" He draped his arm around her shoulder. She snuggled closer.

"Yes, of course I do."

"Look," he began, "I don't know where this is going, but I do know I don't want to waste a minute of this weekend without you. It's been a long time since—"

She lifted her head up to peer at him. "Since?"

"Since I've let myself get involved with anyone."

"Why?" Ali asked, though she suspected she knew the truth.

"Because I was engaged once, and to say it didn't work out would be an understatement."

"Tell me, Joe. What happened?"

Joe looked deep into her eyes with reluctance and regret. Through pain and anger, he admitted, "She wasn't the woman I thought she was."

Ali's heart plummeted. She was filled with dread and self-loathing at her own deception.

"I really loved her, or I thought I did at the time. A man has to think he's in love to offer marriage. It's only logical, right?"

"Right," Ali agreed, her pulse pounding.

"Ali, she worked for me before you came to Global."

He looked at her with guilt as if he'd done something unimaginable, while she was the true guilty one who was playing a dangerous game. "Go on."

"I should have never let it happen. She was a flashy woman, and I knew she was high maintenance when I got involved with her. I should have known better. She wanted me to change. To be someone I'm not. She thought after we got engaged that she'd be able to make me into someone more like Nick, for lack of a better example.

"The truth is, she wanted someone who liked to play at life, someone who tossed his money and power around to climb some sort of social ladder. Well, you know, I'm the green guy in the family. That's just not my thing. When she figured out that it wasn't going to happen, she found someone else. She left me for a wealthier, more powerful man."

"She broke your heart."

"I'm over it now. Have been for a long time."

"Oh, Joe, I'm deeply sorry." Ali meant it. She hated that Joe's heart had been broken, but at the same time she prayed that she wasn't going to do the same thing to him. Her deception haunted her, and she hated the weakness in her that caused her to lie to the man she adored, over and over again.

"I hope not too sorry?" He grinned and caressed her arms until she could barely think coherently.

"What do you mean?"

"You wouldn't be here with me if—"

"Oh." Then she smiled, too. "Yeah, I'm not *that* sorry."

Joe kissed her into oblivion, and she forgot all about her deception, his ex-fiancé and his heartbreak.

Nine

On Sunday morning, Joe took Ali to Chinatown, and as they strolled along the streets hand in hand, window-shopping, Joe found pleasure in buying Ali trinkets that sparked her interest. He held a shopping bag full of hand fans, embroidered handkerchiefs and little China dolls. He'd noticed Ali admiring a jade necklace, the delicate round disk an image of a Chinese garden, and he'd gone back to the store to purchase it.

"Oh, Joe," she said, with surprise in her voice. "I didn't expect you to—"

"I know, Ali. But I saw how much you liked it. I wanted you to have it."

Tears filled her eyes. "Thank you." She held the necklace to her chest. "I'll cherish it forever."

Joe took her hand, touched by her genuine appreciation, and they continued to stroll along. He spotted a shop selling hand-painted tea sets and tugged her along. "You have to have one," he said.

Ali shook her head. "No, Joe." She stopped on the street. "You've already given me too much."

Joe turned to her and cocked his head to one side. "Not as much as you've given me, honey."

And Joe realized the truth of that statement. He couldn't remember a time when he'd been so content. Ali had restored his faith in the opposite sex. He trusted her. They were compatible on every level. She was a decent, hardworking woman who didn't have an agenda where he was concerned.

"What have I given you?" she asked, puzzled.

Joe grinned. "A real good reason to get up and go to work every morning."

Ali let go a little gasp of surprise. "Joe."

"It's true. Now, c'mon. I want to show you the Golden Gate Bridge before lunch."

When they returned to the hotel room after lunch, Joe closed the door behind him and took Ali in his arms from behind. He pressed his body to hers and relished how right it felt to be near her. He kissed the back of her neck. "It was a good weekend." Then a chuckle escaped. "I dreaded coming here. I hate these things. But it turned out almost perfect."

Ali questioned him with a look. "*Almost* perfect?"

Joe nibbled on her neck some more. "You never invited me into your shower," he murmured.

Ali turned around in his arms and gazed deep into his eyes. "You don't need an invitation."

Joe raised his eyebrows. "I don't? Well then, I think you need a shower, Ali. You really worked up a sweat this morning." He sniffed the air around her playfully. "Yes, definitely. Oh, man, you really need to get clean."

Ali turned away from him and headed straight into the bedroom, kicking off her shoes and shedding clothes as she went.

Joe swallowed hard, watching her strip out of her clothes quietly. When she reached the master bathroom, he heard the shower door open then close and water rain down. He wasted no time yanking off his clothes and following her.

He joined her in the shower seconds later, and the sight of her, her hair wet and straight, hanging past her shoulders, her eyes brilliantly green and her body glistening with moisture, stole all of Joe's breath. "I wish we'd thought of this sooner. You're beautiful," he said. "Need some help?"

Ali handed him the bar of fragranced soap. Joe made a thick lather in his hands and stepped behind Ali. Winding his arms around her, he pressed the lather gently to her arched throat, then down along her shoulders, stroking her softly as his body became rock hard. Next, he slid his hands lower, soaping up under her arms and sliding his hands just under her ribs. Her intake of breath amplified his desire. He cupped her breasts, filling his hands with her weight, lathering her in circular motions, giving each perfect globe his undivided attention.

Ali moaned softly as he caressed her. She arched toward him, her body fitting his frame. His lust became almost tangible, his erection straining against her.

Joe spent a good deal of time massaging Ali, teasing and tormenting her breasts until she squirmed under his ministrations and huffed out deep breaths.

Joe was in no better shape. He was ready for more. He slid his hands lower, soaping her navel and just below. Steam built up in the shower, but nothing clouded Joe's vision of Ali, in his arms, bending to his will, allowing him the freedom to bring them both immense pleasure.

Joe cupped her between her legs, and she parted them, her moans of ecstasy mingling with his whispered demands. "Let go, baby. Let it happen."

He stroked her over and over, her body gyrating with his, his finger finding her core and breaching it. Beating rapidly, she moved with him, but Ali held back. He felt her control tight and sure.

Joe wanted to see her release, to see her relinquish that control and let go.

When she called his name like a plea, Joe's control snapped. There was only so much he could endure before realizing his own satisfaction. And Ali had him at his limit.

Joe moved against the thick shower glass and grabbed Ali's hips, sliding a hand along her back, bending her slightly. He leaned over her and cupped her breasts, then entered her soft folds from behind. She accommodated his body and both made quick adjustments to this new position. Then Joe drove a little deeper, holding Ali tight, their bodies joined in an erotic stance that heightened his pleasure even more.

He thrust slowly, deliberately, and Ali's body moved with him in a sensual rhythm. He slid his hand down to torment her most sensitive spot, his fingers urging her to completion as his thrusts grew more rapid, more demanding.

Joe kissed her shoulders, murmured loving words and moved with quicker strokes now, his body at its brink.

"Joe, now. Now," she rasped.

The soft flesh of her buttocks against his groin driving him crazy, he gripped her hips and pulled her against him. He drove deeper into her and split them both in two. Her release matching his, they moved in sync, Joe enjoying every movement, every gyration, until both were spent and fully sated.

They stayed in that erotic position until they caught their breath, then Joe whipped Ali around in his arms. When she wouldn't look into his eyes, he tipped her chin up and kissed her, wondering about her sudden shyness. She puzzled him in many ways, but all that was forgotten when she finally looked at him. Her gorgeous green eyes appeared soft and vulnerable, and a sudden flash jolted him. He was smart enough to realize that what he had with Ali wasn't just about sex.

He cared for her.

Deeply.

And he knew he was in trouble.

Joe left a sizable tip for housekeeping in his suite and then tipped the bellboy with a twenty after he'd brought their bags down to the lobby of the hotel. With Ali by his side, he'd never felt more content, and the staff was reaping the benefits of his good mood. The truth was that he hated to see the weekend come to a close.

As they waited for the valet to bring his car around to the front of the hotel, a familiar voice called to him.

"Joe! Joe, is that you?"

Joe turned around, and his good mood vanished when Sheila Maxwell, his ex-fiancée, strode up, her blond waves bouncing off her shoulders. She walked like a fashion model, her clothes Beverly Hills classy, white on white, and no one could miss the diamonds dripping from her ears and throat.

"Hello, Sheila."

Sheila walked up to him and kissed him on the cheek. "It's good to see you, Joe." She glanced at Ali with assessing eyes before turning back to him.

"This is Ali Pendrake." Joe felt obligated to introduce the women. "Ali, this is Sheila Maxwell."

"Sheila Desmond now," she corrected. "It's nice to meet you, Ali. What are you both doing here? Are you vacationing like I am?"

Ali hesitated, looking to Joe before answering. "No, we're here on business. There's a convention in town."

"Oh, right, the Annual Grapegrowers Convention. I'd heard it was at this hotel. Sorry, I didn't put two and two together. So, you work with Joe in Napa?"

"Yes, I do."

"Ali works for Carlino Wines, and we're lucky to have her," Joe added.

Sheila pursed her lips briefly, looking intently at Ali before focusing her attention back to him. Genuine sympathy softened her eyes, "I'm sorry about your father, Joe. I sent you a note of condolence. Did you ever get it?"

Bumping into Sheila after all this time confirmed Joe's suspicions that he was one hundred percent over her. He decided to put the past behind him. "Yes, I did. Thank you for that."

"So now, you're settled in Napa?"

"For the time being, I am. My brothers and I are running Carlino Wines now." He didn't give her an in-depth explanation. At one time, he'd shared everything with her.

The valet approached Joe, signaling to him. "Well, looks like my car is ready. It was nice talking to you."

"Uh, Joe. If I could have a minute of your time?" She searched his eyes, and he couldn't fathom what she wanted to say to him.

He pushed his glasses farther up his nose. "We really have to get going."

"It'll just take a minute. Would you excuse us, Ali?"

"No," Joe said immediately, glancing at Ali. "You don't have to—"

Ali put her hand on his arm briefly, a gesture Sheila didn't miss. "It's okay, Joe." She reassured him with a smile. "I'll wait in the car."

Joe furrowed his brows and watched her walk off. Then he turned his attention to his ex-fiancée, his annoyance barely hidden. He exhaled and waited.

"She's pretty."

"You didn't ask for privacy to tell me how pretty my assistant is."

"Is that all she is to you? Your assistant?"

"That's none of your business, is it?"

Sheila picked up on his brisk tone. "Listen, Joe, I'm not trying to cause any trouble for you. But as soon as I recognized her—"

"Who, Ali?" Puzzled, Joe frowned. "You know her?"

"Not personally, no. But I know the name, and I've met her mother, Justine. She's known in social circles as the beauty queen, and Ali is the spitting image of her."

Joe jammed his hands in his pockets. "Is there a point to all this?"

"I'm trying to warn you, Joe. Look, I don't want to dredge up past history or anything, but I know I hurt you. I'm deeply sorry about that."

Again, Sheila seemed contrite, which in itself, baffled him. "It's over and done with, Sheila."

"My point is that I don't want you to get hurt again. Ali's mother has dumped more men than a dog's got fleas. Did you know she's on husband number five?"

Joe didn't know that. In fact, every time he tried to ask Ali about her family and her childhood, she evaded the question. He'd figured she didn't like to talk too much about herself.

He remained passive, yet his curiosity was piqued.

"Not to mention how many boyfriends she's had in between her marriages. Each time she married, it was to a wealthier, more powerful man. She's married to Harold Holcomb now. His brother is a senator," Sheila added.

"I know that."

"Okay, just so you know. Justine Holcomb is a social climber. Some have been bold enough to call her a gold digger. Consider yourself warned. You know what they say—the apple doesn't fall far from the tree."

Joe almost laughed. If he wanted to use a cliché, something Sheila was famous for, he'd say her comment was like the pot calling the kettle black. "I've never met Ali's mother, and I'm not going to judge her behavior. But if you're insinuating that Ali Pendrake is going to hurt me, then I'd say you're wrong."

"Okay, Joe," Sheila said on a sigh. "I get it. I'm sorry for intruding. But just remember what I told you. Be careful."

"I'm always careful now. You taught me that."

Sheila blinked.

"Sorry," he said immediately. He'd never been one to retaliate, and oddly enough, he really believed that Sheila had no ill intentions toward him. She was way off base about Ali, though. He surmised that Sheila felt compelled to warn him, out of guilt.

She shook her head amiably. "No, it's probably the truth. I can't fault you for that. But I truly never intended to hurt you, Joe. And if it's any consolation, I'm happy. I'd like to see you happy, too."

"Don't worry about me. Look, I've got to run, Sheila."

"It was nice seeing you, Joe. Take care."

"Same to you," he said, backing away and turning toward the hotel doors. As much as he hated to admit it, Sheila had given him a good deal to think about on the ride back to Napa.

Ali should have been on cloud nine as they drove home from San Francisco. As far as weekends went, she'd never had a better one. The only flaw in her perfect adventure happened at the end of the day, as they were leaving the hotel. What were the chances that they'd come face-to-face with Joe's ex? Yet, there she'd been, holding his attention, looking beautiful.

Sheila had flair. She wore expensive clothes, had perfect hair and makeup and held herself with self-assurance. The twinge of jealousy that Ali felt when Joe introduced them couldn't be helped. Joe had been in love with her once. He'd wanted to spend the rest of his life with her. But it was more than that.

Sheila reminded her of someone. She seemed so familiar. And when it dawned on her, Ali bit down on her lower lip, squeezing her eyes shut. A sense of dread coursed through her system.

She's you, Ali. The Real Ali. The one Joe Carlino had refused to notice.

He'd wanted no part of someone who reminded him of the woman who'd broken his heart. Though Rena had spoken of it, Ali hadn't been quite sure, until she'd seen the woman for herself. It wasn't only that Joe shied away from office romances but it was because Ali had seemed too much like Sheila for him to give her a chance.

Ali snapped her eyes open and glanced at Joe. He was driving his hybrid car down the highway, deep in thought.

A million thoughts flooded her head as Joe remained

overly quiet for the rest of the trip home. Had seeing his ex jarred him? Was he still in love with her?

Oh, my gosh, Ali thought. *I'm the rebound woman and a fake one at that.*

Joe caught her staring at him. He cast her a thoughtful look, then reached for her hand. Entwining his fingers with hers, she felt somewhat better.

"Everything okay?" he asked.

"Everything's fine."

No. No. No, she wanted to scream. I need to know what Sheila really said to you. I need to know if you still love her. Joe's explanation when he got into the car at the hotel hadn't seemed plausible.

"She just wanted to make sure I wasn't holding a grudge," he'd said.

And Fake Ali hadn't probed him for more. She'd merely sat back in her seat and accepted his explanation. The whole way home Ali held her tongue, refraining from asking the questions she had every right to ask.

When they reached her apartment, Joe got out of the car and opened the door for her. He helped her out and then grabbed her bag from the trunk. He took her hand and led her up the path to her front door.

"Here we are," she said, needlessly. She turned to face him.

Joe looked deep into her eyes, removed his glasses, then removed hers and planted a kiss on her to end all kisses. Ali had barely come up for air when Joe kissed her again.

Wow.

Maybe she'd misread him before.

He held her close and nuzzled her neck. "I'm leaving. If I don't, I'd want to stay."

"And I'd want you to," she whispered.

He inhaled sharply and backed away. "It was a great weekend."

"It was," she agreed.

He stared at her mouth, then backed up some more. "I'm going now. I'll have all night to figure out how I'm going to keep my hands off you tomorrow at work."

Ali smiled. "Joe."

"Gonna be a long night." He scanned her body up and down. "A long night," he repeated.

Stay, she wanted to say. Stay and make love to me until the sheets catch fire. But Ali knew they'd have to get back to reality. They'd have to come to grips with their relationship—whatever it was.

"I'll see you tomorrow, Joe. I had a wonderful time."

She turned and entered her home, part of her wanting to jump for joy and part of her ready to shed worrisome tears.

Joe started work early on Monday morning. He'd had a poor night's sleep and figured why not put his energy into something productive. He had Ali on the brain and wondered about Sheila's accusations about her mother. It would be easy to find out more by looking her up on the Internet. He was certain Google wouldn't fail him, but Joe held off. He'd already decided to put no credence in Sheila's comments.

Ali wasn't like her mother, just like Joe wasn't like his father.

Sometimes the apple *did* fall far from the tree.

Joe dug into his work with added ambition, trying hard to concentrate on the task at hand. But the fresh scent of flowers drifted by his nose, and he knew the exact moment Ali had entered the office.

She popped her head inside his doorway, just like she'd done every other day. "Morning, Joe."

Joe sat back in his chair, glad to see her. "Good morning," he said, unable to hide a big smile, but before he could summon her inside, Ali was gone.

"Good thing," he muttered. He'd missed her soft, supple body next to his last night. It had been fantastic waking up with her in the morning and holding her in his arms while in San Francisco. He fought the urge to spend last night with her, because he wasn't sure where it would all lead. An open office romance could spell disaster if it didn't work out. He and Ali had such a fabulous work relationship, and he wanted to keep it that way.

He'd have to be content seeing her after hours, but that didn't stop his imagination from flashing images of hot office sex with Ali that would put his other sexual fantasies to shame.

This morning, he'd lost count during his swim somewhere after twenty-seven laps from thinking of Ali. For a man who banked on his analytical mind, that wasn't a good thing.

Joe ran figures of monthly sales on his computer, getting lost in numbers, but every once in a while, he'd hear Ali's voice as she spoke with a coworker and he'd look up. He found himself staring at her, his heart doing crazy little flips and his body growing tight.

She looked so studious in her glasses, with her hair pulled back with a tortoise-shell clip, wearing a pin-striped skirt and a conservative white blouse.

Ali was beautiful no matter what she wore. Any man with eyes in his head was bound to notice.

And Joe wanted her.

The lust he felt startled him. He wasn't going to make it through the day without touching her. He glanced around his office, cursing the modern decor and glass walls—so much for privacy. The decor had never bothered him before now. Would it be too obvious to lower all the shades in his office and call Ali in?

Hell, why should he care? He was the boss. But he had Ali's reputation to worry about.

He pressed his intercom button. "Hi," he said.

"Hi, Joe." Ali glanced at him from her desk and gave a little wave with her fingers. She was only fifteen feet away in her office, but the distance seemed insurmountable. Employees came in and out of her office almost constantly. Again, he damned the glass walls that allowed them no privacy.

"What are you doing for lunch?"

"I wasn't going to take lunch. I'm swamped with—"

"You're taking a lunch, Ali," Joe rasped.

"I am?"

"Yes, you have to take a lunch break. It's the law, and you wouldn't want me to get in trouble for overworking my employees, would you?"

Before she could answer the rhetorical question, he continued. "Have lunch with me today."

"Yes," she breathed into the intercom softly. "I'd like that."

"Meet me in a half hour."

"Where?"

"At Alberto's."

And a short while later, Joe sat across from Ali in a circular corner booth in the Tuscany-style restaurant the Carlino family had half ownership in. It was just the place for two people who wanted a quiet, candlelit lunch.

"This is nice," Ali said, glancing at the stone fountain that obscured them from view from a good part of the restaurant.

Joe watched her intently as she took a look around. When she finally gazed into his eyes, Joe reached for her hand. "I'm going crazy not touching you." He stroked her fingers, rubbing his thumb over them. "Come closer."

Ali scooted closer to him, and Joe's groin tightened. He leaned over to give her a little kiss, but the minute their lips brushed, his heart rate accelerated, and one chaste kiss wasn't enough.

He took her into his arms and dragged her up against him, driving his tongue into her mouth, taking her in a long, drawn out kiss. He reached down to caress her leg, his hand inching up the hem of her skirt, feeling the soft flesh that had driven him wild over the weekend. He moved his hand farther up her thigh, grazing her skin and inching closer to indecency.

Ali pulled back. "Joe." She glanced around. The waiter was heading their way.

"Hell, I usually don't act like a hormone-crazed teenager, Ali." Joe straightened in his seat and lowered his voice. "I told you yesterday that it'd be hard to keep my hands off you."

The waiter approached their table with menus and offered up the day's specials. "Or anything else, you'd like, Mr. Carlino."

"Thank you, Henry. Give us a few minutes to decide."

"Of course. Would you care for a drink?" he asked Ali first.

"A soda for me, please."

Joe needed something stronger. "Scotch on the rocks."

The waiter left, and Ali peered at him, her eyes soft. "You don't usually drink this early in the afternoon."

"There's a lot of things I don't usually do in the afternoon, like grope my—"

"Your?" Ali appeared curious.

"I was going to say, grope my assistant. But you're more than that to me, Ali. I think the weekend proved that."

Ali put her head down. She sighed deeply and hesitated before lifting up to look at him. "I feel the same way, Joe, but there's something I should tell you about my past."

Joe waited, wondering if she'd tell him about her childhood and what it was like for her having so many stepfathers to contend with and having a mother who bounced in and out of relationships. He wanted Ali to explain to him her mother's motives. He hoped the seeds of doubt that Sheila had planted would be washed away with her explanation.

"I was involved with a man once, at work. He hired me under false pretenses. I thought he'd been sincere, but it turned out he wanted a sexual relationship with me. When I wouldn't comply, he made my life very difficult."

"You're not comparing me to him?" Joe blurted.

"No, of course not. But I'm trying to give you an understanding of why I'm cautious. When I told you I don't do one-night stands, I meant it."

Surprised, Joe frowned. It wasn't what he'd expected to hear. Maybe that's why he'd seen changes in Ali. Had she been scarred emotionally from that incident? Ali took pride in her efficiency and competence in the workplace. He couldn't imagine how much that episode in her life might have hurt her. He had to reassure her that he really wasn't an unscrupulous boss out for a brief fling.

"That's not what this is, Ali. I care about you."

His admission made her smile. He should have made that clearer over the weekend. Maybe that's why he'd sensed her holding back. As good as the sex was between them, Joe knew Ali had more to give.

"I care about you, too, Joe."

"I'm not going to pretend I don't want you every minute

of the day. I'm having a hard time staying focused on work with you just a few feet away."

Ali's lips curled up in a sensual smile. "I know the feeling, Joe."

"Invite me over tonight, and I'll be knocking at your door right after work. Hell, I'll even spring for dinner."

Ali's eyes softened, and his hunger for her grew even more powerful. "You're invited."

Joe nodded, imagining mismatched furniture, soft yellow hues and the scent of lavender drifting by as he made love to her in her bedroom.

That's if they'd even make it that far.

Ten

Anticipation coursed through Ali's body the rest of the day. She hadn't been able to concentrate because she was too focused on the idea of Joe coming over after work. She'd lost her focus countless times during the day, going even as far as forgetting who she'd called three seconds after dialing the phone number. She'd stumbled with her greeting until her mind cleared and she finally remembered. After that first episode, Ali decided it wise to jot down the name of the client she'd called and keep it in front of her before she'd made a fool of herself again.

She lived in a haze of desire and tried to avoid making eye contact with Joe in his office for fear of melting into a puddle of lust. At certain times of the day, she knew he watched her, but she held firm and didn't return his gaze. The clock ticked off the minutes at a snail's pace, and she thought the day would never end.

Finally at six o'clock, Ali straightened some papers on

her desk, filed away the rest then grabbed her purse and stood up. She finally braved a glance in Joe's direction. Thankfully, he had his back toward her as he spoke on the phone.

Ali got in her car and drove home, her nerves raw with tension. Once she entered her home, she leaned against the door and breathed in deeply. Joe would be here soon and Ali would have to hold back her innermost desires. She'd have to be Fake Ali again, the submissive girl with no personality and no sense of style. Her reverse makeover had backfired. The guilt she felt deceiving Joe, the man of her dreams, continued to plague her. He was too good a man to dupe this way. "Oh, Ali, what have you gotten yourself into?"

Ali walked to the kitchen and opened the refrigerator. She pulled out a bottle of water and sipped as she contemplated her situation. The only person who would understand all of this was Rena. She'd have to talk to her again about Joe and how much she hated what she was doing to him.

To both of them.

Rena would help. She'd been the voice of reason and a good friend. Thankfully, Ali could turn to her, and she vowed if things didn't get better by the end of the week, she'd have to ask Rena for more advice.

Not three minutes later, Ali heard a knock at her door and her heart skipped a beat. She walked to the front door, took a deep breath and opened it.

Joe glanced over her body in a quick scan. "Good," he said in a rasp, his brows raised, his expression like a wild animal about to devour his prey. "You didn't change out of your clothes."

"I, what?"

He stepped inside, sweeping her into his arms. Kicking the door shut behind him, Clark Kent turned into Superman.

"I've been fantasizing about stripping you out of these clothes all day."

"Oh, Joe." Ali wrapped her arms around him.

Joe nibbled on her throat, then positioned her against the door, grinding his hips to hers.

"You do this to me, Ali."

The strength of his arousal pressed against her.

"I barely made it here without embarrassing myself." He cupped her head and kissed her hastily on the lips, his hands reaching for the buttons of her blouse. "I need to touch you."

Ali helped. As they fumbled with buttons, Joe nearly ripped her blouse in two. He pushed the material off her shoulders. Then he touched her skin, his hands covering her breasts, his lips crushing her mouth. "You're amazing, sweetheart," he groaned.

Ali's joy mounted. Joe wanted her, and she felt his intense need with his every touch. Her body welcomed his frenzied caresses and openmouthed heady kisses.

Ali stood pressed against her door, inviting his assault with little moans and cries of need. She wanted to strip him of his clothes the way he did her. She wanted to push him down to the ground and play out her every fantasy. "I need you, Joe."

"I know, sweet Ali. I know."

His kisses stole her breath, and his fiery need became hers.

He unfastened her bra, and her breasts sprang free of their constraints. A guttural sound escaped his throat, the sound primal and urgent. He cupped her breast with one hand and stroked her with his tongue—his hot breath on her creating spasms of heat inside her body. Ali's pleasure escalated.

She grew tight and wanton within seconds.

Joe sensed her need. He unzipped her pants and lowered them down. She stood before him naked but for a tiny black thong, shimmering with tiny rhinestones that spelled out, All Yours—the one part of Real Ali that was still intact. Her act of rebellion, she thought.

"Sexy," Joe nearly growled.

"I wore them for you."

A gleam sparked in his hungry eyes. "Hell, Ali. I'm going to imagine you in these every time I see you behind your desk."

"You could take them off."

"Oh, don't worry. They're coming off." Then Joe picked her up in his arms. "Later."

She threw her arms around his neck and held on. Joe strode down the hall, kissing her as he moved. She gestured to her bedroom. "I remember," he said. "I've been dying to see the inside of this room."

"Really?"

"Yeah, really."

Joe pulled her quilt back and settled her onto the sheets. She gazed up at him and waited. He looked at her, his eyes intense and gleaming with dark, hot desire. "How'd I get so lucky?"

Joe unbuttoned his shirt, and Ali watched with keen interest. His bronzed chest came into view, and Ali's throat went cotton dry. She'd never tire of seeing him this way.

Next, he kicked off his shoes, removed his socks and finally released himself from the pants that held his straining erection.

He stood naked before her, and Ali's blood pressure skyrocketed. Everything below her navel throbbed with desire. Her nipples peaked to rosy buds.

Joe noticed. He smiled at her in a way that had her moist

between the legs. That's all it took. One hot look from Joe and Ali was toast.

He reached into his pants pocket and tossed a half dozen condoms on her nightstand.

Ali looked at them with a gasp. "Really?"

"We might need to take the day off tomorrow."

Ali shook her head and giggled. She loved Joe more and more each day.

She wanted to gesture to him to come take her. She wanted to tell him six times might not be enough, but Ali only laid there, watching him, his naked form so enticing, so beautiful that she could easily reach out and touch him, bring him as much pleasure as he brought her.

Should she do it? Real Ali would have jumped his bones ten minutes ago. Ali sensed that's what he waited for. Joe wanted more from her. But Ali's passion was so intense that if she ever unleashed it, Joe wouldn't know what hit him.

The question was taken from her when Joe climbed into the bed beside her and took her into his arms. His kisses shut down her mind completely, and she fell into his embrace, allowing him to lead her to oblivion.

Ali woke in the wee hours of the morning with Joe beside her. They'd made love during the night, not quite the half-dozen times they'd set out for but two rather long incredible and satisfying times that would stay etched in Ali's memory forever.

She glanced at her digital alarm clock. It was four in the morning, and they'd be rising soon. She hadn't expected Joe to stay the night, but it warmed her heart that he did. After their last bout of lovemaking, Joe had taken her into his arms, laying her head on his chest and almost instantly fallen asleep.

He stirred restlessly next to her, and she froze, not wanting to wake him. "It's okay, sweetheart. I'm awake."

Ali lifted up from his chest to peer into his eyes. "It's early."

"How early?"

"Four o'clock."

"I should leave before nosy neighbors see me sneaking out of here."

"I don't care what my neighbors think."

Joe chuckled. "No, neither do I. Just thinking about you." He kissed her forehead and brushed loose strands of hair from her face. "I'm always thinking about you."

"That's nice to know."

"Let's take the day off. Play hooky or *do something else.*" He caressed her breasts and wiggled his eyebrows, villain style.

Ali giggled then flopped her head back against her pillow and stared at the ceiling. "I wish we could, but you can't do that."

"Why not?"

"I've scheduled two meetings for you today. It would be rude to cancel at the last minute."

"What time?"

"One is at eleven and one is at three in the afternoon."

Joe bent over and kissed her soundly. "That's seven hours from now."

Ali wrapped her arms around his neck. "Yes, that's true."

"We could accomplish a lot in seven hours."

Ali stroked his handsome face. "Especially since you're so thorough."

He did the same. "And you're so efficient."

Joe slid his hands over her, gently, sweetly until he'd caressed every inch of her. "I love touching you."

"I love you touching me." But Ali loved more about Joe than that, and she prayed that Joe would return that love someday to the woman she really was.

At ten that morning, Joe was head deep in work at the office. He'd gotten in around nine, and Ali had gone into work a half hour before him. She'd insisted she had work to do, so he'd gone home after they'd made love once more to take a shower and dress. Sometimes he cursed his practical mind. Both he and Ali realized they had obligations at the office that couldn't be ignored.

So much for playing hooky all day.

Sometimes Joe wished he could be a free spirit, acting on a whim like his brother Nick. His younger sibling had no trouble shirking his responsibilities if a good time was to be had.

Yet, Joe wasn't complaining. He glanced at Ali, her head down, going over some papers at her desk. She looked up, and their eyes met. The soft look on her face gave him pause. Something powerful was happening between them. It was more than lust, and Joe told himself to slow down.

There were things about Ali that he didn't understand. He wanted her to talk about her childhood, have her explain about her mother and also explain how suddenly, her entire demeanor had changed, almost overnight. Ali had gone from flashy and vivacious to conservative and subdued in the span of a few heartbeats it seemed.

For all he knew, it was another of Ali's fashion statements. What Joe didn't know about women could fill volumes, so he didn't dwell on it. But he knew one thing: He and Ali were good together—so good that he got a hard-on just looking at her sometimes.

Joe scratched his neck and chuckled. "Get down to

business," he said to himself. "You've got a meeting in less than an hour."

He finished up a call with a client and then his cell phone rang. He took a quick look at the screen and winced. He really didn't want to have this conversation.

"Hey," he said to Tony.

"Hey, yourself. How've you been?"

"I've got no complaints."

"No? Well, I've had a few. Seems the guy I sent in my place to the Grapegrowers Convention was a no-show. You missed a lot of networking, bro. I've been getting calls for two days asking what happened."

"You know that's not my thing."

"But you went, right?"

"Yeah, I showed up."

"So what happened?"

Joe hesitated, refusing to answer.

"Ah, *Ali* happened."

Joe wasn't a kiss-and-tell kind of guy. He kept his mouth shut.

Tony didn't give him the same courtesy. "At least admit Rena and I were right about the two of you. You couldn't go away with her without playing musical beds."

"Isn't that exactly what you and Rena wanted? And listen, Tony, before you go getting ideas, it was just one weekend."

"Yeah, and the moon is made of marshmallows."

"What?" Joe furrowed his brows.

"You care about Ali. Just admit it."

"Of course I care about her. I'm not…Nick."

Tony laughed. "No, you're a far cry from our baby brother. Don't worry. I won't repeat what you said about him. But Ali's a nice girl, and you, Joe, have been alone way too long."

"Leave the matchmaking to someone who knows what they're doing, bro."

Joe didn't need any more encouragement when it came to Ali. He was having enough trouble sorting out his feelings for her. He'd been gun-shy for so long that he wasn't ready to open up his heart again. And there was always the fact that if it didn't work out between them, that he'd lose the best damn personal assistant on the planet.

All of that aside, Joe liked the status quo at the moment. Sex after work hours had its advantages. Joe glanced at his watch. He had a day full of meetings and work to catch up on. Evening seemed a long time away.

Joe took a look at Ali again, never tiring of seeing her. She was laughing at something Randy Simmons said, and then the sales manager touched her arm. An act of friendship he was sure, but Joe immediately turned away from them. A jolting pang of jealousy ripped through him. He squeezed his eyes shut and counted to three. He had it bad if he couldn't stand to see another man casually touch Ali.

"Joe, you there?"

"I'm here. I'm busy, Tony. I'd better get back to it."

"Okay, fine. And listen, don't worry about blowing off the convention. You're the numbers man. You would know whether we're in good shape or not."

"Trust me, Carlino Wines is doing just fine."

"Great then. Say hello to Ali for me. Oh, and be sure not to work her too hard."

Where did that come from? "I…don't."

"Good, and remember women need at least a few hours of sleep at night."

Joe hit the button on his iPhone to the sound of Tony's deep chuckle.

* * *

At home on Friday night, Ali looked at herself in the mirror, and that same sense of self-loathing plagued her. Wearing no makeup but a little lip gloss and a few swipes of mascara, dressed in a tan pin-striped pantsuit with her wild auburn hair confined in one long braid down her back, Ali frowned. She took her glasses off and laid them down on the dressing table. "Who are you, Ali Pendrake?"

But Ali knew the image in the mirror wasn't her. She hated the clothes she wore, and that hadn't changed. She'd hoped that slowly she'd morph into a woman who enjoyed dressing down, who enjoyed the conservative look of a businesswoman.

"You," she said pointing to the mirror, "are not *me*."

It wasn't only the clothes that bothered her. She'd faked her subdued personality, biting her tongue each time a sassy comment came to mind. She couldn't say what she wanted. She couldn't do what she wanted. So many times she wanted to express her feelings to Joe. She wanted to disagree with him about politics and religion and shout at him that rock music wasn't just a bunch of garbage.

She wanted to be herself.

She loved Joe Carlino with all of her heart, but she wasn't being fair to him or to herself with this charade. She was like a little kid who'd caught a big fish and then didn't know what to do with it.

Joe was her big fish. He was the love of her life. But he hadn't been even remotely attracted to the Real Ali Pendrake. One year's worth of hoping had proven that. So why on earth hadn't she let things be?

Now, it was too late. She was in love too deeply to get out without horrid injury. She didn't know if she was brave enough to tell him the truth.

"Who are you?" she asked again to the reflection in the mirror.

The week had been magical on the Joe front. She'd see him at the office during the day, and the hunger in his eyes reassured her that she couldn't let him go. He'd catch her in a private moment at work and steal a quick kiss, saying it was his sustenance until they'd met at night.

He'd come over with dinner each evening after work, but they never managed to eat their meal until the midnight hour, too consumed with each other to feel any other sort of hunger but the sexual kind.

Ali was in heaven while he was with her.

But she was in her own private hell when they were apart.

Tonight, she actually begged off with Joe. She needed an escape from Fake Ali for one night. She needed to be herself.

Joe had frowned when she told him she had a cooking lesson with Royce that would go late into the evening. She could see it was on the tip of his tongue to offer to come over after her lesson, but he'd held back. Maybe he'd hoped she would be the one to do the inviting, or maybe, he realized they needed a short break from each other. They'd been together every day and night for one entire week.

Ali kicked off her brown pumps, slipped out of her pantsuit and unbraided her hair. She ran her hands through the strands, and as her hair loosened from their bonds, so had Ali. She felt free, alive. Herself.

She turned on the radio, and a U-2 song blasted out. Ali danced her way to the shower, stepped inside and sang along with the radio, washing her hair, soaping her body and rinsing off as she moved with the music.

She toweled off, fingered through her hair, allowing it to dry naturally for the time being. Later, she'd take a round brush to it and use the blow-dryer to add more wispy curls.

Ali walked to her closet and spread the hangers wide, ignoring her Fake Ali clothes. She picked out a pair of black jeans and nodded. "I've missed you," she said, stroking the material as she would a long, lost love.

Next she searched for just the right blouse. She found a black silk that had gold tones of op art emblazoned on the front, the neck high on her throat, but the back dipping low with crisscrossing straps. She grabbed her leather boots from the floor of her closet and sighed. "I've missed you, too."

Ali opened her jewelry box and went right to a pair of thin, gold hoop earrings. Without pause, she set them onto her earlobes and stepped back from her dresser to admire them. "Nice."

She put her face on—a little blush on her cheeks, eyeliner and shadow to enhance the jade color of her eyes—and then lined her lips with cherry-red lipstick. She finished off her hair with the blow-dryer, then dressed in the clothes she'd picked out and stepped into her foyer where she could view herself in the full-length mirror. She liked what she saw.

The knock came at her door at precisely eight o'clock, and Ali was ready for Royce.

"Wow," he said, glancing at her with keen interest. He had a nice way about him, and some women might think him incredibly handsome in that blond, surfer looking kind of way. He held a grocery bag full of items for the lesson.

"Come in," she said, allowing him entrance. "What are we making tonight?"

"Well, I uh," Royce didn't take his eyes off her. "You look dynamite, Ali. Are you expecting someone else, later?"

Ali laughed. "No way. I'm up for our cookout."

"Really, because you look too gorgeous to stay home and make dinner. If I had half a brain, I'd offer to take you dancing. I have a friend who plays guitar in a band, and he's got a gig tonight in Yountville."

Ali opened her eyes wide, tempted to take Royce up on it. "Gosh, I haven't been to a concert since I left New York."

Royce narrowed his eyes. "Are you saying you want to go?"

Ali took the grocery bag out of his arms and marched to the kitchen. "How about we make dinner first, and if there's time, I'd love to go."

Royce followed her into the kitchen. "Sounds good to me." Then Royce cast a thoughtful look her way. "Hey, Ali, why'd you call me out of the blue?"

She turned away from the groceries she'd been removing from the bag and smiled. "We're friends, aren't we?"

"Yeah, but you've been busy lately."

"I know I have. The truth is I missed having a friend to talk to."

"You can't talk to your, uh, boyfriend?"

Ali only smiled. She couldn't give Royce a good explanation without spilling her whole sordid deception.

"Is he out of town?"

"No! I wouldn't do that to you, Royce. The fact is, he wanted to come over tonight, but I realized I've been neglecting my friends. Besides," she said, poking him gently in the shoulder, "you need to teach me how to make—" She frowned. She didn't know what they'd be making tonight.

"Beef tenderloin with wild mushroom sauce."

"My mouth is watering already! So go on, teach away."

Royce laughed and gazed at her mouth in a dangerous way. She'd told him countless times they were friends and hoped he wasn't reading more into this evening than that. He'd never really made a pass at her, and she trusted her instincts.

The one really good thing about being with Royce was that he liked her for herself. And she could simply *be,* when she was with him.

Royce immediately began barking commands, teaching her about different cuts of meat and how to look for marbling in the pieces she'd find at the market. He showed her how to prepare it and then went on to teach her how to make the wild mushroom sauce. He was actually a very good instructor, and Ali could tell how passionate he was about cooking.

By nine o'clock the meal was ready and they sat down to eat. Ali felt a measure of guilt when she thought about Joe. What was he doing now? She missed him terribly, but at the same time, she felt good about herself tonight. Like she'd reconnected to Real Ali. So much so, that after they ate the savory meal, she agreed to go dancing with Royce.

"Just for a little while," she said on their way to Yountville. "I've had a busy week, and I'm a little tired," she said.

Royce agreed. "No problem, Ali. We'll have a drink and dance a little. I've been meaning to hear Charley's new band. He'll be glad I showed up. Consider this a favor for the cooking lesson."

Ali relaxed more, glad that Royce didn't view this as any sort of date.

When Royce pulled into the back parking lot of the small club, music blared out from the open doors. He parked the car, and they walked around to the front of the building.

They entered Rock and a Hard Place, and immediately Ali loved the look of the small venue. It wasn't a trendy New York club but a more rustic place with sawdust on the floor and a long wall-to-wall dark oak bar.

"They're on now," Royce said, pushing through a small crowd to bring her closer to the stage. He pointed to a band member with longish hair and ripped jeans. "That's Charley on the guitar."

Royce shot him a quick wave, and Charley nodded.

"What's the name of their band?" she asked.

"Guts and Glory."

Ali laughed and Royce joined in. "I know. Not exactly Bon Jovi or Queen, but they sound good."

"They do," Ali said, clapping her hands and tapping her feet to the music.

Royce leaned over to speak into her ear. "Want a drink?"

Ali had to raise her voice over the band to answer. "Sure. Whatever you're drinking is fine."

A few minutes later, Royce returned with two mojitos. He handed her one, and she took a sip. "It's good. Thanks!"

Royce stood beside her until they'd both finished their drinks. "Want another?" he asked. "Or are you ready to dance?"

"Dance."

Royce took her hand and led her onto the small, crowded dance floor. The band played all fast tunes, and Ali let loose, dancing in sync with the beat, despite bumping into other couples for lack of space. She laughed with Royce over the loud music, tossed her hair to and fro and shimmied with the best of them. After five back-to-back dances, Royce came close enough to ask if she wanted another drink.

Ali debated and finally nodded. "One more. But I'll

get them for us." She felt better about paying her own way. Royce frowned but relented, and she stood at the bar with sweat dripping from her brow. She took a napkin and quickly wiped it away.

She was enjoying herself and burning calories, what more could a girl ask?

The band took a break, and as she waited at the bar for their drinks, she saw Royce speaking with his friend Charley by the stage.

A man sidled up next to her, and Ali turned, coming face-to-face with Nick Carlino.

"You're a great dancer, Ali."

"Nick, hi." Ali kept the panic from her voice. She could only imagine what Nick was thinking. Judging by his compliment, he must have been watching her dance with Royce. "Thanks. I love it."

Nick smiled. "Do you come here often?"

He made his point with the cliché pickup line, and Ali also knew that he was darn curious about her being here with Royce.

"No, I've never actually been here before." Ali brushed her unruly hair from her face, a gesture Nick didn't miss. "My neighbor Royce invited me to see his friend play. He's in the band." She pointed, but Nick didn't bother looking.

"What are you doing here?" she asked.

"I'm on a date."

"Oh, really?" Ali scanned the room but couldn't find the woman he was with.

"She's in the back, taking care of business, I presume. There was a problem with one of her employees."

Puzzled, Ali asked. "What kind of business?"

Nick grinned. "She owns the place."

Ali shook her head and smiled back at him. "I should have known."

"I like you, Ali. In fact, if Joe wasn't in the picture—"

"But Joe's very much in the picture," she finished for him.

"Doesn't look like it tonight."

"We don't spend all our nights together," Ali said in her own defense. Although since their trip to San Francisco, they had been inseparable. "And Royce is a good friend. That's all."

"Hey, I'm not accusing you of anything. I have my eye on your *friend,* though, just in case. If he'd so much as made an improper gesture toward you, I'd have decked him."

"Would you?" Ali asked, not sure Nick was telling the truth. He was a charmer with a killer smile and a man used to getting his own way, yet she didn't figure him as the brute type.

"For Joe. Yeah, I would." Nick braced his arm against the bar and looked her dead in the eyes. "Are you going to tell him about tonight?"

Ali blinked. "I suppose. It's no big deal."

"Just be sure that you do. And don't mention you saw me here."

"Why not?"

"Because then he'd be pissed at me for not telling him I saw you." Nick winked. "He's a good guy, Ali. Don't trample him. He's been there and done that once already."

"I wouldn't hurt Joe for the world."

"Good. Just keep it that way."

Ali sipped the mojito the bartender put in front of her. "You Carlinos stick together, don't you?"

"Like glue."

Ali wished she had someone who watched her back,

the way Nick just had for his brother. Most times she was on the giving end with friends and family. Both her father and mother had sought her out when they needed help, and Ali was glad to give it. But she'd never asked for the same in return. She'd grown up independent of others out of necessity. Her mother's frivolous lifestyle hadn't allowed for her to develop close ties.

It was at this moment that Ali realized that she harbored resentment toward both her parents—maybe a childish notion, but she'd wished they watched her back and put her first, just once.

Nick picked up two drinks the bartender sent his way. "Gotta go find my date." He began to leave, then stopped and turned around, his gaze flowing over her from top to bottom, assessing her hair, her face, her breasts and all the way down to her black leather boots. "I like the look, Ali. I think Joe would, too."

Heat crawled up her neck, and she was darn glad that Nick had taken off before he saw how much his comment affected her. It was almost as if Nick had figured her out.

What if he had? What if he knew the truth? He'd seen her cut loose, dancing like a maniac, drinking and laughing with another man. Did he know she was a fraud? She feared that he did and that would spell disaster.

Ali knew her deception had to end. She had to call it quits and confess to Joe what she'd done. She had to hope he felt enough for her, to give his forgiveness. If she'd injured him in anyway, she'd never forgive herself.

Ali was on unsure footing here. She could think of a dozen worst-case scenarios, and each of them made her cringe with regret and anguish. But one thought preyed on her sense of optimism and gave her hope.

Maybe Joe would laugh it off and tell her he loved her no matter what.

Somehow, she didn't see that happening.

A tremble coursed through her body, a quick shiver of impending doom. Ali couldn't shake off the feeling that things were about to go from bad to worse.

When Royce returned, she handed him his drink. "Please drink it fast," she said to him, urgently. "I need to go home."

Eleven

Ali tossed and turned that night, unable to sleep. She missed having Joe beside her, listening to the sound of his breathing and waking next to him in the morning. She missed his kisses and the steady way he held her.

She finally managed to get a few hours of sleep, and when sunlight beamed its way into her bedroom, Ali glanced at the clock. It was after six, and Joe would be taking his morning swim soon.

Ali rose slowly, reminded of her restlessness from last night by a headache that throbbed in her skull. She rubbed her temples and padded to the kitchen to set coffee brewing. Her motions were by rote, one step in front of the other, and gradually, after she drank a cup of coffee and ate a piece of buttered toast, the ache in her head subsided.

"Okay, Ali. Be brave. Pick up the phone and call Joe."

Ali waited ten more minutes, reciting in her head what she'd planned to tell him. Once she was sure he was out of the pool and dried off, according to his precise timetable, Ali picked up the phone.

She was greeted with a cheerful voice. "Good morning, sweetheart."

"Joe," she said with a sigh. Just the sound of his deep, sexy voice did things to her. "Hello."

"How was your cooking lesson?"

"It went well. I think I could duplicate the dish for you one night."

"I'd like that."

"I, uh, missed you last night."

"Same here, honey."

"What did you do?" *Ali, quit stalling. Tell him about last night and then ask to speak with him in person.*

"Tony and Rena stopped by. They entertained me for most of the night."

"That's nice."

"It was, actually."

"How is Rena feeling these days?"

"She looked great, healthy. She's a lot of fun. She even makes Tony tolerable."

Ali didn't respond to his little jibe. Instead, she began her explanation. "Joe, last night after Royce's lesson, he asked me to do him a favor."

"What kind of favor?"

"Just to go with him to a club. I think it's called Rock and a Hard Place, if you can believe that. He had a friend playing in the band and so I went with him, and we listened to the band and had a few drinks."

"Did you enjoy it?"

Ali decided the truth was her best option. If she was going to come clean with Joe, now was the best time to start. "The band was pretty good, actually. Great dance music. Yes, it was fun."

"You danced?"

"I did, Joe."

She heard Joe take a long, deep pull of air. Then silence ensued for what seemed like an eon. "What are you doing right now?"

"Now? I just finished breakfast. I'm not even dre—"

"Don't go anywhere. I'll be over in less than an hour."

Joe hung up the phone before Ali could respond. "That went well," she said, her body shaking. She couldn't tell if Joe was furious or not. She had no idea what he was thinking. Joe didn't wear his heart on his sleeve. He was steady and even and practical minded most of the time.

Ali hopped in the shower and dressed, with her eyes on the clock. If Joe said he'd be over in less than an hour, she knew he wouldn't be late. She had her clothes all picked out for today. It was Saturday, and she'd thought she'd put on her tight stone-washed jeans and something wild and colorful. But Ali changed her mind at the last minute. She donned a brown knit blouse and beige slacks and then put her curly hair back into a tight ponytail. "You're a chicken, Ali Pendrake," she said, sliding her eyeglasses on.

She paced the room and finally settled down with a *People* magazine. She sat on the edge of her sofa and flipped through the pages until she came upon an article that held her moderate interest. Attempting to concentrate on a blurb about upcoming summer blockbuster movies, the doorbell rang. Ali jumped off her perch and tossed the magazine aside. Her nerves jangling, she strode to the front door.

With one hand on the doorknob, Ali took a deep breath, closed her eyes and said a little prayer. Then she opened the door slowly, afraid of what she might find on the other side.

Joe stood on her doorstep, wearing a grim expression,

yet holding a big bouquet of the most gorgeous white lilies Ali had ever seen. Her mouth gaped open in surprise. Joe strode over her threshold, and after she closed the door, she turned to him in question. Without a second's notice, he pressed his mouth to hers in a long leisurely I-missed-you kind of kiss that would have knocked her socks off had she been wearing any. He backed away after that awesome kiss and handed her the flowers.

"For you, sweetheart."

Tears welled in her eyes. She didn't understand any of this, but she was grateful she'd been given a slight reprieve. "Thank you. They're beautiful. But what's the occasion?"

"No occasion." Joe took her hand in his. "I'm not the most romantic soul, Ali," he confessed, using his other hand to move his eyeglasses up his nose. "But I really care about you, and I don't want to take advantage of our situation. We haven't dated at all. Hell, I've barely fed you dinner this week, much less taken you out."

"We've had other things to do," Ali said aloud.

"Yeah, we have. But you deserve more."

"Joe, if this is about last night, it was completely innocent. Really, I have no interest in Royce. You have to know that."

"I know it, or I'd be beating down his door right now."

Apparently, Nick wasn't the only macho Carlino. Ali almost smiled at the image of Superman Joe, taking on Royce, the surfer dude.

"But it was a wake-up call for me, Ali. I've only been in this partway. It's my fault, and I want to make it up to you."

"It's not your fault. There is no fault." Ali almost couldn't bear to hear him out. *She* was the one at fault, not Joe. Guilt ate at her, weakening her knees. She hugged the lilies to her chest.

"Ali, I've got a vacation coming up in a month. I wasn't going to take it, but I've changed my mind. I want you to come with me to our villa in the Bahamas. I think you'd love it."

Staggered by his offer, and the implications that he wanted to share his vacation with her, Ali needed to sit down. She plopped on the sofa as myriad emotions caught her by surprise. Joy and love burst forth, but then self-loathing and guilt reared its ugly head, destroying her good mood. "Joe, that's so…um, I don't have the words."

"How about yes? That's the word I want to hear."

She couldn't refuse Joe anything, much less a chance to be with him at a tropical paradise. "Yes."

Joe smiled then reached for her, crushing the flowers she held between them, and kissed her again. "Good. I'll make the arrangements. We'll take a week. I'll show you a good time, Ali."

"Joe, you always do."

He grinned and stroked her cheek. "Do you have plans tomorrow?"

She thought for a second, then shook her head. "No."

"Great. I've rescheduled our bike tour. That was our deal, and I'm following through. You still want to see Napa?"

She'd follow him anywhere. "Yes, I look forward to it."

"Great, well, I've got to get busy. How about dinner tonight?"

Ali smiled at him while a little voice in her head nagged that her inner chicken was hiding in the hen house. "I'd love it."

He gave her a quick nod and looked deep into her eyes.

"This time, I'm taking you to the nicest restaurant in Napa."

"But Joe, you don't—"

Joe put a finger to her lips. "Shh, Ali." He bent his head and brushed a soft kiss to her mouth. "I'll be dusting off my tux, so be ready."

Ali leaned heavily on the door as soon as Joe left. Her heart in her throat, she felt as though she'd run a marathon without benefit of water. Everything went limp, including the smile she'd shown Joe.

Tears threatened to spill down her face, but she managed to hold her emotions in check and march over to her kitchen phone. She should have done this much sooner.

"Hi, Rena," she said softly into the phone. "It's Ali, and I need your help."

"It's a good thing I insisted you come over this morning, hon. I could hear by the sound of your voice earlier that you were upset." Rena set a cup of tea in front of Ali on a charming round table for two in the Purple Fields gift shop. "I hated to bother you," Ali said quietly.

"No bother. As you can see, we're not busy this time of day. We have the whole place to ourselves."

"Thanks. But with the baby coming soon and the construction on your house, I didn't want to give you added drama."

Rena chuckled and gestured wide with her arms. "Give me drama. *Please,* give me drama. My life is so sedate these days that I'm ready to pull my hair out. Tony takes care of the business mostly, and I'm done with picking floor samples and paint colors." She patted her rotund belly. "Tony tells me to relax now because when the baby comes, I'll be superbusy, but relaxing isn't easy. I've never been one to sit and let the world go by."

"Right now that sounds good to me," Ali said.

"So, what's going on? I presume there are problems with Joe?"

"Yes, but it's probably not what you're thinking." Ali paused to sigh deeply before sharing with Rena her innermost feelings. "I love him very much. I do, and he's been wonderful to me. We have a great time together. That's why I'm so afraid to tell him the truth. I almost did this morning. I almost told him that I've been deceiving him and that the woman he asked to go away with him to the Bahamas is a fake. He thinks I'm someone I'm not. But I chickened out when he brought flowers and asked me to take a vacation with him. How could I refuse that? It's a dream come true."

"Oh, Ali. Is it really that bad?"

"Yeah, it is." A self-deprecating laugh followed. "Look at me? Look at what I'm wearing." Ali pulled at her preppy-looking cotton blouse. "This isn't me. But worse than the clothes, I'm not being true to myself, and I've hit a wall. I can't stand it anymore. I've bitten my tongue so many times around Joe that it's a wonder I can speak at all. I want Joe but not at the expense of fooling him the rest of his life."

Rena sipped her tea and listened carefully.

"Do you think you and Joe…is it serious?"

"For me, yes. For Joe, I think so. At least I'm hoping so. I know he cares for me." She smiled when she thought about this past week and how hungry they'd been for each other. The overtures Joe made this week had been so endearing and thrilling that she could only assume that their relationship would move ahead.

Yet, she had one more confession to make. "Even in the bedroom I'm holding back," she said bluntly. "I'm not the passive sex partner I've portrayed myself to be." Ali worried that she'd overstepped her bounds sharing that detail, but Rena hadn't even blinked. "Sorry, but I had to tell someone."

"It's okay, Ali. You can share anything with me. I'll keep whatever you tell me confidential."

"I'm such a fraud." Ali stared out the little window she sat beside, looking into flourishing vines in the distance. "And I've been too cowardly to tell him that I'm not the person he thinks I am. I've tried, but I'm afraid of losing him."

Rena took her hand and squeezed. "Ali, if you want my advice, I'll give it to you."

"Please." Ali desperately needed help in sorting this out. "If you have any suggestions, I'm listening."

"Don't tell him."

Ali blinked rapidly a few times. "But that means that I'd have to go on pretending."

"Show him." Rena cast her a reassuring smile.

"Show him?" Puzzled, Ali nibbled on her lower lip and shook her head. "I don't get how."

"Show him who you are. Be yourself, Ali. Dress the way you want. Say what you want, and for goodness' sake, don't hold anything back in the bedroom. If Joe cares enough about you, he'll accept you for you."

Ali saw the logic in that. "It makes sense when you say it, but it still scares me."

"Ali, if Joe can't love you for yourself then do you really want him?"

Ali mulled that over for second or two then nodded in agreement with Rena. "Good point."

"I'm sorry I got you into this, Ali. If I'd known it would have given you so much anguish, I would have never suggested your little makeover in reverse."

"You have nothing to be sorry about. If anything, at least you've given me a chance with Joe."

"I hope so."

Ali gained newfound strength. "I'm going to do it, Rena. I'm saying goodbye to Fake Ali for good. Next time you see me, you might not recognize me." Her mood lightened, and tension released from her body. The cloud she'd been under had lifted. "God, I feel so free, just saying it!" She rose and hugged Rena. "Thank you."

"Let me know how it goes, hon."

"I will. I'm taking a gamble. But that's what I always do. I just hope I snatch the brass ring this time."

"Got a hot date?" Nick sauntered into the living room, just as Joe was pouring himself a drink at the bar.

"Maybe."

"No maybe about it. You don't dress in a monkey suit unless you want to impress the hell out of a woman."

Joe turned to his brother and grinned. "Yeah, I guess you're right." The whiskey slid down his throat easily. He glanced at his watch, wishing the time would go by quickly. He had thirty minutes to kill before picking Ali up.

"I am? You mean, you're admitting it?"

"Yeah, I won't deny it." Joe leaned against the long, polished bar and folded his arms across his middle.

"And you're smiling from ear to ear. Be careful, Joey. You might find yourself—"

"I know all the warnings, Nick. And for once, I don't care. I think Ali is the right woman for me."

Nick walked over to pour himself a drink. He offered Joe another, but he shook his head. "Really? It only took you over a year to figure it out."

"I'm slow on the uptake, but I finish with flying colors," Joe said.

Nick chuckled and took a swallow of whiskey. "I couldn't have said it better myself."

"I said it for you, so you couldn't gloat."

"Oh, don't worry. I'm gloating and a bit envious. Ali's pretty spectacular."

"I agree. She's not like most women."

Nick smirked and shook his head, and Joe didn't know why that look annoyed him so much.

"What?"

"Don't be naive, Joe. One thing I know is women. They all want the same thing—money, power, status and lucky for us, we're in the position to give them that."

"Cynical, Nick."

"Realistic. But hey, I'm glad you're coming out of the cave Sheila trapped you in. I hope it works out for you."

Nick finished his drink, slapped him on the back in a show of real affection and left.

Twenty minutes later, Joe knocked briskly on Ali's front door, anticipating the night ahead. He tucked his hands in his pockets and when she opened the door, Joe's mouth fell open. "Wow."

Ali stood before him, and the first thing he noticed was her auburn hair flowing down her shoulders in a mass of curls. Her hair looked untamed and amazingly free. Glancing from her hair to a face that positively beamed, he peered into jade-green eyes that looked twice their size and weren't hidden behind eyeglasses. Her smile brought his focus to her lips colored to a dark pink hue. Full, lush and so kissable, Joe held his willpower in check, determined to give Ali the romantic night he'd planned.

But as his gaze dipped lower, Joe's intake of breath was loud enough to bring on another smile from Ali. Her sexy black dress clung to her body like a second skin—and how that crisscrossing material kept her beautiful cleavage from spilling out could possibly be the eighth wonder of the world.

Her dress stopped short of her knees. Three-inch black high-heeled sandals supported tanned, gorgeous legs that went on forever.

"You like?" she asked, whirling around in a slow circle.

Joe caught a glimpse of her soft shoulders and lower back and all the skin exposed by her dress before she turned to face him.

"You look beyond beautiful, Ali."

"And you look sexy, Joe. I like the tux." She tugged on his arm and enticed him inside.

"No," he said, stopping short and grabbing her hand. Immediate heat radiated between them. He'd have her out of that dress in two seconds flat if he gave in to what he was feeling.

"No?" Ali asked, her lips forming a pout.

"C'mon, sweetheart. If I come inside, we'll never make dinner. Go get your things. I'll wait for you out here."

Joe stepped outside and waited, telling himself he'd done the right thing. With the way Ali looked tonight, all glittery and beaming, he wouldn't have had a chance if he'd strayed inside her condo with the bedroom only steps away.

Hell, forget the bedroom. He might not have made it that far.

Joe drew in a steady breath, allowing the crisp Napa air to cool his jets. *You promised her a great evening, so stick to the plan, Joe.*

When Ali joined him, holding a small purse and wearing a little black shawl around her shoulders, Joe put his hand to her back and escorted her to the limo.

"I know," he said before she could ask. "I debated, but I conserved water today, recycled cans and planted a vegetable garden."

"With your bare hands?" she asked, looking at him like he could save the world.

"No. The gardener did it, but it was my idea."

Ali laughed lightly, and the sound of her joy made him grin from ear to ear.

"Okay, so you get credit for the idea," she said.

"Is that cheating?"

"Not in my book. It's called clever maneuvering, Joe. To be honest, I'd expect Nick to dream something like that up."

"Hey, at least we'll make up for the limo ride tomorrow when we take our bike ride."

"True," Ali said, and the chauffeur opened the door for them. Ali slipped inside and Joe followed, aware of every movement she made in her dress.

Heat climbed up his neck, and he grew hard instantly.

"What's the matter, Joe?"

"Nothing that can't be fixed in a few hours from now. Just keep to the far side of the seat and don't look at me that way."

"Okay," Ali said with a sweet smile that somehow appeared wickedly sinful.

Joe groaned and kept his focus out the window the entire way to the restaurant.

Joe's blatantly sexy gaze was on Ali as they ate dinner atop a hill in a gorgeous mansion transformed into a top-notch restaurant, called quite simply The Mansion. Ali's mother and one of her right-then husbands had dragged her to many classy country clubs as a child, but no place she'd ever been to could compare to this.

Darkly textured stone walls and romantically lit tables were surrounded by old-world elegance in a tall room with sweeping sheer drapes that opened to the magnificence of the valley below. Crystal chandeliers, plush carpets and waiters dressed in tuxedos made an impressive picture. Soft music played by a five-piece orchestra added to the ambience.

The menu, a leather-bound book of choices, had given her a heart attack as she imagined what each entrée would cost. Joe was a rich man, but this extravagance was totally out of character for him. Yet, he looked good in the surroundings, blending in with the decor and not intimidated at all by the elegance. Thankfully, he'd ordered for both of them and picked a fine wine to go with the meal.

Joe gave her his full attention during dinner, entertaining her with the history of The Mansion and telling stories of his youth, growing up in Napa.

After the meal, Joe stood and reached for her hand. "Dance with me."

Ali rose, and he led her onto the dance floor.

"Is this your first-date way to impress a woman?" she asked as they stepped onto the wooden flooring.

"I don't know." He took her into his arms, bringing her up close. "Am I impressing you?"

"Oh, yeah, Joe. You're impressing the heck out of me."

He chuckled and drew her even closer.

Ali wound her arms around his neck. "You might even get lucky tonight, boss." She nibbled on his throat.

"Ali," Joe warned in a low tone, his sharp inhalation very telling.

"What, Joe?"

"They make a great chocolate soufflé here. I want us to last at least through dessert."

"Then maybe you shouldn't have asked me to dance," she whispered.

"I had to," he said. "In case you hadn't noticed, you turned a lot of heads when you walked in."

How could she have noticed? She only had eyes for Joe. "Oh, so you're staking your claim?"

Joe grinned. "Something like that. And you looked so beautiful in candlelight that I had to touch you."

Ali rested her head on his chest, and he tightened his hold on her. "You're saying all the right things."

"Am I passing the first-date test?"

"With flying colors."

Joe chuckled, and when she peered up at him in question, he simply shook his head, smiling.

"Did I say something funny?"

"Not at all. You just repeated something I'd said to Nick earlier."

Ali let that comment go and didn't question him further. Being held in his arms as the violinist played a sweetly romantic tune was heaven on earth.

They moved slowly, erotically. Ali's hips brushed Joe's, her body flowing into his with intimate little touches—a sort of public foreplay that had her mind whirling.

Joe kissed her forehead, caressed her back and ran his hands through her hair, his body rock hard.

Show him who you are. Rena's advice came through loud and clear, and Ali wouldn't stop now.

"You think we could get the soufflé to go?" she asked urgently in a breathless tone that was true to her nature. "I want to feed it to you myself privately."

Joe stopped dancing and stared at her. He blinked several times and grinned. With a hot gleam in his eyes, he dragged her off the dance floor. "Let's go."

Twelve

They made out in the back of the limo, unable to keep their hands off each other. Ali climbed onto his lap, and Joe's control nearly snapped. He ran his hand underneath her dress and stroked her thigh, skimming the soft flesh. Ali's moan of pleasure had his erection pulsing.

Ali seemed different tonight, but Joe wasn't questioning it. He was as hungry for her as she was for him. They stumbled up to her apartment, Ali tugging at his tie, loosening it. She opened the door, and they fumbled their way in.

When Joe wanted to take her straight to the bedroom, Ali shook her head and led him to the kitchen. "Dessert, remember?"

Joe protested with a groan and wished they hadn't taken the chocolate soufflé to go.

"I promise you that you won't be sorry." She removed

his jacket and then his tie and offered him a seat at her kitchen table.

When he glanced at her puzzled, she gave a little shove. "Sit."

Joe sat.

She came around from the back, her exotic scent invading his senses, and with nimble hands she unbuttoned his shirt. She stroked his chest, running her hands up and down. He loved when she touched him. She rarely took the initiative, which confirmed that something was up with her tonight.

He pulled her down to kiss her, and when he tried to do more, she backed away. "Hold that thought. I'll be right back."

Joe waited just a minute before Ali shut down the lights in the room. She came back with one vanilla scented pillar candle glowing and the chocolate delicacy on a plate with one fork. She set the candle down on the table along with the plate.

Next, Ali stood before him and slipped out of her dress. The material pooled at her feet. She stepped out of it, and Joe looked at the most gorgeous woman he'd ever seen. The strain in his pants was now an ache.

Ali wore a tiny bra that barely contained her ample breasts, the nipples a faint hint through the lacy material. A little black stretch of fabric covered the vee between her legs and enticed him beyond belief. Ali had never undressed before him. She'd never been so bold. "If you're trying to kill me, you're succeeding."

Ali smiled, a sensual curving of her lips. "That comes later, baby. First I'm going to feed you."

Ali straddled his legs and took up the dessert plate. She forked into the chocolate concoction and lifted it to his lips. "Open your mouth, Joe."

Her breasts were at eye level and so beautiful. "My mouth has better things to—"

Ali set the fork into his mouth. The chocolate oozed inside and melted into his mouth.

"How is it?"

Joe glanced at the picture she made straddling him nearly naked. "Amazing."

"Now my turn," Ali said, forking a piece and opening her mouth wide. She inserted the fork in and Joe's throat constricted. She chewed briefly then swallowed, licking her lips. "Delicious."

Then she leaned over to kiss him, and he didn't miss the opportunity to drive his tongue into her mouth. She tasted sweet and sexy, and he took his time with her.

"I think we can do better," she said. She set the fork down and dipped her fingers into the soufflé. She pressed the cake into his mouth then brushed a soft kiss to his lips. He chewed quickly and lifted her messy fingers to his tongue, licking off the chocolate, one finger at a time. The heady maneuver broke him out in a sweat.

"Ali," he groaned. "I can't take much more of this."

She plopped a piece of chocolate cake into her mouth and swallowed. "You have a little on your mouth," she said. She leaned in and swirled her tongue onto his upper lip until he burned with dire need.

Joe's willpower shut down.

He pulled out the chair and grabbed her around the waist. "Wrap your legs around me," he ordered. And once she did, Joe bounded up from the chair, Ali's legs tight around his waist.

He knew his way to the bedroom and made quick work of lowering her down on her bed.

But Ali didn't stay down. She rose up on her knees. "Let me undress you."

Joe surrendered immediately. Ali lowered the sleeves of his shirt and pulled it off. Her hands found his chest again, and her touch made his straining erection throb harder.

She caressed him for a few seconds there before sliding her hands down lower to unfasten his belt. She pulled it free, then brought her tongue to his navel and laved it, moistening his skin thoroughly. Joe kicked off his shoes and slipped his feet out of his socks, waiting. Anticipating. Her next move didn't disappoint. Ali unzipped his pants, lowered them down along with his briefs and then glanced at his manhood. "Impressive," she said with a sexy grin.

Joe didn't need any more encouragement. He was almost at his limit.

Ali cupped him with her hands, and Joe managed to hold on, enjoying every minute of Ali's foreplay. She stroked him gently, her soft hands on his silken flesh. He braced his hands on her shoulders, needing to touch her as she pleasured him. Her hand slid over him in ways that he'd only dreamt about, and he grabbed handfuls of her hair in both hands gently encouraging her to go on. But this was Ali, he kept saying to himself, and he wondered why tonight was different. *She* was different. She didn't hold back in any way. She drove him absolutely wild. The picture she made on the bed was a visual he'd not soon forget.

Then, she took him into her mouth. "Oh, yes," he muttered through gritted teeth. Ali held his hips and worked magic on him with her perfect mouth. Her tongue caressed his shaft and flames erupted. He held her hair tight as she moved on him. Little moans of pleasure erupted from her throat, and Joe's whole body gave in to her, allowing her to have her way. He enjoyed every ounce of her sensual assault, whispering his praise in full surrender.

It wasn't long before he reached his limit. He stopped

Ali, pulled her away and climbed onto the bed, taking her with him. "Hang on to your hat, sweetheart."

He entered her in one fully satisfying deep thrust. She was ready for him, and he could always count on that. He moved quickly, fiercely, his memory of what she'd just done to him, making short work of filling her with his powerful need. They climaxed together, the quick joining just chapter one of a very long night ahead.

Joe dozed after that, with a big smile on his face. He heard Ali rise and the shower go on. He pictured her in there, soaping up, scenting her body with some delicious fragrance, and he thought about joining her. But before those thoughts came to fruition, Ali walked into the room bare naked, wet hair flowing down her back and her face scrubbed clean looking natural and pure. Droplets of water glistened all over her body, her breasts full and ripe, nipples erect. Water clung to the tips, and Joe itched to lick those drops off her.

He lifted from the bed to do just that, but Ali stopped him with a gentle hand. "Lay back, Joe. Tonight I'm the boss."

Joe's eyes went wide. "Sounds good."

"Oh, it *is* good."

Joe imagined the most erotic things a woman and a man could do in a bedroom, and his heart began pumping like an oil rig striking a full-on gusher. And in the next hours, most of those erotic imaginings became staggering and stunning memories.

Joe leaned back with amazed joy as Ali straddled him one more time, riding him up and down, her hair dry now and flowing in wild curls past her shoulders, her beautiful body arching, her breasts tipped toward the ceiling, her face glowing and ready to fracture with the shattering of her next powerful orgasm.

They'd had several through the night, each one different and amazing.

Joe held her, stroked her breasts, flicking the tips, and watched Ali with half-lidded eyes, take him places he'd never gone before with a woman. Not like this. Not this potent and heady and downright sexy.

Ali unleashed her passion and rode him with frenzy. She pleaded and moaned with ahs of sheer breathless delight. Oh God, he'd never seen anything so humanly beautiful.

Joe knew this was it—their last time tonight. There wasn't anything more they could possibly do to each other. They were spent and sated, and so when Ali climbed high, Joe met her there and they shattered together, in unison crying out each other's names.

Ali stayed atop him a minute, looking at him with eyes that were unreadable. Then she climbed off, breaking their connection and lay beside him. Immediately, he wound her in his arms and held her. "That was the best sex of my life, Ali. I'm the luckiest man alive."

With that, Ali burst into tears.

Ali bounded out of bed, her heart broken. Unstoppable tears streamed down her face. She couldn't do this anymore. She hated lying to Joe, and the guilt ate at her each day.

She shoved her arms into her silk robe and walked over to the window, her body wracked with anguish. She hugged her middle tight.

"Ali, Ali, what is it?" Joe came up behind her. He put his arms onto her shoulders. "What have I done to upset you?"

Ali whipped around to face him, wiping her tears with the back of her hands. "Nothing, Joe. You haven't done a thing. It's me. I'm the guilty one here."

Ali moved away from Joe, breaking off all contact. She

put the middle of the room between them. She hated seeing the look of puzzlement on Joe's face. "It's just that I can't do this to you anymore."

"Do what, honey?" he asked, softly, being gentle with her. She was probably confusing the hell out of him.

"I'm not the person you think I am. I'm certainly not the soft-spoken, passive little woman I've been pretending to be since almost the minute you hired me back here. I don't like wearing pencil skirts and business suits and putting my hair up in buns. I don't even *need* glasses. Those are fakes. I always wear contacts."

Joe slipped into his briefs and put on his glasses at the mention of hers. He shook his head. "What's going on, Ali, really?"

"Really? *Really?* I'm in love with you. I mean, the Real Ali is, but you didn't notice her, with her sassy mouth and trendy clothes and flamboyant nature. The whole time when we worked together in New York, you never looked at me as anything but your employee. If my hair caught on fire, you wouldn't have noticed me. And then you kissed me goodbye at the airport, and I knew there could be something great between us."

"It was a great kiss, Ali. But I wasn't looking—"

"I know all about it. I know about Sheila what's-her-name and how she broke your heart. I know you didn't want an office romance and boy, you sure as hell stuck to your guns." Ali softened her voice, "But then you called and asked me to work for you, and I came. I flew across the continent to work for you, Joe."

"Ali, where is this going?"

She shuddered and her nerves went raw. "I'm trying to tell you. You wouldn't notice the Real Ali, so I made up Fake Ali. I changed my whole personality to get your attention. You see, what we have now isn't real. Nothing about me is real."

Joe pointed to the bed. "That's as real as it gets, Ali."

"Yes, that was real. But all those other times, I held back—afraid to show you who I was."

A storm brewed in Joe's dark eyes. "I knew it. I sensed that something was wrong. The question is why the hell you thought you had to deceive me."

Tears pooled in her eyes. "I guess I was desperate to have you any way I could." Ali took a breath to steady her nerves. There was no going back now. She had to own up to all of it. "Tonight I opened up and showed you the real me. I couldn't go through with it anymore. I feel so bad about this, Joe."

He remained quiet, as if trying to absorb her confession.

"I don't want you to fall for a woman who is a fraud. That's what I am, a fraud."

"Noble of you to admit it, Ali." She didn't miss the sarcasm in his voice.

"I've been acting all this time. And I can't do it anymore. I'm sorry, Joe."

More tears spilled down her cheeks. She reached for a tissue and hastily wiped them away. "I'm bold and opinionated, and I say what's on my mind. Men notice me. They want me. But not you, Joe. You never wanted the real me."

"You're blaming me for your deception?"

"No, I'm taking all the blame. It's all my fault."

Finally what she told him began sinking in. He pushed his glasses back and forth on his nose and then shook his head, casting her a look of disdain. "Then what Sheila told me about you was true."

"Sheila?" Ali's heart stopped in that instant. "What, how…"

"In San Francisco. She warned me about you. She told me about your mother—her five husbands and all the men in between. She warned me that you were playing me. I didn't take her seriously. But my curiosity got the better of me. I looked Justine Holcomb up. It's amazing what a person can find out on the Internet."

"You investigated me?" Ali's temper skyrocketed.

"Not you but your mother."

"And what did you find, Joe?" She put her hands on her hips, defying him to answer, while inside her heart was breaking.

"A lot, Ali. Your mother has quite a reputation for her conquests. She did just about anything she could to get a ring on her finger. Oh, I didn't want to believe it. But you," he said, his voice thick with accusation, "you're just like her. You manipulated me, Ali. Admit it."

"You're confusing me with Sheila. She's the one who burned you. And she had the nerve to warn you about *me?*" Ali's shackles rose. The hairs on her arms stood on end.

Joe approached her, his voice firm and filled with disgust. "Sheila isn't the issue here. You are. You knew all along that you were deceiving me, acting out a role to what? String me along?"

"No!"

"Get your hands on my money?"

"No!"

"Blow my mind with sex, so I wouldn't catch on."

She slapped his face.

Joe grabbed her hand and stared at her. Through tight lips, his voice cold and hard, he looked deep into her eyes. "I never wanted to believe it of you, Ali. But it's all clear now. Your clothes, your personality, you changed it all to fool me. Hell, you even changed your bedroom habits. Your mother taught you well."

He dismissed her, just like that. He grabbed his clothes, slipping into his pants quickly, and walked out of her bedroom without a second glance.

She jumped when she heard the front door slam. And burst into tears for the second time tonight.

Tumultuous emotions roiled in Joe's gut. He walked at a fast pace, trying to burn off some of his anger and despair. He'd sent the limo home, thinking he'd be with Ali until the morning. So now he found himself furious, barefoot and half dressed walking down the highway toward home.

It had been on the tip of his tongue to tell Ali he was in love with her. That would have made her charade complete, he thought with disgust.

She'd already made a colossal fool of him.

Yes, he'd noticed changes in her, but who could figure a woman's mind? Joe thought Ali had been a little more contemplative lately due to the newness of her surroundings. Maybe she'd felt out of her element and needed time to acclimate to California living. She had few friends here, and all that combined could have an effect on a woman.

But Ali hadn't felt any of those things. No, she'd simply had one goal in mind—to trick him into a relationship.

She was just like her mother.

Joe had read accounts of how Justine Holcomb left her first husband for a wealthy oilman. Then a few years later, she'd become a caregiver for an ailing supermarket mogul and had divorced husband number two and moved on to husband number three. She had ties to famous male actors, real estate tycoons and clothing designers. More husbands, more boyfriends, the list went on and on. No wonder Ali never wanted to talk about her family. Speaking of it would have tipped her hand.

After Joe's fury subsided a little, he pressed Nick's number on his iPhone. The phone rang several times. "I hope I'm interrupting," Joe grumbled after his brother finally answered.

"What?" Nick sounded flustered. "Joe, is that you? Do you know what time it is? Like two in the morning."

"Early for you. I need a ride."

"Now? What the hell. Can't you call—"

"No, I'm in no mood to explain myself. Just pick me up. And don't keep me waiting." Joe gave him the location and plopped himself down by the side of the road.

Ten minutes later, Nick showed up in his red Ferrari, and Joe got in. "You look like crap, man. Have a fight with Ali?"

"More than a fight. Just take me home, Nick, and don't ask any questions."

Nick cast him a concerned look and didn't offer up any snarky remarks, for which Joe was grateful.

When he got home, he emptied half a bottle of Scotch, drank himself into oblivion, replaying his argument with Ali in his head until he couldn't think anymore. He fell into bed and slept off the effects of the alcohol.

In the morning, he frowned at the clock by his bedside when he saw the time. He'd slept past noon and rose with a splitting headache. Apparently, he hadn't slept off all the liquor he'd consumed. He felt like hell.

He lumbered downstairs for a cup of coffee and found *both* brothers sitting in the kitchen. Tony was here? And Rena, too? They all gazed at him with sympathetic eyes.

He whipped around abruptly to walk away. The quick movement brought pain to his skull. He rubbed his head.

"Sit down, Joe," Nick called to him.

"I'm bad company today," he muttered.

"I'll get you a cup of coffee," Rena said, her voice hopeful.

He turned, and she sent him a sweet look. He could easily blow off his brothers, but his sister-in-law deserved better treatment. "Thanks."

Rena was already up and pouring his coffee. She brought it to him and gestured for him to take a seat at the table. He hesitated a second, then sank down in the seat. He directed his attention to Tony. "What are you doing here?"

"It was my idea to come over," Rena said. "I was hoping you'd come down while we were here."

"Yeah, why?"

"Because, um," Rena began, looking guilty about something. "I know what happened between you and Ali."

"You *know?*" Joe sipped his steamy coffee while holding his head steady. "News travels fast."

"Ali called me this morning. She's very upset."

Joe gave a slight nod. "She should be."

Rena leaned back in her seat and sighed deeply. "Oh, believe me, she is."

"If you ask me, having a woman that amazing go to such great lengths to get you to notice her ain't the worst thing that could happen, man," Nick said. "You've got rocks in that geek brain of yours if you haven't figured that out yet."

"I didn't ask you." Joe sent his brother a grim look.

Nick glanced at Tony, who in turn glanced at Rena. His sister-in-law put her hand on her growing belly, and Joe was reminded to tread carefully with her.

"Joe, she really cares about you," Rena said.

"Until the next sucker comes along." This time he took a big swallow of his coffee and burnt his tongue. "Damn it."

"I think you should hear her out," Rena said quietly.

"If you know what she did, then how can you ask that of me? She's a phony. Just like her mother."

"Oh, Joe," Rena said, nibbling on her lower lip. She glanced at Tony, who sent her a nod of encouragement. "What if I told you I had a hand in that little scheme?"

"I'd say no one forced Ali to follow through with it. You probably thought you were helping. She knew better."

"The last thing Ali wants is to be like her mother. Perhaps you've judged her too harshly."

"I've been burned before, remember?"

Rena flinched. "I know, Joe. But Ali seemed so perfect…"

Joe rose. "Thanks for stopping by. I'll live."

He left the three of them and walked out of the kitchen and up the stairs. At least he had a day to get Ali out of his system—until he had to face her at work tomorrow.

Ali called in sick on Monday. It was the first time she hadn't come to work since Joe had met her. On Tuesday, he walked into his office and stopped short when he spotted a young blond woman sitting at Ali's desk.

He approached her with furrowed brows. "Who are you?"

She smiled wide, showing sparkling white teeth. "I'm Georgia Scott, from the Short Notice temporary agency." She rose from behind Ali's desk and put out her hand. "You must be Mr. Carlino."

"Joe Carlino," he said, still trying to figure this out. He shook her hand absently. "Where's Ali, Ms. Pendrake?"

"I don't know. Ms. Pendrake called our office yesterday and said you needed a temp. That would be me. She faxed me very detailed instructions." The woman lifted up several sheets of handwritten papers.

Joe nodded, unnerved seeing Ali's desk occupied by someone else. "Did she say how long you'd be here?"

The woman shot him a quizzical look. "At least two weeks."

Joe entered his office and listened to his messages. He had four, and the last one was a breathless Ali.

"Hello, Joe. Under the circumstances, it would be best if I didn't work for you anymore. I know you think the worst of me, and I'm not going to beg you for forgiveness. I made a mistake, and I'm truly sorry. I've arranged for a temp and hope she works out until you can find a suitable replacement for me. You'll have my official resignation on your desk tomorrow. If I'm nothing else, I'm efficient." She laughed sadly into the phone before the message ended.

Joe stared at the answering machine for several minutes, feeling a hollow sense of loss.

And that feeling persisted the rest of the week. He'd made several attempts to call Ali, but his pride had him clicking off before the phone could ring. What could he say to her? He didn't even know who Ali was anymore. It wasn't just that the hair, makeup and demeanor had changed but it was the entire idea behind it that galled him. Was she really that calculating and devious?

Made a man think what else she would have done to gain his attention.

By the middle of the next week, Joe dreaded coming into work each day and not seeing Ali behind her desk. He'd thought he'd get used to seeing Ms. Scott there, typing away, bringing him reports, making his appointments, but that surely didn't happen. Worse yet, he hadn't lapped his swimming pool since the day Ali quit her job. He'd lost his desire and found most mornings he dragged himself out of bed and forced himself to go to work. His well-ordered life had taken a nosedive.

This morning, as he walked into the front doors of Carlino Wines, noting that Georgia Scott wasn't at her desk, Joe's mood lifted a little. He'd come to resent the woman who wasn't Ali. Yet as he approached his own office, he slowed when he reached the doorway. His heart rate sped, and hope that he never thought he'd feel again surged forth. Ali sat in his office. Her back was to him, and she sat erect, holding her head up high, her beautiful long auburn hair flowing in curls down her back.

He entered quietly. "Ali?"

The woman turned her head and looked at Joe with stunning jade-green eyes. She smiled Ali's smile, but she wasn't Ali. "I'm Justine Holcomb, Ali's mother. You must be Joe."

Shocked by the resemblance, Joe took a second before acknowledging her. "Yes, Joe Carlino."

She put out her hand, and Joe took it, giving a gentle shake. "Please, if I may have a minute of your time. I came a long distance to speak with you."

Her soft, gentle voice surprised him. She didn't sound like Ali, but she sure as hell looked like her—a slightly older version but Justine Holcomb was every bit as beautiful as Ali.

"Of course." Joe took a seat at his desk and waited.

"I can see why Ali loves you," she began, not mincing words. "And by the hope in your eyes before you realized I wasn't Ali, I think you feel the same way."

"If you came all this way, to tell me how I feel—"

"No, Joe. I didn't. I came to tell you how *I* feel."

And Justine Holcomb poured out her heart to him, explaining how she'd grown up poor and wanted so much from life. She told him how her becoming a beauty queen might have been the worst thing that could have happened to her. That she floundered in relationships, never being satisfied, always looking for something that she could never quite attain.

"I wasn't a very good role model for my daughter. Lord knows, I've finally come to realize that now, in my older years. I'm extremely proud of Ali, Joe. Unlike me, she knows what she wants in life. She's decisive and smart, and she's never wanted to climb social ladders. Believe me when I tell you it's the very last thing on her mind. I know she fears living the same kind of life I've led. She's done everything in her power *not* to be like me, but I know she wants love in her life, Joe. She wants a home and a family."

Joe didn't know what to say to that.

She watched him with assessing eyes. "I see you're thinking this through. That's good. Don't make snap judgments. I've done that all my life, and look where that got me? Finally, after five husbands, I've found true happiness, and it took a near-fatal heart attack for me to see how much I love my husband. Ali's smarter than me. She only wants one good man in her life."

He let go a deep pent-up breath.

"And if you don't believe that and think she's just like me, let me share this with you. Since leaving your employ, she's been approached by two of your most formidable competitors to come work for them. Both have offered her great opportunities with more money and frills than she received working for you, if I might add. Ali turned them both down. My daughter is beautiful, and if I might say, she could have her choice of a dozen rich wealthy men, if that were her goal. She doesn't want that—or them. She only wants you."

Justine rose from her seat and smiled. "Think about it, Joe. Think about Ali and what she really means to you."

Joe stood up. "I will. Thank you for coming by. I know it wasn't easy for you."

"Oh, but it was. For my daughter, I'd do anything. I have a lot of making up to do where Ali is concerned." She cast him a sad smile. "Don't wait too long, Joe. Ali plans on moving back to the East Coast."

And with that, Justine turned and left, again with her head held high.

Joe shuddered as he watched her go.

"I knew that guy was a jerk," Royce said, helping Ali move some heavy boxes into her living room. The movers were coming tomorrow. It had been two weeks since she'd seen Joe on the best and worst night of her life. Two weeks and he hadn't called. Apparently his mind was made up.

"He's not a jerk," Ali said in Joe's defense. "He's just, well, I don't know what he is, but he's not a jerk."

Royce grumbled a reply, but Ali wasn't listening. She focused on her move back to New York. A teeny, tiny part of her thought she should confront Joe and talk it through with him before she left Napa for good, but Ali wasn't sure she could take another rejection from him. The past two weeks had been nightmarish for her. She'd spent all of her tears and had moved on to self-recriminations. She was angry with Joe, but she was even angrier with herself. She should have never concocted that scheme, yet her real anguish came each minute of every day when she realized that they weren't meant for each other.

He doesn't want the real you.

After Royce left to go to work late in the morning, Ali kept busy packing up boxes with her clothes and kitchen items. At noon, when her doorbell rang, she called out, "Coming," and grabbed her wallet for the pizza she'd ordered.

"How much do I owe you?" she asked, opening the door and fumbling with her cash.

"Not a thing. I owe you."

A sharp gasp escaped when Ali recognized Joe's deep voice.

He stood on her threshold, dressed in blue jeans and a black polo shirt, looking more delicious than hot fudge melting over a mound of rich vanilla ice cream.

He smiled, and his dark eyes gleamed; Ali thought she'd be melting soon. "What are you doing here?"

Joe peered over her shoulder, taking note of the boxes she had stacked up. "I owe you two things, Ali. The first one is an apology. I wasn't happy with you the other day. In fact, I was disappointed and well, pissed. No one likes to be made a fool."

"Joe, I said I was sorry. It was a big mistake," she implored. At the very least she wanted him to know she regretted how she'd tried to trick him.

"I know, Ali. But I shouldn't have reacted that way. I didn't let you explain. Instead, I assumed the worst about you. I shouldn't have said those things about your mother, either. She's actually a very honest woman."

Ali put her hands on her hips and ignored the hope that filled her heart. "And you know this how?"

"We spoke."

"You spoke…on the phone? Did my mother call you?" Ali's heart raced.

Oh, God, Mom, what did you do?

"No, she didn't call me. She came to see me. Yesterday. She gave me a lot to think about."

"She was here? In Napa? I didn't know," she said, shocked and fearful of how that encounter went. "I didn't put her up to it, Joe. You have to believe me. I understand how you feel about me. I know we're incompatible. We're different as night and day and you don't want—"

Joe leaned close and put two fingers to her lips. "Shh, Ali." His touch caused a quake to rumble through her body. "You don't know how I feel."

When Joe removed his fingers, she opened her mouth to reply, then clamped it shut.

"I said I owed you two things. The first one is my apology. And I hope you accept it."

Ali nodded. "I do."

"And the second one is our bike tour. I regret not following through on that. I owed you that much for all your help, and I keep my promises."

Her heart could have been swept aside with a broom. All the hope she didn't dare count on faded to nothingness. "It's okay, Joe. As you can see, I'm moving. I don't need to see Napa anymore."

"But you do. At least let me take you to one place that's very special to me." Joe moved away from her door so she could see the two touring bikes with helmets on the seats, waiting for them.

Ali furrowed her brows. He seemed so adamant, and what did she have to lose? At least, maybe the two of them could wind up as friends. Okay, maybe not friends. But they could end their relationship on a better note. It would just about kill her to be with him today, but Ali had always been a fool when it came to Joe.

"Fine. I'll put my tennis shoes on."

And five minutes later, Ali, dressed in her moving clothes, a tank top, workout pants and a slick red-striped helmet followed Joe down the highway. It was a road she'd seen a zillion times. An occasional car whizzed by them, and Joe looked back to make sure she was okay. They'd gotten only a few miles from her condo, when Joe pulled off the road by a white wooden fence that separated two properties. Green grass, with vineyards in the distance, sloped down to a little clearing. There, Ali saw a blanket laid out, with champagne cooling in a bucket and flowers set in a little vase.

Joe removed his helmet and got off his bike. Ali did the same. He approached and led her to the blanket just a few feet off the road. "Joe? What is this?"

"It's the only stop on our bike tour, Ali. Come, have a seat."

Joe waited for her to sit on the blanket and then he took a place next to her. Ali looked out, but all she saw was the road ahead of them and vineyards in the background. Confused, she shook her head. "I don't get it."

Joe took her hand, and a jolt of electricity coursed between them. Ali knew it wasn't one-sided. She could tell by the gleam in Joe's eyes that he felt it, too. "Neither did I for a long time. After our fight the other night—"

"You mean, the night you walked out on me after we nearly burned up the sheets in bed?"

Joe appeared chagrined. "Yeah, that night. I walked and walked and thought. I was angry and hurt. And all sorts of things entered my mind. But the one thing that kept coming back to me, over and over again, was that I was so angry with you because I'd fallen in love with you. It was here, right here, as I waited for Nick to pick me up, that I figured it all out. I was ready to tell you that night, but then…"

"I blew it," Ali said softly.

Joe squeezed her hand. "I was burned really badly with Sheila, and I didn't want to even consider another relationship, much less one with my very best personal assistant. Maybe, I'd been a little obtuse about it."

"You think?" Ali said with a grin, her whole world looking much brighter now.

"Yeah, but I'd always liked you. Maybe too much. That's why I couldn't bring myself to fall for you. I held back, but if you think I didn't notice you, you're dead wrong. I noticed. How could I not? You're smart and fun and gorgeous, Ali. I noticed it all. But I was protecting myself. It wasn't so much that *you'd* changed that drew me to you. It was that *I'd* changed. I was ready to give us a chance, finally. It took me a long time, I know. So sue me. I'm slow on the uptake."

"You make up for it, though. In bed." Ali smiled sweetly, and Joe's eyes widened. Then he chuckled.

"Ali, I don't think I can live without you. You and I are like night and day, but who said that's a bad thing? Opposites attract, sweetheart. And life would never be boring. I love you, Ali Pendrake. Marry me. Be my wife, the mother of my children and please," he pleaded, "come back to work for me."

Ali threw her head back and laughed, her heart filling with joy. "I want a raise."

"You got it."

"And a house of our own."

"You got that, too."

"And children, right away. I'm not getting any younger."

"Right away?" Joe cast her such a loving smile that her nerves tingled. "I'm for that."

"I love you, Joe. With all my heart."

Joe leaned over and brushed a soft kiss to her lips. "I love you, Ali. Just the way you are."

Ali's heart warmed, believing that her mother had finally come through for her this time, and that compounded her joy.

Joe poured champagne, and they toasted to new beginnings. Cars continued to whiz by, but Ali sat back on the blanket off the side of the road in Napa Valley and thought it was the most romantic proposal a woman could ever hope to receive.

* * * * *

THE BILLIONAIRE'S
BABY ARRANGEMENT

BY
CHARLENE SANDS

To Jason and Lindsay and Nikki and Zac.
May your lives always be filled with love, devotion and
joy. The four of you have made our family complete.
Here's to pizza dinners and game nights,
friendly competitions and traditions.

One

Nick Carlino hopped into his Ferrari and drove out of the Rock and A Hard Place parking lot, gravel crunching under his tires as he turned onto the road that led him to his Napa Valley home. He could really use a smoke right now and cursed the day he quit for good. Rachel Mancini had had that look in her eyes tonight, the one that told him she was getting serious. He'd seen that soft half-lidded expression a dozen times in the women he'd dated and each time he'd been wise enough to back off and let them down easily.

Nick liked Rachel. She was pretty and made him laugh and as the owner of the successful bar and nightclub, she intrigued him with her business smarts. He respected her and that's why Nick had to break it off with her. Rachel dropped hints like bombshells lately that she needed more. Nick didn't have more to give.

Moonlight guided his way on the dark patch of highway with vineyard columns on either side of him, the pungent scent of merlot and zinfandel grapes heavy in the summer air. He'd been called back to Napa after his father's death to help his two brothers run Carlino Wines and according to the will they had six months to decide which of Santo Carlino's three sons would become head of the empire. None of his old man's sons wanted the honor. So it was win by default. Yet Tony, Joe and Nick had pulled it together for the past five months and they had one more to figure out who'd run the company.

As Nick rounded a hilly curve, oncoming headlights beamed straight at him. He let out a loud curse. The car skidded halfway into his lane as it took the turn. Those beams hit him straight in the eyes and he swerved to avoid a head-on collision, but not enough to avoid impact. The two cars collided with a loud smack and his Ferrari whipped around in a tailspin. The jolt jarred him and his airbag deployed. He found himself sitting at a perpendicular angle to the car he'd just collided with.

"Damn," he muttered, barely getting the words out. Pressure from the air bag crushed his chest. He scooted his seat far back and then took a deep breath. Once he was sure all of his body parts were in working order, Nick got out of the car to check on the other driver.

The first thing he heard was a baby crying. Holy crap, he thought, fear gripping him tight. He moved quickly, glancing at the damage to the dated silver Toyota Camry as he strode past. He peered inside the car to find a woman behind the wheel, her body slumped forward, her head against the steering wheel. He opened the door with caution and saw blood dripping down her face.

The baby's cries grew louder. Nick opened the back door and glanced inside. The baby was in a car seat facing backward and looked to be okay—no blood anywhere, thank goodness. The car seat had done its job.

"Hang on, kid."

Nick didn't have a clue how old the child was, not an infant, but not yet at the walking stage, he presumed. He focused his attention on the woman behind the wheel, placing his hand on her shoulder. "Can you hear me? I'm getting help."

When she didn't respond, Nick braced her head and shoulders and gently guided her back, so that he could see her injuries. Blood oozed down her forehead—she had a deep gash from hitting the steering wheel. He rested her head back against the headrest.

Her eyes opened slowly and the first thing Nick noticed was the incredible hue of her hazel eyes. They were a mix of turquoise and green. He'd only seen that spectacular color once in his life. He brushed aside blond wisps of hair from her face, "Brooke? Brooke Hamilton, is that you?"

"My baby," she whispered, straining to get the words out, her eyes beginning to close again. "Take care of my baby."

"She's fine."

This woman he'd known in high school, twelve, maybe thirteen years ago, implored with her last conscious breath. "Promise me, you'll take care of Leah."

Without thinking, Nick agreed. "I promise I'll take care of her. Don't worry."

Brooke's eyes closed as she slipped out of her conscious world.

Nick dialed 9-1-1.

When he was through with the call, Nick got into the backseat of the car. The baby's sobs grew to soft whimpers that tore at Nick's heart. "I'm coming, kid. I'll get you outta this contraption."

Nick could write a book about what he didn't know about babies. He had no idea how to remove the little girl from the straps that bound her into the car seat—hell, he'd never even held a baby before. He struggled for a minute, then finally figured out the release, all the while muttering soft words to the helpless child.

To his amazement, the baby stopped crying and looked up at him, her face flushed and her breaths slowing. With eyes wide, she stared at him in wonderment with her mother's big hazel eyes. "You're gonna break hearts with those eyes," he said softly.

The baby's lips curled up. The smile caught him by surprise.

Nick lifted her out of the car seat, holding her awkwardly in his arms. "You need someone who knows about babies," he said quietly.

Nick shifted the baby onto one arm and got his cell phone out again to call Rena, Tony's wife. She'd know what to do, then he remembered the late hour and how much trouble Rena was having sleeping these days. She was nearly ready to have her own baby. He clicked off before the phone had a chance to ring and dialed Joe's number. Joe's fiancée, Ali, would come running to help and he'd be glad to turn the baby over to her tonight.

The phone went straight to voicemail. Nick left a quick message then remembered Ali and Joe were vacationing in the Bahamas this week. "Great," he muttered, taking the baby in both of his arms now. "Looks like it's me and you. That's not good news for you, kid."

Before the paramedics arrived, Nick managed to sift through the woman's handbag and find her driver's license. In the car's dim overhead light, he saw he wasn't wrong. The woman who'd swerved into his lane and caused the accident was Brooke Hamilton-Keating. He'd gone to high school with her. He'd gone further than high school with her once, but that was ancient history.

Nick sat the baby down on the backseat. "Sh, you be quiet now, okay? I've gotta check on your mama."

The second he released her, she whimpered.

Nick gazed at her and made a slow move toward Brooke. The baby opened her mouth and let out a wail.

"Okay, fine." Nick picked her up again and as soon as she was back in his arms, she quieted. "Let's both see to your mama."

Nick held the baby in one arm and opened the front passenger door. He slid in carefully and adjusted the baby in his right arm, so he could look Brooke over better than he had before. She was out cold, but still breathing. He didn't think the collision had been enough to cause internal injuries, but hell, he was no doctor so he couldn't be sure.

Sirens in the distance sent a wave of relief through him. Nick closed his eyes for a moment. It was late and no other cars were on the road. Napa wasn't exactly a party town and the road they were on led to nothing but residential properties and vineyards.

With the baby in his arms, Nick greeted two paramedics in dark blue uniforms that came bounding out of the van. "The baby seems fine, but the mother is unconscious," he said.

"What happened, sir?" one of them asked.

"One minute I'm driving around a curve, the next this Camry is coming at me head on. I swerved the second I saw her car, or it could have been a lot worse."

"The baby yours or hers?" he asked as he examined Brooke.

"Hers."

He looked at his partner. "We'll take them both to the

hospital." Then he turned to Nick. "How about you? Are you injured?"

"No. The air bag inflated and I'm fine. The Camry doesn't have one, apparently."

The paramedic nodded. "Looks like the car seat saved the baby any injuries."

Within fifteen minutes, the police arrived to take a statement and Brooke's gurney was hoisted into the ambulance. Nick stood by, holding Leah in his arms.

"I'll take her now," the paramedic said, reaching for the baby.

"What'll they do with her?"

"Give her a full exam and then try to reach a relative."

The second Leah was out of Nick's arms, she put up a big fuss. Her face turned red and those big eyes closed as she wailed loud enough to wake the dead. Worse yet, when she opened her eyes, she stared straight at Nick looking at him as if he were her savior.

He remembered the promise he made to her mother.

"Let me have her," he said, reaching for the baby. "I'll ride with you to the hospital."

The paramedic cast him a skeptical look and kept Leah with him.

"I know the mother. We went to high school together. I promised her I'd watch out for Leah."

"When?"

"She opened her eyes and was conscious long enough to make sure the baby was taken care of."

The paramedic sighed. "She likes you a heck of lot better than me. Grab the diaper bag in the car and anything else you see they might need. We've got to get going."

Brooke opened her eyes slowly and even that slight movement caused a slashing pain across her forehead. She reached up to rub it and found a bandage there. She didn't know how long she'd been out, but slivers of sunshine warmed her body.

Her first thought was of Leah and a wave of panic gripped her. "Leah!"

She sat straight up abruptly and her head spun. Her eyes rolled back and she nearly lost consciousness again.

Stay awake, Brooke.

She fought dizziness and took slow, deep breaths.

"She's here," a masculine voice announced softly.

Brooke glanced in the direction of the voice, narrowing her eyes to focus. She saw Leah tucked into her pink blanket, looking peaceful and content, sleeping in the arms of a man. Relief swamped her at first. Her beautiful baby was safe. Tears sprung from her eyes when fragments of the accident played over in her head. She'd gotten distracted by Leah's wailing as she navigated a sharp curve in the road. She glanced back for an instant to check on her and the next thing she knew, she'd collided with another car. She vaguely remembered waking for a moment before all had gone black. Brooke took a minute to thank God for keeping Leah safe in the Peg Perego car seat she'd insisted on when she was pregnant.

Her gaze shifted up to the deep blue eyes and self-assured smile of... Nick Carlino? She'd never forgotten the timbre of his voice that oozed sex or the handsome sharp angles of his face. Or the dimples that jumped out when he smiled. It was enough to make a girl get naked in just under a minute.

She knew. She'd been one of those girls, way back when.

Oh, God.

"Leah is safe," he assured her again.

That's all that mattered to her. "Nick Carlino?"

"It's me, Brooke." Those dimples peeked out for a moment.

She reached out for Leah and the movement rattled pain through her head. "I want to hold my baby."

"She's sleeping," he said, not moving a muscle.

Brooke rested her head against her pillow. It was probably better she didn't wake Leah now, she still felt light-headed. "Is she really okay?"

"She was examined last night. The doctor said she had no injuries."

"Thank God," Brooke whispered, tears once again stinging her eyes. "But why are you here?" She couldn't wrap her head around why Nick was holding her baby in her hospital room.

"You really don't remember?"

"I barely know my own name at the moment."

"You came around a turn late last night and crashed into my car. For a minute there, I thought it was lights out for all of us."

"It was your car I hit?" If she were a cruel-hearted woman she'd say it was poetic justice.

"My Ferrari. Yeah."

His *Ferrari*. Of course. Nick always had to have the best of everything. How was she ever going to pay for the repairs? She'd let her insurance lapse when she took off from Los Angeles.

"I'm sorry. I don't know what happened."

"What were you doing driving so late at night?"

"I was looking for my aunt's place and must have taken a wrong turn. The roads were dark and I got distracted. We'd been driving all day and I'd thought we could make it to her place rather than stop at a motel for the night. Are you all right? You weren't injured, were you?"

She still couldn't believe that Nick Carlino was in her

hospital room, holding her baby in his arms like Leah belonged there. A shudder went through her. This was all so surreal.

"I'm fine. The air bag saved my as—uh, butt."

She let go a sigh. "Oh, that's good. What about your car?"

"Needs some repairs."

"And mine?"

"The same. I had them towed to my mechanic's shop."

Brooke wouldn't think about the cost to repair those cars. If she did, the tremors in her head would escalate to a major earthquake.

"You haven't been here all night?" she asked.

The dimples of doom came out on cue and he gave a short nod. Her heart fluttered. "You have?"

He glanced down at Leah then up at her again. "I promised you I'd take care of her last night."

"You did?"

"You were adamant, Brooke. You woke just for a minute to make sure Leah was taken care of. You made me promise."

"Thank you," she said, holding back another round of tears. She didn't need to fall apart in front of Nick Carlino. "I appreciate all you did last night for my baby."

Nick nodded and glanced down at Leah for a second. "Where's her father?"

Brooke blinked. Leah's father, Dan? The man she'd been married to for all of two years, who had told her on her twenty-ninth birthday that he was having an affair with a woman he'd always loved and that he'd gotten her pregnant? He'd left Brooke that night, and one week later she found out that she herself was going to have a baby. That father? "He's not in the picture."

"Not at all?"

Nick seemed amazed by this. Didn't he know how many deadbeat dads there were in this world? Her own father left her mother when Brooke was six years old. She'd rarely seen him, but when he did come around, Brooke would cling to him very tight and beg him to stay longer. He never did. "Daddy's got to go," her mother would say. Brooke never understood why Daddy couldn't live with her any longer. And she cried for him, night after night, praying he'd come home to stay. After she turned ten, he never came around again.

Brooke wouldn't subject little Leah to that heartache and pain. She'd moved away from Los Angeles and Dan, and spent the next months living on her own, managing a small seaside inn on the California coast just outside of San Diego. The little beach town fit her needs at the time. It paid the bills and she liked the cool ocean breezes and smog-free sunshine. It was good for her pregnancy and good for her state of mind.

"No, Dan's not in the picture at all." It felt good saying it. She knew one day she'd have to tell Dan about Leah, but not now. Not yet. She needed to get Aunt Lucy's place up and running and making money before she'd tell Dan about his child. She needed all the ammunition she could get to retain full custody of Leah. That's if Dan would even want his daughter. But Brooke couldn't take any chances. She'd inherited her aunt's eight-bedroom home in Napa Valley and with a little ingenuity she planned to make the place a shining bed-and-breakfast for tourists.

"So, you're visiting your aunt?" Nick asked matter-of-factly, as if he'd already come to that conclusion.

"My aunt passed on three months ago. I inherited her home."

When Nick was ready to pose another question, Leah fidgeted in his arms and made sweet little waking-up sounds. Nick stiffened, appearing confused as to what to do with her.

"She's hungry and probably wet."

On impulse, Nick moved her away from his body, looking at her bottom through the blanket. "You think so?"

"Has she been in the same diaper all night?"

"Yes, no. I think one of the nurses changed her late last night and fed her." He pointed to her suitcases at the other end of the room. "She found what she needed in there."

"Oh, I hadn't even thought about my things. Did you bring them here last night?"

He nodded and stood. She moved her eyes up the length of him and inhaled a steady breath of air. His day-old stubble and wrinkled clothes made Nick look even more appealing, sexier than she'd remembered. She found that he'd filled out his boyish frame to one of a man who could sustain every woman's fantasy.

Good thing he was leaving. "I'll take Leah now. I'm sure I'll be on my way soon," she said.

The doctor walked in at that very moment with a chart in his hands. "I wouldn't be too sure of that." He introduced himself as Dr. Maynard.

Blood drained from her face and her insides knotted. "Why not?"

"While your tests show no damage, you took one nasty bump to the head. You're going to have bouts of dizziness. You won't be able to drive and it's better that you rest for at least two days."

The doctor did a cursory exam, removing the bandage on her head, nodding that it looked better. He checked her eyes with a probing light and used his stethoscope to listen to her heart. "I can release you today into someone's care, though. Do you have help for your baby?"

She shook her head. "I just arrived in town last night."

And what an entrance she'd made. "I can call a friend." She'd kept in contact with Molly Thornton for several years after she'd graduated from high school. Though she hadn't spoken with Molly in two years, she knew she'd lend a hand if needed. Molly was the nurturing type and wouldn't let a friend down.

"Okay, I'll get your release ready. I'm writing you a prescription for pain relievers. Nothing too strong. Are you still nursing the baby?"

Brooke nodded. "Yes."

He glanced at Leah, who was kicking up more of a fuss now in Nick's arms. "She's cute. I have a daughter a few months older than her." Then he glanced at Nick. "I never thought I'd see a baby in *your* arms, Carlino." The doctor glanced back at Brooke. "Next time you come to Napa, I wouldn't suggest you crash into Nick." He winked at her. "It's safer to steer clear when you see him coming."

Brooke had already come to that conclusion, years ago.

Nick twisted his lips. "Funny, Maynard. But you won't be laughing when I kick your butt on the court Friday."

"Keep dreaming." Dr. Maynard turned back to Brooke, his serious face on. "Be sure to have someone pick you up today and stay with you. Take it easy for a few days."

"Okay, thank you, doctor."

When he left the room, she turned to Nick, who had calmed Leah down again. Leave it to Nick to know how to persuade a female. "I'll take Leah now."

Nick walked close to the bed, holding Leah like she was a football tucked close to his body. Her daughter stared at him with wide eyes.

"She seems to like me," he said, mystified. "I don't have a clue about babies. Until last night, I'd never held one in my arms."

"You never had children?"

"No little bambinos for me. I'm leaving that up to my brothers."

She glanced at his left hand looking for a wedding ring and when he caught her, she must have turned a shade of bright red judging by the heat creeping up her neck. Nick always had that effect on her. He'd turn her inside out and then leave her blushing, or worse. The one night they had together, he'd humiliated her so badly she thought she'd die from embarrassment. She must have been the locker room joke of the day for all the jocks on the Napa Valley Victors.

Baseball, girls and partying were Nick Carlino's claims to fame in high school.

Brooke had been crazy to think that Nick would have wanted her. The golden boy, the first baseman with a .450 hitting average, born with a silver spoon in his mouth and heading for great things—Brooke found out just how out of her league she'd been with him.

He'd nearly ruined her seventeen-year-old life. Her self-esteem had hit rock bottom and it had taken her years to recover. All of the negative things she'd believed about herself had been confirmed. And she'd hated him all the more for it.

Now, she glanced at him as he handed over her five-month-old baby. He was looking handsome and sinfully delicious, and she hated the slight trembles invading her stomach. The sooner she got away from him the better. She wanted no reminder of her past and wished she had crashed into anyone else on earth last night but Nick Carlino.

"It's simple, Brooke. You'll stay overnight at my house."

"I can't do that, Nick." Brooke put her stubborn face on

and refused to budge, ignoring the spinning in her head. While he was gone, she'd gotten up and dressed in the hospital room, made three phone calls to Molly to no avail, then nursed Leah on the same leather rocker Nick had sat watch on last night.

When Nick said a casual good-bye earlier, she'd known she'd still have to deal with him regarding the damages to his car, but she hadn't expected him to return to her hospital room two hours later.

She'd found him leaning against the doorjamb, staring at her while she nursed Leah, his lips pursed together in an odd expression. An intimate moment passed between them before he'd started issuing orders like a drill sergeant.

"I'll figure something out," she said quietly, not to disturb Leah. She always had before. She'd supported herself during her pregnancy and managed to deliver a baby without a partner so she could certainly handle this dilemma without a lot of fuss.

"Like what? You're out of options." He could be just as stubborn, she thought, watching him fold his arms over his chest and take a wide stance. "You can't reach your friend and you heard what the doctor said."

"I'll deal with it. Thank you. I don't need your help."

Nick sat down on a chair. Bracing both of his forearms on his knees, he leaned toward her. He looked deep into her eyes and his dark penetrating gaze blindsided her. "Wow, it's been what? Thirteen years, and you're still holding a grudge."

Brooke gasped and Leah stopped nursing. She settled her baby down and waited until she continued sucking, making sure to cover both the baby and her breast with the blanket.

She wanted to be anywhere but here, having this conversation with Nick. It amazed her that he even remembered that night. To her it was a mind-sucking, punched-in-the-gut experience, but she presumed it was business as usual for Nick. He'd probably left dozens of humiliated girls in his wake during his lifetime. "I'm not holding a grudge." It had been so much more than that for her. "I barely know you."

"You know me well enough to accept my help when you need it."

"I don't need it." Even to her ears she sounded contrary. "Why do you care anyway?"

Nick ran a hand through his dark hair and shook his head. "It's no big deal, Brooke. I live in a huge house, practically by myself. You'll stay a night or two and my conscience will be clear."

"You're worried about your conscience?" That sounded like the Nick Carlino she'd known, the one who watched out for Numero Uno first and foremost.

"I promised to take care of Leah last night. And her mother needs a quiet place to rest. Dammit, maybe I'm just sorry I didn't swerve outta your way faster."

Brooke was losing this argument fast and that made her nervous. "You weren't the one in the wrong lane. It's my fault. Besides, who's going to look after us, you?"

Nick shrugged. "I'll hire a nurse for a few days. We'd probably never see each other."

"I can't afford that."

"I can," Nick said point-blank. Not in the cocky way he had about him either. He seemed sincere.

The idea sounded better and better to her, yet how could she accept his charity?

He was right about one thing—she was out of options. With the exception of Molly, she'd broken all ties with her friends from Napa Valley when her mother moved them away right after graduation.

Brooke had never felt like she fit in with the sons and daughters of wealthy winegrowers, landowners and old Napa money. She was one of a handful of students at the school that wasn't of the privileged class. Her mother managed the Cabernet Café down the street from the high school and Brooke had worked there after school and on weekends. It had started out being a wine-tasting room, but after it failed the owner changed the place into a burger and shake joint. The kids at school called it the Cab Café and the name stuck.

When Brooke didn't answer, Nick landed the final blow. "Think about what your daughter needs."

She squeezed her eyes shut momentarily. God. He was right. Leah needed a healthy mother. Having a nurse on duty meant that Leah would be cared for and Brooke would get the rest she needed. Waves of light-headedness had come and gone all morning long. It was barely eleven and she was already exhausted. Every bone in her body seemed to ache at one time or another when she moved. The soreness she could handle, but she needed to be fully alert in caring for Leah.

Damn Nick. While she should be thanking him for his generous offer, she resented that he had the means to provide exactly what she needed. Why did it have to be Nick? It seemed like a very bad, cruel joke.

"Well?" he asked.

The idea of spending one minute under Nick Carlino's roof made her cringe.

"Just let me try calling Molly one more time."

Two

Nick glanced at Brooke sitting there on the passenger side of his Cadillac Escalade SUV. The only indication of the crash that took her to the hospital last night was the bandage on her forehead. "All set?" He leaned over to give an extra tug on her seat belt and met with her cautious eyes.

"Yes," she said, averting her gaze. After a moment of hesitation, she asked, "How did you get the car seat for Leah?"

Nick looked in the back seat where the baby lay resting against a lambswool cushion. "My mechanic, Randy, has two kids. He installed it for me."

"I think I'm supposed to get a new one now. After a crash, a car seat needs to be replaced."

"I didn't know that."

"How would you?"

"I wouldn't," he agreed, not missing Brooke's impatience. He figured her head ached more than she let on. Lines of fatigue crinkled her otherwise stunning eyes and she appeared exhausted. "My house isn't far."

"I guess we haven't got a choice."

We, meaning her and Leah. Nick caught her drift. "I'll drive slow to the House of Doom and Gloom."

Brooke glanced at him. "Is that what you call it?"

"Me? No. But you, on the other hand, look like you're going to your own execution."

Brooke faced him with a frown. "It just wasn't supposed to happen like this."

"What wasn't?"

"Me, coming back to Napa."

"What was supposed to happen?"

"I was supposed to reach my aunt's house by daylight. Walk in and find an immaculate house filled with antique furniture. Leah and I would spend the night and then in the morning, I'd be making plans to open it to the public."

"Guess what? Life doesn't always work out the way you planned."

"That's cynical, coming from you."

Nick started the engine. "Because I'm wealthy and entitled, right?"

Brooke sighed and blew breath from her heart-shaped mouth. Nick didn't dwell on that mouth. If he did, he'd be knee-deep in babies and beautiful blondes with attitude. He was simply being a Good Samaritan here. But it irked him that Brooke thought it so out of character for him to help her.

"Nice car. Whose is it?"

Nick blinked at her rapid change of subject. "Mine."

She smiled, though he saw what that curling of her lips cost her pain-wise. "I make my point."

Instead of being irritated, Nick chuckled. He hadn't seen that coming. He liked a good sparring partner and

Brooke had just surprised him. "So you think because I drive nice cars and live in a big house, I have everything that I want?"

"Don't you?"

Nick shook his head. He didn't have to think twice. "No." He'd wanted something more than all those things and he'd lost it, just when it was within his grasp. "Not everything, Brooke."

He sensed her gaze on him for a few long seconds and then she laid her head against the headrest and closed her eyes, which gave him a chance to really look at her. Unfortunately, he liked what he saw. Silken lashes framed almond-shaped eyes and rested on cheekbones that were high and full. He'd already decided he liked her mouth. He'd kissed her before, but the image of those kisses had blurred with age.

Long, wavy blond locks tumbled down her shoulders and rested on the soft full mounds of her breasts. Her body was shapely, but he'd never have guessed she'd had a child five months ago from her slim waistline and flat stomach.

Don't go there, Nick warned. He wasn't the fatherly type. He had zero plans to get tied down with a family. His past haunted him daily and reminded him that he was better off single, glorying in bachelorhood than trying his hand at anything more.

He drove the car slowly as promised and made his way onto the highway. "Where's your aunt's place?"

"Just outside of the city on Waverly Drive."

Nick knew the area. It was at the base of the foothills, before the roads led to higher ground and the bulk of the vineyards. "You want to do a drive-by?"

Her eyes widened, lighting up her face. "Yes."

"You're up to it?" he asked, wondering if he should have suggested it.

"I am. I'm curious to see what the place looks like. It's been years since I've seen it."

"You never came back to Napa? Even though you had an aunt living here?"

"No," she said. "I never came back."

Nick looked at her and she once again averted her eyes by looking out the window.

They drove in silence the rest of the way.

Brooke didn't want to tell him that her Aunt Lucy was her father's sister. That after her parents' marriage broke up, her mother never talked to Aunt Lucy again. But her aunt would sneak visits to Brooke, coming around after school to walk her partway home. When Brooke was in high school, Aunt Lucy would ask her to stop by the house. Brooke had little family and she liked Aunt Lucy, even if she was a bit eccentric. Eventually, her mother found out about the visits but she never tried to stop them.

When they moved away, Brooke had fully intended to keep in touch with her aunt, but time had gotten away from her. She'd always feel guilty that she hadn't made more of an effort to see her aunt before she died. Inheriting her house had come as a bolt from the blue and there'd been only one stipulation in the will, that Brooke not sell the place for a period of five years. With her mother remarried and living in Hawaii, it only made sense for Brooke to come back and try to build a life here for Leah and herself.

She glanced at Nick, who'd just taken a turn off the highway. He was part of the reason she'd never wanted to come back here. Thirteen years had dulled the pain and she'd almost forgotten that deep sense of rejection—of not being good enough, of falling for the wrong boy and feeling like a fool, but then fate had a way of intervening and turning Brooke's life upside down.

She'd managed to crash into the very man she'd wanted to avoid at all costs. And now she was his charity case. She was going to live under his roof, accept his help and be beholden to him for the rest of eternity.

Good going, Brooke.

"What's the address?" Nick turned onto Waverly Drive and looked at her for direction.

"It's up half a block on your right. It's the only three-story house on the street."

The houses were sparsely spaced, each parcel of land at least half an acre. If Brooke remembered correctly, her aunt owned slightly more acreage than her neighbors. In fact, it was by far the largest piece of land in the vicinity.

"It's there," Brooke said, pointing to the lot she remembered. Eager anticipation coursed through her veins and excitement bubbled up. This was the start of her new life. She remembered driving up here in her beat-up 1984 Chevy Caprice when she was in high school. "The Victorian that looks like…" she began and a sense of doom crept into her gut. Her heart sank. The wrought iron gates that were once pearly white grabbed the sunlight with golden hues of rust and age. The flower garden once bright with pansies, daffodils and lavender was a mass of weeds and as Nick drove into the driveway that led to the house, Brooke's heart sank even further. The house looked like something from an Addams Family television reunion, the only thing missing were the cobwebs. And Brooke even thought she saw a few of those tangled up on the third story.

"Oh," she said, tears welling in her eyes. "It's not like I remembered."

Nick glanced at her. "Do you want to go inside?"

"I should. Might as well face the music." She smiled with

false bravado. What had she expected? Her aunt had been ill for the last few years of her life. Obviously, maintaining the house hadn't been high on her list of priorities. Another wave of guilt assaulted her. Had her aunt been alone when she died? Did she have anyone to sit by her bedside when she was ill?

She looked at Nick. "But Leah's asleep."

"I'll stay. You go in and check the place out."

When she debated it for a few seconds, Nick added, "Unless you want me to go inside with you?"

"No, no. That's not necessary. If you can watch Leah, I'll go in."

Nick got out of the car at the same time she did. He took her arm and led her up the steps. His touch and being so near as he walked with her mingled with all the other emotions clouding her head. She didn't want to owe him, but here he was, doing her a favor again. And touching her in a comforting way that led her mind to other touches, other days when Nick had surprised her with kindness, only to destroy her in one fell swoop. Today, even in her weakened state, she wouldn't let Nick's touch mean anything. She didn't trust him. Not in that way.

She stepped onto the wraparound porch by the front door and stood a moment, hesitating.

"Are you all right?" Nick asked, holding her arm tight.

"I'm fine. Just can't believe it."

Nick smiled and her heart rammed into her chest. "I'll be right out here. Call if you need me."

She removed his hand from her arm and stepped back.

Nick looked at her skeptically, but bounded down the steps and stood watch over Leah, sleeping in her car seat.

She turned toward the front door and reached into her purse for the key.

Five minutes later, Brooke had seen all there was to see

and it wasn't pretty. The house had been let go for years. The only rooms that were in halfway decent shape were the kitchen and her aunt's bedroom. Those rooms looked somewhat cared for, but the others needed quite a bit of work. It would take a whole lot of elbow grease and some of her hard-saved cash to make it shine, and right now, the whole situation overwhelmed her.

She stood on the porch and found Nick leaning against the side of his car, the open door letting air inside for her daughter. "Well?"

"Let's just say the inside makes the outside look like Buckingham Palace."

"That bad?"

Brooke walked down the steps a little too fast and everything spun. She fought to keep her balance, wooziness swamping her. She swayed and was immediately caught. Nick's arms came around her. "Whoa."

Her body pressed against his. He was rock solid and strong, yet his arms around her were gentle. He pressed his hands to her back and rubbed. "Are you okay?"

"I will be as soon as you stop spinning me around."

He chuckled.

She clung to him, trying to find her balance. Breathing in his sexy musk scent wasn't helping matters. He felt too darn good. She hadn't had a man hold her like this for a year and a half. She'd been deprived of masculine contact for a long time. That was the only explanation for the warm sensations rippling through her body. She'd gotten over Nick Carlino ages ago.

"Bad idea," Nick said softly in her ear.

Oh God. She stiffened and backed away. Did he think she'd thrown herself at him? "I know."

"I shouldn't have suggested bringing you here. You're not up to it."

Stunned, Brooke didn't respond. Clearly, she'd taken his "bad idea" comment the wrong way. She could only look into his eyes and nod. "I think you're right. But I'm feeling okay now, the world's not spinning."

He took her hand and led her to the car. "C'mon. I'll get you home. You need to rest."

Brooke got into the car and closed her eyes the entire way to Nick's house. Partly to rest and partly to block out how good Nick felt when he held her close. He was solid and steady and caring. If he were any other man, she might have enjoyed the sensations skipping through her body, but since it was Nick, she warned them off. He'd been out of her league the first time and nothing had changed, except now she knew better than to take Nick Carlino seriously.

She rubbed her temples and adjusted the bandage, thinking fate had a great sense of humor.

Only Brooke didn't find any of this amusing.

She'd heard about the Carlino estate, driven past its massive grounds in her earlier years many times, but nothing in her wildest imaginings had prepared Brooke when she entered the home for the first time. While she expected opulence and cold austere surroundings, she found…warmth.

That was a shock.

The stone entryway led to rooms of creams and beiges, golden textured walls, rich wood beamed ceilings and living spaces filled with furniture that she would describe as comfortable elegance. A giant floor-to-ceiling picture window in the living room lent a view of lush grounds and vineyards below.

The architecture of the home was more villa style than anything else. It was an open plan on the first floor but the upstairs spread out to four separate wings, Nick explained.

He followed Brooke to the stairway, carrying her bags as she held Leah.

"You doing okay?" Nick asked from behind as she climbed the steps.

"Great, you won't have to catch me again."

"No, I'm not that lucky."

Was he flirting? Boy, she was struggling to keep her head from clouding up and one comment from him had her head spinning again.

When she reached the top of the stairs, she stopped and turned. "Which way?"

Nick stood on the step below her and their eyes met on the same level. He stared at her, then cast his gaze lower to where Leah had clutched her blouse, pulling the material aside enough to expose her bra. Nick flashed Brooke a grin, dimples and all, then looked back at Leah, who seemed absolutely fascinated with him. He poked her tiny nose gently and the baby giggled. "Go into the first set of double doors you see."

Brooke entered the room and then blurted, "This is your room."

She couldn't miss it. His baseball trophies sat on a shelf next to pictures of Nick with his brothers and one family photo from when both of his parents were alive. The entire room oozed masculinity from the hardwood floors covered with deep rust rugs and a quilt of the same color covering his king-size bed. Another picture window offered an amazing view of Napa from the hilltop.

"Yes. It's my room."

She whirled around and narrowed her eyes at him. "Surely, you don't expect…" She couldn't finish her sentence, her mind conjuring up hurtful images of the last time she'd been with Nick.

Nick set her bags down and leisurely looked her over

from the top of her bandaged head to her toes inserted in beach flip-flops. Tingles of panic slid through her.

"It makes the most sense, Brooke. There's an adjoining room where the nurse will sleep." And finally, he added, "I'll take the guest room, two doors down."

Her sigh of relief was audible and so embarrassing that she couldn't face him. What made her think he was at all interested in her anyway? He probably had scores of women dangling, just waiting for a call from him.

She scoured the room looking for a safe place to lay Leah down to sleep. Finally, she glanced at Nick, who was busy taking out a few items of clothing from his dresser. "There was a little play yard for Leah in the trunk of my car."

"It's here."

"It is?"

He nodded. "I got the rest of your things out of your trunk this morning."

"And you brought them here?"

He shrugged. "I figured the kid needed them. I'll bring them up later."

Overwhelmed with gratitude and ready to cry, she didn't know what to say. "I, uh…thank you, Nick."

"No problem. Use whatever you need. There's a great shower and tub. Climb into bed if you want to. The nurse is due in half an hour. I'll send her up when she gets here."

"What about you? You must have had plans today. Don't let us keep you."

"Sweetheart, no one keeps me from doing what I want to do." He winked and walked out of the bedroom.

How well she knew.

"Well, Leah, that was Nick Carlino."

Leah looked around, her eyes wide, fascinated by her new surroundings. She made a cooing sound that warmed Brooke's heart. All that mattered was that both of them were safe and provided for at the moment. She sat down on Nick's bed and bounced Leah on her knee. "Promise me you won't go falling for him, baby girl," she said, clapping their hands together and making Leah giggle. "He's not to be trusted. Mommy did that once and it wasn't good. Not good at all."

"That's a first for you," his brother Joe said, as he toweled off from his swim in the pool. "You're letting a woman and her child stay at the house."

"It's not like I had a choice." Nick glanced at his middle brother with disdain. "What was I supposed to do? She's got a kid. She's injured and has nowhere else to go. I couldn't walk away. Her head's not right."

"Must not be, if she moved in with you." Joe toweled off from his swim and put his glasses back on. He was building his fiancée a house and though he lived at Ali's condo currently, Nick had to put up with his gibes when he came over to do his hundred laps in the pool. Joe was the geek in the family and swimming was his only means of physical activity.

"Good thing you know your way around a computer. You'd never make it as a comedian."

Joe ignored him. "Who is she?"

"Her name is Brooke Hamilton. We went to high school together."

"Brooke Hamilton? That name sounds familiar."

Nick kept his mouth shut. Let his brother figure it out.

"Oh, she's the one who worked at that Cab Café, right?"

Bingo.

"I remember her now. She was the waitress who had a big crush on you."

"Ancient history." Nick didn't want to bring up the past.

It had been the one time in his young life he'd done the right thing. The one time, he'd put someone else's needs above his own. He'd let Brooke off the hook. Still, after all these years, when she looked at him, it was with wariness and contempt. Could it be she still held a grudge over what happened?

"So you're the Good Samaritan now?"

"Something like that," Nick muttered, squinting into the sun. "Like I said, she's here temporarily. A few days at most. Just until Maynard gives her the okay to be on her own."

"Yeah, speaking of that, how is it that my little brother gets in a car crash and doesn't tell his brothers?"

"I tried calling. Then I remembered you were in the Bahamas. Or were supposed to be."

"We got back late last night. If you got our voicemail, it's probably because we were sleeping. So, how are you?"

Nick lifted his arms out wide. "I'm gonna live."

"Amen to that, little brother. How old's the kid?"

"Leah is five months old."

"A baby?" Joe looked at him with suspicion. "You're not—"

Nick shook his head. "I just laid eyes on Brooke last night. I haven't seen her since high school. But thanks for the vote of confidence, bro."

"Hey, don't take offense," Joe said. "But you do have a reputation with the ladies."

Nick couldn't deny it. He liked women and they liked him back. They had a good time together and then Nick would let them down gently and walk away. Or they'd get fed up with not getting a commitment from him and leave on their own. He never led them on or lied to them. From the beginning, he'd always let the women in his life know what to expect from him. It had been that way since he could remember. As a young man, he assumed he'd grow out of it when the right woman came along, but his father had taken that option away from him in his attempt to control Nick. Santo Carlino had wanted one son to take over the family business and once Tony left to race cars and Joe took off to New York to develop software for a global company, the youngest son got the brunt of his father's manipulations.

Santo had done a number on him and Nick had taken a hard fall.

"I'm not interested in Brooke Hamilton. Hell, give me a break, Joe. I'm doing a good deed here, not looking for an instant family."

Damn it! Nick glanced up to find Brooke standing behind Joe. The baby bottle she held slipped from her hand. Flustered, her face turned color and Nick couldn't tell if she was angry or embarrassed.

Angry, he decided.

Joe swept up the bottle quickly and handed it to her. "Here you go. Hi, I'm Joe."

"I remember. Hi, Joe." She took the bottle graciously and smiled at him. Those knock-out hazel eyes, the shade of tropical waters, lit up her whole face.

"Sorry to hear about the accident," Joe said. "I hope you recover well from your injuries."

"Thank you." As if she had forgotten about her head injury, she touched her forehead. "I'm doing okay."

"Shouldn't you be resting?" Nick asked. He'd shown the nurse to their room an hour ago and she'd promised to watch over both mother and child.

She glanced at him and the light in her eyes faded as fast as her smile. "I couldn't calm down so I thought I'd get some air."

"With that?" Nick pointed to the baby's bottle. Seemed she only had a smile for Joe.

"Oh, I was on my way to the kitchen to store this. It's expressed breast milk."

Nick blinked. "Expressed?"

"I think this is my cue to leave," Joe said, adjusting the glasses on his nose. He darted glances at both of them then bid them good-bye and left.

"Sorry to bother you," Brooke said to him, not sounding sorry at all as she turned to leave.

"Brooke?"

She stopped and whirled around. "It's not as if Leah and I have a choice in this, Nick. I don't mean to sound ungrateful, but I don't want to be here anymore than you want us here."

"If I didn't want you here, you wouldn't be here. Why couldn't you calm down?"

Brooke fidgeted with the bottle in her hands. He didn't want to think about how she'd expressed the milk into the bottle. Some things were beyond male comprehension. She glanced away, looking at the pool, then the grounds, and finally back at him. "I, uh, it's the accident. I keep replaying it in my head. Every time I close my eyes, it's there. I hear it. I see it." She took a swallow and her voice cracked then lowered to a bare whisper. "And when I think what might have happened to Leah…"

Nick walked over to her and put his hands on her shoulders. "But nothing happened to Leah. You're going to be fine."

"My brain knows that." She closed her eyes for a second, then when she opened them again, granting him a soft look, something pierced through his gut. It was *something* that he didn't recognize. *Something* that was new and strange to him.

He touched her cheek and got lost in her eyes. He had a need to protect. To comfort. He brought his mouth close and brushed his lips to hers. The kiss was meant to reassure, to help her find some peace, but Nick didn't expect the sensations to rip through him. He didn't expect to want more. Sure, he'd once been attracted to Brooke. She'd been different than the other girls he'd been with in high school. There was substance to her, a depth that other girls didn't have at that age. She hadn't been a party girl. Maybe that's why Nick had been attracted to her. She was unique and special and Nick had realized that during the one night they'd spent together when he'd almost taken her virginity.

For years after, he'd wondered if he'd been really noble or scared that she was the one who could tie him down. And for years after he'd also imagined what it would have been like making love to her. Her first time. He'd wanted it to be with him, yet, he knew enough to back off. He'd done the right thing back then.

Her lips were warm and inviting. Devouring her heart-shaped mouth until she was swollen and puffy would be easy, but Nick pulled away. She gazed at him with a question in her eyes. He circled a lock of her long hair with his finger and tugged gently. "Just so you know, there aren't any strings attached to you staying here."

"I know," she said abruptly. "You're doing a good deed and you don't want an instant family. You're not interested, and buddy, neither am I."

She turned on her heel and walked off. He watched her stop to fight off a dizzy spell before climbing the stairs. He waited until she made it up to the second floor before looking away and smiling. Now he remembered why he liked her so much. She wasn't afraid to speak her mind and tell him off when she thought he needed it.

Three

Brooke lay in Nick's bed as fading sunshine spilled through the window. She'd never been one to sleep away the afternoon, but the doctor ordered rest and she would do anything to get out of the Carlino house as quickly as possible. So with Leah sleeping in her little playpen next to her and Nurse Jacobs in the adjoining room, Brooke punched the pillow and placed it under her head then forced her eyes closed.

But rest wasn't coming easy. Her little episode with Nick down by the pool played over in her mind. *Stupid, Brooke. You let him kiss you.*

Nick Carlino wasn't lacking in the kiss department. He knew what he was doing and always had. He was sexy down to the bone. Even with a dozen internal warnings screaming at her to back away from Nick, the second his lips touched hers, magic happened.

Foolishly, she'd gotten lost in his touch and taste, wanting more. More comfort. More reassurance. More magic. But Brooke wouldn't let the need inside her grow. She might have had a weak moment, but she'd be on guard now.

She took slow deep breaths, calming her nerves and letting all the tension ooze out of her body. The events of the past twenty-four hours had finally caught up to her. Her head ached less and less and sleep seemed possible now.

Nick left his group of friends at the window booth in the Cab Café, and headed her way. The minute Brooke spotted him approaching the counter her heart skipped some very necessary beats. Every time he came into the café with his friends she wanted to run and hide.

She wasn't one of them. The baseball jocks and their cheerleader girlfriends had their own exclusive club. Their friendliness ended with casual hellos. They wouldn't let her inside their circle, even if she wanted to be let in. She worked at the Cab Café and wore a purple and white uniform with an apron decorated with lavender grapes. She lived on the wrong side of town.

"Hi," Nick said, straddling the stool in front of her.

"Hi. What can I get you?" Brooke asked, as she passed him to set down coffee and a slice of peach pie for a customer.

"Would love a vanilla shake, but I'm in training. Just a lemonade." He smiled.

"You got it," Brooke said, trying not to stare at him. Nick Carlino had a set of dimples that made mush of her brains. "How's the team doing?"

"We won last night. I hit home run number twelve."

Brooke poured his lemonade and slid the glass over. "Is that a record?"

"Not yet, but I'm getting close. You should come to the games."

"I, uh, thanks. Maybe I will." Brooke had to work on the weekends. That's when they were the busiest. But Nick didn't know about things like that. He came from the privileged class and she doubted he knew anything about sacrifice or paying the bills.

"I hope so." He stared into her eyes so long, heat traveled up her neck.

Why did he care if she came to his baseball games? "I'll try."

He sipped his lemonade. "How'd you do on the trig test?"

"Got an A, but I sweated that one. You?"

"You beat me, Brooke." His blue eyes twinkled with mischief. "I don't like to lose."

It was official now. It wasn't just her brain melting—her entire body turned marshmallow-soft hearing him say her name. "Try studying. I hear it's a sure way to ace a test."

Nick chuckled and rose from the stool, taking the last sip of his lemonade. He laid down some money on the counter. He was a good tipper for a high school student. She moved on to her next customer at the counter and Nick walked away. When he reached the middle of the café, he turned back around and caught her eye one last time. "I've got a game tomorrow at three."

She nodded her acknowledgment just as the Victors' head cheerleader, Candy Rae Brenner, slipped her hand into Nick's and pulled him along, giving Brooke a dismissive look.

The dream startled her awake. But it wasn't a dream—it was a real memory. Brooke hadn't thought about that day in a long time. She didn't know why that particular scene entered her dreams, but it must have to do with the fact that she'd hit Nick's car and was sleeping in his bed.

She glanced at Leah beside her, all rosy cheeks and dark blonde curls wrapped into a sweet sleeping bundle. Leah made everything possible. She held her mama's heart in those tiny little hands.

Concentrate on her, Brooke. Forget about Nick. And the past.

But Brooke couldn't do it. The dream had been so real, so vivid that it triggered more memories of Nick. Those next few weeks entered her mind with stunning accuracy.

"You didn't come to the game." Nick caught up to her *as she walked down the hall past the chemistry lab. School was out and she had a long walk home.*

She glanced at him. Tremors of excitement erupted inside and she felt queasy from the turmoil stirring her stomach. Why was he walking with her? "I had to work. You know, some of us have to earn a living."

"Little Miss Attitude today, aren't you?"

"Me?" She pointed to her chest then realized her mistake. Nick's gaze followed the direction of her finger and he studied her chest. He raised his brows and stared some more. It figured she'd be wearing a tank top that revealed a modest amount of cleavage today.

She scurried past him but he caught up to her. "Hey, are you working after school?"

"Why?" she asked, curious what he wanted with her. "Need a study buddy for trig?"

Nick laughed. "Hell no. I'm getting a passing grade, that's good enough. As long as I keep my grades up, I'm on the team."

"And that's all that matters?"

Nick was a sure thing for the major league draft. The entire school rallied around him. He was the golden boy who earned okay grades and had a batting record that brought the scouts out in droves.

"For me, yeah. I'm not going to college. And I'm not working for my old man. It's baseball or nothing."

He had dreams, Brooke thought, and he'd probably attain them. He was after all, the golden boy. While Brooke faced community college and working to help her mother pay the bills, others would be off pursuing a life that would mean something important to them.

"So, are you working or not?"

"Later tonight I am," she answered.

"I'll drive you home."

She was ready to say no thanks, but then she looked into Nick's midnight blue eyes and hope swelled in her chest. Her heart wanted to say yes, but her brain got in the way. "Why?"

"Why what? Why do I want to drive you home?"

She furrowed her brows and nodded.

"Maybe I'm going that way." Then he leaned in closer and lowered his voice. "Or maybe I like you."

She laughed, thinking that would be the day, and looked away.

Nick moved in front of her so she had to face him. "Brooke?"

He said her name again in a tone that sounded sincere and...hopeful. It was the hopeful part that swept through her like a hurricane, obliterating all rational thought. She nodded and smiled. "Okay."

His world-class dimples emerged, stealing her breath. "C'mon, my car's in the parking lot."

Those last weeks in June before graduation were a combination of highs and lows. Whenever Nick didn't have practice after school, he'd drive her home and they'd sit on her front porch and talk about everything and anything. She'd learned a lot about his childhood, his baseball dreams and when he spoke of his mother, it was with fondness and love. Each day, Brooke had fallen more and more in love with him. It was a young girl's fascination, but the feelings she had for him were real. He'd never asked her on a date or tried to kiss her, which contradicted his reputation. He'd dated every popular girl on campus, Candy Rae being the latest in the string. Rumor had it that they'd broken up and Nick had alluded to it, but one thing he didn't talk about with Brooke was other girls.

She'd resigned herself to the fact that she was Nick's "friend" who lived on the other side of town. When prom came, Brooke had waited, but Nick never said a word, so she accepted a date with the busboy that worked with her at the Cab Café. She'd shown up in a dress she'd splurged on from her meager savings. Her mother, who had a great sense of style, had curled her hair and helped with makeup. When she spotted Nick at the dance with Candy Rae her heart sank. Though Nick had never promised her a thing, she felt hopeless and dejected, but was determined not to take it out on poor Billy Sizemore, her date. They'd danced and danced, and took pictures under the corny grapevine arbor inside the hall where the prom was held.

She came out of the ladies room and was instantly grabbed by the waist and pressed against the wall of a secluded corner by the bathroom. "Nick? What are you doing?"

"Just wanted to say hello."

"Hello," *she droned without emotion.*

The dimples of doom came out and Brooke had an uncanny urge to touch her fingertip to one.

"You look amazing." *His gaze swept over her hair, her dress, her body and then he looked deep into her eyes.* "You have incredible eyes. It's the first thing I noticed about you."

Nick was deadly handsome and so near, she could

hardly breathe. What she couldn't figure out was why he was torturing her.

"I didn't want to bring Candy Rae here," he confessed. "The fact is, she made me promise months ago."

"And you don't break your promises?"

"Try not to. Her mother called my father last week to make sure I'd follow through. He put the old Italian guilt on me."

"Why are you telling me this?"

He looked at her quizzically. "You don't know?"

She shook her head.

He reached out to touch her hair, his gaze flowing over her face. A long moment passed and then he bent his head and kissed her.

Brooke couldn't believe this was happening. His lips were just like she imagined, amazingly warm and giving, a prelude and a promise of more to come. Brooke had waited so long for this, for him, that at first she just remained there enjoying the sensations rippling through her, frozen like an ice sculpture and melting a little at a time.

He wrapped his arms around her and she found herself immersed in Nick Carlino, his touch, his scent, his body pressed to hers. And she was through holding back. She returned his kiss with everything she had inside. He kissed her again, his mouth more demanding now, and a wild sort of frenzy built. Lust combined with the love she held in her heart for him and everything else faded from her mind. He parted her lips and drove his tongue into her mouth. Sensations whirled and she let out tiny gasps as he devoured her, his desire overwhelming.

Overhead, an announcement rang out calling for the last dance.

"I've got to go," he said with a low rasp. He backed away from her but the regret in his eyes bolstered her spirit.

Things had gotten out of control. Wonderfully so and she knew that when she went to sleep that night, her dreams would be of Nick.

Nurse Jacobs entered her room to take her blood pressure and temperature. Brooke waited patiently, sitting upright on the bed, while the older, sweet-faced woman removed the cuff and took the digital thermometer out of her mouth.

"All looks good, Mrs. Keating. Your blood pressure is normal and so is your temperature. How about the dizzy spells?"

She'd told the nurse once already not to call her Mrs. Keating. She hated the reminder of her marriage. "It's Brooke, remember? And I had a slight dizzy spell earlier, but nothing for a few hours."

The nurse looked pleased. "The rest is doing you good. Now, if I could get you to eat something. Mr. Carlino said that dinner would be ready at six. Are you up to going downstairs or shall I bring food up to you?"

"Oh, no. That's not necessary. We'll go down."

Leah began to stir and she knew her baby had enough of napping. She'd want some stimulation and learning about these new surroundings would satisfy her curiosity. Brooke would take her outside later to get some air as well.

"She's a good baby and a good sleeper." Nurse Jacobs smiled at Leah. "My children weren't good sleepers. I tried everything, but they were determined to keep their mom up most of the night. But they were good kids after that. Didn't give me a wink of trouble as teenagers."

"I guess you can't ask for more than that," Brooke said, suddenly curious about the nurse. "Are they grown now?"

"My son is finishing up college at Berkeley. My daughter,

she's the older one, is married and I'm hoping she'll make me a grandmother one day."

Brooke thought about her own mother. She'd had a tough life and was finally married again and living in Hawaii with her new husband, a widower and former naval officer with a kind heart who thought the sun rose and set on her mother's shoulders. Brooke was glad of it and though they missed each other, she knew her mother would spend some extended visits with them once Brooke and Leah settled into their new home.

"My mom is really crazy about Leah," Brooke said. "We saw her last month and—"

Leah fussed, letting out a complaining cry. Brooke stood up to go to her, but the room spun instantly and she reached out for the bed to steady herself. She closed her eyes until the feeling passed.

Nurse Jacobs was beside her quickly and braced her around the waist. "You stood up too fast," she said softly. "Move slow and make each step deliberate. How's your head now?"

Brooke glanced at her. Everything began to clear. "Better."

"Let me get Leah for you. Have a seat and I'll diaper her and bring her to you so you can nurse her."

Brooke did as she was told. The sooner she recovered, the better. She didn't want to be beholden to Nick for anything more. She already owed him for the damages to his car and for room and board, not to mention for the private nurse he'd hired to care for her. Brooke vowed to pay him back once her establishment started making money.

An hour later, Brooke had showered, changed her clothes, put a little blush on her pale cheeks and felt human again. She dressed Leah in a sundress and sandals that matched her own—a gift from Grandma "for her two girls," her mother had written on the gift card. Thankfully, her mom was provided for now and could spend money without pinching pennies and she'd lavished so many wonderful things on Leah.

Brooke smiled.

"That smile looks good on you. Feeling better?"

"Much. I'm ready to go down for dinner."

"I'll take Leah, if you can manage the stairs."

"I'll help Brooke down," Nick said, standing in the opened doorway and nodding at the nurse. He wore a black Polo shirt that displayed lean muscles and tanned olive skin. His pants were beige, expensive and fit his frame perfectly.

"I can manage."

Nurse Jacobs touched her arm. "Let him help you, Brooke. Just in case."

Brooke hesitated, but now wasn't the time to be obstinate. "Well, okay."

Nick waited until they reached the top of the staircase before putting his arm around her waist. She felt the gentle pressure of his touch all the way down to her toes. If nurse Jacobs only knew what a dizzying effect Nick had on her, she wouldn't have encouraged this.

"I'm glad you decided to come down for dinner. I thought you were still annoyed at me from before."

"I'm not in a position to be annoyed. You're being very… gracious."

"So out of character for me, right?"

"No comment," Brooke said, but she smiled and Nick didn't seem to take offense.

Once they made it down the stairs, Nick led them to the terrace where a table was set under a slatted patio roof held up by stone columns. "We're between cooks right now, so I ordered in. You'd end up back in the hospital if I tried my hand at cooking."

"That's fine, thank you," she said, then reached for Leah. "Come here, pretty baby." She kissed Leah's cheek the minute Nurse Jacobs handed her over. She settled Leah onto her lap. The baby was still groggy from her long nap.

The housekeeper, Carlotta, made a big fuss over Leah, offering to hold her while Brooke ate her meal, but she kindly refused. She still hadn't gotten over the accident and what could have happened. She wanted Leah near and she'd eaten this way, with Leah on her lap, dozens of times. It was a ritual that she'd soon have to break. Leah was growing in leaps and bounds and would need a high chair soon.

Carlotta made sure they were served and wanted for nothing. Brooke was amazed at how hungry she was, satisfying her growling pangs with shrimp salad, pasta primavera and creamy pesto chicken. She ate with gusto as Nick and her nurse conversed about growing up in Napa. Nick was a charmer and by the end of the meal, her middle-aged nurse was surely smitten. Every so often, Nick would catch Brooke's eye and they'd exchange a glance. Heat traveled through her body even as she pretended not to notice his effect on her.

Carlotta served a decadent Italian dessert catered from a restaurant Nick's family owned. The oozing lava cake exploded with melted chocolate the minute Brooke touched her fork to the center. Leah grabbed at her fork with her chubby grasp and a spray of liquid chocolate splattered onto Brooke's chest. The baby giggled and swiped at the confection again, tipping it over.

"Leah!" Brooke shook her head as she glanced at her freshly stained white blouse and the puddle of chocolate her child made on the table.

Carlotta and her nurse rushed into the kitchen to repair the damage, leaving Brooke alone at the table with Nick.

"Look what you've done to Mommy." Leah giggled again and Brooke had to smile, unable to feel any anger at the situation. Though she imagined she looked a total mess now. "You're getting me all chocolately and—"

"Delicious," Nick said softly, gazing into her eyes. He slipped a forkful of dessert into his mouth, but his eyes remained on her.

She didn't know how to react. Was he coming on to her? Any embarrassment she might have felt dissolved just seeing the spark of intensity in Nick's eyes. Did she want his flirting, even just for her own deflated ego?

"Here, Carlotta gave me this." Nurse Jacobs returned and handed her a wet dishcloth. "It might not stain if you get to it quickly."

"Oh, I'll probably just take it off upstairs and work on it," she said, holding Leah on her lap with one hand while dabbing at the splashes of chocolate with the other hand.

Carlotta walked onto the patio with a pained expression. "Nick, you have a visitor."

Nick glanced up as a sultry dark-haired woman breezed onto the patio.

"Hi, Nicky."

"Rachel." Nick got out of his seat.

The woman was stunning, even if she was a bit older than Nick. Looking proprietary, she placed her hand on his shoulder and lifted up on her toes to kiss him.

Brooke looked away rather than intrude on an intimate moment. She wondered what Rachel would say if she knew Nick had kissed her just hours ago, on this very same terrace.

"Who are your friends?" the woman inquired, staring at Nick.

He made the introductions without qualms. Rachel followed the direction of Nick's gaze and swept a quick glance at Brooke and the baby, noting her stained blouse without missing a beat.

Brooke had learned not to give in to humiliation anymore. She lifted her chin and greeted Nick's girlfriend with a poise that could win her an Oscar. "It's nice to meet you, Rachel."

"Rachel owns A Rock and A Hard Place," Nick offered.

Brooke furrowed her brow. "I don't remember it."

"It's a bar and nightclub," Rachel explained. "I opened it about three years ago and I guess you could say it's my baby." Rachel looked at Leah. "Until the real thing comes along, that is." She glanced at Nick, who held an unreadable expression, then turned her attention to Leah. "She's adorable."

"Thank you. She's quite a mess at the moment. Both of us are. I should probably clean us both up."

When Brooke rose from the table, Nurse Jacobs stepped up and reached for Leah. "I'll take her for you."

"Thank you," Brooke said, her glance darting from Rachel to Nick. "I'll leave you two alone. Have a nice evening."

Nick met her eyes. "Think you can make it upstairs okay?"

Brooke nodded. "I'm feeling better. Thanks for dinner." She waved her hand over her blemished blouse. "For as much as I managed to get into my mouth, it was *delicious*."

Nick's eyes went wide, then he chuckled and Brooke walked off feeling his gaze on her.

She heard Rachel question him with one word. *"Upstairs?"*

And she scurried a bit faster into the house.

* * *

Nick leaned against the railing that overlooked the valley below, his beer held between two fingers as he took a swig. He'd sipped champagne with the monks in France and enjoyed the best wines in all of Europe, not to mention imbibing from the best-ranked vintages in the family wine cellar, but tonight he needed good all-American beer.

His father would cringe seeing the cases of beer Nick had stocked in the house. Carlinos didn't drink beer. Carlinos were winemakers. His father never came to grips with the fact that none of his sons wanted to be winemakers. They had separate interests, which were, of course, of no concern to the man who'd fathered them. Once Nick's mother died, the boys were treated to Santo Carlino's constant demands on how they should live their lives.

Tony and Joe had escaped relatively unscathed, but Nick hadn't been so lucky. His father had managed to ruin Nick's career, before it had even started.

"I'm pregnant, Nick," Candy Rae cried into the phone right before his debut minor league baseball game. "I'm scared and I need you. Come home."

Nick couldn't come home. He'd been drafted by the Chicago White Sox. He was making his first start on the triple AAA squad on the Charlotte Knights and he needed to perform. He needed to make his mark and prove himself.

While he assured Candy Rae he'd come home and deal with the situation as soon as he could, she wouldn't let up. She'd called him every day for weeks and the calls sapped his concentration on the ball field, so much so that he stopped taking her calls. Next thing he knew, Candy Rae showed up at the ballpark and pleaded with him in person to come home. She was six months pregnant and the evidence of his child growing inside her couldn't be missed. He didn't love Candy Rae, but he'd make sure his child wanted for nothing. He'd have a part in raising the baby but that wasn't good enough for her. She wanted Nick home. She wanted marriage and the white picket fence fairy tale. Candy Rae was spoiled and stubborn and she put up a huge fuss, crying, screaming and stomping her feet. They argued, Nick not giving in to her tantrum and an hour later Nick walked onto the baseball field.

Distracted and pissed off, he'd collided with his teammate trying to make a catch in the outfield. He'd dislocated his shoulder, requiring surgery and a long recovery time.

"Should've been a piece of cake," Nick muttered, sipping his ice-cold beer in the warm Napa night, thinking about that catch *and* the recovery.

The house on the hill was quiet. Only a few stars lit the sky and it was the remote silence surrounding him that brought back his desolation and disappointment. His life could have been so different.

He'd found out late that summer that Candy Rae's baby wasn't his but he'd also found out that his father had put her up to the deception. They'd schemed together to get what they wanted and both wanted the same thing, Nick to come home to Napa. Candy Rae claimed she loved him and Santo wanted a son he could groom to take over the family business.

Nick was released from his minor league contract after that injury and to this day, he'd bet his life his father had his hands in that. Santo was an unscrupulous manipulator. He'd had a reputation for being a ruthless businessman and his business always came first with him.

Nick never forgave him for that…for messing with his dream.

After that fiasco, he'd moved out of the country for many years, becoming the foreign liaison for Carlino Wines in European markets. This was all he could stomach to do, working for the family business—needing time and distance away from Santo. Nick managed other interests overseas, making sound real estate investments. He'd become wealthy in his own right before long.

Nick heard footsteps on the grounds and turned to find Brooke coming out of the house, barefoot, wearing a silky robe. Her long blond hair spilled onto her shoulders. He watched her take a few steps onto the terrace.

She hadn't seen him yet—he was in the shadows—and that was fine with him. He could look at her without her defenses going up. Cascading terrace lamps lit her in a halo of light. Her movements graceful, she stepped farther out onto the terrace, taking in deep breaths of air. She looked troubled, as if searching for peace.

When she spotted him, she jumped back. "Oh, sorry," she whispered. "I didn't think anyone would be out here this late."

"Neither did I. Couldn't sleep?"

"Not tired. I think I got too much rest this afternoon. Looks like you're enjoying the peace. I'll just go back upstairs." She turned and took a step.

"Don't go." Nick cursed under his breath. He was in a dangerous mood and it would be better for her to go inside.

She stopped but didn't turn to face him. "I should go up."

Nick pushed off from the railing and strode over until he was behind her and near enough to whisper in her ear. "You should. But I don't want you to."

Nick put his arms around her waist and brought her close. He'd always liked Brooke. She was unique and fresh with a clever sense of humor. She could make him laugh and he admired her gutsy attitude, while being beautiful and sexy at the same time. She was the girl that got away and she'd remain so, but right now, he wanted her company. And maybe a little bit more.

He felt her trembling in his arms. "What happened to Rachel?"

"She wanted something I can't give her."

Brooke hesitated, then finally whispered quietly, "What's that?"

"All of me."

Nick reached up and took Brooke's hair in his hand. He moved soft strands off her neck and kissed her there. Goose bumps erupted on her nape and Nick drew her closer to whisper, "And you want none of me. Are you holding a grudge?"

"Not a grudge. I told you before."

"Then what, Brooke?"

She turned around to face him. He was hit with an immediate jolt when she stared at him with those beyond-beautiful eyes. "Why does it matter?"

"You were important to me. We were friends once."

Brooke's mouth gaped open then she hauled off and shoved at his chest. Startled by her sudden move, he struggled to keep his balance.

"You are so dense!" Brooke seemed to shout, though it came out in a loud whisper.

Nick looked at her and the absurdity of the conversation struck his funny bone. He laughed. "What the hell are you talking about?"

"You see, you don't even know!"

"So why don't you tell me?" Judging by the look on her face, maybe he didn't want to know.

"You used the 'F' word."

"I did not," he said adamantly and then it dawned on him. He arched a brow. "Oh, okay. So I said we were friends."

Brooke turned to leave. 'I'm not having this conversation," she said as she stepped into the house.

Damn it. The woman was always walking away. He marched after her. "Sit down, Brooke."

She stopped in his living room and glared at him. "Is that an order?"

Nick was through being amused. Why he cared to clear the air with her was beyond him. Maybe it was the mood he was in. Maybe it was hearing Rachel accuse him of using her that got to him tonight. Maybe it was because she'd also accused him of not having a heart. Or maybe it's because he thought he'd done the right thing for once in his life and Brooke was punishing him for it.

He shouldn't give a damn.

But he did.

"Hell, Brooke. Cut me some slack. Talk to me."

Brooke glanced at the sofa and twisted her lips. "I could claim fatigue. I think I feel a dizzy spell coming on."

"Sit," he said, keeping his tone light.

She sat down on the sofa and he took the seat across from her. A glass and wrought-iron coffee table separated them. The room was dark but for the dim lamp light from the terrace filtering inside.

Nick waited.

Then Brooke began. "You were the last person on earth I ever wanted to see again."

"I know that. Now tell me why."

Four

Brooke's memories came rushing back of that one night that had changed her life forever. It wasn't what Nick had done but what he hadn't done that had devastated her young heart.

The pounding on the door startled Brooke out of a sound sleep. She raced down the hallway in her nightie, certain that something was wrong. Her mother was visiting her best friend in San Francisco for the weekend and Brooke feared something terrible had happened to her. Why else would someone be pounding on her door after ten o'clock at night?

She hesitated behind the door, until she heard his voice. "It's me, Brooke. It's Nick. C'mon. Open up." She heard the excitement in his voice and immediately yanked the door open.

He stood in the moonlight, grinning from ear to ear and she came alive right then, as if she'd been an empty shell until Nick appeared to breathe new life into her. She smiled instantly, his obvious joy contagious. "Nick? What is it?"

He lifted her off her feet and twirled her around and around in dizzying circles. "I did it. I did it. I'm going to the major leagues. I got drafted by the White Sox in the fifth round."

Before she had time to react, he set her down, cupped her face in his hands and kissed her with such intensity she thought she was still floating above ground. When he broke off the kiss, the hungry look in his blue eyes held her captivated. "Nick, that's great. It's what you want."

"I know. I know. I'm going to Charlotte to play for the Knights. It's Triple A ball, but if I play to my potential, Coach thinks it won't take long to make it to the majors."

"Oh, Nick. You'll get there. If you want it bad enough, you'll get there."

Without his knowledge, she'd gone to a play-off game and watched him play once. He'd been the star of the team. Everyone cheered for Nick when he stepped up to the plate. He'd hit three home runs in that weekend series and the team had gone on to win the championship.

"I came right over to tell you. I wanted you to know. I wanted to share this with you first."

He'd come to her, before telling his friends? Warmth rushed through her body and when he reached for her again and kissed her, Brooke's world turned upside down.

"I want you, Brooke," he whispered urgently, bracing her waist and tugging her close. Her legs rubbed against his jeans. "I've always wanted you."

He lavished kisses on her forehead, her eyes, her nose, her cheeks and then devoured her mouth in another long, fiery crazed kiss that lit her body on fire. "My mom's out of town," she whispered and Nick wasted no time.

"Where's your room?"

Brooke led him there and stood by the bed. He smiled and in one smooth move, he lifted her nightie and filled his hands with her breasts. The exquisite feel of his palms on her sent a hot thrill through her body. Deft fingers stroked her nipples and she ached for more. When he put his mouth on her, she squeezed her eyes shut from the exquisite, sweet torture.

Nick had her naked on the bed in seconds, then he removed his shirt and joined her. She was glad she'd waited, glad to have her first time be with Nick, the boy who'd been out of her reach for so long. Now, he was here, wanting her.

She loved him with a fierceness that stunned her. His touch sent her spiraling out of control. He kissed her a dozen times, driving her insane with his tongue, as he caressed every inch of her body.

Inexperienced and awkward, Brooke didn't know what to do. What would he expect from her? Should she be touching him back?

"This is a good night...being with you," he whispered, nibbling on her throat. His softly spoken words abolished her insecurities.

His hand traveled lower, his fingers seeking her warmth, and electric shocks powered through her body. She stiffened from the new sensation. She'd never felt anything like it, the intimacy of the act, the way he knew how to find her most sensitive spot and stroke her until she was breathless and mindless.

The sensation built and built and she arched and moaned until only little cries of ecstasy escaped her lips. Wave after wave of release shattered her and Nick stroked her harder, faster, drawing out her orgasm, his eyes dark and filled with desire. He murmured soft words but she didn't hear

*him, didn't recognize what he was asking until she felt the
last tiny wave leave her.*

"Are you protected?" he asked again.

*And she looked at him and shook her head. "I don't
have, I mean I don't—"*

*He stood up and reached into his pocket, then something
stopped him. She'd never forget the look on his face, the
way he studied her as she lay naked on the bed.*

*"Nick?" Dread beat against her chest and her stomach
coiled.*

*He stared at her and blinked. His gaze roved over her
again and this time she truly felt naked and strangely alone.
Then the unthinkable happened. Nick shook his head,
closing his eyes to her and taking deep breaths. "I can't
do this, Brooke. I'm gonna have to leave."*

"Nick?" Panicked, Brooke lifted up to reach for him.

*To her horror, he backed away, as if repulsed by her
touch. "I gotta go, Brooke. I can't. I'm sorry."*

*Mortified, Brooke watched him grab his shirt and walk
out of her bedroom.*

"Brooke?" Nick asked, glancing at her intently.

Sudden anger strangled the words she wanted to say to
him. She wanted to blast him with full guns and then walk
out of his house and forget she ever laid eyes on him again.
But she bit back her remarks and calmed down to a rational
level. "You hurt me, Nick. That night. The night you got
drafted."

His sharp breath was audible. "None of that was supposed
to happen."

That's all he had to say? He'd broken her heart and left
her shattered, wishing that she'd been enough for him. The
girl from the right side of town. The girl he'd want to take

out on a date and introduce to his family, the girl who didn't work at the local diner and sewed her own clothes.

She'd dared to hope, but that hope had been crushed.

She wasn't even good enough to have a one-night fling with. He'd rejected her and left her lying there, exposed and vulnerable and humiliated.

"How do you think I felt when you walked out on me?"

"You should have been relieved," Nick said in earnest, and she wanted to shove him in the chest again.

"Relieved? How can you say that? You…you led me on. You came to my house that night with one thing on your mind."

"Things shouldn't have gone that far, Brooke. I realized that and I walked out before we made a mistake."

"A mistake?" Inwardly she cringed. Now she was a *mistake*. This conversation was going from bad to worse and Brooke wanted to scream out in frustration.

Nick leaned forward, bracing the back of his elbows on his knees. "You were special to me, Brooke and—"

"I was your good buddy," she spit out.

"No, you were the girl I wanted the most and the one I couldn't let myself have."

Brooke shook her head. "I don't get it. Your memory must be failing you. Age does that to a person. You must be old before your time."

"You see," Nick said with a grin. "You're clever and feisty and pretty. Listen, I may have had a reputation back then—"

"Similar to the one you have now," she butted in.

"R-right. But I didn't want to lump you in with the other girls I dated."

"You never *dated* me. Are you going to tell me that's because I was so special?"

"I was afraid of you."

"What?" Brooke sat back in her seat, thunderstruck. Nothing he said was sinking in, but this, *this* was too ridiculous to even consider. "Big, bad Brooke."

"Sweet, special, smart Brooke," he said.

Her anger rose. His compliments meant nothing to her. "Stop! Just stop, Nick," she rushed out. "Why don't you just admit the truth! I didn't measure up to the other girls in your string. You got me naked and decided you could do better. Isn't that what really happened? I was inexperienced and I don't know, maybe I wasn't doing the right things and you—"

"Let me get this straight," he said, between clenched teeth. "You're angry because we didn't screw like rabbits all night long? Here I was trying to be noble, to do the right thing, and you're upset because I didn't take your virginity?"

"I cared about you," she said, raising her voice. "I wanted it to be with you."

"And I didn't want to use you. Damn it, the one time I do the right thing I get kicked in the ass. Listen, Brooke. I wasn't sticking around. At that time, my life, my future was baseball. I was leaving the next week for the minor leagues. And yeah, you scared me, because of all the girls I'd been with you were the one girl who could tie me down. The one girl I'd miss when I took off. It wouldn't have worked. I didn't want to hurt you. I never meant to."

"But you did," she said quietly. "You devastated me, Nick. I never heard from you again. Ever."

I was deeply in love with you.

She opened up to him, finally confessing what she'd held back all these years, "Just think of all the worst things you think about yourself, your secret innermost thoughts that nag at you day after day, that you're nothing, not pretty enough, not smart enough, not wealthy enough, not *anything* and to have those very thoughts confirmed by the one person in the world who can change your opinion. You leaving me there that night confirmed the worst about myself."

Nick came around the coffee table to sit beside her. From the dim lights, she could see into his eyes, the sorrow there and the apology. He didn't try to touch her, but those eyes penetrating hers were like the tightest embrace. "I'm sorry. I thought I did the right thing for you. I've never been one to hold back when I wanted something, but what I did that night, it was for you. I wanted you, Brooke. But it wouldn't have been fair to you."

Brooke had clung to her perceptions about Nick for so long it was hard to let them go. She wanted to believe him and release the bitter feelings that had only dragged her down these past years. She wanted to be done with it. She had a future to look forward to now with Leah. Finally she resigned herself to accept Nick's claim as the truth as he saw it. "Okay, Nick."

It still didn't make up for the months of anguish she'd experienced or for the heartache of loving someone like Nick, but she realized it was finally time to move on.

"Okay?" Nick said. "We've cleared the air?"

She nodded. "Yes."

And they sat in silence for a long while, just absorbing the conversation.

"I think I'm well enough to leave tomorrow," Brooke said finally. "I've got a new life waiting for me." She rose from the sofa. "I should go."

Nick nodded, but his response left room for doubt. "We'll see."

Brooke dressed Leah in a blue-and-white-polka-dotted short set with a ruffled collar and bloomers. She combed her hair and hummed the *Sesame Street* song, laughing as Leah's stubborn curls popped right back up the minute she put the brush down. The morning seemed filled with promise. She'd had a lot to absorb from her encounter with Nick last night and she'd slept on it, waking this morning with a better attitude and ready to put the past behind her.

"It's gonna be a good day, baby girl," she said, lifting Leah up and twirling her around. A wave of light-headedness hit her and Brooke stopped and let it pass, clutching her child tight. "Your mommy is pushing her luck," she whispered.

Nurse Jacobs entered the room, dressed and ready to take over. "Time to take your vitals," she said to Brooke.

Brooke complied, having her blood pressure and temperature taken. When the nurse finished her exam, she gave her a reassuring smile. "You look well-rested."

"I'm feeling much better today."

"You got dizzy just a second ago."

Brooke didn't think she'd seen that. "Stupid of me to spin Leah around. I won't do that again. We're going down for breakfast."

"Okay, I'll hold Leah on the way downstairs."

"Actually, I'd like to hold her."

Nurse Jacobs narrowed her eyes and debated until Brooke added, "You'll be right by my side. We'll go down together."

Once it was all settled, they headed to the kitchen. They heard cupboards being opened and slammed shut and curses being muttered by Nick in hushed tones. The odor of burnt toast filled the air. Brooke walked in with Leah in her arms, took one look at the kitchen in disarray with greasy frying pans on the stovetop, blackened bread in the toaster and Nick, dressed in a pair of jeans and a white T-shirt that hugged his male frame, looking frustrated and out of sorts.

Brooke immediately grinned. "I didn't feel the tornado this morning. Did you, Leah?"

The baby looked at her quizzically.

Nick cast Brooke a quick glance. "Carlotta's got the morning off, not that she cooks anyway, but at least she can boil water and make toast. Looks like I can do neither."

Brooke took in the state-of-the-art appliances and fully functional workstation. "It's a great kitchen. You don't have a cook?"

"Not since my father passed away. The cook retired and we've managed without her up until now. Tony's gone and Joe spends his time at the office or with his fiancée. Which leaves me. I've been fending for myself, not very well I might add, interviewing a little, but no one's worked out." He picked up the phone. "I'll call for delivery. What would you ladies like for breakfast?"

Brooke shook her head. "Jeez, that bump on my head didn't obliterate my cooking skills. I'll fix breakfast. It's the least I can do. I make a mean omelet. Let me at this kitchen and I'll have breakfast on the table in half an hour." Nick put the phone down slowly and Brooke took over. "Here, hold Leah a minute while I raid your refrigerator."

She put Leah in Nick's arms and her daughter snuggled in looking comfortable, while Nick looked anything but. He tried to hand her off to Nurse Jacobs and the wily nurse stepped back and shook her head. "*Brooke* is my patient." She winked at Brooke. Nick sat down at the kitchen table with a twist of his lips and Leah latched onto his shirt.

Brooke opened his double stainless steel refrigerator and

began taking out ingredients. "It's well stocked, which is good news." She immersed herself in her task, enjoying the process. She quickly whipped together three of the lightest, fluffiest omelets she'd ever made, pan-fried potatoes and a fresh fruit salad. Coffee brewed in the pot and while she cooked, Nurse Jacobs set the table.

"How's Leah doing over there?" Brooke asked. She'd been keeping an eye on the two of them.

"Is she always this fidgety?" Nick asked as Leah tried to crawl her way up his chest. She pulled at his shirt and brought her little hand up to swipe at his chin. He set her back down onto his lap. "I think I liked her better when she was sleeping."

Brooke smiled. "She's an absolute *angel*…when she's sleeping. Okay, all set. I'll dish it up. I hope you like lots of veggies and avocado."

There was still tension between them, but she wouldn't have to deal with it too much longer because Brooke was leaving today. She was eager and excited at the prospect of starting her own business.

She served the meal and silence ensued. With Leah on her lap, she dug into the omelet and tasted. Not bad. Then she glanced at Nick's plate to find he'd gobbled up the omelet already and was working on the potatoes. "Want another?" she asked.

"In a heartbeat. Finish yours first. I'll work on what's left on my plate."

A few minutes later, Brooke started cooking Nick's second omelet and Nurse Jacobs took Leah outside for a little stroll.

Nick leaned over the black granite counter, elbows folded, watching her put the bell peppers, onions, bits of ham and grated cheese onto the egg mix and top it off with avocado. "So we're good, about last night. No hard feelings?"

Brooke met his gaze, waiting for the hurt, anger and bitterness to emerge. When it didn't appear, her heart lifted. She and Nick came from different worlds. They were never destined to be together and maybe…just maybe she might believe that he had spared her that night. Yet her initial thoughts from her high school days hadn't changed. He was way out of her league. If she were looking for a man, he wouldn't be last on her list—he wouldn't be *on* it at all. He wasn't a man to stick around. Nick was a player and Brooke had already played the game and lost. And while that might be okay for her, it wasn't all right for Leah. Her daughter's needs always had to come first.

"No hard feelings. But we have to talk about something else. Have you heard back from your mechanic?"

"I have."

"And? What's the bad news?"

He frowned. "Your car might live."

"That's not bad news! That's great."

She flipped the omelet over and lifted it with a spatula then grabbed Nick's plate from the table. "I was hoping it wasn't totaled." She loaded the omelet onto the dish and set it in front of him.

He took his fork and began eating. "How do you do it? This is better than the last one and that one was pretty damn good."

"I'm amazing. I can make an omelet."

Nick scoffed. "You're a good cook, Brooke. Admit it."

"I do okay. So how much is it gonna cost for the repairs?"

"It's taken care of."

She blinked and stood completely still. "No, Nick. It's not. Both of our cars were damaged. I owe somebody, something. I plan to pay. Do you have an estimate?"

"I do."

"Well, where is it? Show it to me," she ordered.

Nick scratched his head and stared at her. She glared back and held her ground. He reached into his pocket and pulled out two pieces of paper from Napa Auto Body Works. Unfolding the papers, he laid them onto the counter and turned them her way.

"Thirteen thousand dollars for your car! You can practically buy a new car for that!" Of course she'd had to collide into *Nick* and the *most* expensive car on the planet.

"My insurance will cover most of it."

Relieved about that, Brooke peered at her estimate. "Forty-eight hundred dollars." She breathed a heavy sigh. That would cut heavily into the money she had saved to start her business, not to mention fixing up the place. The broken interior door would have to wait, and so would the painters and new linens she'd need for the beds. And fixing the bathrooms. Still, she couldn't make *any* repairs without her car. She needed wheels. "When can I have my car back?"

"Maybe you should get another car. Randy said it was borderline. He could fix your car but it's almost not worth it."

"I can't do that. I can't afford a newer car."

Annoyed that Nick would think it just that easy for her to buy a car, she turned away, working out her frustration by scrubbing the frying pan in the sink.

A long minute stretched out in silence.

"Brooke, turn around." Nick was sure bossy this morning. She turned. "Listen, I have a proposition for you. I've got a 2006 Lexus just sitting in the garage waiting to be driven. The insurance is paid up on it for the rest of the year. It's yours if you want it."

She laughed at the thought, shaking her head. "Yeah, you'll just give me a car."

"Not give. You'll work it off."

"Work it off?" Her smile faded instantly. She closed her eyes to small slits. "I feel the need to slap you coming on."

"Cooking," he explained.

"Cooking?"

"You need a car. I need a cook. Correct that, I desperately need a cook. Carlotta's been a pain about who she'll let into the house. The last cook I tried to hire had Carlotta threatening to quit, but she'll jump for joy at having you here."

She immediately began shaking her head. "No, it wouldn't work. I've got a job. I'm going to be spending all my time at my aunt's place. My place now."

"You said yourself, it's in bad shape. You can stay here while you work on your place." The idea seemed to take hold, snowballing as Nick became more adamant. "I'd only need you for breakfast and dinner. You'd have all day to work at the house."

"I'm not staying here."

"You shouldn't have made me that omelet, Brooke. My stomach's involved now. You need the car. I'm tired of eating restaurant food. It'll work out for both of us. Think about it."

She didn't' want to think about it. She didn't, but his offer was too good not to at least give it some thought. "How long before I earned the car?"

"For as long as you need to get your place up and running. A couple of months?"

"That's very generous of you, but I can't—"

"Your car doesn't have air bags," he pointed out none too gently. "You'd be foolish to fix that car."

She squeezed her eyes shut, reminded of what might have happened. The accident could have been far worse.

"Think of Leah," he added without missing a beat.

She was thinking of Leah, constantly. And harrowing thoughts of that accident struck her with fear. She'd actually lost consciousness when they'd collided. What if she hadn't run into someone she'd known? What would have happened to Leah then? She didn't want to take Nick's offer. But Leah's safety came first. She remembered what the flight attendants always said in their little welcome aboard speech about putting an oxygen mask on yourself first, before putting one on for your child. The bottom line, in order to care for your child, you must take care of yourself.

Brooke craved independence and wanted to be indebted to no one. Living under Nick Carlino's roof wouldn't be an option if she were thinking only about herself. But of course, Nick had the upper hand and was on the right side of the argument. Small wonder—he negotiated for Carlino Wines, and knew when to finesse and when to land the crushing blow. This time, he'd used Leah as his weapon and Brooke was defeated.

"That's low, Nick. You know I always have Leah's welfare at heart. What's in it for you?"

"I'm selfish enough to want to eat good meals. And keep the housekeeper from walking out. Do we have a deal?"

Brooke's mouth turned down as she accepted. "Hand over the keys and tell me what you want for dinner."

The dimples of doom came out when he smiled and Brooke didn't find them attractive at all.

Not even a little bit.

"You're joking, right? You've got Brooke Hamilton *living* with you now? I thought it was only temporary." Joe glanced at Tony as they sat at their monthly meeting at the Carlino offices in downtown Napa. His two brothers shook their heads in disapproval. "You're good, little brother," Joe said, "but I didn't know how good. You met her what, twenty-four hours ago?"

Normally, Nick didn't let his brothers get to him, but right now he wasn't in the mood for their wisecracking. He spoke through tight lips. "It was two days ago. And more like she met with the front end of my Ferrari. She's working for me, to pay off her debt." Hell, he made her sound like an indentured servant. With a brisk wave of the hand, he added, "It's complicated."

Tony's laughter filled the air. "Complicated as in a honey blonde with pretty blue eyes."

"You liked her back in high school," Joe said. "You know what they say about the one that got away."

"She's got a baby," Nick said in his defense. "Or are you forgetting about the kid?"

"You think that's gonna stop you?" Tony looked skeptical.

"Hell yeah." Nick wasn't father material. He'd learned from the master. He had enough of his old man in him to know he wouldn't make a good daddy. The blood ties ran thick. He never planned on having children, thus saving some poor child his ruthless tendencies.

"We think not," Tony said glibly, leaning back in his chair and stretching out. He darted a glance at Joe.

"Then, you think wrong," Nick said, ready to change the subject.

After Candy Rae's deception, Nick had lost faith in the opposite sex. Not that he didn't love women, but he wouldn't be foolish enough to place his trust in a female again. He'd lost out on his dream because of Candy Rae's lies and his father's self-serving manipulations. He'd been crushed and trampled on like the precious grapes that his father had loved so much. For that, he hated what he did for a living, feeling his father had won. Nick spent most of his time in Europe, away from the place that caused him such heartache. He'd made enough smart financial investments to break loose of his father's ties forever and was about to do so, but then Santo up and died. Nick came home because his brothers needed him. He was here because of them even though they were a pain in his rear end. Nick liked things simple and getting too involved with Brooke and her bundle of trouble would only complicate his life.

"Want to put money on it?" Tony said, baiting him.

"Damn right," Nick said. "A betting man always likes to take money from suckers. Name your price."

Joe sat straight up in his seat and Nick saw his brother do mental calculations. "What if it's not for cash? What if we wager something more important?"

"Like what?" Nick furrowed his brows.

"Like if you fall for her, you take over the company."

Nick fell back against his seat in shock.

"I like it," Tony said. "The nameplate on the door will read, Nick Carlino, CEO."

"Don't go counting your chickens. I haven't agreed to this yet. Seems this is a little lopsided. What do I get if I win?"

Joe didn't hesitate to answer. "Easy, if you win and you don't fall hard for that gorgeous woman and her little girl, you're completely off the hook. You'll get your fair share of the empire but you won't have to run the company." Joe looked to Tony. "Does that sound fair?"

Tony nodded. "That's right. If you win, it'll be between Joe and I."

"You said if I fall for Brooke. Define *fall for.*"

"The whole enchilada, Nick," Joe said. "Love, marriage and baby carriages."

Nick grinned. He'd never been in love before. He didn't think himself capable and marriage to any woman wasn't in his game plan. Ever. Just because the two of them found their so-called soul mates, didn't mean Nick wanted to follow in their footsteps. He wasn't like his brothers. He didn't do long-term relationships. "This is a piece of cake. You've got yourself a bet." Nick stood, eager to shake hands with his brothers and seal the deal. "And thanks for making this easy for me."

Joe looked at Tony and they both smiled smugly.

Nick would relish wiping the smiles off their faces and then he'd be off the hook to go about living his life. There was no way he'd let one woman and her child take him down.

No way in hell.

Five

The Lexus was a really great car, Brooke thought, running her hand along the smooth black leather seat. With dual temperature settings, a CD player and all the other bells and whistles, this was five-star luxury at its finest. She couldn't wait get behind the wheel and take it for a drive. She sat in the passenger seat glancing at Nick behind the wheel as they drove to Dr. Maynard's office.

He wouldn't let her drive until she got the okay from the doctor this afternoon and she couldn't blame him for that. Still, she hated leaving Leah behind. Though she trusted Nurse Jacobs and Carlotta to watch her baby, she hadn't spent much time apart from her since the moment she'd been born.

"She's okay," Nick said, glancing at her. He had an uncanny way of knowing what she was thinking.

"I know. It's just that I feel lost without her."

"We'll get her a new car seat after your appointment, then you won't have to leave her behind again."

"Thanks for doing this, Nick."

"No problem. I've got a vested interest now." He winked.

She cocked him a wry smile. "I live to cook for you."

"That's the attitude," he said.

"So what would you like for dinner?"

"First, let's see what Steve says. If all is well, you can surprise me."

"All will be well."

Nick looked her up and down and the heat of his gaze made her quiver. "Looks good from where I'm sitting."

Brooke had to remind herself not to melt into a puddle just because he complimented her. It was Nick being Nick. She wouldn't fall for his charm again.

Thirty minutes later, after a thorough exam, Dr. Maynard gave her a clean bill of health. "I'm feeling so much better today," Brooke said, as he walked her out of the room.

"Good, well just take it slow for a while. Don't overdo anything," the doctor said.

"I won't."

Nick rose when Dr. Maynard walked her to the reception area. The two men shook hands.

"Well?" Nick asked her with a hopeful expression.

"I'm fine. I get to pass Go and collect two hundred dollars."

Nick smiled and his dimples appeared. She ignored them, telling herself the thrill she felt was only because she was finally back to square one and she could begin working on the house. Then she turned back to the doctor. "Oh, Dr. Maynard, can you recommend a pediatrician for Leah?"

"Sure can." He walked around to his reception desk,

pulled out a business card and handed it to her. "Dr. Natalie Christopher. She's excellent. And right in this building."

"Thanks for everything," Brooke said, glancing at the card. "I appreciate it."

"You take care now," he said to her, then turned to Nick. "I'll see you Friday."

Nick nodded and when he walked away, Brooke walked up to the desk and spoke to the receptionist, taking out her checkbook. "What do I owe you?"

The receptionist shook her head. "There's no charge."

"No charge? Really? But—"

Nick took her arm and led her away. "It's taken care of."

"You paid for me?"

"Not exactly. The doc owes me and he just settled up the score."

"What? I can't let you do that." Her voice elevated enough to cause stares from the patients in the waiting room.

"It's done, Brooke. Trust me. He's getting off cheap. Come on, we have to go car seat shopping."

Frustration rose and settled in her gut. She didn't want to make a scene in the waiting room, so she marched out of the office. She couldn't figure out why she was so angry with Nick. Ever since the accident, he'd been kind to her, so why did she want to lash out at him all the time? Was it because he could still push her internal buttons with a look or a smile? Was it because he was still the golden boy with all the money, good looks and charm one man could ask for? Or was it because he always seemed to be in control, always took care of things. He was someone she didn't want to rely on and yet, that's all she'd been doing lately was letting Nick make her life easy. It wouldn't last and she didn't want to get used to him being there for her. In the long run, she knew Nick couldn't be counted on.

Once they reached the parking lot, Nick took her hand and looked deep into her eyes. He was amazingly handsome and being near him complicated her life in ways she couldn't begin to deal with. She stilled from his touch, feeling a sharp jab of emotion, knowing she should pull her hand away.

"It's all yours," he said, dropping the keys into her palms.

Brooke stared down at the keys, speechless.

"You want to drive, don't you?" he asked softly.

Brooke nodded, holding back tears. Why had she gotten so emotional? Maybe, because Nick Carlino had just given her a car.

A car.

She wouldn't fool herself into thinking that her culinary skills could have earned her enough to pay for this car. This was the nicest, most decent thing anyone had ever done for her. Her lips quivered. *Don't cry, Brooke. Don't cry.*

But the more she tried to hold back, the more moisture pooled in her eyes. Then the dam broke and tears spilled down her cheeks.

Nick appeared puzzled, then he pulled her into his arms. "Hey," he said quietly, tucking her head under his chin. He stroked her back. "It's just a car."

"It's not just a car," she blubbered, feeling like a fool and hating Nick for being so sweet. Why on earth couldn't he just be the bastard she'd hated all these years and leave her alone?

She clung to him for an awkward minute then pulled away. "It's more than a car…it's safety for Leah and my future, and—"

"Don't cry," he said, lifting her chin and gazing at her. Her eyes were probably red and swollen, her nose all wet and ugly.

He bent his head and kissed her softly on the lips.

It was a warm, sweet, gentle brushing of the lips meant to console and comfort. It did just that, making Brooke feel safe and protected. She sighed deeply and allowed soft feelings for Nick to filter in, just this once. Fighting them would be futile, so she surrendered to her emotions and took what he offered.

When he lowered his head again, ready to do more consoling, Brooke's nerves rattled, not because she didn't want him to kiss her again, but because she did. She turned her head into his chest, denying another kiss, and announced with a whisper, "Men don't like seeing women cry. They think they've done something wrong and don't know how to fix it."

Nick cupped her chin gently and lifted her face to his. "Did I do something wrong?"

She shook her head. "No, you did something...nice."

His gaze lowered to her mouth. "And for the record, that's not why I kissed you."

She didn't want to know why he kissed her.

"I kissed you because you're a brave, honest woman who's been through a lot these past few days and..."

When he stopped speaking, Brooke searched his face, waiting. "And?"

Nick appeared slightly taken aback. He blinked and seemed a little flustered, then he moved away from her. "And, nothing. You looked like you needed a kiss, that's all." He headed for the passenger side of the car. "Are you ready to test this baby or what?"

Surprised by Nick's sudden change of demeanor, Brooke had no choice but to bolster her emotions. She took a deep, cleansing breath. "You bet. I'm ready."

She got into the car, put the key into the ignition and started the engine, then glanced at Nick. He looked at her oddly for a moment as if he were trying to figure something out, then he pointed to the road. "It's all yours, Brooke."

Sudden nerves took hold. Maybe she wasn't ready yet. Apprehension led to fear as she replayed the collision in her mind. The images rushed back to her fresh and vivid. She'd never been one for panic attacks, but she could see one happening now. "This is my first time behind the wheel since the accident."

"First times can be rough. Just do what comes naturally and you'll do fine." Nick sounded so confident.

"Really?" She nibbled on her lip.

"Gotta jump back onto that horse."

"I'm afraid of horses," she said.

Nick shook his head. "We'll remedy that another day. Right now, you're going to hold onto the steering wheel and put the car in gear, then gas it." He was back to being bossy again.

"Okay, don't go getting smug on me. I know *how* to drive."

Nick grinned. "That's my girl. Let's go."

Brooke pulled out of the parking lot and onto the road, doing what came naturally. Nick was right, she was doing fine. It was like riding a bike in some ways, everything seemed to come back to her and she'd overcome her initial fear.

"You've got it, Brooke," he said after a minute on the road.

"Thanks." She breathed a sigh of relief and wondered how she would have done without Nick sitting beside her, giving her courage. She felt more confident with each mile she drove. Now if she could only get the "that's my girl" comment out of her head, life would be peachy keen.

Nick helped Brooke install the car seat and was amazed at how intricate the danged thing was. Pull the strap here, tug there, make sure it fits tight enough and after all their struggles, Brooke finally said, "I'm going to have a professional look at it. Make sure it's safe."

"Doesn't look like it's going anywhere to me." He gave a final tug.

"Just to be sure," she said, staring at the car seat with concern. "Can't be too careful."

Brooke looked cute with her hair pulled back in a ponytail, her blonde curls falling past her shoulder, wearing an oversized T-shirt, jeans and flip-flops on her feet. She'd changed into different clothes once they'd returned home from Napa, calling them her "mommy clothes." It shouldn't be a turn-on, Nick was used to women in slinky clothes that left little to the imagination. But on Brooke, the clothes suited her and he found no matter what she wore, he was more than mildly interested.

"Thanks for helping me get it into the car," she said. "Maybe the experience will come in handy for you one day."

Nick winced. "I doubt it."

"You might change your mind. Don't be too sure of it, Nick." She glanced at her watch. "What time do you usually eat dinner?"

"I'm usually through working at seven."

"Okay, I'm going to surprise you tonight."

"You always do," he said and Brooke's soft laughter made him smile.

He thought back on their kiss this afternoon in the parking lot. That had been a surprise. It was nothing, something to soothe her fragile nerves, but he hadn't expected to be thrown for a loop by that kiss, or by holding her and bringing her comfort. Usually a master of self-control, Nick hadn't been able to stop himself and the rewards he'd reaped were those of protecting and calming her. It had felt good, damn good in a way he hadn't experienced before.

He scoffed silently at the notion. Just hours ago, he'd made the deal of all deals with his brothers. He was so certain he'd win his bet, that he'd started making plans for his return to Monte Carlo in the fall. He had a house there and planned on moving in permanently once the renovations were done, hopefully by late September.

By then, Tony and Rena would have their child. Joe would have married Ali, and Nick would be free to come and go as he pleased.

With no ties and no one to account to but himself.

Nick's stomach grumbled as he admitted to himself that he was ready for home cooking again. His mother had been a great cook and he remembered as a child being lured into the kitchen by pungent aromas of garlic and rosemary and bread baking in the oven. His mother would hum a melodic tune as she prepared the family meals, happy to be nourishing her young family. She'd been a saint to simmer Santo's volcanic nature. When Nick's mom was alive, the house had been a home. Nick had almost forgotten what that felt like.

He'd been smart to hire Brooke for the time being. He was really looking forward to sitting down to a meal that hadn't been boxed up, frozen or delivered from a local restaurant.

At least that was one craving Brooke could satisfy while under his roof.

"I guess it's time to say good-bye to Nurse Jacobs," Brooke said with a note of sadness. Brooke glanced down the driveway to where Leah was being strolled around the garden by her nurse. "She's a sweet woman."

"Are you sure you don't need her a little longer?" he asked.

"I'm sure," she said firmly. Bracing her hands on her hips next to the car, she hoisted her pretty chin. "I just drove you all over town. And installed my daughter's car seat. I'm fine, Nick."

"Correction, *we* installed the car seat."

"Fine, burst my bubble. *We* installed the car seat. But I really hate saying good-bye. And you know what's crazy? I don't even know her first name. She doesn't like it and wouldn't divulge it."

"It's Prudence. I was warned not to call her Pru, Prudy or Trudy. Otherwise, she might walk out."

Brooke's mouth gaped open for a second. Then she tossed her head back, giving way to spontaneous giggles that made Nick laugh too. She braced herself on the side of the car, her whole body jiggling as she tried to stifle her amusement.

Fully caught up in her laughter, Nick watched her breasts ride up and down her chest from underneath that loose shirt. He sidled next to her by the car. Her fresh citrus scent that reminded him of orange blossoms filled the air around her.

"I'm sorry," she said amid another round of giggles. "It just struck me as funny. You should have seen the look on your face when you were telling me that."

Nick smiled along with her. "Pretty unbelievable, isn't it?"

"Why didn't you tell me before now?"

"I forgot all about it. It was on the terms of her agreement."

"It's not a bad name at all," Brooke said, still smiling. Her entire face lit up when she was happy. "I don't know too many women who really like their name."

Nick tilted his head. "You don't like your name?"

She shook her head. "Not really. Brooke sounds so…I don't know, boring?"

"It suits you."

"So you think I'm boring?" Her amusement faded.

Nick winced. He'd stepped in it now. "Hell no. It's a strong name, like the woman. That's all I meant." He wouldn't tell her that her eyes reminded him of streaming clear aqua waters. What better name than Brooke?

Thankfully the conversation was interrupted when Nurse Jacobs approached with Leah in the stroller. "She's ready for a feeding."

"Okay," Brooke said, bending down to lift the baby out. "How's my pretty girl?" Brooke planted a kiss on Leah's forehead. "Did you like your walk?"

Leah clung tight to her mother, then focused her wide blue eyes his way and gave him a toothless smile.

Nick looked at mother and baby and an off-limits sign posted in his head.

"I'll take her inside and feed her, then I'll make dinner."

Brooke walked off with the baby and Nick stood in front of the house with the nurse. "As you know, Brooke got a clean bill of health from the doctor. I want to thank you for all you've done, and on such short notice."

"You're welcome. It was a treat for me too. I don't often get a chance to care for a young family. Leah's precious."

Nick nodded politely.

"Brooke is a determined young woman. It's a hard life, being a single mother. I hope she finds someone to share her life with." Nurse Jacobs cast him an assessing look. "You'll look out for her, won't you? As her friend?"

The "F" word. Brooke wouldn't want that label put onto their relationship. He didn't know how to label it, but they weren't friends. Exactly.

"She'll be working here for a while, so you don't have to worry," Nick replied, sounding as noncommittal as he could.

She nodded. "I'll go inside now and say my good-byes."

He shook her hand and thanked her once again, watching as she walked inside the house, leaving Nick alone with some nagging thoughts.

Brooke nursed Leah, knowing that pretty soon the pediatrician would probably encourage her to begin feeding the baby solid foods. Leah's appetite was growing and she was ready to have more substance in her diet. Brooke gazed down at her daughter—the bond they made through eye contact during this special time touched her heart. She'd miss these daily feedings, when she could forget all else, put her feet up and simply enjoy this special time with her baby.

Brooke's guilt came in sudden waves now when she thought about Leah's father. Her ex-husband didn't know he had a daughter. He didn't know Leah existed. Would it matter to him? A little voice in her head told her he had a right to know, but her fear had always won out. And if she were honest with herself, she'd have to admit that both fear and *anger* were at the root of her holding the truth from Dan.

Their marriage hadn't been perfect, but she would never have guessed that her husband was capable of such deception. Right under her nose, Dan had been carrying on an affair with another woman. He'd been sleeping with both of them.

She'd been blindsided by the betrayal and wasn't in any frame of mind to divulge her own pregnancy to him, not when he'd made it clear that he no longer loved her. But deep in her heart, Brooke knew she would have to confront him one day and reveal the truth to him. One day...but she didn't want that day to be anytime soon.

Brooke took Leah down to the kitchen and set her into her little playpen positioned by the granite island in the middle of the room. "Watch Mommy cook."

Leah looked up with wide curious eyes and picked up a pretzel-shaped teething ring and stuck it into her mouth. She gnawed on the ring with glee, as if it were a one-hundred dollar steak.

Brooke grinned. Her little girl would be cutting her first tooth soon.

"Okay, what shall we surprise Nick with?" Brooke scoured the refrigerator and pantry and decided on her meal. Cooking soothed her nerves. There was something therapeutic about producing a fine meal for someone who would appreciate it. She'd always enjoyed the nearly instant gratification she'd felt when it all came together better than expected. Working as a waitress while in high school, then managing the inn more recently, where she'd lend a hand in the kitchen, had taught her a thing or two about taste, presentation and nutrition.

By seven o'clock dinner was ready and the table was set. When Nick didn't appear, Brooke picked up Leah and went in search. She found him sitting in the downstairs study behind a desk, head deep in paperwork. The room was so masculine, with dark walnut panels combined with warm russet textured walls, massive bookcases and a wood-framed bay window that looked out to verdant vineyards, that Brooke felt uncomfortably out of place.

Leah's little baby sounds brought Nick's head up.

"Hi," she said, witnessing Nick's power and status once again, as he sat in the Carlino office. Sometimes, when he was adjusting her baby's car seat or holding Leah in his arms, she'd forget that he was a wealthy wine magnate with a vintage heritage that went back for generations. "Dinner is on the table."

"Okay, smells great from here." Nick rose and smiled at her. "What's for dinner?"

"It's a surprise. Come and see."

Nick followed her into the kitchen and she filled his plate and set it on the table. "Have a seat."

He glanced at the table set for one. "After you."

"What? No, Leah won't sit still. This is her fussy time. You eat. I'll have something later."

Nick glanced at the baby in her arms. She was peering straight at him with a look of contentment on her face.

Leah, don't make a liar out of your mommy.

"I'd like to have your company during dinner, Brooke. Set yourself a place."

"Why?"

"Why not? You have to eat too. Why should we both eat alone? Besides, how else can I critique your meals?"

"Oh, so you're going to rate my cooking."

"I'd like to *taste* your cooking. Are you going to sit or what?"

"You're grumpy when you're hungry." Brooke moved the playpen closer to the table and set Leah down, then dished herself a plate. She sat across from Nick and he watched her carefully. "Dig in," she said. "It's pork loin with tangy mango sauce. Cinnamon sweet potatoes and creamed spinach. Carlotta said you eat your salad last."

"I do."

"Why?"

"I like to get to the good stuff first," he said, casting her a look so hot, she could have burst into flames.

He dug into his food and Brooke waited patiently for a comment.

"You gonna eat or watch me clean my plate?" he asked after about a minute.

She passed him the basket of warm Italian bread she'd sliced and toasted under the broiler then coated with olive pesto. "I can do both, you know."

Nick looked at her with admiration. He pointed with his fork to what was left on his plate. "This is delicious."

She breathed a sigh of relief. "Carlotta said it was one of your favorites."

"Yeah, but I've never tasted anything this good."

"Helps when you have an amazing kitchen to work with. And good cuts of meat."

Nick shook his head. "You never could take a compliment."

"I didn't get that many from you," she blurted.

Nick smiled. "Now who's grumpy?"

Brooke clamped her mouth shut, hating that she made a reference to their past. She wanted no reminders of that time in her life.

Nick got another plate of food and demolished it before Brooke had a chance to finish her first helping.

"It was hard to say good-bye to Nurse Jacobs." She took a small bite of her potatoes.

"Was it? She could have stayed on longer."

"It wasn't necessary. I'm feeling fine. It's just that I've never really remained in one place long enough to have a lot of close friends. She and I sort of bonded. I'm hoping now that I'm in Napa for good, I'll be able to make some friends."

Leah fussed and Brooke put down her fork to lift her out of the playpen. "You want outta there, baby girl, don't you?"

She set Leah on her lap and continued with her meal while Nick looked on. "I've left another message with Molly and I hope she calls me back. I'd like to reconnect with her. Not that I won't have enough to keep me busy," she said as she tried the spinach. Leah's hand came up and she grabbed the fork from her and giggled. "Leah!"

The next time she tried to get a forkful into her mouth, Leah twisted in her lap, squirming so much that Brooke had to put her silverware down. "What, you want to play now?"

She was just about to stand up, when Nick reached for Leah. "Here, let me have her. Finish your meal, Brooke."

Leah went willingly to Nick, nearly bounding out of Brooke's arms and into his. Leah adjusted herself onto his chest and settled in, her small body against Nick's strong chest. Brooke's heart gave way a little.

"Let your mama finish her meal," he said in a stern tone and when Leah twisted her face, ready to let go big tears, Nick softened his voice. "Okay, okay, Leah." Then he bounced her on his knee.

Brooke smiled wide and Nick shot her an annoyed look. "What? You think I don't know how to bounce a kid on my knee?"

"I didn't say a word." Brooke finished her meal with her head down, refusing to give in to the tender emotions that washed over her as Nick consoled her baby daughter, speaking softly and charming her with sweet words.

That night, Brooke had a slight argument with Nick over their sleeping arrangements on their way upstairs. She wanted to give him his room back, since she'd be staying on for weeks. But Nick wouldn't budge claiming she needed the extra space for the baby's things and the guest room had everything he needed for the time being.

Stubbornly, she wasn't ready to give up until Nick walked over to her in the hallway near the master suite, ready to compromise. "Or we could *share* my room," he suggested with an arch of his brow. He began taking his shirt off.

Brooke froze on the spot, watching one button after another open to his tanned chest. She was very much aware that they were alone in the house. Carlotta, much to her surprise, didn't live in the house. She used a downstairs room for sleeping when the Carlinos had a big party or special occasion; otherwise she went home before dark to spend time with her husband. "Fine, you made your point. I'll take your room. Th-thank you."

Nick backed away then, satisfied.

She entered her room and closed the door. After she bathed Leah and nursed her one last time before putting her to bed, she took a long hot soak in the bathtub and fell into a gloriously deep sleep.

Brooke woke in a great mood. She fixed Nick a breakfast of bacon and eggs and home-fried potatoes, grabbing a quick plate for herself before heading out. Nick had called Randy, arranging for Brooke to drive by his shop this morning so he could double-check the car seat for Leah. Randy had been nice enough to make a few adjustments and she drove away relieved to know Leah was as safe as she possibly could be. Still, Brooke drove five miles under the speed limit all the way to the house, garnering some dirty looks from the drivers behind her.

"Here it is, sweet girl," she said once they arrived. "This is our new home."

Brooke spent the better part of the day making assessments and writing up a list of all the repairs she'd need, setting her priorities. Yesterday, she'd called to have the electricity turned on, and that made her work much easier. She noted the sizes of the beds in each room and checked the bed linens in the closets. There were antique quilts that she could have cleaned but the bed sheets and all the towels would have to be replaced. Thankfully, the kitchen appliances were in working order, though on the old side, their dated look added charm to the kitchen. The dining room was full of dust and debris but the table and chairs were made of fine wood that would polish up nicely.

Brooke contacted a few local handymen and painters in the area by phone and set up appointments, then she called to make Leah an appointment with the pediatrician. She also placed another call to Molly Thornton, hoping her friend was still living in Napa.

She felt an odd sense of belonging here. She'd never owned a home of her own. Even the house she'd shared with Dan had been a rental. At least during their quickie divorce, she didn't have to deal with property settlements; he'd taken what was his and she'd taken what was hers.

But this house was all hers and an overwhelming sense of pride coursed through her system. Tears pooled in her eyes as she looked around the old house, seeing it not as it stood today, but envisioning how it would be one day. Her dream was finally coming true and it had been a long road getting here. Often she'd wondered if this was her aunt's way of making up to Brooke for what her father had done to her. Nothing really could. How can you make up for a man who'd abandoned his family?

But she was grateful for her aunt's generosity. Because of her, Brooke would secure a future for Leah without any outside help. If she didn't rely on anyone, then she couldn't be disappointed. Her ex-husband had taught her that hard lesson.

Yet it was Nick's face that had popped into her mind. It was so unexpected that her breath caught in her throat. Why had she been thinking of Nick? Was it because he'd disappointed her once, or was it because she wanted to make sure he wouldn't have the chance to disappoint her ever again?

"I don't know about him, Leah," she said, sweeping up her daughter and planting kisses on her cheek. Leah was fascinated by her new surroundings and had been quietly curious since they'd arrived, letting Brooke make her phone calls without interruptions.

By mid-morning, Brooke had accomplished what she'd hoped to and decided a trip into town was necessary. She packed up Leah and made their first stop at a hardware store to pick up cleaning supplies, some small appliances and a beginner's tool kit. Next she went to Baby Town to purchase a new playpen for Leah that she could keep in their house, eliminating the need for her to continually cart it back and forth. After picking out a jungle-themed playpen, she drove to the grocery store and bought beverages and food to stock in the kitchen. It was a funny thing, just having milk and bread in the refrigerator made her happy. She smiled the entire way home.

Hours later Brooke glanced at her watch to find it was time to head back to Nick's house. The time had flown by and she was extremely happy with her progress. She'd managed to clean up the refrigerator, wash the kitchen floors and counters and arrange a new toaster, food processor and coffeemaker in strategic places in the kitchen. She'd had a full day and now was off to make dinner for Nick.

She arrived a little later than she'd planned, so dinner was a rush of getting Leah nursed and down for a nap, and creating something wonderful to eat. The something wonderful ended up being a quick stir-fry with shrimp and scallops, scallions, and veggies over brown rice.

"I know I must look a mess," she offered when she heard Nick walk into the kitchen, precisely at seven. "And dinner's going to be a little late today." Steam from the wok rose up and heated her face. She wiped her forehead with her arm, feeling like a slug from the earth. She hadn't had a chance to change her clothes or clean up before starting dinner. "Give me a second and I'll have it all ready."

Nick approached her in a slow easy stride. "Why, do you have somewhere you need to be?"

She snapped her head up. Heavens, he looked like a zillion bucks today. His tan trousers and a chocolate brown shirt brought out the bronze of his skin and accented those dark blue eyes. His appearance made her feel even more a mess, if that were possible. She caught the subtle scent of his musky cologne and knew immediately it probably cost more than her entire wardrobe at the moment. "No, of course not. I'm sorry I'm running late."

She took the wooden spoon and stirred, as if that would make the dinner cook faster.

Nick sidled up next to her and covered her hand with his. Stir-fry steam continued to drift into her face, but that wasn't what caused her body to flame. Having his hands on her was doing a great job of that.

"There's no rush," he said quietly and her heart pounded in her chest. He stroked her gently and she didn't dare look at his face and show him the turmoil he caused her. Instead, she focused and took a deep breath.

"Brooke?"

"What?" she barked out and Nick smiled.

He took the spoon from her and shut off the burner on the stove. "Don't make yourself crazy about this, honey. If you're running late, just tell me. I'm a big boy, I can wait for dinner."

"You said seven."

"Or later. Today it's going to be later. Go up and take a minute for yourself."

"Is that your way of telling me I look like something the cat dragged in?"

"You look fine, Brooke. You've had a busy day. And I want to hear all about it."

"You do?"

He nodded.

She glanced at Leah asleep in her little playpen. "But Leah's down here."

"I've got some reading to do. I'll stay in here and watch her."

Nick had a determined look in his eyes and she decided to take him up on his offer, rather than argue about it. "Okay, I'll be down in a few minutes."

She raced upstairs and tossed off her clothes, jumped into the shower and reveled in the refreshing spray that not only cleansed her, but relaxed her as well. She changed into a pair of clean jeans and a black sleeveless tunic and brushed her hair back, away from her face, letting it fall in curls down her back. Taking a look in the mirror, she liked this image reflecting back at her much better than the harried, uptight woman she'd been just twenty minutes ago.

When she entered the kitchen again, she found Nick standing over Leah's playpen, watching her sleep. The moment caught her by surprise. She walked over to stand beside him and they stood there silently like that for a few seconds.

Finally, Nick looked at her. "She made some sounds. I thought she was waking up."

"Those are her baby noises. She's not a quiet sleeper. You'll get used to it."

Nick glanced once more at Leah, then took a long assessing look at her. "Feel better?"

"Much."

The appreciation in Nick's eyes told her he liked what he

saw. Her nerves went raw and she resumed her position at the stove to finish cooking the meal and ignore the flutters threatening to ruin her dinner.

Nick set the table, putting out plates and utensils and Brooke opened her mouth to stop him but then clamped it shut again. He'd said it point-blank tonight—he was a big boy. If he wanted to set his table who was she to tell him not to?

So she sliced bread and stirred the meal as Nick set the table and Leah slept. For anyone walking in on the three of them in the kitchen, they'd think it a homey domestic scene. Only it wasn't, and Brooke had to remind herself that Nick was her employer and she was leaving him as soon as humanly possible.

Nick ate every bite on his plate and went to the stove to get a second helping. When he sat down again, instead of diving into his food, he leaned back in his seat looking her over. "So how did it go today?" He poured himself a glass of wine and gestured for her, but she shook her head. She couldn't drink alcohol while nursing her baby.

"You really want to know?" She didn't think her day would be of any consequence to him, but if he'd rather make small talk than eat then she would oblige.

"I wouldn't have asked if I didn't want to know." He sipped his white zinfandel thoughtfully.

"I got a lot accomplished. Actually, I'm feeling pretty good about things," and Brooke went on to explain the details of her day. To her surprise, Nick asked quite a few questions and seemed genuinely interested in her progress. In fact she felt so comfortable discussing the subject with him, she asked him for advice. "I was hoping you could help me figure out a good promotional plan to advertise and attract guests, once I get my place ready."

Nick thought for a second, scratching his jaw. "I've made a lot of contacts in the area. I'm sure I could call in some favors."

"I wasn't asking for your help, just a point in the right direction."

"Right, heaven forbid I should help you."

Nick focused his attention on her face then lowered his gaze to her chest and the hint of cleavage her top revealed. He didn't seem to mind that she'd caught him in the act. He merely sipped his wine and continued to look at her until heat crawled up her neck.

"I appreciate you will—"

"Get your place registered with tour books and guides. You'll need a Web site. You'll also need to work out arrangements with other bed-and-breakfasts so that they refer tourists to you if they can't accommodate them. Initially, I'd say to visit local wineries and make your place known. Carlino Wines will put you on top of our referral list for visitors." Through tight lips, he added, "Unless that's against your rules too."

Brooke took offense to that. "I don't have rules, Nick."

He finished off his wine and poured another glass. "Sure you do. You don't want anything from me."

"I don't want anything from any man," she said, her anger rising. She was sorry she'd asked him for advice. "It's not personal."

His brow furrowed. "Is that because of what happened between us in high school?"

Brooke had heard enough. She rose from her seat and took up her plate, unable to hide her annoyance. "Maybe you don't know this, but there is *life* after Nick."

Nick shot up and followed her to the sink. "What is it then? Why are you so damn stubborn? Is it your ex? Did he do a number on you?"

She winced at the mention of her ex. "I don't want to talk about it."

"Hell, maybe you should. Maybe it'll knock off that chip on your shoulder."

She whirled around and faced him straight on. "I don't have a chip on my shoulder. I have a baby to raise by myself and I'm trying my best not to get hurt again. That's all, no chip, just survival. But you wouldn't understand that."

"Yeah, because I've got everything I want."

"Hell, it looks like it from where I'm standing!"

Nick ignored her accusation and wouldn't let up. "Tell me. What did he do to you, Brooke? Why isn't he around for Leah?"

Brooke's defenses fell at the mention of her daughter. Emotion roiled in the pit of her stomach making her queasy. Her heart ached for Leah and all that she'd lost. Dan's betrayal had cut her to the core, because it meant her daughter wouldn't know her own father. It meant, when she did tell Dan about his daughter, he might not care to know her. He might abandon Leah, the way he'd abandoned Brooke. And that would be too much to take. Too hard to deal with.

Brooke lashed out at Nick because he was there, and because he'd asked for the truth. "He isn't around for Leah, because he doesn't know about Leah! One week before I found out I was pregnant, Dan came to me with the news that he was having an affair. She was pregnant with his child. He left me and the child he'd didn't know about. And," she said, her tone and bravado fading, "my beautiful baby girl isn't anyone's castaway. She isn't." Tears spilled down her cheeks and she let them fall freely, shedding her heartache with each stinging drop. "She'll never be. And when I tell Dan about her, it'll kill me if he hurts her the way he hurt me."

Nick ran a hand through his hair. "Christ, Brooke," he said in a low rasp.

"I know," she said, between sobs. She swatted at her shoulder. "Knocked the chip right off."

Nick closed his eyes briefly, then grabbed her around the waist and drew her into his chest. She wound her arms around him and sobbed quietly while he held her, making her feel safe and protected.

"Damn him," he muttered. "The jerk."

"I know," Brooke replied over and over again. "I know. I know."

"Want me to have him killed?"

Even through her heartache, she chuckled. "How would you do it?"

"He would just disappear one day, never to be heard from again."

Brooke nestled into his chest a little more. "I appreciate the thought," she whispered.

"I'm a helluva guy."

"Don't be nice to me, Nick," she pleaded.

"Don't be so damn brave and beautiful and sexy."

"I'm none of those things." She wasn't. She was just muddling her way through life, making mistakes and trying to cope the best way she knew how.

Nick lifted her chin and met her eyes. "You're all of those things, Brooke." Then he lowered his head and kissed her.

It wasn't a consoling kiss, but an all-out Nick Carlino kiss filled with demand and passion. He cupped her face, weaving fingers into her hair and tilted her head to get a better angle, then he kissed her again, his mouth hot and moist and intoxicating. Brooke fell into the sensations swirling down her body in a spiral of heat.

He pressed her mouth open and drove his tongue inside,

taking her into a more intimate place—a place Brooke hadn't been in a long time.

She wanted more. She wanted *him* but she knew it would have to stop. She couldn't do this. Not with Nick. Those thoughts turned to mush when he drizzled kisses down her throat and cupped her breasts with his hands. He groaned with need and backed her up against the counter, their bodies hard and aching for each other. His thumbs stroked over her blouse, making her nipples peak, tormenting her with slow circles that sent shockwaves down her body.

It felt good to be kissed this way by Nick, to have him desire her, and she would die a happy woman if he made love to her now. But Brooke thought about Leah again, and the mistakes she'd already made in her life.

Nick would be another one. And she couldn't afford that luxury.

"No, Nick." She broke off his kiss, and regretted it immediately, but she was determined to stop him. "We can't do this."

He gazed at her with smoky eyes that promised a hot night between the sheets. His hands were halfway up her blouse. He removed them and waited.

"I haven't had sex in a long time," she confessed.

"You haven't forgotten anything."

She squeezed her eyes shut for a moment. "You're good at bringing it all back."

"Somehow I don't think that's an invitation."

"It's not. It's an explanation of why I let things get out of control. My life is complicated right now."

Nick sighed. "Sex doesn't have to be."

She breathed in deep and his scent on her lingered. "I'm not ready."

Nick backed up and gave her breathing room. "When

you are, you have an open invitation. You know where my room is."

She swallowed past the lump in her throat and nodded.

They stared at each other a long moment, then Nick turned away, picked up his keys and walked out the front door.

Brooke stood there, bracing herself against the granite counter, her body aching for completion. She needed the physical act, but she also needed the intimacy of being held and loved and cared for. She wanted the bond and connection that lovemaking at its finest could bring. Knowing she had an open invitation with Nick rattled her nerves and made her imagine things she shouldn't be imagining.

When Leah stirred, Brooke glanced down to watch her daughter's eyes open to the world, her blond curls framing her chubby cheeks and a little pout forming on her mouth. She believed with her whole heart that she'd done the right thing by pushing Nick away tonight.

For all three of them.

Six

The week flew by uneventfully. Brooke got into a routine of waking early enough to cook breakfast and get out the door by nine to work at the house. She'd come back to the Carlino estate in the late afternoon to shower and make dinner. All in all it was working out better than she'd hoped.

Nick came and went as he pleased, and she was grateful there was no tension between them. At least not on the surface. They'd share their meals, talk about their day and have a few laughs. After dinner, they'd head in opposite directions.

She didn't think about Nick during working hours, when her focus was on getting the place cleaned up. She had a handyman there during the week, fixing doors and repairing damage to the walls as well as bolstering the railings that wrapped around the house on three sides. The painters were due next week and Brooke had to begin building a website for her project. She could write the text herself, but she couldn't add photos until the house transformed from the deteriorating Addams Family house to one that looked appealing and inviting. She'd made plans to visit wineries in the area this weekend, reacquainting herself with local vintners and getting the word out about her new establishment.

That would be the hardest part. She'd never felt as though she belonged in Napa and during the night she struggled with old feelings of not being good enough and of not fitting in—only this time, she was able to talk herself out of those nagging thoughts. She'd come a long way since her teen years, having been through some rough patches and learning from them. This was her chance for independence and happiness.

But while she could talk herself out of those old feelings, new feelings had emerged that were harder to keep down. At night, she'd lie across her bed and think about the temptation that lay just a few steps away. Nick had let her know in no uncertain terms that he was available to her if she wanted him. She had an open invitation. And every night since, she'd thought about his offer and him and what it would be like making love to Nick.

The passion they experienced in the kitchen in those few unguarded minutes had been two-sided. She'd opened up to Nick and bared her soul to him and he'd understood her pain. He'd approached her not from self-fulfilling lust, but from shared desire. Each night, as she turned down her covers and crawled into bed, she'd secretly wished Nick was beside her and as the nights wore on, it was getting harder and harder to sleep knowing what she craved, if just in body, was so close to her.

And yet, never further out of her reach.

That afternoon, Brooke stopped work early, deciding Leah needed a break from the drudgery of the old house.

As much as she wanted to accomplish her tasks as soon as possible, she never wanted to lose sight of Leah's needs. She'd stopped off at the store and bought Leah a turtle-shaped inner tube and a two-piece pink bathing suit. Leah loved water, her bath time being one of her favorite activities. Today, they were going for a swim in the Carlino pool.

"Oh, don't you look sweet in your new suit," she said as she dressed her daughter on Nick's big bed. She adjusted the straps on Leah's two-piece swimsuit. "There, all set." Leah giggled and kicked her legs up. "Let's go. Mr. Turtle wants to take you for a ride."

Brooke wore her own two-piece suit covered by a sundress. She grabbed the already inflated turtle—a bad move on her part, she should have blown it up downstairs—picked up the diaper bag full of towels, sunscreen, bottled water, Leah's hat as well as her diapers, then lifted Leah up in her other arm. "Here we go, little girl."

She made it out the door and headed toward the staircase, balancing baby and everything else in her arms, precariously.

"Need some help?" Nick strolled out of his bedroom and didn't wait for an answer. He slipped his hands into the straps of the diaper bag, taking it from her, then lifted Mr. Turtle off her shoulder. "Did you load the diaper bag down with lead?" he asked.

"Not quite," she said, and a chuckle escaped. "It's just a girl thing. Thanks."

Nick followed her down the stairs. "I take it Leah likes water."

"We'll see. She's never been in a pool like thi

"Really? This I've got to see."

"What are you doing home?" she asked m
It was his home and he could come and g

pleased, but Brooke was really looking forward to having this special time alone with Leah. And if she were honest, she didn't really want to parade around in her swimsuit with Nick looking on. Her body wasn't perfect, not in the way Nick was accustomed to seeing a woman—she had stretch marks still in the process of fading that never really bothered her until now.

Suddenly, the idea of using the Carlino pool lost its appeal, but she couldn't back out now without looking like a complete idiot. Besides, Leah deserved some splash and play time.

Suck it up, Brooke.

"I only work half a day on Friday. It's a guy thing," he said with a wink. "Maynard wiggled out of our tennis game, claiming he had a patient in need." A wry grin spread across his face. "A likely story. He didn't want to get beat again."

"Yeah, and owe you any more favors like treating me for free."

Nick only smiled.

Once they reached the pool, Nick set her things down on the chaise lounge. The day was gloriously warm, the sky a clear blue and the pungent scent of new grapes nurtured on the vine filled the air.

Brooke laid out her towels on the chair, then set Leah down and lathered her with sunscreen before plunking a pink bonnet on her head. "I called Dr. Christopher today and she said Leah could be out in the sun for thirty minutes as long as she was protected."

Nick took a seat in an adjoining chaise lounge and spread his legs out. He was dressed in slacks and a white button-down shirt with the sleeves rolled up. "You're a good ther," he said and she waited for the punch line, but when me she realized he'd meant it.

"Thank you." She stepped out of her flip-flops. "I never thought I'd be a single mom." She shimmied off her sundress and let it pool down her legs. Then stepping away, she reached down to pick up Leah and the turtle tube.

When she finally glanced at Nick, she found he'd put on sunglasses, which was a good thing because now she couldn't see his eyes measuring her. Thankfully, her suit wasn't a bikini thong. She'd picked out a more conservative two-piece suit, yet there was more skin exposed than she'd like Nick to see.

"I like the suit," he commented immediately.

It suddenly got ten degrees warmer under the direct sun. "I, uh…it's nothing special."

"Leah could be a model for *Baby News* in that pink getup."

Oh, he meant Leah. Now, Brooke wanted to die of mortification.

She turned away and took her first step into the pool. The water felt cool enough to be refreshing, but warm enough to enjoy.

"Brooke?"

She tossed the turtle into the water and watched it land with a little splash in the shallow end. Then she turned to face him, holding Leah close in her arms.

"Your kid looks cute, but I was complimenting you."

"Let's just leave it at, Leah looks cute." Brooke took another step in, and then another. Normally, she wasn't the wait and see type of swimmer—she loved to dive in and feel the unexpected shock of the water, but of course she couldn't do that now. Once she got in up to her waist, she splashed water on her daughter's legs. Leah bent down to touch it. Her chubby fingers reached out again and again and Brooke had to cling onto her tight for fear of dropping her.

Nick sat forward, straddling the lounge, and tipped his sunglasses down. "She's fidgeting again."

Brooke tossed her head back and laughed. "Now I've got you saying words like fidgeting."

Nick smiled and those dimples popped out and caught sunlight. "I guess you do."

He leaned back in his lounge, getting comfortable as Brooke finally managed to get Mr. Turtle to accept Leah's weight. Once she was sitting on the floatation device comfortably, Brooke breathed easier. She pushed Leah around and around, her daughter's big smiles and cackles of delight warming Brooke's heart.

Then a thought struck and she hated to ask, but she also hated to miss this moment. "Nick, a big favor? Since it's Leah's first time in a pool, will you take a picture of her?"

He narrowed his eyes as he made his way over. "Depends, what are you feeding me tonight?"

"Anything you'd like. Name it."

"I'll let you know later. Where's the camera?"

"In the diaper bag."

Nick sorted through her things and came up with the camera. She didn't have to instruct him how to use it—he seemed knowledgeable. He asked for smiles, and Leah obliged immediately, staring straight at Nick. He bent down close to the steps and clicked off a few shots.

"You look hot," Brooke blurted, noticing beads of sweat on his brow.

Nick cast her a charming grin. "I'm taking that as a compliment."

"You know what I mean," she said, spinning Leah around on the tube again.

"Do you swim?" he asked.

Brooke glanced with longing at the long kidney-shaped pool. "Like a fish. I'm a good swimmer."

"Hang on. I'll be right back."

A few minutes later, she heard a quiet splash from behind and turned toward the deep end. Nick swam underwater the length of the pool and came up just inches from her and Leah.

Leah's eyes rounded and she clapped her hands with glee when she saw Nick. He patted her on the head and she followed the course of his hands, watching his every move with fascination. "I'll watch her for a few minutes. Take a swim."

"You don't have to do that." Brooke stood close enough to Nick to reach out and touch the droplets of water trickling down his chin onto his chest. His dark hair was pushed off his face and she noted a small scar cutting into his forehead she didn't know he had. It was just enough of a flaw on a perfectly handsome face to make him look dangerously sexy. Brooke figured it safer to take him up on his offer than stand in the shallow end drooling over a well-muscled hard body.

"Have at it, Brooke," he commanded, pointing to the water. He grabbed hold of the turtle tube and gently pushed it through the water. "The kid and I will be just fine. When you get done, I have a favor to ask you."

"Ah, that makes more sense. You have an ulterior motive."

Their eyes met with amusement.

Brooke turned to kiss her daughter's cheek. "Watch Mommy swim."

"Don't worry," Nick said with a sinister arch to his brow. "We will."

Brooke turned and dove into the water, freeing herself from all worries and simply enjoying her swim. She lapped the pool several times, slicing through the clean rejuvenating water with her breaststroke and several minutes later, she came up to take a breather on the opposite end of the pool.

With a hand on the edge, she glanced at Leah, who was now out of Mr. Turtle and being swirled around by Nick. He held her under her arms and lifted her high in the air, then lowered her feet into the water, letting her kick and splash before lifting her high again. Next, he twirled her around above the water, holding her like a little horizontal helicopter then swooped her down again to let her feet and legs splash through the water.

Leah loved it. Her joyous cackling tore into Brooke's heart. The scene they made, the way her daughter looked at Nick—it was almost more than she could bear to watch.

She swam over to them and Nick turned to her as she straightened up to face him with Leah clinging to his neck.

"She's a swimmer, just like her mama," he said. "Did you enjoy your swim?"

"It was very refreshing."

"For me, too. It isn't every day that I have a gorgeous dripping wet blonde standing in front of me."

Brooke ignored his comment, but it was hard to ignore the earnest expression on his face. "Thanks for the swim. I enjoyed it. Here," she said, reaching for Leah. "I'll take her now."

Nick tried to untangle Leah's arms from around him, but she didn't want to let go. Brooke coaxed her with another ride in Mr. Turtle. After she set her into it and moved her to and fro, she turned to Nick. "You said you had a favor to ask?"

Nick sat down on the pool's step and stretched out his long legs, his face lifted to the sun. "My sister-in-law, Rena, is dying to meet you. Well, actually, she's dying to see Leah and pick your brain about babies and labor and everything else." Then he met her eyes. "My brother Tony said she's going stir-crazy. She's as big as a house, but don't tell her I said that. And she wants a night out. I invited them to dinner tomorrow night."

"That sounds okay," she said with reluctance. She didn't want to enmesh herself any more into Nick's life than necessary.

Nick picked up on her reluctance. "I know it's Saturday night. If you had plans—"

"I'm a single mom with a five-month-old baby. Not exactly hot date material, Nick. I'll cook for your family."

"I wasn't suggesting that. We'll go out for dinner. And then come back here for drinks, maybe some of that blueberry pie you made the other day."

"I don't have a sitter for Leah."

"Not a problem. She'll come along."

Fully surprised by the suggestion, Brooke tossed her head back and a deep rumble of laughter spilled out. "You can't be serious."

"Why not?" Nick looked truly puzzled.

"Leah will disrupt everyone's meal. You see how *fidgety* she is, especially if she's not in her own surroundings."

"So? It'll show Rena and Tony what they're in for." His grin was a little too smug.

"As in, it serves them right for having a baby?" Brooke wasn't sure she liked Nick's suggestion to use Leah as a means to taunt his brother.

"It's not really Tony's baby. At least not biologically, but he's in it for the long haul and no one could be happier about becoming a father than Tony. He'll love meeting Leah. Both of them will and it'll get them off my back. They've been hounding me all week about you."

Brooke's internal alarm sounded. "They don't think that you and I are, uh…"

Those dimples popped out with his sly smile. "You can set them straight."

"Darn right I will."

It shouldn't matter to her what Nick's brother thought about their living arrangements, but it did. She had a good deal of pride. She wasn't one of Nick's bimbo girlfriends that he could toss aside when he was done. She'd never put herself in that position.

"I'll take that as a yes."

"Okay, I'll go to dinner." Did she really have a choice without coming off as sounding ungrateful? She recalled all the questions she had before Leah was born and how nice it would have been to talk to a friend who had gone through it already. And since Molly hadn't returned her calls, Brooke didn't have any female companionship in Napa aside from Carlotta, who seemed to be on the opposite schedule from hers. When Brooke was home, Carlotta wasn't working and vice versa.

Nick's comment about the parentage of Rena's baby spiked her curiosity. She'd left Napa and never looked back and apparently, a good deal had happened during that time. "Is there anything I should know about Tony and Rena, just so I don't put my foot in it?"

Nick shrugged. "The short story is Rena was married to Tony's best friend. Right before David died, Tony promised him he'd take care of Rena and the baby."

"How tragic. She lost a husband and he lost his best friend."

"Yeah, it was rough, but Tony and Rena had past history and my brother worships his wife. They're one of the few happily married couples I know."

"Does the *long* story have something to do with your father?"

Nick drew in a sharp breath and uncharacteristic pain crossed his face. "Santo had a hand in ruining lives and Tony and Rena were drawn into all that."

Leah squawked, letting go a little cry of complaint. Brooke wanted to hear more about Tony and Rena, but it was time to get out of the water. She lifted Leah off the float. "I think it's time to get out or my little girl will turn into a prune. She's ready for a nap."

Nick stepped out first and wrapped a towel around Leah. Together they wiped her down, before he stepped away. "Thanks," she said. It was a simple gesture that lasted no more than a few seconds, but being here with Nick, doing things together was starting to get too comfortable and feel too right.

When Brooke knew in her heart it was all wrong.

Nick hated to admit how much he was looking forward to having dinner with Brooke tonight. Whenever he thought about her, it was with a smile. She made him laugh and he enjoyed her company more than any other female he had or hadn't been sleeping with. She was off-limits in so many ways, yet he found himself drawn to her. Part of that was due to the challenge she posed. She didn't want him and she'd made that clear.

She was also at the root of the deal he'd made with his brothers.

Falling for Brooke was a deal breaker and Nick didn't like to lose.

He showered, shaved and combed his hair, then dressed in a pair of casual beige trousers and a black shirt. They agreed on having an early dinner because of Leah's schedule and so Nick knocked on Brooke's door at precisely six in the evening.

"I'll be right there," she said, her voice hurried. She yanked open the door and rushed off, putting earrings on as she moved to the bed. "Leah took a longer nap today and I'm running late."

She dashed about the room, tossing a few things in the diaper bag and checking on her own purse. While standing before him in a knockout black dress that hugged her curves and reached her knees, she slipped her feet into heels. "I'm sorry."

"Don't be. I'm enjoying the show."

She glanced at him and rolled her eyes, too harried to see his humor. "Okay, what do you need me to do?"

"Stop teasing me, for one," she said.

"Done. What else?"

"Leah needs to be fed."

Nick shrugged, blinking, recalling the time in the hospital when he'd witnessed Brooke feeding her baby. "Sorry, can't help you with that."

"Sure you can." She grabbed a bottle out of her diaper bag and shoved it into his hand. "Give her this. She'll do the rest. She'll take enough to last her until tonight. It'll keep her content through dinner."

Nick sat on the bed and she put Leah into his arms. "Here you go. I've got to comb my hair."

"It's okay if we're a few minutes late you know."

"Good to know," she called out. "Because we will be."

A chuckle rumbled in his chest at her answer. Then he looked down at Leah who seemed happy enough at the moment. "You want this?" he asked. Her big hazel eyes followed the bottle until Nick got it near her mouth. She grabbed hold and tipped it until the thin milky fluid flowed into her mouth. She sucked in a steady rhythm and Nick watched as she drank.

Leah kept her gaze focused onto his eyes as she drained the bottle, her little chubby cheeks working for all she was worth. "You like that, don't you," he said quietly, getting the hang of it. Leah made it easy. She'd taken to him from the moment he'd wrestled her out of the car seat after the accident.

"She looks pretty," he called out, thinking it wasn't a lie. Leah had golden curls, big eyes, rosy cheeks and Brooke had dressed her in a sunny yellow dress that made her look like a sunflower.

Brooke walked out of the bathroom, appearing beautiful and calmer, her blond hair curling past her shoulders in waves and her smile lighting up the room. "Thank you. Compliments to my daughter will always win you points."

"I'll remember that," Nick said, taking a leisurely look at her. "How about compliments to you?"

"I don't count."

"You do to me," Nick blurted, then stood with Leah in his arms, surprising himself for his uncanny appraisal of both of them. "Like mother, like daughter. You both look amazing tonight."

"Thank you," Brooke said slowly, refusing him eye contact. She reached for the baby. "I'll take Leah if you wouldn't mind taking the diaper bag."

"Got it. Toss me your keys. I'll drive. I hope you like Italian. We're going to Alfredo's. We own half the place so there won't be much chance of Leah getting us thrown out."

"Funny, Nick. You'll see. She can be quite a handful. And for the record, I *love* Italian."

Twenty minutes later, Nick walked into the restaurant

holding the handle of the car seat that transformed into Leah's baby seat. Brooke was by his side carrying Leah. "Oh I forgot to tell you, my brother Joe invited himself to dinner and he's bringing his fiancée."

Nick knew Joe and Tony were conspiring against him, trying their damnedest to bring Brooke and him together for their own reasons. Nick was slightly amused at their efforts. He was a worthy opponent and while he might be a sucker for blondes with big eyes and pretty smiles, he wasn't a fool. He might want Brooke in his bed, but that's where it would end.

His brothers underestimated him if they thought they would win their bet.

Brooke glanced at him. "Is this the whole family?"

"Except for a few cousins on my mother's side, living in Tuscany, yeah. This would have been the end of the Carlino line, except now Tony is having a boy."

"I'd like a boy one day," Brooke said quietly and he noted a sense of defeat in her tone. "It's lonely being an only child. I wanted Leah to have a brother or sister."

"Maybe one day you'll get your wish."

Brooke shook her head. "No. That's an impossibility." Her gaze flowed over Leah with softness in her eyes. "Leah's enough."

Nick didn't pursue it. He never talked to women about having babies. He didn't care to know their dreams and hopes for the future because it would never include him. He was destined to be the family's favorite uncle. And that suited him just fine.

Tony and Rena had garnered a large corner table at the back of the restaurant. Fresh flowers adorned the table in cut crystal vases. Flowing fountains lent an air of old European charm with richly appointed stone floors and Italian marble statues.

Nick made quick work of the introductions and helped Brooke to her seat. Rena asked to hold the baby immediately and the two women began a discussion about pregnancy and labor that left Nick and Tony to catch up on some business.

Joe and Ali arrived just as the wine was being served. Nick introduced Ali to Brooke and the three women conversed until their waiter arrived with menus. "The chef will prepare any special entrées you would like."

Nick asked Brooke if she wanted anything special. "I'm sure everything is wonderful. I'll order off the menu."

After they placed their orders, the women took turns holding Leah with looks of longing on their face and talked "baby" for twenty minutes. Finally Nick changed the subject. "Brooke's going to need a Web site for her bed-and-breakfast."

"I don't know what I'm doing really," she offered. "I'm going to start researching what I need beginning next week."

Ali grinned. "Are you kidding? Joe is a computer genius."

"Tell her like it is, Ali," Nick said with a grin. "He's a geek."

"He could probably whip you up a site in less than an hour," Ali said, looking at Joe with adoration.

Joe took her hand and winked at Brooke. "I don't walk on water, but I can help with that, if you'd like. Probably wouldn't take me very long once I had a clear picture of what you wanted."

"Really? That's...well, it's awfully nice of you but—"

"She accepts," Nick butted in, then shot Brooke a warning look. Hell, the woman had trouble accepting help, but there was no one better to get her started on her Web site than Joe.

Brooke shot him an angry glare then smiled at Joe. "Apparently, Nick doesn't think I can speak for myself."

"It's a trait of all the brothers," Rena said. "You'll get used to it. Just stick to your guns and they back down." She smiled sweetly at Tony, who seemed totally unfazed.

Nick sipped his wine and watched as Brooke interacted with his family. When the food came the women fought over who would hold Leah while Brooke ate her meal. It was only when Leah fussed, making frustrated baby noises that she was handed back to Brooke. From across the round table, he watched Brooke handle her child with care and patience. She had loving smiles for Leah even though the baby's complaints grew louder and louder. Finally, Brooke set down her fork and gave up on eating.

Nick stood and strode over to her. "Let me have her. I'm finished with my meal," he said, reaching for Leah. The baby's cries stopped and she lifted her arms to Nick. He picked her up and, having learned not to be stern with the baby's sensibilities, he said softly, "You gonna let your mama eat in peace now?"

Leah's cheeks plumped up, giving him a big smile.

"That's a girl."

Nick didn't miss Tony darting a quick knowing glance at Joe.

"Look at that," Rena said. "Nick's got a way with babies."

"I wouldn't have guessed," Ali said, in awe. "Looks good on you, Nick."

He took his seat as Leah laid her head on his chest and looked out toward the others. "She's a sweet kid, but children aren't in my future. Rena and Ali, it's up to you to carry on the Carlino name."

"We plan to," they said in unison then both laughed.

"Good, then you won't miss me when I'm gone. You'll have your own families."

Brooke's head shot up and all eyes at the table noticed her surprise.

"Of course, we'll miss you," Rena said, glancing from Brooke to Nick. "Where are you going?"

"If things go as planned, I'm leaving for Monte Carlo in a couple of months."

"For good?" Ali asked.

He nodded and when Leah squirmed, he rocked her in his arms to soothe her. "I'm itching to get back there."

"Nick?" Rena said, looking disappointed.

"I'm not going anywhere until your baby is born. And I'll be back for holidays. I'll be your kid's favorite uncle. Promise."

Joe shook his head. "I wouldn't plan ahead too far, bro."

Tony chimed in, glancing at the baby in his arms. "You never know what might happen."

"I'm going," Nick said adamantly. "As soon as we meet the terms of Santo's will."

Nick glanced at Brooke, sitting there, looking beautiful but wearing an unreadable expression. He had no idea what she was thinking. She seemed quieter than usual yet Rena and Ali took to her right away. Both Tony and Joe seemed to like her; Tony offering to help spread the word about her bed-and-breakfast and Joe setting up a date to design her website. Nick knew they had ulterior motives and were trying to trap him into losing the bet. Yet, watching Brooke interact with his family disturbed him on a number of levels, not the least of which being that she fit in so naturally.

Since Leah fell asleep shortly after the meal, they decided to order dessert at the restaurant rather than go back to the house. "Sorry," Brooke said, looking at Leah sleeping soundly in the infant seat, "but with a baby you have to be flexible."

"Oh, we understand," Ali said, "you'll just have to invite us over for coffee another day."

"Once I get my bed-and-breakfast going, I'll invite all of you over for dinner."

"Sounds good to me. Nick says you're a fantastic cook," Tony offered.

"Nick's been staying home nights," Joe added. "Can't say as I blame him."

Brooke blushed, her cheeks turning a bright shade of pink. "If that's a compliment, thank you. But just to make the record clear, Nick and I have a deal. He's been generous to me since the accident and I cook breakfast and dinner for him. But that's all I do for him." She glanced at Tony and Joe, and both men sat back in their seats.

"You tell them, Brooke," Ali said.

"I think we've been properly put in our place," Tony said with a grin. "Are we still invited for dinner?"

"Of course," Brooke said, her eyes going soft again. "I'd love to have you all as my guests."

"Great," Ali said. "I can't wait."

Coffee was served and a variety of desserts were put on the table; cannoli, tarimisu, almond pound cake, pastries and cookies. Nick sipped his coffee and leaned back. Every so often, he'd catch Brooke's eye and they'd share a look.

He wanted her and it was becoming increasingly harder to sleep under the same roof and not share a bed.

Something had to give.

Soon.

Brooke was pleased with the progress she'd made in just a few short weeks. Every day, she spent the morning weeding and planting flowers in her front yard as workmen painted the exterior of the house and a handyman did repairs to the bathrooms and bedrooms. She'd gone shopping for bed linens and fluffy bath towels and bought new curtains for the kitchen.

Joe had helped her with the website—they were now in the preliminary stages of the design. Ali had offered to take her shopping at her favorite out-of-the-way antique shops one day last week. They had a fun time, returning with some really beautiful items to decorate the rooms. Ali's friendship was both unexpected and welcome. By the end of the third week, Brooke felt her bed-and-breakfast would soon become a reality. Her dream was finally within her scopes.

She'd even heard from Molly Thornton, who finally returned her call to say she'd been out of town with her family for nearly a month and she'd been thrilled to hear from Brooke. Molly explained she was a schoolteacher now and had taken the summer off to do some traveling. She'd promised to stop by the house this afternoon.

Brooke had just finished feeding Leah in her new high chair, when a knock sounded at her door. Her daughter had graduated from a breast milk only diet to eating solid foods and managed to get half the jar of carrots anywhere but in her mouth. "Whoopsie!" she said to Leah, wiping clean her mouth and chin. "That'll be Molly. Can't have her meeting your carrot face, now."

There was additional pounding on the door, and Brooke called out, "Coming." She scooped Leah up in her arms. "You're going to like Molly. She's a nice lady."

Brooke opened the door wide, excited to see her friend again after so many years and her heart stopped for a moment, when instead of finding Molly, she came face to face with Dan Hartley, her ex.

A dozen questions entered her mind as her body began

to tremble. How had he found her? Why was he here? She noticed his eyes on Leah and hugged her tighter as she backed away.

He looked from her to the baby. "When were you going to tell me I had a daughter?"

"Dan, what are you doing here?"

"Don't you mean, how did I find you?"

She'd hoped she'd never have to lay eyes on him again. Though she knew she'd have to tell him about Leah soon, she wanted it to be on her own terms, once she'd thought things through, not unexpectedly like this. She didn't want Dan to have the upper hand, ever again.

"How could you do this to me, Brooke? I have a daughter and you don't tell me? You run away and hide her from me?"

"You didn't seem to mind taking off with your bimbo girlfriend, without a thought or care about me."

"You're not denying she's mine."

"I'm not having this conversation with you. I'm expecting someone to stop by at any moment. You want to talk to me, you call me on the phone."

"You want me to *call* you? I'm here to get to know my daughter, Brooke." His gaze roamed over Leah as if memorizing each little detail of her body. "She looks like you."

Leah turned away from him, nestling her face into Brooke's shoulders.

"Let me come inside. I want to see her."

No. No. No. Brooke wanted to scream. "You left us to have a child of your own, remember?"

Dan's expression changed to defiance. "I didn't know you were pregnant!"

"Would it have mattered? Sure didn't seem like it to me. You couldn't wait to pack up your things and get out.

You had something better waiting for you—the woman you really loved and the baby you were having with her. So, why don't you go back to your *something better.*"

He winced as his brown eyes went dark. "She lost the baby. Things didn't work out between us."

Brooke's anger rose and her sense of betrayal intensified. Her entire body shook. "So now you want to get to know Leah? So now you want to impose on our lives? I'm sorry for the loss of the child, but that doesn't excuse your behavior. And I'm going to tell you this *just once,* Leah isn't anybody's second choice. Would we even be having this conversation if things had worked out? Would you even care about the child you abandoned?"

"Hell, Brooke, be reasonable. I didn't know you were going to have my child."

"That might be true, but you were having an affair behind my back and you managed to get another woman pregnant while you were married to me."

"I know. I made a mistake."

"You slept with both of us at the same time. That makes you a snake in my book. I don't want you anywhere near Leah, ever."

"You're hurt and angry."

"Damn right I am. But I'm over you and moving on with my life. I want you off my porch right now. If you want to talk to me, call me. You're not coming into my home."

With that, Brooke slammed the door in his face and bolted it shut.

She waited and it was several minutes before she heard him get into his car and pull away. She stood there shaking and wishing this were all a bad dream. She had trouble fusing her thoughts together, trying to make sense of what just happened. She still didn't know how he'd found out about Leah or how he knew how to find her,

Thankfully, Leah went down for her nap without a fuss and she'd just walked out of the downstairs bedroom when another knock came at her door. She nearly jumped out of her skin. She moved to the parlor window, carefully parted the sheer draperies and peered out. Relief seeped in when she saw a woman on her porch.

Brooke opened the door and found Molly's smiling face. She hadn't changed much over the years. Her hair was a darker shade of auburn and she wore it shorter in a stylish cut. "It's good to see you, Brooke. You look exactly the same."

"Molly, come in," she said, trying to hold it together. "It's good to see you, too." A friendly face was exactly what she needed at the moment.

They fell into a heartwarming embrace.

Then Brooke broke down and cried.

Seven

Brooke entered the Carlino home a little later than usual that afternoon, her routine disrupted by seeing her ex and the implications that involved. Thankfully, Molly had been as sweet as ever and lent an ear to her troubles. Just having someone listen, just being able to open up to a friend, made her situation seem more than hopeless. They'd spent the better part of the afternoon talking and catching up. Brooke hadn't had this type of outlet in a long time and it felt good. She had her mother to talk to, but her mother had had enough grief in her life and had finally found happiness. The last thing Brooke wanted to do was burden her with her troubles. So Molly's timing today had been perfect. Brooke didn't know how she would have made it through the day without her.

Now, at the Carlino house without Molly's strong shoulder to lean on, Brooke's fears returned and a knot twisted in her stomach. All she could think about was seeing Dan's angry face. What would he do? She'd literally kicked him off her property and she knew he wouldn't let it go. He'd be back. Deep in thought and worried to death, she cooked the meal quickly and didn't say much to Nick all throughout dinner. She couldn't eat a thing and he asked her three times if anything was wrong, but she denied there was and rushed out of the kitchen and away from him as soon as she could.

Of all nights for Leah to go to sleep early, tonight wasn't the night. Brooke wanted to hold her and play their silly little games and read her a story, keeping her close and feeding off the love they had for each other. Instead, she sat on her bed and watched Leah sleep, worried about her future. When Brooke laid her head down and tried to sleep, old haunting feelings of betrayal, of not being good enough for Dan, of hating him and what he'd done to her, came rushing forth. Her thoughts wouldn't go away, they wouldn't give her peace.

Tears streamed down her face, as Molly's words came back to her. "You've come so far, Brooke." And she had. She wasn't the wilting wallflower from the wrong side of the tracks anymore. It wasn't her, but Dan, who'd done wrong. She shouldn't be torturing herself like this. She deserved better. She deserved more.

She heard footsteps going down the hallway and Nick's bedroom door closing shut.

She was through denying that *the more* she wanted was Nick.

He'd given her an open invitation to join him in bed.

He was the balm she needed to soothe her restlessness.

And why not? They were two consenting adults and he'd made it clear that he wanted her with no strings attached. Her life was complicated enough—she didn't want strings either. He was leaving the country soon and that would ensure no complications.

"He's just down the hall," she whispered into the darkness and rose from the bed. She dressed in a sheer white summer nightie, checked on Leah, who was still sound asleep and tiptoed downstairs. Her bravado needed a little help. She grabbed a bottle of fine Carlino merlot and two goblets and went back up.

Behind Nick's door, she heard the television. She knocked and didn't bother to wait for him to answer. She slowly pushed open the door.

Nick gazed at her from his bed. He clicked off the TV. "Brooke, is something wrong?"

This was Nick Carlino, the boy she'd once loved, the boy she had wanted to claim her virginity. It was too late for that, but she'd never stopped wondering about Nick. She'd dreamt about this moment so many times through the years that she had trouble believing she was actually standing here, offering herself to him. "You said sex can be simple."

Nick peered at her with assessing eyes, his gaze flowing over her lacy white gown that bared more cleavage and leg than she'd ever let him see before.

He stood up. "It can be."

He looked like sex personified in a pair of jeans and nothing else. His body tight and muscled, his skin a golden bronze. Brooke wondered how she'd been able to stay away from him so long.

"I need simple, Nick. With you."

He walked over to her and took the wine bottle from her hand. "You want to tell me what changed your mind?"

She closed her eyes. "No."

"You really want wine right now?"

"No."

He set the wine bottle down and then the glasses. "I've been waiting for you," he said softly, then took her into his arms, bringing her in close. Their bodies meshed perfectly and she ran her fingers across his chest, stroking him before he had a chance to kiss her. She heard his intake of breath.

"It's a long time coming, honey." Then he bent his head and brushed his lips to hers gently, teasing, stroking her lips with his tongue until she whimpered his name.

His kiss went deeper and deeper until they simultaneously mated tongues, the potent sensation sweeping them both up into a hot raging storm of desire. Nick cupped her neck and angled her head to take her fully then he wove his fingers into her hair and muttered quiet oaths between kisses that only spurred her passion further.

He moved his lips lower, to her throat and down her shoulders, planting moist delicious kisses there, his hands riding up and down her sides. She arched for him and he didn't bother getting tangled up in her nightgown, he removed it with one quick yank of the spaghetti straps down her shoulders. The garment slowly dropped down her legs to the floor.

Her breasts sprung out—now her tiny white thong was all that was left on her body. Nick's gaze filled with lust and admiration. "No more mommy clothes."

Throaty laughter spilled out. "Not tonight."

Nick cupped her breasts and stroked with nimble fingers, driving her completely insane. He whispered, "I don't care what you say, those clothes are still a turn-on."

"Are you saying I turn you on, night and day?"

"Pretty much." He bent his head and kissed one breast, then the other. "Whatever brought you here, I'm damn glad." He cupped her behind and pressed her belly to his erection.

"I see how glad you are."

He groaned when she rubbed harder against him.

"Don't tease me, Brooke."

"Why," she said breathlessly. "What will you do?"

He grinned wickedly then picked her up and lifted her until she was over the bed. "This." He dropped her a few inches and she bounced once, before settling in. He didn't give her time to react, joining her on the bed, covering her with his body.

"You feel good."

The heat of his gaze and the hungry look in his eyes told her playtime was over. Her throat constricted and she managed, "So do you, Nick."

She wove her hands into his hair, threading her fingers through the dark locks, gazing into his eyes, then lifted up to brush a quick kiss to his lips. He lowered her down and pinned her hands above her head, then proceeded to make love to her body with his mouth. She was trapped by his hold, but more by the way he touched and caressed every inch of her. Little moans escaped her throat as she closed off her mind to everything but the pleasure Nick gave her.

Nick released her hands then lowered himself down on the bed, and kneeled before her. He lifted her legs and pressed his hand to her core, the heat of his palm creating hot moist tingles of excitement. He rubbed his palm over her several times then angled his head and brought his mouth to her.

She arched and gave him access, feeling every kiss, every stroke of his tongue in her most sensitized spot. The pleasure was exquisite and torturous and Brooke thrashed her head back and forth, absorbing the sensations whipping through her.

Pressure built quickly and she panted out breaths, the tension almost too much to bear.

Nick released her then and lay beside her, unsnapping his jeans. "Let me," she whispered, turning toward him and lowering his zipper. She helped him out of his jeans and then took his manhood in her hands, stroking him lightly.

"You're wicked cruel," Nick said with a smile.

"You're welcome."

He lay back, taking heavy breaths as she continued to stroke him, his erection thick in her hands. She felt so free and open with Nick, the final culmination of years of wondering and dreaming about this night that she wouldn't hold back.

Tonight was all about sex and she couldn't think of a better partner than deadly handsome, dangerous Nick Carlino.

Brooke could be dangerous too and she was about to show him how much. She slid her hand up and down his length, enjoying the contrast of hard muscle against silken skin. He grew harder in her hands and when she rubbed her finger over the tip, a guttural groan emanated from his throat.

A slim path of moonlight streamed into the room casting shadows on his perfect body. "I want you on top," he demanded, his gaze burning hot.

She gulped oxygen and waited while he took care of protection. Then he lifted her over him and she straddled his legs, her back arching slightly.

"Do you have any idea how beautiful you look right now?"

A charmer and a sweet-talker, Brooke often didn't take Nick seriously, but there was a rich sincere tone to his voice now and even though she didn't think her body was beautiful, not after stretch marks and breasts that had lost their ripeness, she peered into his half-lidded, sex-hazy eyes and saw that he believed it.

He took her hips in his big hands and guided her down. She felt the initial touch of his penis and a dam of desire broke as her body opened for him. She lowered down a little more, taking him in slowly, deliberately, absorbing the feel of him inside her.

She closed her eyes to feel the height of every sensation. It was sheer heaven. She'd gone so long without this natural act. At this time in her life, she needed Nick and the sexual satisfaction he could provide for her.

Nick moved his hips and thrust into her, testing her and tempting her to take all of him. She complied easily, her body moist and ready to accommodate his needs. She sunk down deeper and through the dim light, she witnessed his expression change. He whispered words of encouragement as she moved on him, up and down, each intense thrust bringing her closer to the brink of fulfillment.

Nick lifted up and wrapped his arms around her, holding her tight as she moved on him. He cupped her derriere and brought his mouth to hers, slanting fiery hot kisses over her lips. She was ready, so ready.

"Together," he said, between kisses. "We're doing this together."

Brooke understood and when Nick rolled her onto her back, she accommodated his full weight. He adjusted his position and took control. He fondled her breasts as he kissed her, driving her nearly insane. His thrusts were powerful and deliberate, each one meant to arouse and tease until she couldn't hold back her release. Her breaths came fast and hard. Nick was relentless, his body covering hers. She held him around the neck as he drove his thrusts home.

Hot waves swirled and electric jolts coursed through her body. She cried out with little moans, her face contorting as she took on the extreme, heady pleasure. Their release erupted, shattered and consumed. Just as he'd promised, they came at the same time and the notion left her with a breathless smile.

Nick lowered his body down and she breathed in the scent of man and musk and sex. He stroked her face gently and kissed her again before moving off her to roll onto his back. "That might have been worth the wait."

Brooke chuckled. "It's only been a few weeks."

Nick moved onto his side and with a finger to her chin turned her face to his. "More like thirteen years."

Her throat tightened and she tried to make light of it. "Ancient history."

"I wanted you back then, Brooke. I know you don't believe it, but it's true."

Brooke didn't believe it. "Let's not talk about the past."

Nick bent his head to kiss her lightly. "Okay, let's talk about how amazing you are."

The compliment made her uneasy. "I bet you say that to all the girls."

Nick remained silent and Brooke realized that she had really stepped into it now. Her obvious attempt at humor failed.

"Listen," Nick said in a serious tone, "I don't sleep with a different woman every night. That's never been my style. I actually have to like the woman and respect her, before I take her to bed."

"Okay," Brooke said, oddly believing him. He was a man with integrity.

"What happened between us just now was amazing."

Brooke agreed with a nod. "For me, it was."

Nick took her into his arms and laid her head on his chest. "For me too."

She could stay in his arms all night, but thought better of it. "I'd better check on Leah."

She found her nightie and tossed it over her head then made a move to go, but Nick stopped her, taking her hand. "Come back."

"I, uh, we're still keeping this simple, right?"

"Simple," Nick agreed without hesitation, releasing her from his grasp.

"Okay, then I'll be back."

Nick put on his boxers and got out of bed to pour two glasses of wine. He didn't know what brought Brooke to him tonight and he wasn't going to look a gift horse in the mouth. But he couldn't help wondering. She'd been bold and vulnerable at the same time, but it was the underlying trepidation in her eyes that she'd tried to hide that bothered him. Something was up with her—something had changed to bring her to his bed. Maybe he shouldn't want to know and maybe he was better off not knowing but the hell of it was, he did want to know.

Sex with her was better than he'd imagined. And he'd done a lot of imagining over the years. Whenever he was at his lowest points in life, he'd think about Brooke Hamilton and her image would make him smile. But at the same time, it would leave him empty.

He'd done the right thing back then, but it was different now and Brooke seemed to want what he did. Simple and uncomplicated. Two words Nick knew a lot about when it came to women.

He set the bottle down, the Carlino Wines label facing him, a constant reminder of the sacrifices forced down his throat for the sake of the company. He wanted out. He wanted away from here and the sooner the better. His old man wouldn't win. Not ultimately. Nick would win his bet with his brothers and that would be that.

When Brooke reappeared in his doorway, he was swept up by the look in her stunning blue-green eyes. It was a turn-on just seeing her framed by the moonlight, her blond hair tousled and the strap of her nightie falling down her shoulder.

"Hi," she whispered.

"How's Leah?"

She smiled. "Sleeping like an angel."

Nick walked over to her and took her hand. "Come back to bed."

She hesitated and peered at him with eyes that seemed haunted. "This isn't a mistake, is it?"

Nick put his hands on her shoulders and caressed her lightly. Touching her spurred something fierce within him and he followed the path of her slender body, his hands roaming down her sides until he reached her waist. He pulled her close and she squeezed her eyes shut.

"Doesn't feel like a mistake." He brushed a kiss to her lips. "Does it to you?"

She shook her head and those gorgeous eyes caught him in a spell. "No, but it's just that I…"

"Just that you, what?"

"Nothing, Nick." She pulled away from him to pick up the two goblets of wine. She handed him one, then took a sip of her own, her demeanor changing. "I haven't been able to drink wine or anything alcoholic in a while. This tastes delicious."

Nick blinked and wondered about her sudden mood change but not enough to destroy the evening. He had a beautiful woman in his room, drinking wine after a wicked time between the sheets and he wanted her back in his bed. He wasn't through with Brooke Hamilton yet.

She took a few more sips then set the glass on the nightstand. Nick polished his merlot off easily, then sat down on the bed and grabbed her hand. With a tug, he pulled her onto his lap. She fell onto him gracefully and wrapped her arms around his neck.

He nibbled on her throat and his voice took on a low rich rasp. "I want to make love to you all night long."

"That's why I'm here," she answered softly.

Nick's questions were quelled with her response. He gave up trying to figure her out and simply enjoyed the fact she was so willing. He lifted her off him and laid her down on the bed. She reached for him with outstretched arms causing his heart to hammer and his body to tighten instantly.

He made love to her slowly this time, peeling away her clothes and relishing each morsel of her body. He took care and time and enjoyed her as he'd never enjoyed another woman. She was hot and sexy and fun and feisty in bed. She gave as much as she took and as the night wore on, they made love again and again.

Each time was different and better than the last. Nick hadn't had sex like this in a long time. It was almost as if Brooke had been dying of thirst and once she was offered a drink she couldn't get enough. Lucky for him.

Sometime during the late night, Brooke must have tiptoed out of bed, because Nick woke up alone. Oddly, the sense of loss he experienced when he found her gone puzzled him. They'd certainly had a satisfying night between the sheets and it wasn't unusual for him to wake up alone after being with a woman. Usually, he preferred it that way.

Nick showered and dressed and made his way down the hallway. He knocked on Brooke's door softly, and when no one answered, he opened it to find both mother and baby weren't there.

He strode downstairs and found them in the kitchen.

Brooke stood at the kitchen counter feeding Leah her breakfast. The little girl was outgrowing her infant seat quickly. Brooke was so intent on spooning squash into her mouth, she didn't notice him enter the room. He walked up behind her and wrapped his arms around her waist. "Morning," he said. When she turned around, he planted a kiss to her lips.

"Morning," she said, taking only a second to look at him before turning back to her daughter. "Watch out, Leah's in a squash-tossing mood this morning."

Nick patted Leah's head, her loose little blond curls bouncy under his palm. "You need a high chair, kid. I'll order one and have it delivered today."

Brooke put Leah's spoon down and stared at him. "Nick, you will not."

"Why not? She's outgrowing that seat she's in."

"Because for one, she has a high chair at my house, and for two, we'll be moving out in a few weeks. We can make do until then."

"Hey, did you get up on the wrong side of the bed?"

Brooke's defiant expression changed to something more reasonable. "No, I didn't." Then a little smile emerged and she softened her tone. "I got up feeling pretty wonderful this morning."

"You can thank me for that later." He grabbed a cup by the coffeemaker and poured his coffee.

"I thought I showed my appreciation last night."

Nick chuckled and was glad feisty Brooke was back. They drove each other crazy last night, a memory that would stay with him long after she was gone. He sipped his coffee. "What are you doing tonight after work?"

"Cooking for you and then falling into bed. I didn't get a whole lot of sleep last night. Why?"

He shrugged. The thought just popped into his head.

"There's a new pizza place in town and I hear it's pretty good. I thought you'd like to try it. Nothing fancy, sawdust on the floor."

The incredible hue in her eyes softened and just when he thought she'd agree, she turned her attention away and shook her head. "I don't think so."

"We'll take Leah."

"It's not that. I just don't think it's a good idea."

"Pizza is always a good idea."

She wiped her daughter's chin then the rest of her face and removed her from the infant seat. With Leah on her hip, she turned to him. That underlying worry he'd seen last night reappeared. "I've got a lot going on right now, Nick. I…can't."

"What's going on?"

"Nothing." She clammed up and again he wished she'd tell him what had put that wary look on her face. "We're keeping this simple and I really need that right now."

"It's what we agreed on. I'm a man of my word."

She sighed deeply. "Your breakfast is on the stove. I'm not hungry this morning."

Hell.

"Don't cook tonight. I'll bring pizza home."

She turned away from him and busied herself with dishing up his meal. "Okay. If that's what you feel like having tonight. It's fine with me."

Nick spent the morning at the Carlino offices in town. More than once he thought about Brooke and that haunted look on her face. He told himself to butt out, that *simple* meant not getting involved too personally. Leah's face popped into his head and he figured Brooke's worry might have something to do with her baby. If that were the case, she might need his help. But Leah looked like the picture of health. He didn't know much about kids but he knew that Leah was a happy child.

Brooke was a fantastic mother.

After lunch, Nick found himself in front of Brooke's bed-and-breakfast. He had no reason to stop by other than he couldn't stop thinking about her. He got out of his car and the first thing he noticed was how manicured the front lawn appeared. New grass grew along the walkway leading up to the front door. A garden of yellow, pink and lavender flowers sprouted from the borders on either side of the front porch. The exterior walls of the house were painted with a fresh coat of yellow paint and half of the shutters were gleaming white, the other half layered with primer.

Nick knocked on the door. When Brooke didn't answer, he knocked again, louder. He saw her part curtains in a big box window and glance first at his SUV, then gaze at him. The look of pure relief on her face gave him pause.

A second later, the door opened and he grinned, seeing the splotches of cornflower blue paint on her nose and chin. Her oversized T-shirt and denim jeans were splashed with streaks of paint in various colors. In the background, he heard Leah's cries of complaint. "Did you get any paint *on* the walls?"

"Funny, Nick," she said, heaving a big sigh and opening the door wider to allow him entrance. "Come in."

As she waited for him to step inside, he noticed her scanning the street before shutting the door and bolting it. "I'm painting one of the bedrooms and Leah's not happy about it." She headed toward the sound of Leah's cries.

Nick followed her past the parlor and up the staircase. "I don't want her inhaling the fumes, so she's complaining about being out in the hallway."

Once he reached the hallway, the baby gave him a big smile from inside her playpen and lifted her arms out toward him. He bent to lift her up and Leah tucked her little body against him. Nick stroked her soft curls as her baby scent wafted to his nostrils.

Brooke looked at the two of them together and her lips pulled down in a frown. "What are you doing here?"

Was this the same woman who'd been sweet, sexy and loving in his arms last night? Brooke seemed to be out of sorts and jumpy as if she'd lose it at any second. It was exactly why he'd come here today. Something was wrong and she wouldn't confide in him. The truth was, he was worried about them though he wouldn't say it out loud. "I had an appointment with a client. It was on my way and I thought I'd stop in and see your progress. The outside is taking shape."

"Thanks. It's slow going today though. Leah's not cooperating."

"She's fine now." He couldn't help it if the kid liked him, could he?

The furniture was in the middle of the room covered with a big drop cloth. Brooke must have dragged it there and covered it without any help. Hell, he could have a crew of painters out here tomorrow and every room painted to her specifications if she'd allow him. But he wouldn't even suggest it. She budgeted for the exterior to be professionally painted and took on the interior work herself. He had to admire her work ethic and pride. He knew she loved working on this place. *That* was not what was making her edgy.

"She'll be worse once you're gone."

"Then I won't leave."

Brooke glanced at him. "You've got better things to do."

Leah bumped her head against his chin and he flinched

from the hard knock that gnashed his teeth together. He ground out, "Can't think of anything."

Brooke shook her head and laughed. "She's got you conned, Nick."

"I'll help you paint. We can take turns with her."

Brooke scoffed and the look on her face annoyed him. "You're dressed like a million bucks."

"I'll take off my clothes. Anything to accommodate a lady."

"Thanks, but no thanks."

"I'm serious, Brooke. I have a free afternoon. I've got an old pair of sweats in my car."

Before she could answer, her cell phone rang. Nick glanced at it vibrating on the window ledge. One ring. Two rings. Brooke's eyes went wide but she didn't make a move to answer it.

"Want me to hand it to you?" he asked.

"No! Don't get it." Brooke's face froze with fear. She glanced at the phone as if it were death warmed over. "I'm not going to answer." When the phone stopped ringing, her body slumped and she let her breath out.

Nick set Leah down in her playpen and strode over to Brooke. "What the hell's wrong? The phone scared the crap outta you."

"Nothing's wrong." She tried to smooth over her fear by softening her tone, but Nick saw straight through that. "I can't talk right now. I have to finish painting, that's all."

"And you don't want to know who it was?"

"It was Molly," she said without skipping a beat. "You remember Molly Thornton, don't you? She's teaching school now and I told her to call, but I'm too busy to talk. You know how women are, once they get on the phone, they don't stop. I'm really eager to finish this room today."

Nick narrowed his eyes. "You're a terrible liar."

Brooke squeezed her eyes shut. He watched turmoil cross her features. When she opened her eyes to him, she hoisted her chin, her stubborn face on. "Are you going to help me paint this room or what?"

"Yeah, I'll help," he said, angry that she'd lied to him. Why the hell he cared baffled him. She wanted simple and so did he.

He walked out to his car and got his sweats. He couldn't remember the last time he'd picked up a paintbrush.

If ever.

Eight

Nick was true to his word. He helped her paint the bedroom and they took turns with Leah when she fussed. It was a sight, seeing Nick with paint smudging his usually impeccably groomed face. Half an hour into it, his sweats were in no better shape than her clothes. She kept fixating on the speck of blue paint on Nick's eyelid whenever they spoke to keep from thinking about the *call*. She suspected it was Dan but she hadn't listened to her voicemail. It could have been Molly leaving her a message. Wishful thinking, she supposed because from the look on Dan's face yesterday, she didn't think he would give up. Oddly, having Nick with her today calmed her nerves.

By six o'clock they'd finished the room. Both stood back to admire their work. "Looks nice, a soft shade of blue and once I get the furniture back in place, I can call this room ready to rent. Only three more to go."

It was a good thing too, because the money she'd saved

for repairs and renovation, meager as it was, had been stretched to its limit.

"I'll call for pizza and once the paint dries, we'll put the furniture back."

Brooke had a protest on her lips, but Nick had turned his back on her, his cell in hand making the call. "What kind do you want?"

"Vegetarian."

He winced and ordered two pizzas, one with veggies and one fully loaded. "They'll be here in thirty minutes," he said. "Where can I clean up? I need a shower."

"Oh." That caught her off guard. Images of Nick naked in the shower made her mind sizzle with promising thoughts. Making love to him last night had been better than any of her wild imaginings.

Nick grinned as if reading her mind and approached her. "You could use one too."

The dimples of doom emerged on his face in a way that beckoned and brought even more lusty thoughts. After a full day of being shuffled back and forth, played with and read to, Leah had conked out. Her naps usually lasted at least an hour, so Brooke couldn't use her for an excuse.

Not that she wanted one.

Nick came within a breath of her and their eyes met. Once again, she focused on that blue fleck of paint on his eyelid and inhaled sharply. He dipped his finger onto his wet paintbrush coming up with a dollop of cornflower blue and spread it across her throat in a slow caress. "You're gonna need a good scrubbing to get all that paint off." His brows lifted, then he bent his head and brushed a lingering kiss to her lips.

Brooke trembled and her eyes fluttered closed. Every nerve in her body tightened. She couldn't refuse Nick and the promise of pleasure he would give to her. For a few minutes, he could take her away from her troubles and make her forget.

It was simple sex, she reminded herself. She took his hand and led him to the upstairs shower in the corner room. "It's small. We'll have to squeeze in together."

"I like the way you think." Nick lifted his sweatshirt over his head and tossed it in the corner. With his muscled chest bare, she itched to touch every inch of taut skin then devour him with her mouth.

He skimmed the edge of her shirt, pushing it up and over her head, exposing her white cotton bra. His dimples popped out and an appreciative smile spread across his face. "You've changed my opinion of soccer moms."

Brooke swatted at him, but he grabbed her wrist and wound her arm around his neck. He pressed his lips to hers in a more demanding kiss, one that had them pushing and tugging off the rest of their clothes. Nick pulled her into the shower stall, turned the water on to a hot steamy spray then backed her up against the tiled wall.

He was beautiful and sleek and tan, built like a superior athlete and at the moment, he was all hers.

They didn't even try to scrub each other, but allowed the steam to do that job while they kissed and touched and played in the shower. Brooke devoured him with her mouth as she'd planned and he, in turn, did the same. His hands slid all over her—pausing in her most erotic spots long enough to drive her completely crazy.

Nick had expert hands and a mouth that was made for pleasure. He brought her to the brink of climax with just a few exquisite touches to her inner folds, then he bent down and took her into his mouth. She grabbed his hair in her hands when she no longer could hold on and the rush of raining waters drowned out her little cries of ecstasy as her body convulsed.

She lay back against the tile, her gaze hazy and her body sated. Nick smiled at her. "I like that look on you."

"Feels pretty good too."

Nick kissed her again and his massive erection rubbed her belly. She reached down and took him into her hands, smiling when his face grew taut and his eyes closed with pleasure. "Wicked cruel."

"That's me," she said, sliding him through her fingers, his shaft growing even larger. He only allowed a minute of stroking before he stopped her. "No more," he said then lifted her up in his arms and wrapped her legs around his waist. He kissed her hard, stroking her with his tongue, then plunged deep into her moist body, his hands on her waist guiding her movements.

She arched back and he thrust harder and harder. "Brooke," he muttered, his voice deep and primal. His release came shortly after, in hard bursts of power that stirred her to another amazing climax. Her body shuddered for several long seconds and then she went limp in his arms. He held her that way for a long time after he shut the water off.

Nick made her forget her troubles for a short time and gave her more pleasure than any man she'd known. She was grateful to him for that, but reality knocked her hard when Dan's angry face stole into her mind. It was like a splash of freezing cold water on her sated body. "I'd better check on Leah," she said hastily. "And the pizza will be delivered soon." She left Nick standing there, gloriously naked with a puzzled look on his face.

"She's cutting her first tooth," Brooke said to Molly on the phone much later that night in her bedroom. Leah had fussed all evening long requiring all of Brooke's attention.

"I can see the first buds coming through her gums. No wonder she's been out of sorts."

"Oh, I remember that phase. Sometimes they wake up with teeth in their mouth and sometimes it's a major trauma when a tooth comes in." Molly had two children, a six-year-old boy and a four-year-old girl.

"I think Leah is somewhere in between. She's really such a good baby most of the time, but I know her little gums are bothering her."

"Teething rings work well," Molly said. "Do you have one?"

"Yes and she likes it. She gnawed on it until she finally fell asleep." It was ten o'clock, late for Leah to fall asleep. But between a late nap and the teething, it had taken a long time for Brooke to get her down.

That late nap allowed Brooke time alone with Nick, always a risky proposition. He was her guilty pleasure and as long as she thought about him that way, she'd manage okay. No hearth and home thoughts of Nick, she warned herself.

"Brooke, what happened with your ex? Did you hear from him today?" Molly asked, more than mildly curious.

"He called, but I didn't pick up the phone. The voicemail was not pretty. I don't know what to do. He's so angry with me but at the same time, there's an undertone of civility. I think he wants a second chance, for Leah's sake."

"He told you that on the voicemail?"

"It's the impression I got."

"And how do you feel about that? Would you ever take him back?"

"No. Never. I'm not in love with him. He killed that a long time ago. He's Leah's father and I'm going to have to deal with that sooner or later. I'm just so scared."

"Well, you're not alone. I'm here if you need me."

"I know, Molly. Thank you." But it was Nick's image that popped into her mind whenever the fear got to her. She slammed her eyes shut to block him out. She didn't want to rely on him. She wouldn't allow herself to feel anything for him. He was a walking heartbreak and she'd be a fool to fall for him. Yet, she knew in her heart, he'd be there for her, if she really needed him. That's why she wouldn't confide in him about Dan. She couldn't afford the luxury of getting that close to him. She had to be strong and independent. She'd never place her trust in another man ever again. "You've always been a good friend. I'm sorry we can't meet for lunch tomorrow. I don't know how fussy Leah will be."

"That's okay. We'll do it another time. Remember, I'm here if you need me."

"I know and I'll call you soon, I promise."

Brooke hung up the phone and walked over to Leah's little bed. Her baby looked peaceful, sleeping soundly. Instead of undressing, Brooke had something on her mind, something that had occurred to her after two slices of pizza and a beer tonight, in the aftermath of making love with Nick. But this was the first chance she'd had to address it.

She left her room, keeping the door open in case Leah woke, then strode down the hall to Nick's bedroom. She knocked and waited.

He opened the door with his cell phone to his ear and gestured for her to come in. She thought she heard a woman's voice on the other end of the phone and immediately her jaw clenched. A sense of dread coursed through her system and raw jealousy emerged. It hit her hard and she denied it over and over in her mind.

Nick could do whatever he wanted.

She had no hold on him.

Was he making a date with another woman?

He'd told her he didn't see more than one woman at a time. Had he lied? She fought her trust issues, reminding herself that she and Nick had an uncomplicated relationship. Still, her ego would be trampled if Nick were seeing someone else.

"Hi. That was Rena," he said to her, looking thoughtful after the call ended. "She couldn't sleep and needed to talk. Tony's out cold."

"So, you're her sounding board," she asked, ridiculously relieved he'd been speaking with his sister-in-law.

His grin spread wide and stole her breath. "Yeah, I'm willing to listen to complaints about my brothers anytime."

"She was complaining?"

"Venting. Tony's been hovering and protective. She's due in just a week or two."

"It's an emotional time," Brooke offered. "I remember my mood swings were like a roller-coaster ride, up and down, mostly down."

It was ironic that the subject led to this, because that's exactly why she'd come to his room tonight.

"Yeah, that sounds like Rena too."

He glanced at her, as if finally realizing she was there. He focused on her mouth, arched a brow and waited.

Suddenly, Brooke's throat constricted. She'd thought it would so easy to bring this up, but now found herself unbelievably speechless. "I, uh, about this afternoon."

"The best shower I've ever had."

"Nick," she said, glad he was the one to mention it. "We didn't use any protection."

Nick studied her a moment, his gaze roaming from her eyes to her nose, to her mouth and lower still, taking his time. When he lifted his gaze back to hers, once again he appeared thoughtful. "I'm healthy, Brooke. I'd never endanger you."

"Okay." She took a big swallow and nodded. "But it's more than—"

"If you're worried about getting pregnant, don't. I can't have children."

That came out of the blue and was so unexpected, her mouth dropped open in surprise. "You…can't?"

He shook his head. "No, but it was my choice."

"What do you mean, it was your choice?"

Nick took her hand and led her to the bed. He sat down and pulled her next to him. His fingers laced with hers and he let out a heavy sigh. "About five years ago my father pissed me off, as usual. That wasn't new, but I was so angry with him I wanted to do something that would show him he couldn't control me any longer. I fixed that part of my anatomy so I couldn't give him an heir."

"Wow," Brooke said, her brows furrowing together. "You must have really wanted—"

"I wanted to hurt him. It was wrong, but a cocky twenty-something, and my rage at my father made me do some crazy things."

"Oh Nick. I'm sorry. You must regret that."

Nick squeezed her hand. "I don't. I'm not father material. I knew I'd never make a good father. I wasn't lying when I said I'd be happy being the favorite uncle. Joe and Tony will take care of the baby-making in the family."

Brooke felt like crying for Nick. Imagine that, the sexy dangerous and wealthy wine magnate had Brooke's sympathy. "What did your father do when he found out?"

"The hell of it was I never told him. My brothers talked me out of it and I wasn't sure that was the right move, but they convinced me. Now that he's gone, I'm glad I didn't, so I owe my brothers for that."

"Nick, what did he do to make you hate him so much. Was he…abusive?"

Nick smiled with sadness darkening his eyes. "No, never. But he was ruthless when he wanted something. He destroyed my career."

Brooke remembered Nick had told her a few times, he didn't have everything he wanted. Searching her memory, she recalled his one passion. The one thing that he'd wanted above all else. "Baseball?"

He put his head down and dragged her hand to his lap, holding tight. "I was just a kid with a dream." Deep emotion weighted his words. "I was good, Brooke."

"I remember."

"I'd made the minor leagues and was on my way to the majors, but dear old dad wanted his boys to run the wine business. He wanted us to love his legacy as much as he did. None of us did. I was his last chance."

Nick went on to tell the details of the incidents that crushed his baseball career. The lies, the deception and the manipulations. He spoke about Candy Rae and Brooke's spine stiffened when she learned about her part in the deception. Nick had been just a young boy with his whole life ahead of him. How devastating for him to go through that, knowing his father disregarded his wishes to manipulate him into a life he didn't want. Brooke finally understood why Nick wanted nothing to do with the company. It signified all he'd lost.

"Then I had my accident during the game. I know in my head my father didn't physically injure me so I couldn't play again, but he sure as hell put pressure on me and had me rattled enough to make a fool move on the field. I was recovering from the surgery too, but before I knew what happened, the team released me. I know my father had something to do with that."

Brooke had heard rumors about Santo Carlino when she'd lived in Napa as a young girl. He'd been a powerful and ruthless businessman. "I'm sorry."

"Don't be. I'm only telling you this to ease your mind about being with me."

"Is that the only reason, Nick?" She shouldn't have asked. She never knew when to keep her trap shut.

He turned to face her, his gaze piercing hers. "It's been a long time since I've spoken about this. And only to my brothers. I guess I figured you'd understand."

"I do." She smiled and stroked his cheek gently, his day old stubble rough under her palm. "But I'm sorry for more than what you've gone through. I'm sorry for thinking having money and good looks meant you had everything you wanted."

"You like my looks?" he said, in an attempt to lighten the mood.

"Yes, I like your looks," she said, not taking the bait to banter. This was serious and she wouldn't let Nick make light of it. "I've misjudged you and I apologize."

He brought her hand to his mouth and gently kissed the inner skin of her palm. "Thanks."

They sat in the dark, holding hands, the intimacy of the moment more profound than the sex they'd experienced these past few days. Brooke's heart ached for him in a way she'd never be able to justify or explain to another person.

Because this was Nick.

And she was falling in love with him.

"Stupid, stupid, stupid," Brooke muttered, as she gave the dining room table a second polish, the cloth in her hand circling faster and faster, to match the crazy beating of her heart. "How could Mommy do that? How could she fall in love with Nick again?" she asked Leah, who played with a Baby Elmo music box on the floor. Leah looked up with a questioning pout on her little lips. To add insult to injury, her daughter's eyes rounded and searched the room at the mere mention of Nick's name. Even her child was smitten with him.

Her life was in shambles and she didn't have a solution to either of her dilemmas.

Dan wanted to know his daughter and start over, and Nick, the man she loved, wanted to be rid of Napa in the worst way. One man was coming back into her life, another leaving for good. And it was all wrong.

When her cell phone rang, Brooke didn't jump and she didn't panic. It was time for her to come to terms with her life and fix what she could. She noted Dan's number on the screen and took a deep breath before answering. "Hello."

"It's Dan, honey."

Honey?

"I'm only in Napa for a few more days. I'd like to come see you. We have things to talk about. Things to work out. I know I made a mistake leaving you."

"Yes, you did, Dan. But that's over now."

"It doesn't have to be. I want to talk to you, Brooke."

There was a calm and amenable tone to his voice today, but she still didn't trust it, or him. "I suppose we do have things to talk about."

"Can I come over?"

"Today's not good, Dan. Come tomorrow afternoon. We'll talk."

After Brooke hung up the phone, she slumped down in a chair and put her head in her hands. She couldn't afford a court battle with Dan, but she'd do anything within her power to keep Leah. There was no way she'd give him joint custody. At the very most, she'd allow him the right to come for a visit every now and then. She'd stick to her guns and not budge an inch.

She glanced at Leah who had rolled onto her back on the pink flowered quilt, her chubby legs kicking in the air, as she nibbled on her teething ring. "He doesn't deserve you," she whispered, holding back tears.

The only good news she had all week was that her mom was coming for a visit in a month. She's promised to help Brooke with her first paying guests and with any luck she'd be open for business by then. With Joe's expertise, her website would be operating soon and she'd managed to meet local merchants, hand out flyers and spread the word about her establishment.

"It's good news," she said to Leah. "I've gotta keep reminding myself that all this hard work will pay off one day."

Brooke got down on the floor and sat cross-legged on the quilt. She put Leah in a sitting position facing her. "Wanna play a game with Mommy?"

She took Leah's hands in hers and spread them wide. "Open," she said, drawing the word out. Then she closed their hands together, relaying in a sing-song voice, "Close them."

Leah giggled with joy. She loved this game. "Open," she repeated. "Close them." Brooke's mood lightened instantly just seeing her daughter's fascinated expression.

There was a sharp knock at the door, a knock she recognized. She braced herself, glancing outside at the parked car, before opening the door. Nick stood on the threshold, looking like a zillion bucks as usual and her heart thumped hard in her chest. He was eye-catching no matter what he wore, but today, he had on a tailored, and from the look of it, very expensive dark suit. "Hi," he said with a sparkling gleam in his blue eyes.

The sight of him blew her away. "Who died?"

He smiled. "You don't like my going-to-San-Francisco-on-business look?"

"You look nice, Nick," she relented, a gross understatement. "You didn't mention your trip this morning, though."

"It just came up. I'll be staying overnight. I came to give you the key to the house, just in case you miss Carlotta when you come in."

She let him in and they walked into the dining room. "Hey, kid," Nick said when he spotted Leah on the quilt. She gazed up at him and immediately lifted her arms for him to take her.

"She cut her first tooth. She's in a better mood today."

"Really," Nick said, taking off his jacket and getting down on the floor. "Let Nick see your tooth." He picked Leah up in his arms. Leah smiled at him, opening her mouth just slightly but not enough for him to catch a glimpse of it. He tickled her chin to make her laugh, then bent his head, searching until he came up with a grin. "Hey, there it is." He kissed Leah's forehead and Brooke's stomach twisted. How this man thought he wasn't good father material, she couldn't fathom. Granted, she'd thought so too, until she'd seen him interact with Leah and gotten to know him again.

Her heart broke thinking he'd never have a child of his own.

He looked up at Brooke, the smile still on his face. "Let's move furniture."

"What?"

"You have three more rooms to paint, don't you?"

"Yes, I was going to start on the next one when Leah took her nap this afternoon."

Nick rose, taking Leah in his arms. He tilted his chin and gestured upstairs. "It'll take me a few minutes."

"You're all dressed up."

"Are you going to stop arguing with me?" He glanced at Leah. "I hope you won't be this stubborn when you grow up."

Her daughter responded with a soft touch to his cheek.

"Okay, fine," she said. It was killing her seeing Nick holding Leah and how easy they were with each other. "Let's move furniture."

Half an hour later, after they'd arranged the furniture in the center of each of the three remaining rooms, Nick glanced at his watch. "I'd better get on the road. My meeting is in a couple of hours."

Brooke walked him downstairs and handed him his jacket. He slung it over his shoulder and strode to the door. "See you tomorrow night."

She nodded and glanced at his mouth.

He inhaled a sharp breath. "Keep looking at me that way and I'll never get out of here."

Heat rushed up her neck to warm her face. He was smooth, a charmer to the umpteenth degree, but he'd shown her a different side of himself last night and she feared she'd never get enough of him.

He took her into his arms and brushed a light kiss to her lips. Then he groaned and pulled her up tight against him, deepening the kiss. It lasted a gloriously long time and when they finally broke apart, both of them were breathing heavily.

"You make a man want to stay home nights," he whispered with a rasp, before turning and exiting the house.

She stood on the porch and watched him get into his car and pull out of the driveway. Then she entered the house and leaned back against the closed doorway. "Damn you, Nick. Don't say those things to me."

Nine

"So how long have you been teaching English at the high school?" Brooke asked Molly as they sat at the bed-and-breakfast's newly spruced up dining room table. It was tea for two with her aunt's Royal Albert English Chintz china teacups looking wonderful on the lacy rose tablecloth she'd laid out.

Molly juggled having Leah on her lap and sipping chamomile tea without the slightest pause. It was clear her friend knew a thing or two about children. She was glad she was finally able to have Molly over for an early brunch.

"This is my fifth year at the high school. I started teaching English and History a year after Adam was born and it's working out very well. We have our summers together and during the school season I'm home early. My husband works out of the house a few days a week, so he's Mr. Part-time Mom."

Brooke chuckled. "Is that what you call him?"

"Yeah, I do. John's got a great sense of humor. We laugh about it all the time."

"It's important to have someone to laugh with. Dan never laughed much. It's a wonder the two of us ever got together."

Molly reached for her hand. "You're doing the right thing by moving on. He wasn't right for you."

"Don't I know it! He'll be here in a couple of hours and I have no idea what I'm going to say to him."

"Just listen to what he says," Molly offered, touching her hand. "Let him speak his mind, but don't give him an answer. Tell him you have to think things over and then do that. There's no rush. You don't have to make any decisions quickly."

Having Molly here soothed her fragile nerves. She'd given her good advice and made her wish they hadn't lost touch with each other in the past. "Thanks, Molly. I will do that. It's the sane, rational thing to do." Then Brooke thought about it some more, shaking her head. "It's hard to be objective. He's such a snake."

A quick smile brought light to Molly's amber eyes. "Take the high road. Only call him a snake behind his back."

"I'll try," Brooke said, arching her brow as she pondered. "It won't be easy."

Brooke rose from her seat to arrange little round lemon pastries she'd made earlier this morning on a plate. She set out a bowl with fresh strawberries and raspberries topped with a special cream she'd prepared and a platter of sliced cranberry bread. "I'm practicing on you. Tell me what you think."

Molly tasted each one of the dishes and nodded. "Excellent. You get an A. The lemon tarts are amazing. When did you have time to do all this?"

"Last night and early this morning. Nick was gone, so I had free time."

Molly grinned. "Nick?"

"I mean, I usually cook him breakfast and dinner and the house was empty so I took advantage of the time to whip these up."

"Okay, I get it. He wasn't home to *occupy* your time, right?" Molly shot her a wicked smile. "What's up with the two of you?"

"He's a fr—" she began, then quickly stopped herself from calling him a friend. The "F" word wasn't a label she wanted between the two of them. "He and I have an arrangement. And no, it's not what you're thinking."

"Oh, so you're not sleeping with him? Too bad. Remember when he won Desert Island Dream in high school? The girls got to pick the one guy they'd like to be stranded on a desert island with."

"I remember," Brooke said with a groan. The girls wouldn't have been disappointed.

When Leah began to fidget too much, Molly set her down in her playpen and gave her a toy. "There you go."

Molly lifted up to stare into Brooke's eyes. "You had a thing for him and now you're living under his roof."

"Just temporarily. We'll be moving out soon. And he'll be off to Monte Carlo. He's got a house there and can't wait to leave the country."

Molly continued to stare at her, narrowing her eyes. "You're in love with him."

"I've got enough problems at the moment, thank you very much."

Molly spoke with gentle regard. "Doesn't change the fact."

"No, it doesn't," Brooke admitted, lowering her tea cup slowly to confess her innermost feelings. Maybe it would help to discuss this with someone. "It just happened. I had my eyes wide open, knowing it was impossible."

"To coin a cliché, love is blind. You can't help who you love."

"But you can be smart about it, can't you?"

Amusement sparked in Molly's eyes when she shook her head. "I don't think so. Intellect has very little to do with matters of the heart. Nick must be more than a hot hunk loaded with money for you to fall for him. The girl I knew needed more than eye candy." Molly was forever astute and that's why they'd gotten along in high school.

"Nick always let me see a side of him he rarely showed anyone else," Brooke said soberly. "I told myself over and over it was ridiculous and impossible, but there he was, opening up to me and being so good with Leah." Tears welled up in her eyes as she glanced at her baby sucking on her fist. Brooke had dressed her for company and she looked so pretty in her frilly flowered dress and bloomers. "Leah adores him."

She sniffed and halted her feelings of melancholy. "It's not going to work with him, Molly. My life is so complicated right now. I just want to have it all simple again."

Brooke and Molly talked for half an hour more and before her friend left she gave her a big comforting hug. "Call me anytime, Brooke."

"Don't worry, I will."

Brooke braced herself for Dan's visit. She didn't want this, any of it. She scooped Leah up in her arms and thought about running away, but it was just a wishful dream. She had to face him today and there wasn't much she could do about it. She sat down on the sofa and rocked Leah, giving her a bottle of formula and hoping she'd be sound asleep when Dan came by.

Less than an hour later, she heard a knock and rushed

to the door to keep Leah from waking up. "Come in," she said the second she saw Dan.

He entered the house. His hair was groomed, his face shaven, and he had on the same type of business casual clothes he always wore; khaki pants and a brown Polo shirt. She looked at him and felt nothing but disdain. At one time she had thought he was handsome, with his angular lines and sharp facial features. "Let's have a seat in the parlor."

She moved ahead of him and sat down in a wing chair that faced the sofa. Dan took the sofa and stared at her. He leaned forward. "You look good, Brooke. Pretty as always."

She refrained from rolling her eyes. "How did you know where we were?"

Dan glanced around the parlor taking it all in with assessing eyes as if doing mental calculations. "There's a lot of antiques in here. Are all the rooms furnished like this? How old is this place? "

"Old," she replied, refusing more information. "Please answer my question."

"Okay, fine, Brooke. I've been searching for you for months. I realized I'd made a drastic mistake. I hired a private detective to find you only to get a report last week that you'd had a baby and moved back to Napa."

"How touching," Brooke said. Was she supposed to cave just because he paid someone to find her?

Dan's face reddened and he looked ready to wrestle a bear.

She hoisted her chin.

"Look," he began. "Let's try to be civil to each other. We have a daughter."

Brooke hated hearing it. She hated that Leah had a drop of his blood and that he did have a legal right to see her. "Her name is Leah Marie and she's a Hamilton."

Dan's lips twisted. "She's a Hartley, Brooke, whether you want to accept it or not. Now, can I see her?"

Brooke's stomach quaked. "Fine, but please don't wake her." Brooke rose and took him into the downstairs bedroom where she'd set up a little crib she'd recently purchased on sale. Slowly, this place was becoming a home to them.

She led him into the bedroom and Dan gazed down at his daughter sleeping in the crib. He stood there a few minutes, just watching her as Brooke studied him. Something odd happened. Dan's expression didn't soften. It didn't change at all. His gaze didn't flow over Leah with loving adoration. Maybe it was because she was a stranger to him, or because he'd already lost one child, but Brooke had expected something more from Dan than the stony face staring down at the crib. Granted, he'd seen her several days ago, but that was for only a few seconds.

After half a minute, Brooke cleared her throat and Dan got the message. He exited the room with Brooke steps behind him.

"I remember you talking about this place," he said as they reentered the parlor and took their seats again. "Now it's all yours. What will you do with it?"

Brooke was taken aback by his question. Didn't he want to know about Leah? When was she born? How was the delivery? What is she like?

"I'm converting the house into a bed-and-breakfast. I have to support myself somehow."

"How many rooms does it have?"

"Eight, but six upstairs that I'll use for patrons."

"You were always good at homemaking, Brooke."

"Funny, but I never heard that from you before."

Dan gritted his teeth, making the words flowing from his mouth seem implausible. "I'm sorry I hurt you."

She wasn't sure that he really was. "That's not enough. Being sorry won't make up for anything. You abandoned me."

"I didn't know you were having a child. You should have told me."

"You shouldn't have gotten another woman pregnant and left me the way you did. You just packed up and moved out the same day I'd learned about it. I was in shock for months and picking up the pieces. I don't owe you anything, Dan."

"We can be a family again."

"That's not possible."

"Anything's possible, Brooke. Give us a second chance."

Leah cried out and Brooke prayed she'd fall back asleep, but the cries continued and she excused herself. "I have to get her. She's probably hungry and wet."

"I'll come with you."

"No. Stay here. I'll be back in a few minutes. I'll bring her in."

And Brooke walked out of the parlor on shaking legs.

Nick stepped onto Brooke's porch, a gift for Leah in one hand, another for Brooke in his pocket. He'd made it back to Napa after his late morning meeting with customers for Carlino Wines in good time and decided to stop by Brooke's house first before heading home this afternoon.

He told himself that Brooke might need a hand putting the furniture back in place after painting for the past two days, but in truth he was anxious to give the girls the gifts he'd picked up in San Francisco.

He heard a man speaking to Brooke from inside the house. The somber tone of his voice had an edge to it that

Nick didn't like. He pushed through the front door, without bothering to knock, and turned toward the parlor.

"Don't be unreasonable, Brooke," the man said. As he held Leah in his arms, the baby's lips turned down in a pout, tears ready to spill from her eyes. "Things could go so much easier if you agree to give us a second chance. I have rights and if you don't think so, I might have to take you to court."

Distressed, Brooke reached for her baby. "Give her to me, Dan. She's upset."

The man backed away from Brooke, refusing her the baby. "She needs to know her father."

"She *doesn't* know you and she's scared." Brooke said, panicked.

Nick stepped farther into the room, his emotions roiling. Seeing Leah in that man's arms and Brooke clearly agitated infuriated him. "Leah's not a pawn in this. Give her back the baby."

Both Brooke and Dan seemed startled to see him standing in the room.

"Who the hell are you?" Dan asked, raising his voice even more. He turned to Brooke, "Who is he and why is he issuing orders about my daughter?"

"Nick Carlino. He's been like a father to Leah, the only one she's ever known. She should be so lucky."

Nick's gaze darted straight to Brooke and from the firm resolve on her face he knew she meant what she said.

"But he's not her father. *I am.*"

The roughness of his voice carried across the room and Leah's face turned red as she burst into tears. The jerk was too selfish to realize he'd upset the baby.

"Give her to me," Brooke said quietly between gritted teeth.

"I will in a minute." Dan tried to calm Leah but it wasn't working, her cries grew louder.

Nick set Leah's gift down and strode up to Dan, his anger barely contained. Immediately, Leah turned toward him and reached out her wobbly arms, her sobs quieting down. Nick put his hands on Leah's waist, her body twisting toward him. He stared at Dan, his jaw tensing. "Let go of her."

The man glanced at Brooke then sighed. He released his hold on Leah. She flowed into Nick's arms. Her baby scent wafted up as she hung on tight, attaching herself to him. He held her for a few long moments and stroked her hair, before handing her back to Brooke. He eyed Leah's father with contempt and spoke with deadly calm. "Don't come in here and threaten them ever again."

"Nick, I can handle this," Brooke said, intervening. He didn't think so, but he backed off for her sake. "Dan was just leaving. We've said all we have to say for now."

"I'm not giving up, Brooke," Dan said. "We can make this work. I want you both back."

Brooke squeezed her eyes shut. "And I told you, that's not going to happen. Just go, Dan."

Dan shot a quick glance at Leah, then his gaze went to Brooke. "This isn't over." He sent Nick a hard look and strode out of the house with Nick at his heels. He waited until the guy was off the property before returning to Brooke, who had collapsed on the sofa with tears streaming down her face.

Nick stood staring at Brooke, his anger dissipating but other emotions clicking in with full force. When he'd walked into the house seeing another man holding Leah, claiming he wanted Brooke and Leah back in his life, surging waves of anger and jealousy destroyed his good mood. He'd never experienced anything like it, this fierce instinct to protect and comfort.

Brooke's defiant words from just minutes ago stuck in his head.

He's been like a father to Leah, the only one she's ever known.

Was that true? Was he getting that close to both Brooke and Leah? Or was Brooke just using those tactics with her ex to drive her point home, that Dan hadn't been any kind of father to Leah? He had walked out on Brooke and never looked back until what? What had happened to make him seek Brooke out?

She should be so lucky.

That comment had touched Nick in ways he didn't want to think about. Brooke couldn't possibly look at him as a role model for her child. Could she? Could she think of him in a way that he'd never thought of himself, as a man who could be a good father?

The *simple* they both wanted was getting real complicated.

His best bet would be to walk away now, but Nick knew he couldn't without helping Brooke one more time. He wouldn't leave until he was sure she and Leah would have the life they deserved. Dan had some rights to see his daughter, he was Leah's biological father, but Nick wouldn't stand by and watch the jerk hurt either of them.

He could be a hard-ass when necessary and this was the time and place for that.

Later that night, Nick watched as Brooke sat cross-legged on the floor opposite Leah in his living room, playing with the music box he'd brought home for the baby. Brooke opened the ornate silver box and a miniature ballerina twirled around to a classical tune that had Leah mesmerized. She kept trying to touch the ballerina and Brooke caught her hand each time. "Let the pretty ballerina dance," she said in a soft sweet voice.

Leah bobbed up and down with excitement from her sitting position and gurgled with laughter at the music box.

"She loves it, Nick."

Nick leaned forward in his chair, bracing elbows on knees, seeing Brooke finally calmed down from today's debacle. "Looks like it."

"Did you pick it out yourself?"

"I did. The ballerina reminded me of Leah."

Brooke's gaze met his. "You're an old softy."

"Just don't tell anyone."

Brooke glanced away for a few moments then turned to face him with regret. "I'm sorry you had to witness that today."

"I'm not. I seriously hope you don't plan on letting that guy back into your life."

"Not if I can help it," Brooke said, closing the music box. "But what choice do I have if he takes me to court?"

"He won't do that." Nick had connections and already had someone on it. He'd managed to memorize Dan Hartley's license plate and coupled with the information he'd gathered from conversations with Brooke, he'd know a lot more about him and his motives very soon. "How much are you willing to give him as far as Leah goes?"

"Nothing, but I have to be realistic. She may want to know her father one day. At the very most, I'd grant him visitation rights with me being there. That's all I can imagine for now."

"That might be doable."

"I'm not that sure, Nick. I'm going to have a lot of sleepless nights over this."

"He's the reason you came to me that first night, isn't it?" It didn't take a rocket scientist to figure that one out. "You were upset."

"That was part of the reason," she confessed with apology in her voice.

Nick arched his brows. "Part? What was the other part?"

"Maybe you're just irresistible."

Nick scoffed at that. "Come on, Brooke. Tell me."

Indecision marred her pretty face as she debated a few seconds before finally owning up. "It was partly because Dan had contacted me and I was frightened, but it was also because I wanted to be reckless for once in my life. I wanted something just for me. I've dreamed about being with you for a long time and well, you were just down the hall giving me an open invitation."

Nick swallowed down hard. He didn't know what to say to that.

"I know you're leaving, and I've got my own plans. I figured no harm could come of it."

"You want simple, I get that," he said. "I've lived my whole life that way."

"Right. Simple is as simple does."

Only Brooke and Leah were complicating the hell out of his life lately.

Nick stood and walked over to Brooke, reaching for her hand and when she placed it in his, he helped her up. He wound his arms around her waist and kissed her gently. "It's late. You've had a rough day. Let's go to bed."

"Together?" she asked.

"I'll be waiting for you."

Brooke's eyes softened and she smiled. "As soon as I get the baby to sleep, I'll be there."

Nick would hold her all night long if that was what

she wanted. He'd never done that with a woman but with Brooke, all his rules were shot to hell.

He picked up Leah and walked up the stairs side by side with Brooke, Nick kissing the baby's cheek before handing her off to her mommy.

He was in deep. But he hadn't changed his mind about anything. Brooke knew the score—he was leaving for Monte Carlo in just a few weeks.

He wanted no ties to Napa at all and that included this beautiful blond mommy with her equally beautiful blond baby.

Brooke got Leah to sleep easily. All that crying today had worn her out. She checked on her one last time, before she donned the oversized T-shirt that Nick liked and went to his room. She knocked softly and Nick was there, immediately opening the door and taking her into his arms. He held her gently and kissed her forehead, cheek and chin before bringing his warm inviting lips to hers.

"I don't think I can leave Leah," she whispered, a sense of urgency she couldn't explain, niggling at her. "I'm sorry. I thought I could, but I can't. It's going to be hard enough for me to fall asleep tonight."

Nick kissed her forehead again. "Then I'll come to you."

She gazed into his eyes.

He winked and pulled her against his chest. "I miss my big old bed."

"I'm not feeling—"

"I know, honey. We'll just *sleep* together. Just don't tell anybody, it might ruin my reputation."

She punched him in the shoulder. "You're so bad, Nick." Then she added, "In a wonderful way."

A chuckle rumbled from his chest. "That might be the nicest thing you've ever said to me."

She turned to go back to her bedroom, but Nick grabbed her hand just in time and she swirled around to face him. "Wait a second." He moved to the dresser and pulled out a black velvet box from the top drawer. "When I saw this, I knew you had to have it."

He handed her the square box. "This is for you."

Her heart pounded and she was totally confused. "What, why?"

"Open it, Brooke."

She held the box with trembling hands and opened it slowly. "Oh, Nick, this is beautiful." She fingered the green-blue oval gemstone surrounded by inset diamonds on a long silver chain.

"It's tourmaline. This stone is the exact color of your eyes."

"I don't know what to say, except thank you...and why?"

Nick shrugged. "Why not? When I saw the necklace it reminded me of you and I wanted you to have it."

"But it's probably worth more than my old clunker car."

"Your point?"

"I don't really have one, except that it's too generous, Nick. You've already done so much for me. How can I possibly accept this?"

He gave her a smoldering kiss, loving her mouth and charming her into submission. "Just say you love it."

She shook her head, ready to refuse his gift even after that mind-blowing kiss. She had pride and Nick had given her so much already, but she couldn't insult him by not accepting such a thoughtful gesture. Happy tears pooled in her eyes. "You're impossible, you know."

"I've heard that before."

She reached up on tiptoes and pressed a sweet kiss to his lips. "I love it. But you shouldn't have done it."

"I do a lot of things I shouldn't do, but giving you this gift isn't one of them."

Nick put out the light and took her hand, leading her back to the master bedroom. Quietly, they slipped in between the sheets and he took her into his arms and held her until she fell asleep.

Brooke woke early in the morning in a better mood. She'd had a good night's rest after all, cradled next to Nick during the night. She breathed in his expensive musky cologne and smiled from ear to ear at the position they were in. He lay on his back, his legs spread out, while she was on her stomach, her thigh thrust over his, and his full thick erection pressing against her hip.

"It's about time you woke up," he said, stroking her back.

Stunned, she let out a gasp. "How long have you been like this?"

Nick groaned a complaint. "Too long. Am I taking a cold shower this morning?"

Brooke kissed his neck and whispered, "Sometimes that can be fun when we do it together."

"Brooke," he warned then he rolled her over onto her back and kissed her until her lips burned from the scorching heat. He gazed into her eyes until she nodded and smiled. He wasn't a man to be denied, not that Brooke could even conceive of that now. She wanted him in all the ways that complicated her life. She wanted him in any way she could have him.

Nick made love to her with slow hands and sexy words that sent her mind spinning and her body aching for more. He was an expert at making a woman feel desirable and beautiful. She relished every illicit touch, every gliding stroke of his hands and every moist sensual thrust of his tongue.

With his encouragement she touched him back, her assault a partial revenge for the tortured pleasure he'd given her. She inched her palms up his muscled chest, through the coarse hairs surrounding his nipples. She kissed him there, then suckled on him until a heavy impatient groan erupted in his throat. She smiled and moved farther up, kissing him hard then outlining his mouth with her index finger, swirling it around and around, then slipping it into his mouth. He suckled her finger and pressure built, his chest heaving as much as hers. Heavy heat consumed her and when Nick held her tight and rolled her on top of him, instincts took over.

He helped her off with her T-shirt and she slid him out of his boxers. Naked now and consumed with lust, Brooke took his thick shaft in her hands and stroked him, sliding her open palm up and down the silken skin. She bent and put her mouth on him, loving him with fiery passion. She sensed when he was at the brink and rose above him. His face was emblazoned with desire, his rough stubble and dark hair tousled. He was the sexiest man alive.

She lowered her body down in a straddle and took him inside her. It felt so right, so perfect that she wanted to cry. Nick watched her ride him, his eyes heavy-lidded. He brought his hands to her breasts and caressed her, sensitizing her pebble-hard nipples even more. She ached for him, wanted him and loved him like no other man before.

Her climax came first and she splintered, her nerves tight, her body convulsing and finally giving up to the intense pleasure of being joined with Nick.

Nick watched her with awe in his eyes and when she was completely through, she rolled off him and accommodated his weight. He filled her again and she welcomed him. He thrust into her hard and fast, his climax coming just seconds after hers. She felt another wave of fulfillment just witnessing the satisfaction she could give to him.

She was so much in love with him her heart ached.

Afterward, they lay in each other's arms silently.

Brooke felt content and happy, but distraught at the same time. She knew this wouldn't last. She knew she was in for a gigantic fall.

When Leah made her early rising sounds, little complaints as she woke, Brooke lifted up to get her. Nick put a stopping hand on her arm. "I'll get her."

Brooke shook her head. "She'll need to be changed."

Nick winced, his lips pulling down in a frown. "Really?"

"Of course, really. She's slept all night in the same diaper."

Nick thought about it for half a second then gave her a quick kiss on the lips, slipped on his boxers and rose from the bed. "I'll take care of it. Just relax."

Brooke laid her head down on the pillow and grinned as she heard Nick struggling with the diaper change, but after a while Nick brought Leah to her. "Here she is."

He sat Leah on the bed between the two of them and Brooke inspected his handiwork. "Well, you're no speed demon, but it looks good."

With a satisfied look on his face, he winked. "I learned from the best."

She hated when Nick said nice things. She hated when he did nice things. And he'd been doing and saying nice things for so long now. Maybe she should have clung to her anger and not let him charm her into liking him. Because aside from being head-over-heels in love, she really liked the man Nick had become.

Deep down in her heart, Brooke knew this wasn't a good idea. Nick hadn't made her any promises. He'd been up front and honest with her. She was the one who wanted "simple."

What she'd gotten was a whole lot more.

Sure, she feared Leah was getting too attached to Nick. But her mommy was already a terribly hopeless case.

Ten

Three days later, Nick showed up unannounced at the bed-and-breakfast just as Brooke had finished dusting the entire house from top to bottom. She met him at the front door, wearing an apron with her hair pulled back in a ponytail. "Hi," she said, looking at him with confusion. "You didn't say you were stopping by this morning."

"I have some news," he said, his face grim. He made his way into the house and walked into the kitchen. Brooke followed him inside the room, curious. He gestured to a chair. "Here, have a seat."

Brooke's heart pounded with dread as he waited for her to sit down. "What is it?"

He sat in a chair adjacent to her. "I had your ex investigated. Don't ask me how or why, but it's done."

Brooke ran a hand down her face, taking it all in. She was more than a little stunned. "Okay," she dragged out, "but I don't understand."

"He's bankrupt. Seems his girlfriend cleaned him out and he's desperate for money. He knew that you'd had his child, months before showing up here."

Brooke blinked and shook her head. "What are you saying?"

Nick studied her face and spoke quietly, "I'm saying that he didn't search for you for months. He found out where you were right after Leah was born. He knew about her almost from the time of her birth. He didn't come for you and Leah, until he found out that you inherited this house. The house is probably worth what, three quarters of a million dollars? He probably figured you'd inherited a huge pile of cash along with it."

Brooke squeezed her eyes shut momentarily. "That bastard."

When she opened her eyes again, she saw the whole startling truth. It hurt to know what little she'd ever meant to Dan, but it hurt worse knowing he didn't really care about his daughter. "He was after my money?" Brooke asked, already certain of the answer.

Nick nodded.

Her heart in her throat and her stomach in knots, she was ready to cry. "It's hard to believe I once loved him. Shows you what a poor judge of character I am."

"Don't beat yourself up too badly. He only showed you a side of himself he wanted you to see."

"He's Leah's father and she deserves more."

"He won't be around much."

Brooke snapped her head up and stared into eyes that didn't meet hers. "What did you do? You didn't make him disappear, did you?"

Nick cast her a crooked grin and scratched the back of his neck. "No, I had a little chat with him. I told him you and Leah were off-limits. You'll decide when and where you want Leah to see him."

"How did you get him to agree...?" Then it dawned on Brooke. "Oh Nick, you paid him off, didn't you?"

Nick kept his expression unreadable. "All that matters is that you and Leah won't be bothered by him from now on."

"It does matter." Brooke rose from her chair. "How much was my little girl worth to him? How could he put a price tag on that?"

Nick stood and cupped her shoulders in his big hands, holding her still while she wanted to throw things. He spoke calmly. "It doesn't matter, Brooke. He was never in Leah's life. You can move on and forget about him. Will you do that?"

Brooke stared at Nick, wondering if she should take that same advice about him. She was a bad judge of character. She'd fallen for a guy who'd flat out told her he didn't want a family—a man who was leaving to live halfway across the world. Was he also telling her to move on and forget about him?

Nick's cell phone rang and he excused himself to answer it. Brooke took that time to check on Leah, then wash her face and comb her hair. She removed her apron and by the time Nick reentered the kitchen, she had new but heartbreaking determination.

"That was Tony. He's a giddy mess. Rena had the baby. They named him David Anthony Carlino." Nick's grin broadened across his face.

Brooke's heavy heart warmed. Babies brought such joy into a person's life. "That's wonderful. Is Rena okay?"

"According to my big brother, she's doing fine. I'm going to see them now. Want to come?"

"No, no. You go. Tell Rena I'll visit her another time. I want to see the baby. But this time is for family."

The thought of seeing Rena, Tony and their new baby, a child that wasn't Tony's biological child but one he'd love like his own, hit a little too close to home. Brooke had wanted that so much for herself, but it wasn't to be. And after the news she'd gotten today about Dan, she couldn't take witnessing the happy threesome with their whole future ahead of them.

Nick cast her an odd look. "She wouldn't mind if you came with me."

"No, Nick," she said with resolve. "I'm not coming with you. I'm not part of your family."

And I never will be.

That night when Brooke entered the Carlino house, her courage bolstered by the words she'd rehearsed all day and knew by heart, she found Nick's suitcase by the front door.

"Hi," Nick said, coming to greet her when she walked in. "You should have seen the size of that baby. He was almost nine pounds." He held two flutes of champagne. "I've been waiting for you to celebrate."

Leah clung to her shoulder, nearly asleep. "I can't right now, Nick. Leah's not feeling well. She's a little warm and her nose is running. I'm going to put her to sleep."

Nick's face fell and she could barely stand to watch his cheerful expression transform. He gazed at Leah with concern, his eyes soft and caring. "I'll go up with you." He set the flutes down, ready to help.

"No, that's okay. She's a little clingy right now. Are you going somewhere?"

Nick glanced at the suitcase in the entry. "I've got a

crisis at the Monte Carlo house. I'm leaving on the red-eye tonight. I hope to be back in three days, tops."

Brooke stopped when she reached the base of the staircase and seized on her chance to say her rehearsed words. "Nick, now's as good a time as any to tell you, Leah and I are moving out. The house is ready for us now. I don't have much more to do before I can open my doors. We'll be gone before you get back."

Nick furrowed his brows. "You're leaving?" He sounded as if it were news to him. This had always been their deal, though it broke her heart to see the look of confusion on his face. Women didn't walk out on Nick Carlino.

"It's time for me to go. I want to thank you for everything. I don't know what I would've done without your help these past few weeks. I promise, I'll find a way to pay you back. And I'm still in shock about how you handled Dan. I don't know what to say about that."

"Damn it, Brooke, you don't owe me anything." His mouth tightened to a thin line. "And you don't have to move out right now."

"Yes, Nick. I do. That was the deal." He was the classic dealmaker in the family, so he should understand. She may owe him a few weeks of work, but he'd just have to make do. She couldn't live in the house with him another day. "This was always a temporary arrangement."

His eyes darkened with anger. "I know that."

"I've learned something since coming back to Napa, Nick. You can't dwell on the past. You have to move on and look to the future. You've helped me see that."

Nick stared at her without blinking.

"Just think, you'll have the house back to normal, no more baby things to trip over."

Nick ignored her little jest. "This is because of what that jerk did to you, isn't it?"

Brooke smiled with sadness in her heart and shook her head. How could she explain that her leaving had nothing to do with Dan and everything to do with protecting herself and her daughter from getting attached to Nick, a man who was bent on running away from his past, a man who wanted a lifestyle that didn't include a ready-made family. "You've given me so much and I want to return the favor the only way I know how. My friend Molly says the high school is in desperate need of a baseball coach for the boys. You should think about it."

Nick looked at her like she'd gone crazy.

"Okay," she said with a heavy sigh. Saying good-bye to Nick was one of the hardest things she'd ever had to do. She summoned all her courage and held her ground, when she wanted to throw herself into his arms. "I've got to go up. Leah and I have a long day tomorrow." She whispered softly, "Good-bye, Nick."

Nick remained silent. She sensed his gaze on her as she climbed the stairs to the room she'd sleep in one last time. When she reached the top of the staircase, she heard him pick up his suitcase and open the front door.

There was a long pause before finally, the front door slammed shut.

Silent tears rained down her face as she carried her precious child to her bed. Brooke had no one to blame but herself. She'd come into this with her eyes wide open yet couldn't help falling in love with him again regardless of her constant internal warnings.

But by far, this time hurt the most.

She'd never get over Nick Carlino.

Not in this lifetime.

Nick sat on the deck of his Monte Carlo home and sipped wine, gazing out at the Mediterranean's classic blue waters.

He had everything he wanted here, a gorgeous view of the ocean, twelve rooms of modern conveniences and old world charm, friends to party with and a world-renowned casino only minutes away.

He'd gambled there last night and had gone out with friends afterward. He had offers from women during his time here, but Nick wasn't interested in them. Somehow their sleek clothes and sultry looks didn't stir his juices as they once had. Images of Brooke in her mommy clothes would seep into his mind instead. But he balked at that.

Thoughts of her stayed with him constantly, but he knew that would pass. Nick wanted an easy life and now that he was away from all that Napa represented, he decided to stay on a few more days.

The Italian marble "crisis" his contractor had called him about had been straightened out and it turned out not to be a big deal after all. The renovations he'd ordered were almost done and not a minute too soon. He was only weeks from winning his bet with his brothers, and by all accounts he'd already won. He'd be through with his father's wine business once and for all and he could come and go as he pleased. He would enjoy rubbing his brothers' faces in the win, smug as they both had been about the bet.

But with those thoughts also came Brooke's words that she'd spoken just days ago. *You can't dwell on the past. You have to move on and look to the future.*

He'd helped her see that?

A smile spread across his face. If he had, then he was damn glad. He couldn't deny that he wanted to see her happy. She'd always been special to him and she always made him smile with her sassy tongue and witty comebacks. She had a chance for a good future with Leah now.

During the next few days, Nick refused more party invitations than he accepted and he refrained from entertaining females at the house. He took walks on the beach, spent a more active role in the renovations and watched sports on television.

After dinner on Thursday night, he placed a call to Rena and Tony. The baby was almost a week old and Uncle Nick wanted to hear how the three of them were doing.

Rena picked up and said hello.

"Hi, it's Nick. I'm checking on my favorite uncle status."

"You're still it, but don't tell Joe I said so. And least *he* isn't thousands of miles away. He didn't abandon the family."

Nick chuckled at Rena's teasing.

"I'll be back in few days and I'm bringing gifts."

"Oh, so you're spoiling my child already?"

"That's the plan. How's the little guy?"

"He's doing fine. Eating like a Carlino and growing like one too. I never knew breast-feeding could be so challenging."

Nick laughed and an image popped into his head of Brooke holding Leah to her breast, the baby nursing until she was good and satisfied. The serene picture they'd made would be forever imbedded in his mind. "I bet you could ask Brooke for advice. She seemed to take to it naturally."

"Brooke?" Rena paused. "That girl's got her hands full right now."

"What do you mean?"

"You haven't heard?"

"No, I haven't spoken with her. We don't have that kind of relationship," Nick said, convincing himself of that fact.

"The baby's in the hospital."

"What?" Nick's good mood vanished. His heart pounded hard and he thought he heard wrong. "Leah's in the hospital?"

"Yes, she had a febrile seizure."

"A seizure?" Nick couldn't believe it. "But she's such a healthy kid."

"It's caused from a high temperature. The baby was sick and her fever spiked really fast. It's pretty scary, but they say it happens to some children. Because she's so young, they're doing tests to make sure it's nothing more serious."

"Damn! It better not be." Nick couldn't fathom that sweet baby having to suffer. "How's Brooke?"

"She's a brave one. She's all alone and I tell you, I don't know how she does it. Ali stopped by the hospital when she found out to check on both of them. She said Brooke is holding up. She has no choice, but it's rough. Her world revolves around that baby."

"Oh man." Nick put his head down and took a few deep breaths. His stomach felt hollowed out, like someone had gone in and scooped out his guts with a shovel.

"You should call her, Nick. She doesn't say it, but I know she misses you."

"I'm not so sure." He couldn't call her. He didn't know what to say to her. He'd walked out on her just like every other man in her life. He'd let her down and he'd done it without realizing it. He should have known better than to get involved with someone like Brooke. She didn't need him in her life. She needed stability. She needed someone who would be there for her, through thick and thin. She needed a man who would love the hell out of her and her beautiful daughter.

He's been like a father to Leah. She should be that lucky.

Had Brooke meant it? Had she seen something in him that he hadn't seen in himself?

Nick hung up the phone and paced the length of his living room, darting glances around his home, noting the textured walls and marble flooring, the pillared terrace with its sweeping vista overlooking the Mediterranean. The place was perfect. He'd gotten what he wanted. He could Pass Go and Collect $200 and as an added bonus he'd received the Get Out of Jail Free card, his prison being Napa and all it signified.

He admitted that he had decided to stay on longer in Monte Carlo to keep as much distance from Brooke as possible. She would have moved out of his house by now. He could go back to living his bachelor life, yet he didn't like what he was feeling about her. He missed her, but he was no good for her. He wouldn't succumb to those emotions. A few more days away would help purge her from his thoughts.

"Hang on, Nick," he muttered to himself. "Don't go nuts because the kid got sick. Brooke's a survivor. She'll be okay."

And to prove to himself that he was better off without them and vice-versa, he went out that night. He gambled in Monaco and had dinner with an acquaintance he'd met months ago at the roulette table. She was beautiful and willing, but he made up an excuse and spent the night alone in his bed.

Nick woke up feeling like crap. If someone had taken a hammer to his head, he couldn't feel worse. The hell of it was, he knew why. He hadn't caught too many winks last night and he had two blond-haired, blue-eyed females to thank for that. He rose from his bed and padded to the kitchen for some aspirin.

Only Nick knew beyond a doubt now, aspirin wouldn't cure what was really wrong with him.

Brooke took Leah out of her car seat in the back of the Lexus and gazed at her daughter with pride. "You're my pretty girl." Leah returned her compliment with a two-toothed smile. She'd dressed her in a brand-new white dress dotted with bright red cherries and green stems. Atop her baby blond curls sat a cherry red bow.

"We're going to visit your new little friend, David Anthony today," she said as she walked up the path to the house at Purple Fields. Brooke had dressed to match Leah. She wore a red and white sundress, minus the cherries. It felt good to dress up for a change and go out with Leah. Since the move into the bed-and-breakfast, Brooke had felt somewhat isolated and lonely, just the two of them in that big house.

Leah's medical episode had taken its toll on Brooke. The febrile seizure had come on so suddenly and had scared her half to death. She'd called the paramedics and they'd taken Leah to the hospital. By the time they arrived, Leah was alert and awake again. The doctor explained that the seizure was the body's natural reaction to such high temperatures and as soon as Leah's body adjusted, she came out of it. They also explained that febrile seizures in themselves were not life threatening.

Thank God for that.

They'd kept Leah in the hospital to do some tests and when they released her with a clean bill of health, Brooke had broken down and cried her eyes out. Now, just three days later, Leah was a happy girl again and both were looking forward to spending time with Rena and the new baby.

She knocked on the door and just a few seconds later Rena appeared, looking beautiful and well rested. "Hi, Rena. Leah and I are so excited to see you and the baby."

"I'm glad you accepted the invitation." Rena smiled at her and patted Leah's head. "She looks happy and healthy, Brooke. Is all okay now?"

"Yes, she's perfect. Thanks for your support and friendship. It means a lot to me."

Rena opened the door wider. "Come in, please."

Brooke stepped into the entrance hall and followed Rena to the living room. Once they reached it, Rena turned to her with apology in her eyes. "I just want you to know this wasn't my idea. I think there's a better way to do this."

Puzzled, Brooke looked at Rena then followed the line of her gaze into the room. Tony, Joe and Ali were there. "Oh, I didn't realize you were having the family over."

Rena sighed and shot Tony a hard look.

"Meet little David Anthony." Tony walked over to greet them and Brooke forgot all else, thrilled to see their new child.

"He's beautiful. You must be so happy."

"We are," Tony said to her, then Rena walked over and Tony put his arm around her. "We're thrilled."

Leah reached a hand out to touch the baby and Brooke made sure she was gentle, helping guide her hand to his cheek. "Isn't he sweet, Leah?" And after they'd fawned over little David, Brooke turned to say hello to Ali and Joe. They inquired about Leah's health and made her feel welcome, then the room became awkwardly silent. Brooke wondered what was up.

"Sorry, Brooke," Ali said finally.

Rena joined forces with Ali. "We didn't know about the bet."

Brooke looked from one woman to the other, sensing their discomfort and feeling some of her own. "What bet? What's going on?"

Nick appeared, coming out of another room and startling her. He stood in a solid stance, his gaze flowing over her from head to toe with hunger in his eyes, then he glanced at Leah and his gaze went heartbreakingly soft. He looked drop-dead gorgeous and dangerously confident about something. Just seeing him again squeezed her heart and coiled her stomach. He'd hurt her when he hadn't called about Leah. He must have known. He must have realized how much agony she'd been in when Leah was sick. He'd taken her at her word when she'd asked for *simple,* but she never thought he'd be so cold and uncaring. He should have called and asked about Leah.

"Hello, Brooke," he said.

She couldn't keep her disappointment from showing. She pursed her lips.

"Tell her," Nick demanded, looking at his brothers.

Joe glanced at Nick. "You're sure? This could spell doom for you, bro."

Nick nodded. "I want her to know the truth, all of it."

Tony handed the baby off to Rena and she shook her head at him. "We were on your side, Brooke. In all of this," Tony said in a defensive tone.

"All of what? What's going on?" she asked.

As soon as Leah spotted Nick, she put her arms out to him and she bounced with excitement until Brooke could barely contain her. "Leah!"

The dimples of doom broke out on Nick's face and he strode over to Brooke. "Let me hold her."

"I can't seem to stop her," she said, disgruntled.

Leah reached out for Nick and when he took her, she clung to his neck. He kissed her cheek and stroked her hair. "Thank God you're all right."

Ali's and Rena's expressions softened.

"Tell her the truth," Nick demanded again of his brothers.

"Why don't you tell me, Nick?" Brooke said, angrily. "Since it's obvious this was all set up and your doing. Tell me what you have to say."

Nick looked at his brothers who refused to speak. "Cowards."

"On that note, we'll leave you two alone." Joe grabbed Ali's hand and walked outside.

"That's a good plan. Let's take the baby for a walk," Tony said to Rena and the three of them left the room.

Once they were alone, Nick turned to her. "Okay, I'll tell you the truth. When you first came to live with me after your accident, my brothers were so damn sure I'd get involved with you. I mean, here you were vulnerable and alone and you had this adorable kid. They were so damn smug about it. I told them what I told you, I don't do permanent and I'm not father material. I was so sure of how I felt," he said, stroking her daughter's hair again, "that I made them a wager. I bet them I wouldn't fall for you and want the whole enchilada. I bet them my stake in the company. If I didn't fall in love with you, I get a free pass with Carlino Wines. I wouldn't have to run the company and I wouldn't have to stay in Napa. I'd be out of the running and it would be between Joe and Tony."

Brooke's mouth dropped open and she was stunned speechless.

Nick went on, "I told you how much I hated it here. How much I wanted revenge against my father. So much so, that I wanted nothing to do with his legacy. So much so, that I couldn't see past my anger. But you made me see things differently, Brooke. You made me realize that I shouldn't live in the past. That's all I've been doing, living in the past and running away."

Brooke regained her composure and finally spoke. "You actually *bet* you wouldn't fall in love with me? Not very good for a girl's ego, is it?"

"I wasn't looking for permanent, Brooke. But man, was I wrong. I lost the bet. I'm the new head of Carlino

Wines. I'm the CEO now and rightfully so. Joe and Tony are staying on too. We're brothers and we're going to help each other. Thanks to you I'm facing my past and moving on to my future."

Brooke swallowed hard. "Nick." She didn't know what to say.

"I put in a call to the high school too. Looks like they might want me to coach the Victors this season."

"Oh, Nick. That's wonderful."

"You've made it all possible, Brooke. You helped me see that I was wasting my life away. This is one bet I was glad to lose. Because I'm crazy about you and Leah. You're all that matters to me. I don't want to lose you and if it means me staying in Napa and running the company, I'll do it. I want you that much. I love you that much."

Brooke got past the initial ego deflation, to hear him, to really hear what he was telling her. He loved her. He loved Leah. It was quite a lot to take in. He was making sacrifices for her and the idea warmed her to the point of melting. "What's the whole enchilada?"

Nick spoke with reverence and a hopeful tone. "Marriage. The three of us being a family, everything I thought I never wanted."

"And now you do?"

"I took the CEO position to prove it to you." He lowered his voice and spoke with sincerity. "With your help, I think I could be a good father to Leah."

Oh my God. That did it. Any anger she felt over the stupid bet he made just faded to nothingness. She couldn't hold it against him. He'd always been honest with her. But hearing him say he loved her and that he wanted to be Leah's father turned her insides to jelly. Tears welled in her eyes and raw emotion overwhelmed her. She struggled to get the words out yet she felt them with every beat of her heart, "You don't need my help being a good father. Leah's already crazy about you."

"What about you, Brooke? How do you feel about me? Still trying to keep it simple?"

Her smile spread across her face and her heart burst with joy. "Nick, you've complicated my life since the day I set eyes on you in high school. I loved you then and I love you now."

Nick breathed in deep. "Then will you marry me?"

Brooke gazed at him holding Leah in his arms. "You don't play fair asking me with Leah looking at you like you could paint the moon."

"I could, with both of you in my life."

Brooke sighed with utter joy and spoke the words she'd never thought she'd ever say to Nick Carlino. "Yes, I'll marry you."

Nick bundled her up close, the three of them in a huddle and Nick kissed her with sweet tenderness. "I've missed you, Brooke. I've missed you both. I promised you that night of the crash that I'd take care of Leah. I want to do that and share my life with you. We'll be a family, the three of us."

"Oh, Nick. That's all I've ever wanted."

Brooke would have the family she'd always hoped for, but she was getting a bonus.

Her very own drop-dead handsome, dangerously sexy Desert Island Dream.

What more could a girl ask for?

* * * * *

Don't miss Sarah Morgan's
next Puffin Island story

Some Kind of Wonderful

Brittany Forrest has stayed away from Puffin Island since her relationship with Zach Flynn went bad. They were married for ten days and only just managed not to kill each other by the end of the honeymoon.

But, when a broken arm means she must return, Brittany moves back to her Puffin Island home. Only to discover that Zac is there as well.

Will a summer together help two lovers reunite or will their stormy relationship crash on to the rocks of Puffin Island?

Some Kind of Wonderful
COMING JULY 2015
Pre-order your copy today